MW00780112

THE MEDICI RETURN

ALSO BY STEVE BERRY

NOVELS

The Amber Room
The Romanov Prophecy
The Third Secret
The Templar Legacy
The Alexandria Link
The Venetian Betrayal
The Charlemagne Pursuit
The Paris Vendetta
The Emperor's Tomb
The Jefferson Key
The Columbus Affair
The King's Deception
The Lincoln Myth
The Patriot Threat
The 14th Colony
The Lost Order
The Bishop's Pawn
The Malta Exchange
The Warsaw Protocol
The Kaiser's Web
The Omega Factor
The Last Kingdom
The Atlas Maneuver

WITH GRANT BLACKWOOD

The 9th Man
Red Star Falling

WITH M. J. ROSE

The Museum of Mysteries
The Lake of Learning
The House of Long Ago
The End of Forever

THE MEDICI RETURN

STEVE BERRY

NEW YORK BOSTON

Cover design by Eric Fuentecilla
Cover image of map by Sepia Times/Getty Images
Cover image by Shutterstock

Grand Central Publishing
Hachette Book Group
1290 Avenue of the Americas, New York, NY 10104
grandcentralpublishing.com
@grandcentralpub

First edition: February 2025

Grand Central Publishing is a division of Hachette Book Group, Inc. The Grand Central Publishing name and logo is a registered trademark of Hachette Book Group, Inc.

Copy of portrait of Giuliano di Lorenzo de' Medici by Raphael, Metropolitan Museum of Art, New York. The Jules Bache Collection, 1949.

Library of Congress Cataloging-in-Publication Data

Names: Berry, Steve, 1955– author.
Title: The Medici return / Steve Berry.
Description: New York : GCP, 2025. | Series: Cotton Malone ; book 19
Identifiers: LCCN 2024036441 | ISBN 9781538770566 (hardcover) | ISBN 9781538770597 (ebook)
Subjects: LCSH: Medici, Giuliano de', duca di Nemours, 1479–1516—Fiction. | Medici, House of—Fiction. | LCGFT: Historical fiction. | Novels.
Classification: LCC PS3602.E764 M44 2025 | DDC 813/.6—dc23/eng/20240812
LC record available at https://lccn.loc.gov/2024036441

ISBNs: 9781538770566 (hardcover), 9781538771105 (large print), 9781538770597 (ebook)

Printed in the United States of America

LSC-H

Printing 1, 2024

For Jillian and Benji Stein,
along with Evan and Kristie Wells,
elves extraordinaire

In bocca al lupo. Crepi il lupo.
Into the wolf's mouth. May the wolf die.
—An old Italian idiom

ACKNOWLEDGMENTS

My sincere thanks to Ben Sevier, senior vice president and publisher of Grand Central. To Lyssa Keusch, my editor, whom I've greatly enjoyed getting to know. Then to Tiffany Porcelli for her marketing expertise; Staci Burt who handled publicity; and all those in Sales and Production who made sure both that there was a book to read and that it was widely available for sale.

A deep bow goes to Simon Lipskar, my agent and friend, who makes everything possible.

A few extra mentions: Katie and Brent Gledhill, who introduced me to Tuscany and the Palio and were there for the research (especially Katie, who handled some valuable extra reconnaissance); Camilla Baines, local guide in Florence extraordinaire and Medici expert, along with Daniele Calabritto who drove us everywhere; Caroline and Amy Zongor my resident horse experts; and Gayle Rowland for simply listening.

As always, to my wife, Elizabeth, who remains the most special of all.

This book has an unusual dedication, which requires a short explanation. We live in a neighborhood where Christmas decorating rises to the level of a blood sport. There are some spectacular displays. Christmas in our house has always been a big deal, both inside and out. In years past it would take Elizabeth and me several days to bring it all out, then weeks later another few days to pack it all away.

But for the past four years we've had some help.

During 2021 and 2022, on the third weekend in November, Jillian and Benjamin Stein flew down from Pennsylvania to assist in putting everything up (you might recognize both names from *The 9th Man*). They then came back at New Year's and helped take it all down. For 2023 and 2024 the four of us were joined by Evan and Kristie Wells (who will have their own named characters in a coming book). Among the six of us, what I call Elizabeth's Christmas World both comes to life, then disappears.

So this book is for the Keystone Holiday Elves.

Thank you.

One and all.

THE MEDICI RETURN

PROLOGUE

Cathedral of St. Mary of The Assumption
Siena, Italy
May 9, 1512

Giuliano di Lorenzo de' Medici knew this was his family's last chance at redemption. A single attempt. That is all fate would allow. Their legacy was one of risk and reward but, of late, only failure had come their way. He was thirty-three years old and the titular head of the ancient Medici clan, the great-grandson of Cosimo de' Medici, son of Lorenzo the Magnificent. Quite a pedigree. And quite the accomplishment for a third son. Since 1494 he and his entire family had lived in exile, banned from his beloved Florence, stripped of all rights and titles as punishment for his older brother's grave political mistake.

"Piero was a fool," Pope Julius II bellowed. "Feeble, arrogant, undisciplined. We knew him."

An insult? For sure. But not a lie.

The Medicis had effectively ruled Florence since the start of the fifteenth century. Piero assumed the family leadership in 1492 when their father, Lorenzo, died. Two years later Charles VIII of France crossed the Alps with an army, intent on conquering the Kingdom of Naples. To get there, though, Charles had to pass through Tuscany, so he sought out Piero to both support his claim to Naples and allow his army to pass. Piero, ever the arrogant fool as the pope had just described, waited five days before responding that Florence would remain neutral in the conflict.

Which enraged Charles.

So the French invaded Tuscany.

Piero attempted to mount a resistance, but he received little support from the Florentine elite, who had no taste for war. Eventually Piero, on his own, met with Charles and acceded to every French demand, including surrendering control of key Florentine fortresses and towns. His attempts at a negotiated peace were met with outrage and the Medici were forced to flee, the family's grand palazzo in Florence looted and burned. Piero, for all his mistakes, acquired an insulting moniker.

The Unfortunate.

To say the least.

"My brother has been dead nine years," he calmly said to Julius. "Drowned after the Battle of Garigliano."

"And you were but a boy at the exile, a gifted youth I am told, moving from court to court, searching for a home."

"That is true. But now I am grown and do not intend to repeat my brother's mistakes."

The pope pointed a finger his way. "What you wish, is a reprieve."

He let the insult pass and merely said, "We simply want to return to our home."

The Medici started as farmers, from the Mugello region north of Florence, who tended their vines and oxen. The origin of the family name remained a mystery. *Medici* was the plural of *medico*, medical doctor, yet there were no healers in the lineage. Instead, they became bankers, insanely wealthy, connected to most of the other elite families—the Bardi, Altoviti, Ridolfi, Cavalcanti, and Tornabuoni—through marriages of convenience, business partnerships, or employment. They were the spoke of the wheel, the *gran maestro*, unofficial heads of the Florentine republic for over a hundred years.

Until Piero the Unfortunate's mistake.

"Come closer, Medici," Julius said, adding a wave of his arm.

The pope sat on a marble seat beneath the cathedral's unique octagonal pulpit. Eight granite and marble columns supported sculpted scenes that narrated the life of Christ, the message one of salvation and the last judgment. Fitting for this confrontation.

Giuliano stepped forward, but stopped a comfortable distance away. He'd been advised not to approach too close. His spies had also reported that the pope, nearing seventy years old, was riddled with gout and syphilis, in constant pain. The old man's head hung bent with exhaustion, the brow still high and wide above a large and pugnacious nose. A beard fell from the chin, a sign he'd been told of Julius' personal mourning of his recent military loss of the city of Bologna. Beards had been forbidden by canon law for centuries but, as was common with Julius, he lived by a different set of rules.

The pope had been born near Savona in the Republic of Genoa, of the House of della Rovere, a noble but impoverished family, then educated by his uncle, a Franciscan monk. He rose to be a cardinal at age twenty-eight thanks to his uncle, who became Pope Sixtus IV, and steadily climbed within the church through three more pontificates until finally claiming the throne of St. Peter in 1503.

A soldier in a cassock was how Julius had come to be described. *Terribilità*, awe inspiring, that's what the Italians called him. One of the most dynamic personalities to ever reach the papal chair. Nothing of a priest existed about him except for the dress and name. Never much of a diplomat, always a warrior. Plain-spoken to the point of rudeness, he belonged to a class of men who simply did not rest. Every moment, every thought was geared to a purpose. He drank, swore, was willful, coarse, bad-tempered, and impossible to manage. Yet he was also incapable of baseness or vindictiveness and he despised informers. Everywhere he saw and sought greatness. His faults arose from his relentless candor and uncontrollable temper, both of which Giuliano had to guard against.

"Medici," Julius said, "people are flattering us, telling us grand things, but we know better. We cannot stand on our feet for more than a few moments. Walking has become a chore. Food is revolting. The trip here today took all the energy we have, and our strength diminishes from day to day. Pain is a constant companion. We will not live much longer."

He refused to take that bait. He knew that Julius had been near death before, the latest incident a few months back when he supposedly lay dying and the cardinals began openly plotting his succession. But the old man had rebounded thanks to that famed iron constitution. And many of those cardinals had been fired or dismissed. They learned the hard way not to assume a man of Julius' power and strength would die easily. Better to wait until the body was cold and in the ground. But for what Giuliano had in mind for the Medici family, he needed Julius alive, strong, and feared.

"Did you travel here from Urbino or Venice?" the pope asked.

"Venice, Holiness."

"But that is not your home."

"It is where most of my family is centered. I wished to consult with them."

"How is your leader, the doge?"

"He is well. He sends his regards."

Julius chuckled. "We doubt that. Instead, he surely wishes us to be dead and gone."

He stayed silent, because the observation was correct. The pope and the Venetians were not friends.

"We have always wondered," Julius said, "what would happen when we arrive at the gates of Heaven, finally facing St. Peter."

Giuliano imagined that awkward scene in his brain.

Julius motioned with a wrinkled hand. "We would say to him that we have done more for the church and Christ than any pope before us. We annexed Bologna to the Holy See. We led an army and beat the Venetians. We jockeyed the Duke of Ferrara. We drove the French out of Italy, and we would have driven out the Spaniards too, if the fates had not brought us to this state of physical decline."

No doubt.

"We have boxed all the princes of Europe by the ears. We have torn up treaties and kept great armies in the field. We have covered Rome with palaces. We owe nothing to our birth or youth, for we were old when we began. Nothing to popularity either, for we are hated all around. Then we would say to Peter that all this is the modest truth, and that our friends in Rome call us more god than man."

"And hope Peter is not offended," he added.

Julius chuckled. "To be honest, we hope he is."

The bravado was consistent with all he knew about this forceful, ruthless, violent man who, for the past nine years, had kept Italy in war and turmoil. But Julius had also brought order to Rome and had elevated the papacy to the dominant political and military force of Italy. He had a keen eye for the arts as well, developing close friendships with Michelangelo, Bramante, and Raphael, however confrontational those relationships might have been. He'd established the Swiss Guards, commissioned a magnificent ceiling in the Sistine Chapel, founded the Vatican Museums, and begun the construction of what he wanted to be the greatest basilica in the world dedicated to St. Peter.

Amazing accomplishments.

"You know we have the same first name," Julius said. "We were born Giuliano della Rovere. But I have not been called that in a long time. It means 'youthful.' We still think of ourselves as youthful."

"Death seems not to favor you," Giuliano said.

A smirk came to the thin lips. "There was a time, Medici, when we rode our horse right up the Lateran stairs and tethered him to our bedroom door. We were a rock. We knew no fear or irresolution. Difficulties only roused us to work harder. We think it all consistent with our family crest. An unbending oak."

They were alone, inside Siena's grand cathedral. A favorite of Julius', if his spies were to be believed. His brother, a cardinal, and his cousin, a priest, were close with Julius. So he'd utilized both as intermediaries to request an audience. He'd expected an unequivocal no—after all, the Medicis had been persona non grata for a long time. No one wanted to be seen or associated with the family. Anyone caught scheming with them would be punished by death, and one man had lost his head. So he'd been surprised when the pope had accepted the offer to talk. But not in Rome. Instead, a neutral site.

Siena.

Which had made him wonder. What did this man want?

"We are aware," the pope said, "of your admirable character, your generosity and sympathetic nature. We are told that you oppose violence and cherish honesty. You are a fair and capable man. But you are the third son. The firstborn is dead. The second a cardinal. So it fell to you to head your family. That is a rare opportunity."

He agreed.

"We also are aware of your ambition. You want back what Piero the Unfortunate lost."

He'd been instructed to be direct. "I also want the Spanish gone from Florentine territory."

"Agreed. Now we will tell you what we want."

Giuliano waited.

"Money."

The request was not unexpected.

The church had long been corrupted by gold and silver.

"Though we have been careful with our household," Julius said, "mindful of our resources, when we assumed the papacy there was enormous debt thanks to our predecessor."

That he could believe, since Alexander VI had been a degenerate who cared for nothing much besides pleasure. It was well known that the Borgia pope had drained the treasury.

"We have also financed many wars," Julius said. "All necessary in order to expel our enemies and restore the Papal States to their glory. It is such an insult to have lost them in the first place."

That precious territory, which had long belonged to the papacy, stretched across the Italian peninsula from the Mediterranean to the Adriatic, then north toward Venice. The holdings were a physical manifestation of the temporal power of the popes, but Alexander VI had allowed a large swath of the territory to be appropriated by Venice. In 1508 Julius personally led an army and subjugated Perugia and Bologna. Then, in 1509, he defeated Venice and restored the Papal States. Hence why the doge would wish nothing but pain and death on this pope.

"Those wars were costly," Julius said. "But we have also supported the arts and erected grand buildings, along with being generous to the poor. Our charity has caused the treasury at Castel Sant' Angelo to draw nearly empty. We are ashamed to say, Medici, that we have resorted to selling offices, benefices, and indulgences to raise funds. Shameful, I know, but necessary. We want, before we die, to restore the treasury."

"Our bank no longer exists," he pointed out. "We are not in the business of making loans."

The Peruzzi, Scalia, Frescobaldi, and Salambini were well-known lenders, but the Banco dei Medici had been the largest and most respected in Europe. Giuliano's great-grandfather Cosimo had been a master financier, using his wealth—spread across art, land, and gold—to acquire political control over Florence. But the Medici after him were not as astute. Overspending and bad management combined to send the bank to the brink. For all his political canniness, his father, Lorenzo, had been a terrible banker. Eventually bad loans and too many defaults led to bankruptcy. With his brother's disastrous political moves and the family's exile to Venice, some of the family assets had been seized and distributed to creditors. All of the bank's branches throughout Europe were dissolved. But the Medicis' vast personal wealth survived.

"Do not think us a fool," Julius said. "True, there were great losses when your bank collapsed. But those were borne mainly by your customers, not by you. Your family escaped with its riches."

"Our home was pillaged and burned," he told Julius.

"But most of your art and gold had already been removed."

This pope was remarkably well informed.

"We are aware that your wealth has grown immeasurably during the past eighteen years. Though you deflect all attention, you remain the wealthiest family in Europe."

No sense being coy. "How much do you seek?"

"Ten million florins."

His father had taught him the first rule of negotiating. *Never reveal what is on your mind.* So he did not react to the incredible sum. There were also a couple of other lessons. *Never cut what you can untie.* Advice passed down from Cosimo himself. Along with, *Necessity does not make a good bargain.* Not a muscle twitched on his face, and his eyes remained rock-steady as he weighed his options.

The past eighteen years had been tough on Florence. The city had been nearly destroyed by corruption, misgovernment, and heavy taxation. Everything had come to a head two months ago. The papal forces, plus Spain, had met the French in Ravenna. Both sides fought hard and the French lost their commander, but the Spanish won, driving the French northward to the Alps. That's when Julius laid siege to Florence, intent on changing its wanton ways. That army was still there. Along with the Spanish. Waiting. Outside the walls.

"Forgive me, Holiness," he said. "But my family has not been a lender to the Mother Church for a long time. We were... dismissed, in favor of another bank."

"We are aware of such. But that was another pope's action, not ours. True, we have a bank to handle church affairs, and it will continue to do so. What we are asking of you is something far more personal. More secretive. An arrangement only a few will know exists."

Secrecy brought with it a multitude of problems, especially when it came to repayment. The Medici had learned long ago that kings and emperors never wanted others to know they were borrowing money, which made it easy for them to default.

"In our closing time of life we are concerned about the church's grandeur," Julius said. "Some call us the savior of the papacy. We rather like that description. Popes before us were corrupt, stupid, or weak. But no more do kings and emperors laugh at Rome. Now they fear us. We require you to ensure that legacy remains intact."

"Ten million gold florins would be the largest loan ever made," he had to say.

Julius shrugged. "It is what we require for the treasury to be restored. For your family to once again live in Florence and Tuscany. But it does not have to be all in gold. Property that can be converted to gold later would be welcomed."

Now the main question. "What would the collateral be for such a large risk?"

"An army outside your precious Florence is not sufficient?"

"Hardly."

"Yet you are here."

"And you need money."

He was pushing things.

"Our word means nothing?" Julius asked.

"No. It does not. Especially considering that your army is outside the gates of Florence. And by your own words, you are dying."

He was not going to be bullied. He came with nothing and he could leave with nothing. If his ancestors had been equally as cautious, perhaps the family would not have found itself in its present predicament. True, this pope was stern, passionate, impatient, keen to move from one fight to another, and never happy except at war. All bad. If Julius reacted with his characteristic rage and cast him away, then so be it. Better that than losing everything. The pope was right. The family's wealth was at an all-time high, and he intended on keeping it that way.

The old man cast him a wiry glare. "The talk is, once we are gone, the next pope will be your brother. If such be the case, Medici, you will have direct access to the church and its treasury for any repayment."

"Those are mere possibilities, not collateral. Also, any arrangement we might make must also include that your army, and the Spanish, immediately withdraw from Florence."

Julius shrugged. "They are only still there since we agreed to speak with you. We wanted to see if you were as reasonable as people say."

"And if I had not been?"

"Then our army would have breached the walls and taken Florence by force."

Not an idle threat coming from this man.

"All right, Medici. You produce the ten million gold florins and we will withdraw our army and grant to you the best collateral on this earth."

He was intrigued.

"We will give you what few in history have ever possessed."

He waited.

"Pignus Christi."

The Pledge of Christ.

PRESENT DAY

CHAPTER 1

Dillenburg, Germany
Monday, June 30
12:40 p.m.

Cotton Malone had committed burglary before.

Many times, in fact.

Just not in such an august place.

He stood inside a four-hundred-year-old residence, built of olden brick and stone, first erected during the seventeenth century at a time when the German states, Sweden, and Poland were beset by religious conflict. Catholics fought Protestants in the long and destructive Thirty Years' War. The building around him was a picturesque relic of that violent history that had somehow escaped razing by the Protestants. It likewise survived later conflicts, including both world wars. It remained the rural home of a cardinal, owned by the Archdiocese of Cologne, whose duly authorized representatives in Rome had granted Cotton permission to surreptitiously enter the premises.

So technically this wasn't a burglary.

Still, it definitely felt like one.

Germany possessed nine cardinals. Three were beyond the age of eighty, meaning they were ineligible to attend the next conclave and vote for a new pope. Six remained active, the youngest, Jason Cardinal Richter, serving as the current archbishop of Cologne. The house served as Richter's private retreat, a place outside the city that he enjoyed from time to time.

Dillenburg sat about seventy miles east of Cologne, in a narrow valley cut by the River Dill. The town was one of those out-of-the-way places that had once been much more important. Its healing spring and brine works, renovated a few years ago, were back open for visitors, which helped with tourism. Once, a wooden castle had dominated the hill above the town, but all that remained were ruins, along with an impressive stone lookout tower that had become a local landmark. The cardinal's residence sat in sight of the watchtower atop the thousand-foot hill, with a spectacular view of the valley below.

Cotton was surreptitiously working with the Swiss Guard, on special assignment through the Magellan Billet. His former boss, Stephanie Nelle, had called a few days ago asking for help. An extraordinary situation was developing at the Vatican. Six defendants were on trial for fraud, embezzlement, corruption, money laundering, and abuse of office. The charges centered on the church's multimillion-euro purchases of investment properties located throughout Ireland and England. The deal, investigators argued, was nothing more than a way for the defendants to launder money and refinance their own debts through embezzled funds.

Two of the defendants were monsignors, employed within the Secretariat of State. Two more were former heads of the Vatican's internal financial overseer, charged with making sure frauds never happened. The final pair were an Italian financier and an investment manager. The whole thing seemed a wide-ranging conspiracy better suited for spy novels. Certainly not something that might happen within the Holy See.

Thankfully, as with most complex criminal enterprises, mistakes had been made that led to its discovery. A special Vatican court had been empaneled to try the defendants, the judges selected by the pope from among an array of former Italian prosecutors. The trial itself had started months ago, the evidence trickling out at a snail's pace through a parade of witnesses. It was being held inside a spacious hall within the Vatican Museums to accommodate the many media representatives and spectators. Two weeks ago things had taken an unusual turn when one of the defendants, a monsignor from the secretary of state's office, offered prosecutors a deal. In return for immunity he would provide them with incriminating information on one, so-far unnamed, individual.

A prince of the church.

Jason Cardinal Richter.

A secret proffer of information had occurred to prosecutors, and the Swiss Guard had been quietly ordered to confirm its veracity. The trial itself had been recessed on the pretense of the court performing a partial review of the evidence so as to be able to rule on motions filed by the defendants. A totally plausible scenario, as similar recesses had also occurred. So sensitive was the situation that outside help had been requested through the United States attorney general, who involved the Magellan Billet, which had led to Stephanie calling Copenhagen.

"We need a sneak and peek. There are too many eyes and ears at the Vatican. No way to keep something like this secret. So they want us to quietly check it out. How tough could it be? He's a cardinal, not a mafia boss. Just see what's there."

Right. How hard could it be?

The actual entry into the house had been simple. The locks were easy to pick, and the old building came with no cameras or alarms. But why would it? It was more a getaway than a residence, kept by the diocese as a perk for its resident cardinal. A place to enjoy on the weekends or in summer. No one lived there full-time, but the information they'd been given stated that Cardinal Richter used the house as a repository for, if the informant was to be believed, about four hundred thousand euros in cash. Far more money than any prelate could have ever legitimately accumulated.

He stood at the top of the stairs on the third-floor landing. The stale air carried a musty smell. The walls were heavy plaster, painted a soft cream, broken by arches, the ceilings coffered wood, the mullioned window in the alcove at the end of the hall leaden and in need of cleaning. He assumed this place harbored lots of nooks and crannies. One in particular was of interest. A unique anomaly. The fifteenth-century equivalent of a safe room.

When the Protestant armies rolled through Germany during the Thirty Years' War, Catholic priests were a favorite target. They liked to hang them. To avoid that priests took to hiding, many inside homes where concealed compartments just big enough to squeeze into were secretly constructed. They were artfully contrived not only to hold a priest, but also as a place where vestments and sacred vessels could be hidden away. Those secret compartments had been built into fireplaces, attics, and staircases, concealed in walls, under floors, and behind wainscoting, designed to blend in with the architecture and escape detection.

They even had a name.

Priest holes.

This olden house had its own. His task was to open it, take a look, and photograph what he found.

A classic sneak and peek.

He stepped down the hall, his steps cushioned by a soft carpet runner, and entered one of the guest bedrooms. Fluted columns jutting from the walls filled the corners. All part of the décor to go along with more moldings that adorned the room, everything glazed with a thick coat of paint. He'd been told that what he sought would be to the right of the door.

He studied the column and caressed the slick surface, the wood painted to a high sheen. The mechanism to release the panel was at the bottom. Not olden. Instead it had supposedly been updated a while back by Cardinal Richter to be more reliable. He crouched, found the hole beneath the base, and pushed on the metal inside.

He heard a soft click.

The front part of the fluted column separated from the rest.

Okay. Step one done.

And though he was no longer a first-stringer in the intelligence business, he still knew how to come off the bench and play the game. Ben Franklin said it best. *Distrust and caution are the parents of security.* And if nothing else, he was cautious.

Which told him not to open the panel any further.

A dark crack about half an inch wide had formed from where the wood had separated. Interestingly, it had not swung out any farther. Was that significant? Only one way to know.

He found his phone—Magellan Billet issued, a gift from Stephanie—and activated the light. He aimed the beam into the crack and started examining the opening, slowly moving upward toward the top.

About halfway he stopped and felt a familiar surge in his pulse.

"Gotcha," he muttered.

CHAPTER 2

Piazza di Santa Croce
Florence, Italy
12:55 p.m.

Stefano Giumenta stiff-armed the man in front of him, then lowered his shoulder and prepared to force his way through the sea of sweaty bodies converging onto him. He spotted a teammate who indicated that he should pass the ball. No way. This was his play.

His day.

He loved Calcio Storico.

Henry III had been right. *Too small to be a real war, too cruel to be a game.*

The first match was held in 1530, during a time when Florence was besieged by the armies of Charles V and Pope Clement VII. Instead of celebrating the annual carnival, the Florentines played a match of Calcio Storico to mock the attackers. They did not even keep score, the whole idea was to show their enemies that they were not afraid. That legendary game had made it into history books as the *partita dell'assedi.*

Game of the siege.

Its popularity increased through the 18th century, enjoyed on the streets and in the city squares. A way to vent youthful excesses, rivalries, and passions. The last official match happened in 1739. Two centuries passed before it was revived. Since 1930, except for the World War II period, games among the four historical neighborhoods of Florence had been held annually. The Bianchi of Santo Spirito wore white. The Azzurri of Santa Croce sported blue. The Rossi of Santa Maria Novella were noted for their red. And his beloved Verdi of San Giovanni donned green. All of the players wore baggy puffed trousers and shirts in their respective colors, lightweight so as not to hinder movement. Many, including himself, had already lost their shirts, playing bare-chested under a Tuscan sun.

Three defenders crashed into him, their powerful arms wrapping in a tight embrace. But he spun around, freed himself, and deflected their attempts to take him down. He cradled the ball close to his chest, which was coated in sand and sweat. Once, the balls were shells of cloth or animal skin, cut into sections, sewn together, and stuffed with straw or feathers. Today they were leather filled with air, like a football.

Probing hands tried to pry the ball from him, but he repelled their efforts and kept moving forward.

Nearly every town and village in Tuscany had a festival that paid tribute to history. Siena had its Palio. Arezzo, its Giostra del Saracino. Montepulciano, the Bravìo delle Botti. But none of those compared to Florence's Calcio Storico.

More than a game.

A show of art.

Each team fielded four goalkeepers, three fullbacks, five halfbacks, and fifteen forwards. Fifty-four men engaging in close fights and continuous melee for possession of the ball on a five-thousand-square-meter sand arena set up in the heart of Florence, surrounded by four thousand cheering spectators and half a dozen ambulances ready to transport the injured to the hospital. And there were always injuries. Some quite serious. And a problem, since no substitutions were allowed for either injury or expulsion.

The game was a version of American football that combined boxing, wrestling, and rugby-style tackles. No pads. No helmets. Twelve men tried to score, fifteen defended. The objective? Advance the ball to the end of the opponent's side of the field and toss it over a meter-and-a-half-high fence to score a goal. Shoot and miss? The other side received half a point.

So you could not miss.

Four hundred years ago the winning team was given a Chianina white heifer to eat. Today they enjoyed a meal at a Florentine restaurant. But the real prize was the bragging rights that came from winning for the colors of your neighborhood.

He dug his shoes into the soft sand.

Violence was not just expected but encouraged by the cheering crowds that populated the bleachers, in an atmosphere reminiscent of millennia-old gladiator games. Each game started when the fifteen forwards began kicking, punching, tackling, and wrestling one another, all designed to tire the other side's defenses. Once players were on the ground they could not get back up until a goal was scored. Many of his team were down, being held there by defenders. Calcio Storico came with five other rules. No choking. No ganging up on a single player. No criminals. Limited use of martial arts. And if a player said they were hurt, leave them alone.

Other than that, anything went.

Three Blue defenders converged on him. Two of his Green teammates managed to pry the arms and hands off him, adding a few well-placed punches to make the point. He rolled and tossed the ball to one of his teammates.

One other thing.

The ball had to remain in constant motion. If not, it was brought to the center of the field and placed "at bat," up for grabs.

He pushed himself away and ran.

The day was hot and arid, typical for summer. Good thing, as spring had been especially wet. There'd been flooding north of Florence, and the River Arno's banks had been tested as it wound itself through town. Nothing like the catastrophic flood of 1966, though.

That one had wreaked havoc.

Once only noble gentlemen—those who'd acquired lineage or military rank—from ages eighteen to forty-five were allowed to play. No commoners. Now it was open to all. He'd first played at nineteen. Then a scrawny kid, he was now ninety-five kilos of muscle, which he worked hard to maintain through diet and exercise. The neighborhood in which you were born determined which team you were eligible to play for. And it remained that for life. No switching sides. Every year the four teams squared off. Two semifinal matches, the winners advancing to the final. Always held the last week of June. He was now thirty-eight and this was his fourteenth contest, the sixth in the finals.

The crowd were all on their feet.

He shifted right toward the other side of the field. The ball was still heading toward the end, two of his teammates trading it back and forth, buying time until everyone could get in position. One of the Blues blocked his way, fists raised.

A challenge.

He halted his advance, planted his feet, and delivered a solid right uppercut to the jaw, sending the man to the sand.

Where he had to stay.

The ball was heading back toward him. Over half of each team was on the ground, out of play. That opened up the field.

He smelled success.

And signaled for a pass.

The ball arched across above the players and into his grasp. He tucked it tight to his chest. No match could end in a tie, and this game was locked 3–3.

Time to end this.

Wild throws to the net were not common. It would be easy to hurl the ball from a long way out and hope for the best. But a miss would cost the Greens half a point and the match.

In this game you had to be sure.

In life too.

The Blues were closing in. One slammed into him from behind and tried a quick tackle that failed. His shoes dug in and out of the soft sand, which was great when you were taken down, plenty of cushion for the fall, but terrible for traction. Usually, the pitch became firmer the closer to the goal. He'd noticed that was the case twenty minutes ago when they'd last scored.

Use that.

He gripped the ball between his hands, leading with it as he made a dash for the end. Blues and Greens engaged all around him, his teammates trying to provide an opening, the defenders intent on stopping them.

Spilled blood did not always come from the players. Games had often turned into full-blown brawls involving both players and supporters. His family was among the spectators today, minus his mother, who never cared for the Calcio. She tolerated it, as a good Florentine mother would, but her displeasure was no secret. His father, brothers, and sister loved everything about the game. His brother-in-law was on the field with him.

He'd made nine goals during his career on the pitch. So he knew how to get it done. Shift. Move. Stay loose.

Twenty meters.

Two Blues converged.

The crowd roared.

Ten meters.

He managed to dodge one Blue defender but not the other, who reached for the ball in his outstretched hands. There'd be only one chance to make the goal. But if he missed the Blues would get half a point, enough for victory as the clock was winding down to zero.

More Blues appeared.

He'd never make it to the end.

A Blue defender slammed into him. He mouthed a prayer and launched the ball into the air.

Down he went.

The ball flew over the players high enough that no one could leap up and stop its flight. He'd not been able to apply enough force for it to go all the way to the goal. But thankfully there were no players between the ball's flight and the field's end. So it hit the hard ground about two meters before the fence, bounced once into the air, and dropped cleanly over.

A shot of gunpowder signaled a goal and victory.
The Green supporters exploded in joy, their flags held high.
His teammates leaped in victory.
He rolled in the sand and stared toward heaven.
Thank you, Lord.

CHAPTER 3

Vatican City
1:00 p.m.

Eric Gaetano Casaburi knew he was being played. There really was no other way to view it. He'd been ushered to the second floor of the Apostolic Palace by two Swiss Guards who wore the traditional blue, red, and yellow uniforms, along with black berets. Supposedly, Michelangelo designed the original costumes using the colors of the Medici coat of arms. But who knew for sure? No one of any official stature or standing had been waiting when his car arrived. No cardinal, bishop, or monsignor, not even a priest or nun. Just the two young guards who said they were there to escort him.

A rebuke? Without a doubt.

All consistent with the arrogance that the Roman Catholic Church loved to display.

He'd been waiting now for nearly fifteen minutes, alone, ensconced in what appeared to be some sort of conference room. But not anything ordinary. Far from it. The space was huge, with a vaulted ceiling and walls dotted by an array of impressive Raphaels. There was something to be said for symbolism and imagery. He'd used both tactics, going all the way back to his teenage years when he was part of the Youth Front in the Italian Social Movement, a neo-fascist political party founded by former followers of Benito Mussolini. He worked his way up through a series of administrative posts to finally being appointed, at age thirty, Italian minister of youth. Twice he'd run unsuccessfully for the European Parliament and once in Rome's municipal elections. Then he won a seat in the Italian legislature, the popularity of his National Freedom Party growing in direct proportion to the ruling government's steady decline. Nine years he'd labored as party secretary, overseeing the entire apparatus using plenty of symbolism and imagery. Now national elections were set for September and his job was to secure the prime minister's post for the party's popular head. But to do that they had to achieve a working majority in the legislature, and to accomplish that they needed the help of the godforsaken Roman Catholic Church.

The door opened and a rotund man wearing a simple black clerical suit and collar strolled inside.

Jason Cardinal Richter.

Not dressed in scarlet for the occasion.

More symbolism? Damn right.

"I apologize for the delay," the prelate said, closing the door. "It was unavoidable."

Surely. No doubt.

Richter stepped over and took a seat at the end of the table. "How are you today?"

This was not their first talk. There'd been many before. Most short. Happenstance. At a restaurant. Social gathering. Once in a church. Three on the phone. Overtures. Feeling out the other. But never had they met like this. In the open. Official. Inside the Vatican. For all to see.

But that time had come.

"I came for an answer to my question," he said to Richter. "Which I posed to you three weeks ago. I have patiently been waiting."

"You may not like what I am about to say."

Nothing unusual there. After all, he was a right-wing populist. An avowed nationalist. His party's motto? *God, fatherland,*

and family, but not necessarily in that order. It was opposed to abortion, euthanasia, same-sex marriage, and anything relating to gays or lesbians. For them a family meant male/female with the male at its head. There, at least, the party and the church saw eye-to-eye. They despised globalism and supported a naval blockade to halt immigration. They'd been accused of xenophobia and Islamophobia, which had never been denied. But they supported NATO and, surprisingly, the European Union, with limits. They hated Russia and were not fond of the United States, which was considered equally imperialistic. All in all the National Freedom Party was just the sort of group the Roman Catholic Church would never freely choose to support.

"I have spoken to many here in the Vatican," Richter said. "Trying to gauge the measure of support. I have to say . . . the popularity runs quite cold. The various candidates from your party, which you want us to support for election to parliament, are all unappealing."

"Our polling numbers are nearing 60 percent."

Italy was a democratic republic with an elected president. The executive department was composed of a prime minister, appointed by the president, along with a council of ministers. The prime minister was usually the head of the majority coalition, or some new leader emerging from the majority coalition, or, in extreme cases, someone asked by the president to form a unity government. One caveat, though. Whoever was chosen had to receive the approval of parliament since any prime minister could be ousted with a vote of no confidence.

Which had just happened.

The president had already appointed two different candidates as prime minster, but neither had been able to form a working government. Instead of trying a third time new elections had been called so the people could decide. Eric knew that he was not the only person seeking the church's endorsement. Everyone would want it.

"Did one of your members once call Mussolini a *good politician in that everything he did he did for Italy*? I believe that person was further quoted that Il Duce was the *best politician of the last hundred years.*"

Eric shrugged. "And the problem?"

"The fact that you do not see a problem *is* the problem."

"We are not fascists," he declared. "We have denounced fascism in every form. The fact that we might admire how Mussolini governed is not reflective of our political beliefs. If you recall, we dismissed a member of the party for openly praising Hitler. We are a believer in the new right, not the old. We think differently."

"The catchphrase of your party is taken directly from the Italian fascists. *God, fatherland, family,*" Richter said.

"Those are three admirable things to strive toward. Are they not?"

"Did your party not also say that *fear and insecurity produce much more controllable people*?"

He shrugged. "It is true."

"Eric," the cardinal said. "The church will not back your party. I made the inquiries, as promised. But there are other choices far more palatable."

Was this unexpected?

Not in the least.

Thankfully he knew his adversary.

The church, for all its pontifications, was nothing more than a grand political entity, subject to whims, trends, and, above all, pressure. Especially pressure. Always in the past the church had succumbed to pressure. Changing. Adapting. Yes, it took time. Sometimes centuries. But it always survived. It was perhaps the only institution man had created that had lasted for over two thousand years. And it had done that by not being inflexible. Or foolish. The church did what the church needed to do. The trouble was, he did not have centuries to wait.

So do it. Now.

Apply maximum pressure.

CHAPTER 4

JASON CARDINAL RICHTER HAD OFTEN FANTASIZED ABOUT THE DEVIL. Was he real? Was he even a he? Like many, he thought of the devil in the abstract. A concept. The reverse of God. The epitome of temptation. Then there was John 8:44. *Whenever he speaks a lie, he speaks from his own nature, for he is a liar and the father of lies.* One other thing was also certain. The devil never came dressed in a red cape, with pointy horns, holding a pitchfork. Instead, he always appeared as nothing you'd ever wished for.

So he wondered.

Why had the devil come to see him?

"I am not naïve," Casaburi said. "I fully understand that some of the positions my party takes on various issues could be... uncomfortable... for the church. But let us be real. That could be said of everyone. We all have our bias and prejudices. Our loves and hates. But we have a 60-plus percent approval rating from the Italian electorate. We control nearly a majority of parliament. After the coming elections that will most likely be a majority. Which means our esteemed president will have no choice but to appoint our party leader as prime minister."

"But to achieve that majority status in parliament you have to win thirty-eight of the contested seats. That might prove insurmountable."

"Not if the Vatican focuses its considerable resources on swaying the electorate."

He chuckled. "You overestimate us."

"The church's influence is enormous, and we both know that. Your priests can change hearts and minds across the peninsula."

"The Curia will not authorize it," he said. "I explored that possibility. I truly did. Tell your party leaders that they will have to find another way."

Luckily, he'd anticipated rejection. So he'd come prepared.

"Try again," he said. "This time use these two words. *Pignus Christi.*"

Had he heard right? The Pledge of Christ? He was curious. "What do you know of such things?"

"A great deal. They are not secret. History records them. An ancient promise that the church instituted from its beginnings, yet rarely gave."

He wondered about Casaburi's interest. He knew the man to be forty-two years old, born to the north, in Tuscany, to a working-class family. He had a modest education that included a university degree. He was a member of parliament, longtime secretary of the National Freedom Party, charged with its everyday administration.

Nothing really remarkable about him.

Including his appearance.

Tall, lanky, the face raggedly handsome with a strong jaw, a straight nose, and a pair of pale, almost artless brown eyes. A thick patch of dark hair, graying at the temples, contributed to an accommodating look that was easily photographed. He was impeccably dressed in a pin-striped charcoal suit, crisp white shirt, and purple tie. Everything he knew about this ambitious politician signaled trouble—truly the devil—and he regretted becoming entangled with him.

But entangled he was.

Casaburi sat straight in his chair. "One of the *Pignus Christi* in particular is relevant here. In 1512 Pope Julius II was dying. He'd been a busy man. He'd reclaimed the Papal States. Driven most foreign invaders from Italy. Rebuilt Rome. Ordered the Sistine Chapel painted. Furthered the arts. Started construction on St. Peter's Basilica. Restored the papacy to a political superiority. He was a great pope. The Warrior Pope. But he also bankrupted the church in the process. Of course, the Vatican was already deep in debt thanks to the Borgias and Alexander VI. So before Julius died he made a deal with the Medici. The family had been banished from their beloved Florence and they wanted to return."

"All of that appears in the history books," he said. "Except the part about a deal."

"Giuliano di Lorenzo de' Medici was head of the family. A likable young man. Capable too. But being the third son, he had quite the inferiority complex. So, trying to make a name for himself, Giuliano made a deal with Julius II. He loaned the church ten million gold florins. An enormous sum at the time. Lucky for Julius the Medici possessed gold and property in abundance. But to secure that loan Julius had to give the Medici collateral."

"As I recall my history," he said. "Julius had Florence surrounded by an army, ready to lay siege."

"That he did. But Giuliano didn't care. He wanted real collateral. Julius had none, other than the *Pignus Christi*. A pledge, in writing, signed by the pope himself, under a sworn oath to God, promising in perpetuity to repay the debt. Which Julius signed, and after 513 years that debt remains unpaid. Surely you know about such things."

Yes, he did. He served on the Commission of Cardinals, a five-member body appointed by the pope to oversee the Institute for the Works of Religion or, as it was more commonly known, the Vatican Bank. Which was not a bank in the traditional sense. Instead, it collected, accounted for, invested, and distributed the church's wealth. The problem? That had historically been done with remarkable confusion, official bungling, no independent oversight, and outright corruption and abuse. Not even popes knew the truth about its dealings, a willful ignorance that many had seemed to bask within. Scandals had become all too frequent, and there'd been many attempts at major reforms. The latest pope had tried his hand and appointed five cardinals whom he thought capable of making changes. But instead of positive moves, more corruption had seeped to the surface through the ongoing fraud trial of six defendants.

A five-hundred-year-old promise from the Middle Ages?

What possible relevance could that have?

"Why did you come to me? There are other cardinals much more politically connected. I work only with the bank."

"Which is precisely why I chose you. You alone will understand the gravity of the debt the church owes."

He shrugged. "Could we not simply ignore any pledge, assuming for a moment it still even exists? That was a long time ago."

Casaburi chuckled. "Which the church is quite the expert at doing. But really? That would be your solution? The pope gave his word, in writing, upon an oath sworn to God, and you simply ignore it? What do you think 1.2 billion Catholics would think of that?"

Not much, he silently admitted. But still. "It is ancient history."

"How hard would it be to have the faithful obey the commands of the pope when the church itself is a liar?" Casaburi asked. "What kind of panic do you think will ensue when people realize that something so basic and fundamental as their church is founded on nothingness. No honor. No integrity. No nothing. Have you not taken enough abuse with your questionable positions on sexual predators? What has that cost, just in terms of credibility?"

He knew the answer. A lot. "You seem quite the expert on this Pledge of Christ."

Casaburi nodded. "It was memorialized in two writings. Each identical. Both signed by the pope. One was kept with the church, the other with the Medici."

He needed to make clear, "The Medici family effectively ended in 1737, when the last male royal heir died. Then, six years later, the final female heir died. There are no more legitimate royal Medicis in that line. It is extinct. So even if this Pledge of Christ exists, it would only be viable to a lawful Medici."

"I am a legitimate Medici. A legal royal heir."

"That's impossible."

"I assure you, it is not."

From everything he knew about Eric Casaburi, the man was regarded as braggadocious and narcissistic. As a minister in parliament Casaburi had never sponsored a single piece of meaningful legislation. He spent the majority of his time managing the National Freedom Party, talking to the media, and speaking at political gatherings, promising only that he and his party would deliver the direct opposite of the current ruling majority. What that might be was never detailed. He, and his party, were the precise definition of style over substance. But in today's Italy, where the people were clamoring for change, tired of the same old, same old, that empty rhetoric had found a welcome home.

"You have DNA evidence of your ancestry?"

"I do. My family's Medici roots are not something we speak of in public. The story of the *Pignus Christi* signed by Julius II has been with us for generations. And DNA evidence does not lie."

"You will have to prove all of that," he made clear.

"I will. But keep this in mind. The Florentine florin was struck from 1252 to 1533, with no significant change in its design or metal content. It contained 3.5 grams of pure gold. The Medici loaned ten million florins to the church. In today's value that is 2.3 billion euros."

"A significant sum," he said.

Casaburi stood. "Then interest, for over five hundred years, has to be added to that. Which is substantial. Ten percent, I am told. The resulting balance would be in the hundreds of billions of euros."

He stayed seated and kept a calm demeanor. "You seem to know a great deal about this pledge. Do you have the Medici copy?"

"Of course. I would not be here without it."

"Why is this only being demanded now?"

"You have to ask that?"

Of course. "I assume that in return for our political support, this matter will never see the light of day?"

"It would not be in our best interests to bankrupt the Holy See. We prefer to be in partnership with you. But if you decide to support our opponents? Then our empathy would wane, and we would see what the people think of another example of Catholic hypocrisy."

"Does the party know of your... Medici connection?"

"Not in the least. My task as party secretary is to advance our aims. How I do that is my concern. Results are what they want." Casaburi stepped for the door. "I look forward to hearing from you."

"Soon? I assume."

"I will give you until Friday at noon."

Four days.

Casaburi opened the door.

And left.

CHAPTER 5

SALISBURY, ENGLAND
12:15 P.M.

THOMAS DEWBERRY DROVE HIS SILVER-GRAY MERCEDES AT AN unhurried pace, enjoying the mental release he always felt with being out in the countryside. He savored any escape from London's hurriedness and its microscope, where nosy eyes and ears seemed everywhere. That apprehension all came from leading a solitary life, one devoted only to God, church, and his work, in that order.

The motorway ahead seemed a 110-kilometer-an-hour traffic jam steadily snaking its way west across southern England. Thoughts speckled through his brain like insects darting across water. More and more of late he'd found himself thinking introspectively. Analyzing. Wanting to fully understand himself. But always seeming to fail.

When had it all started?

That was easy.

As a child, when he tortured and killed stray cats and dogs. He'd come to learn that he did not commit those atrocities because he was born bad, or was inherently evil. Instead, as his former psychologist said, he was the product of systematic violentization.

"Experiences that make people dangerous happen over a long period of time. They do not occur all at once. They come gradually, like water over sandstone, and slowly change the shape of things."

Yes, they did.

He now fully understood the five-step process.

It started with brutalization—when a child routinely witnessed and experienced violence. For him that came from his father, a fearsomely violent Welshman who beat his two sons, eventually killing one of them. He could still see his little brother lying in a pine box, not understanding why he wasn't waking up. He'd begged him to get up, since his brother was the only other person he had, the only one who knew what it felt like to be him.

And he lost that.

Violent coaching by an authority figure came next. His started the day he was severely beaten in the neighborhood and came home bloodied and bruised. His father slapped him across the face and made him go back and fight.

He did and nearly beat a boy to death.

Belligerency followed, the conscious decision to use violence to protect yourself. For him that happened at Catholic school. When he acted out the nuns would rap him across the knuckles with a metal-edged ruler. One day he told the nun that if she hit him one more time he'd smash her head.

She did. So he did.

The fourth stage was violent performances.

That came when you asked yourself if you'd be able to hurt someone bad enough to keep them down, make them bleed, and do great bodily harm. He'd known exactly what the therapist meant, since he had no reservations about any of those. As a young man people began to view him differently. Some called him mentally unstable. Others dangerous. Most gave him a wide berth. And as he willingly accepted that newfound status, he quickly drifted into the final stage.

Virulency.

A commitment to act violently.

To hurt at will. Without regret or remorse.

He'd experienced all five stages by age seventeen. That's when he first killed, beating a local bully to death with a rugby bat.

He then tossed the body in a car he stole, drove it two hours to a bridge, and threw the corpse into a river. That was the moment he became what he'd hated most.

His father.

One of his biggest regrets was not killing that man before he died of a heart attack.

He exited the highway and navigated a series of back roads to his destination, which lay outside Salisbury on a broad, grassy plain.

Stonehenge.

Some say it came from the Neolithic Age. Others called it a Druid place of worship. An important burial site. Or something else entirely. On a midsummer's day the sun definitely rose in a direct line with the avenue of stones. Did that make it a calendar? Was it some sort of religious site for sun worshipers? Nobody knew.

He parked in the public lot and stepped out into a warm summer afternoon. Physically he was unassuming. He had a friendly-looking face, a bit on the fleshy side, with pale-colored eyes. With his generous physical build, he dressed in a casual style that suggested not a lot of thought had gone into it. He looked like someone you might be happy to know, a contradiction that never hinted at his true self. He was not one to tell jokes or make comments that anyone would find unsettling. Nor was he a person with no interests, likes, or desires, someone who responded like a machine to the pulling of levers. Not at all. He was well read and enjoyed movies, especially the black-and-white classics. He thought of himself as curious of all things, especially nature. Years of therapy had taught him one sobering fact. He possessed no conscience, few moral values, and little to no emotional structure. Which all made his job so much easier.

He paid his admission fee and headed for the shuttle bus, which would take him and the other visitors over to the two horseshoe-shaped rows of rock. Thirty-five stones stood upright, some supporting huge carved lintels. The innermost circle was of smaller rocks, one even dubbed the altar stone. The whole structure was surrounded by ancient grassy earthworks. But he'd not come for the mystery or history or even the special tour. On the bus he'd noticed one of the other visitors. Coarse features, cob nose, satchel mouth, and a scrubby salt-and-pepper beard that dusted the cheeks, chin, and neck of coffee-colored skin. Another one of those unassuming individuals, the kind of person no one gave a second glance toward.

This one went by the name Bartolomé.

Thomas kept his distance as the tour group stepped off the bus and fanned out with the guide. Once visitors could roam at will. Not anymore. That privilege now came only to those who paid for the VIP experience, which involved a guide. He'd been told to be on the 11:30 A.M. tour and here he was.

He stayed casual in his movements and kept his focus, like everyone else's, on the monument. Finally, after a few minutes, he approached Bartolomé and quietly asked, "Did you know the Anglo-Saxon name for this place means 'hanging stones'?"

Bartolomé scrutinized him with a pair of dark rheumy eyes. "That is not correct. Most antiquarians today believe it to mean 'stone gallows.'"

The voice was deep and gravelly, and the reference to the hanging stones and gallows signaled the correct code words.

A necessary precaution.

If a different phrase had been uttered he would have known there was trouble and that this man, his personal envoy, had been compromised.

But all was good.

"There is an additional request," Bartolomé finally whispered to him. "It came a short while ago."

He was listening.

Bartolomé ambled toward the blue stones in the center of the horseshoe. The guide was rambling on about how they might not be native to England, perhaps coming from Wales or the continent.

He followed, staying close.

"There's a tale," Bartolomé said. "Legends recount that this monument was built by Merlin himself, the great blocks moved into position by magic powers without the aid of human engineering. These blue stones were supposedly brought here by magic from a quarry in the Preseli Mountains in Wales."

He'd learned to indulge his intermediary.

Bartolomé could not be rushed.

They strolled around the stones, drifting even farther from the VIP tour and the guide. He'd actually been here before. Gray as the stones themselves seemed the lives at which they hinted. Some unknown race who liked to erect huge standing megaliths, most times in great rows or circles under an open sky. Similar monuments were found all over England. But this was the most impressive of all. Monstrous powers, born in half-lit minds, had been worshiped here, surely with great pomp and ceremony.

All pagan.

Heathen.

"You still have not mentioned the additional request," he softly said.

"I've been doing some reading. In 1563, at the Ecumenical Council of Trent, headed by Pope Pius IV, it was written that nothing is more necessary to the church of God than the pope associating with himself, as cardinals, the most upright and competent shepherds. The words used then were clear. *Our Lord Jesus Christ will require the blood of the evil government of shepherds who are negligent and forgetful of their office.* Apparently, one has become a problem."

That was a first.

He'd killed people, but it had always been in tough spots of the world. Retaliation for some previous violence. Message sending. He took his cue from the 1578 edition of the *Directorium Inquisitorum*, the standard Inquisitorial manual. *Quoniam punitio non refertur primo, per se in correctionem, bonum eius qui punitur, sed in bonum publicum ut alij terreantur, a malis committendis avocentur.* For punishment does not take place primarily, and per se, for the correction and good of the person punished, but for the public good in order that others may become terrified and weaned away from the evils they would commit.

"They offer double the usual fee for this additional service," Bartolomé said.

"This is different."

"I agree."

"When would this need to be done?" he asked.

"By the end of the week."

Proper preparation was important to success. Speed was not his strong point. Creativity took time and required coordination and flexibility.

So he was hesitant. For a variety of reasons.

"I understand this is unusual," Bartolomé said. "I question that too. But the situation itself is unusual and requires definitive action."

"I have never killed a prelate before."

"Do you accept the job?"

He looked deep into the eyes, shrewd and watchful. Their benefactor paid generously, which Bartolomé shared in. But it was also always his choice. "I do."

"Here's some additional information you may need." And Bartolomé handed him a sealed white envelope. "There is also one special condition that is critical. It must be easily determined to be a suicide. No questions. And the original assignment remains. Keep proceeding there."

His envoy walked off.

Their business concluded.

All communication came through Bartolomé, then money appeared in a Swiss account. The arrangement suited him. He had little curiosity to know more, since people with questions often wound up dead. So he did what was asked, went where sent, and left it to others to ponder its meaning.

But this was different.

He stood among the stones and gathered his thoughts, parading them in mental order as if unruly soldiers. A lot was apparently happening. Serious enough that the killing of a cardinal was required. *Our Lord Jesus Christ will require the blood of the evil government of shepherds who are negligent and forgetful of their office.*

Okay.

He would deliver.

CHAPTER 6

DILLENBURG, GERMANY

COTTON STARED THROUGH THE CRACK MADE BY THE PARTIALLY OPEN door into the priest hole and spotted a thin metal wire running from the panel back into the hidden compartment.

A trip wire?

Possibly.

He'd expected something. There had to be more security here than simply a remote location that no one would suspect as a secret repository. But cardinals could not be too overt with security since, after all, why would they need such measures? They supposedly lived a life of chastity and poverty as princes of the church. Most of them were bishops and archbishops, leading dioceses around the world. Some were merely titular bishops, officials within the Roman Curia. A small number were priests, recognized for their extraordinary service. The duties of a cardinal were *in addition* to those other responsibilities. Their selection came solely from the pope at his discretion, and their most solemn obligation was to elect a papal successor.

He'd done his homework and knew that Jason Richter was a German who'd first studied in Paris, then obtained a doctorate in theology from the University of Mainz. A learned man for sure but unskilled in economics or finance, which had made observers wonder why he was appointed to the commission that oversaw the Vatican Bank. Perhaps it was his connections? He'd served as a member of the Congregation for the Doctrine of the Faith and as president of the Council of the Bishops' Conferences of Europe. He entered the Curia upon his appointment as vice president of the Pontifical Council for the Laity, then as president of Pontifical Council Cor Unum. He'd also served as a papal envoy to hot spots around the world. The current pope counted Richter as a friend, which, more than anything else, explained his selection. The pope had once publicly called Richter *a clever theologian.* A comment that would surely come back to haunt, if a scandal ever broke. He knew that Richter had no idea he was under suspicion. Which should allow for an uneventful sneak and peek. So he focused on the trip wire and saw that it led downward into a leather satchel. The wire was attached to the door panel by a screw. Gently, he moved the hinged door inward just enough to create slack then reached in and unwound the wire from the screw, freeing it. That was probably the way Richter would gain access too, knowing the trap existed. With the phone's light he further examined the gap and saw no more wires.

Okay. Here goes.

He opened the panel.

The space beyond was a rectangle about two feet deep and six feet high. Hell of a place for a person to hide. Like a vertical coffin. Just looking at it brought on a wave of anxiety. Tight spaces were not his favorite. He hated them. But he assumed hiding here was definitely better than the alternative, which would have been torture and death for those medieval priests.

He gently opened the top of the leather satchel and saw that the bag was full of neatly bound euros. Lots of them. The wire ran into one of the bundles on top. He knew what that was. A dye bomb. Normally used in bank robberies. Camouflaged as money and rigged to explode once a robber left the building, staining the bills, making them useless.

He carefully removed the bundle that accommodated the dye

pack, laying it on the compartment floor. The wire was connected to a metal pin that, once withdrawn by opening the door, would have activated the booby trap. He was now able to further examine the money and saw it was all in crisp hundred-euro notes.

The intel had been correct.

He found his phone, snapped a few pictures, and sent them off to Stephanie Nelle.

Okay. Mission accomplished.

He replaced the satchel and re-inserted the dye pack. He re-attached the wire and closed the panel door, which clicked back into place. He was about to leave when he heard the growl of an engine, then the screech of brakes as tires grabbed pavement. He stepped over to the window and gazed down at the semicircular drive.

A police cruiser had arrived.

Doors opened and three uniformed officers emerged.

Through the open bedroom door he heard them enter the house. There'd been no door forced. Which meant they had a key. One of the explicit conditions of his assignment was that no one know that he'd been here, and he'd assured the Swiss Guard that this would not be a problem.

But it had just become one.

He stepped to the open bedroom door and peered out. Footsteps bounded upward. The officers came to the second-floor landing and turned up toward the third. They were definitely coming his way.

Had he triggered some sort of alarm?

Hard to say.

He shut the door and locked it.

One thing he'd never done was romanticize his work. As an intelligence officer he'd learned that the job was a constant struggle with three emotions. Uncertainty, fear, and, the worst, panic. Master those and your odds for success increased exponentially. Skills could be taught. But desire was innate. You were either born with it or not. And he was definitely born with it. He missed being a full-time Magellan Billet agent. Retirement, though welcomed, came with its limitations. Most of them were good. Some not so much. Thankfully, his usefulness remained and his actions generally met with success.

So be successful.

He rushed over to the window and opened it, easing himself out onto the narrow sill he'd noticed a few moments ago, wondering if his nearly fifty-year-old muscles could stand the strain. He kept his spine ruler-straight against the outer wall and fought hard not to tip forward. Thankfully, the sill was about ten inches wide and heights were never a problem for him. He reached the corner and stared down at the high-pitched roof of a wing that extended out from the main house ten to fifteen feet down. Steep. But an iron exhaust pipe protruded about halfway down. Could he snag it?

One way to find out.

He jumped, arms swinging to add momentum to the leap, hands reaching out for support that wasn't there. He hit the slate feetfirst and his knees collapsed, fingers probing for a hold as his body slid downward. He threw all of his weight up through his hips and shoulders, swinging his legs in a scissors motion, arms stretched out, trying to slow the skid. His hands found the iron pipe and he grabbed hold, stopping his slide.

He faced downward toward the slate and lay still, allowing the blood to flow back to his extremities. Then rolled over. The sun moved in and out of clouds, casting harsh moving shadows. All he had to do was get off the roof. The window he'd escaped from was around the corner, out of sight. Four more windows faced him from the main wing, looking down.

One of them opened.

A policeman appeared, poking his upper body out.

And aimed a gun.

CHAPTER 7

COTTON RELEASED HIS GRIP ON THE STEEL PIPE EXTENDING FROM THE roof and rolled his body across the slate.

Just as the cop fired.

The bullet ricocheted off the roof.

He kept rolling until he came to a valley, which allowed him to get to his feet, balancing a foot on either side. Before the man could readjust his aim and zero in on the new target, he leaped over the top edge to the other side of the roof. But the pitch was so steep that he had no choice but to hang on to the peak with his hands. At least he was out of the line of fire, except for his fingers.

Another round found the roof on the other side of the gable.

He let go and started a slide down the steep slate finishing with his feet catching in the copper gutters. How far a drop from there to the ground? Only one way to find out. He wiggled to the left and swung himself around on his belly until he faced the tarnished gutter. A quick glance over the leading edge and he saw the drop down was about ten feet.

But he could minimize that.

He gripped the gutter and swung his body off the roof, holding on and hoping the copper could handle his weight.

It couldn't.

The gutter broke free from its attachments.

He straightened out his arms and cut about eight feet off the ten. An easy matter to drop from there to the ground.

Here he was again.

Right in the middle of the fray.

He started in the navy, graduating from Annapolis, then choosing fighter pilot training. But friends of his father—a submarine commander who died when he was ten—had other ideas and enrolled him in law school. After obtaining a juris doctorate he was assigned to JAG and billeted to Pensacola, Florida. From there a career Justice Department employee, Stephanie Nelle, plucked him away for a new agency she was creating.

The Magellan Billet.

So he switched career paths.

Again.

Twelve years he worked for Stephanie as one of her intelligence officers, handling whatever she tossed his way. He decided to retire out early after being shot in Mexico City. Not the first time, but he definitely wanted it to be last. So he resigned his commission, quit his job, divorced, sold his house in Georgia, and moved to Copenhagen, opening an old-book shop. Books had been a lifelong passion. Now they would be his livelihood. Naïvely, he thought his time in the crosshairs over. But Stephanie had other ideas. And from time to time, he helped her, and others, out. Favors here and there. Some for money, since he did have to pay the bills. Most out of loyalty.

Which kept him in the game.

He surveyed where he stood.

On the back side of the residence. Away from trouble for the moment. But it would only take the police in the house a few moments to regroup. His car was parked down the street, closer to the stone watchtower that had once been part of the old castle. He headed off through a thin stretch of woods behind the house and backtracked to his rental car.

To be honest he hadn't expected to find anything in that priest hole. A cardinal with four hundred thousand euros? True, some of them could be gregarious, outspoken, controversial. But to outright take a huge cash payoff? That was really bold and foolish. Nothing like that ever stayed secret. Which made him wonder. What was going on here? The source of the information itself was suspect. A criminal defendant with everything to gain by lying. Yet it had turned out not to be false. He'd had many encounters with the Catholic Church over the years. Some good, others bad. Duplicity? Oh, yeah. Plenty of it. Especially with all that happened in Malta. But something did not ring right here. What had James Garner once said. From one of his favorite old television shows. *The Rockford Files. That plant is so obvious it needs watering.*

Yep.

He made it through the foliage and found the small paved parking lot near the old castle site. His rental waited among a handful of other cars. He climbed inside, cranked the engine, and backed out. He shifted into drive and was about to speed off when another police car appeared from around the corner and blocked the way. He floored the accelerator and sped straight at them, clipping the driver's-side front end, spinning the car off the pavement.

He'd violated the terms of his assignment and allowed his presence to become known. Not good. His grandfather had been perhaps the smartest, most insightful person he'd ever known. For a young boy who'd lost his father, that man had filled every void. Dead for over twenty years, he still missed him. He'd been a man of stories, which were nothing but metaphors for life lessons never to forget.

"Cotton, did I ever tell you about a barber who whispers to his customer, 'Let me show you something. This is the most foolish kid in the world. Watch while I prove it to you.' The barber laid a dollar bill in one hand and two quarters in the other, then called a young boy over and asked, 'Which do you want, son?' The boy immediately took the quarters and left. 'What did I tell you?' the barber said. 'That kid never learns.' Later, when that customer left the barbershop, he saw the same boy coming out of the ice

cream store. 'Hey, son, may I ask you a question? Why did you take the quarters instead of the dollar bill?' The boy licked his favorite ice cream and said, 'Because the day I take the dollar, the game is over.' "

Proverbs 14:15 was right.

Fools believe every word they hear, but wise people think carefully about everything.

And he was no fool.

So he took the quarters and kept going, speeding ahead.

Out of Dillenburg.

CHAPTER 8

ERIC ARRIVED BACK AT HIS ROME RESIDENCE, A SPACIOUS APARTMENT on the Via Sistina, in an elegant neighborhood located near the Spanish Steps. The rent was outrageous, but the party paid the bill as a perk for his job as secretary. He'd followed a familiar maze of twisting streets and urban chaos back from the Vatican, leaving one nation and entering another. Above him, the Italian sky loomed sodden and sullen. Featureless. A battleship gray without a hint that a sun existed.

Like his mood.

He'd kept his composure, which had not been easy considering Cardinal Richter's negativity. It galled him how righteous the church tried to be, considering that, for centuries, though it projected itself as above politics, above kings, queens, and emperors, above reproach, nothing could be further from the truth. The church had always been heavily involved in secular matters. Especially Italian politics. It was a practice that dated back to the earliest times and Emperor Constantine who, in the 4th century, called the bishops of all the various Christian factions to Nicaea and ordered them to hammer out one doctrine, one religion, one faith. Once done, he proclaimed that form of Christianity the empire's choice, and from that the Roman Catholic Church was born. Which grew and prospered, provided it kept Constantine, and the emperors who came after him, happy. Which it did. Masterfully.

So to say the church was unconcerned with politics? That was a lie.

But he had his own problems with lies.

He'd run a bluff, one he'd hoped would have borne fruit.

But it had not.

It was memorialized in two writings. Identical. Both signed by the pope. One was kept with the church, the other with the Medici.

He'd told Richter that he had the Medici copy. But he did not. And if forced, he could not press the collection of the debt or apply any pressure without that writing.

A disconcerting thought.

He entered the kitchen and decided he was more thirsty than hungry, so he found a drink in the refrigerator. His favorite. An obscure cola that some called Beverly. Why that name? He had no idea. Once made by the Coca-Cola Company as an apéritif, it was now only bottled for a few select American markets. He'd become friendly with the Italian producer who kept him supplied. Most hated its sharp citrus bitterness, which came from grapefruit rind, but he'd acquired a taste for it as a child.

He sipped the drink and found his phone.

Going to the Vatican had been a calculated act. He'd delayed the visit for as long as possible. But time was running out. Campaigning was about to begin. Everybody would want the church on their side, and he had assured party leaders that he would obtain the support. So he'd made a move, trying to leap to the front of the parade. And failed. Badly.

But he still had three days to rectify things.

His grandmother had been the first to explain the ancient connection. Was it a wild story? Or fact? He prided himself on being a realist, harboring no false illusions about how the world worked. And contrary to what opponents like Cardinal Richter might say, he was sincere in what he said, firm in his beliefs, and dedicated to a cause he thought just. The media loved to call the National Freedom Party a populist organization.

But it was more.
Much more.
Like him.

The sun shone bright, the air heavy with the scent of new-mown hay. One of those mornings steeped in dewy freshness when sounds and sights were brought near, and the Dolomites appeared taller than usual. The Tofana di Mezzo, the third highest peak, rarely seen without a turban of clouds, rose sharp and clear in the distance against the azure sky.

He walked with his grandmother, hand in hand, his nine-year-old eyes focused on the village cemetery that lay opposite the church. Its gate stood ajar, the space beyond crowded with a weed-grown wilderness and ancient trees. A confusion of rough stone heaps marked most of the graves, the markers long since collapsed. A few marble tablets and iron crosses stood near the outer walls recording the names of the better-class dead. Everywhere was coarse deep grass, thistles, nettles, loose stones, broken pottery, and trampled clay. Not a flower in sight, not a touch of poetry or pathos in the place. Nothing but indifference, irreverence, and neglect.

And the silence of the dead.

"Why are we here?" he asked her.

"It is time you see something."

She led him farther into the cemetery. They passed a battered alms box bearing an inscription—WE IMPLORE CHARITY IN THE NAME OF THE BLESSED MARY. *Clearly, no one had left anything inside it for a long time. His nonna stopped before a collection of stones lying among the wiry grass.*

An unmarked grave.

"There is where he is buried," she said.

He was both puzzled and intrigued. "Who's there?"

"An ancestor of our family. Remember what I am telling you, Eric. Never forget."

He was excited to hear what she was about to say.

"You carry royal blood in your veins, just like me. It stretches back centuries. The man in this grave was Gregorio Cappello. He lived here in the mountains a long, long time ago. He died in 1786."

He was amazed. "How do you know that?"

"My father told me. Now I am telling you."

"Was he an important man?"

"He was Medici."

"What is that?"

His grandmother stared down at him. "It is your bloodline. Your heritage. You, Eric, are Medici."

He'd had no idea at the time what that meant. So he'd questioned his nonna, trying to learn more. But as usual, she'd been evasive.

"How do you know this?" he asked.

"Take the soldier. What is it that allows him, with courage, to face the rifle's mouth? It is faith. The painter, what inspires the frescoes and the images? Faith. Think of the patience and labor required to build a grand building. What supported the workmen through their trying task? Faith. The engineers who began the Mont Cenis tunnel at opposite ends of the great mountain. After years of digging, they met in the middle. To what power must we attribute such perseverance, crowned with success? It is the supreme and vivifying power of faith. It is faith that we know we are Medici."

Forty years ago there'd been no way to know for sure. DNA testing was just getting started. But today? That was a different story. He'd run a genealogy but had not been able to obtain any information before 1810. Five years back he'd raised money and financed a renovation of that cemetery. It now looked much different. The graves were restored, the remains disinterred then reverently reburied. His efforts had made the national media, and he'd garnered some praise for the humanitarian effort. Along the way it had been easy to retrieve enough bone and tissue samples to run a DNA analysis, which had confirmed that he was, without a doubt, genetically related to Gregorio Cappello, the person in the grave his grandmother had shown him.

So it was not some fanciful story.

But were they both Medici?

Faith would not be enough to answer that question.

He had to know for sure.

And there was only one way to find out.

CHAPTER 9

JASON REALIZED THAT HIS MEETING WITH ERIC CASABURI WOULD quickly be known throughout the Vatican. Eyes and ears were everywhere. But there was no avoiding it. The Vatican ran on a constant dose of rumors and secrets. As did the bank. Which prided itself on discretion. Even its name, the Institute for the Works of Religion, screamed anonymity. The whole thing was operated by a convoluted system of tiered authority. At the top stood the five-member Commission of Cardinals, which appointed a prelate, who acted as secretary of the commission. Then there was a six-member Board of Superintendence that defined strategy and supervised operations. Finally, a directorate was in charge of everyday operations, accountable directly to the Board of Superintendence. Lots of layers. Plenty of people. All designed, in theory, to make corruption less possible.

Historically, the Vatican published little about its finances. Such a small place. Encompassing only 110 acres. With a population of under a thousand. But while small in size, it had a huge impact in the financial world through investments in banking, real estate, and private enterprise. Revenue poured in from a variety of sources. Donations from Catholics and dioceses around the world made up a large part. Admission fees from museums, tours, stamps, coins, and the sale of publications generated more millions. But investments accounted for an ever-growing percentage. Historically, the Holy See spread its money between stocks and bonds, buying and holding only proven performers. Mainly in industry. The portfolio also included Western European currencies and bonds, some activity in the New York Stock Exchange, and real estate around the world. Lots of real estate. But revenues had long not kept pace with expenses. Deficits were routine. Currently they ran about fifty million euros a year in the red. Popes, the present one included, had routinely ordered a reduction in operating costs. But that had proven impossible. Pundits loved to float a total net worth at around thirty billion euros. The famous quote, attributed to no one in particular, was that *if the church would sell everything it had, it could eliminate poverty in the world.*

But he knew how false that statement was.

True, the Holy See was land-rich from its churches, schools, presbyteries, hospitals, nursing homes, office buildings, condominiums, even a huge number of mobile telephone towers. Tens of thousands of properties scattered around the world. But no one knew their true value, appraisals either nonexistent or woefully out of date. Further complicating things was the fact that many of the properties were aged and run down, their maintenance costs enormous, which more than offset their value. Of course some of the greatest artistic treasures in the world, accumulated throughout two thousand years of Christian history, lay within the Vatican. Their worth? Immeasurable. But not a one would ever be sold.

Last year the bank reported a profit of $41.5 million. The bank's assets—valued at about $6 billion—consisted of investments and deposits from almost fifteen thousand account holders, which included clergy, Vatican employees, and Catholic religious orders around the world. The math was simple. Fifty million in revenue from the budget. Forty-one million in profits from the bank. Which, while not eliminating, definitely cut into the deficit. So the pressure was on to maximize profits. And they'd made some bold moves. Diversifying the portfolio and increasing the annual return by multiple percentage points. Then they'd taken the next step and bought even more real estate, the idea being to flip it for a quick profit. Some of those purchases were made in Ireland and England. Where all the trouble began, with the bribery and corruption that had resulted in indictments and now a trial.

He stood outside.

Another warm, humid summer day in Rome.

He was more accustomed to the mild temperatures and dry air of central Germany, where he was born and raised. But this was the center of the Catholic world. Where everything meaningful happened.

And he loved being a part of it.

His friendship with the pope, which dated back over a decade, had been one of those fortuitous things. He had the papal ear. He wondered if his old friend knew anything about a *Pignus Christi* from the sixteenth century. An obscure piece of Catholic trivia from a long, long time ago. It certainly had no place in the modern world. Collateral now had a much different substance and definition. But five hundred years ago the pope's word had carried much weight. Accompany that with a sworn promise to God? And you had a powerful document.

His first inclination was to make inquiries and conduct a search. But anyone in their right mind at the Vatican would have destroyed that promise long ago. No writing, no debt, no obligation. Of course, the Medici would have a copy. But if they did, and it still existed, why had it not been discovered? True, the Medici died out in the mid-eighteenth century. But what about before then? Two hundred and thirty years passed after 1512 without a mention.

Which was strange.

He started walking.

He'd kept to his schedule for the afternoon, trying not to seem anxious or alert to any of those eyes and ears that were everywhere. He'd waited until nearly 5:00 P.M. before leaving his office. The entire situation with the ongoing fraud trial was a problem. Thankfully, that did not involve him. The Commission of

Cardinals had been briefed on all the particulars of the case, and prosecutors had been assured that there would be no Curial interference. The trial would go where the evidence led. That statement had been supported by personal assurances from the pope himself. Everyone was genuinely shocked by the allegations. The conspiracy was far ranging and deep, exposing many flaws in the Curial system that had allowed the thefts. No surprise there, though. The entire Holy See was overloaded with bureaucrats and competing departments that stayed in foot-dragging mode.

"Eminence."

He stopped at the sound of someone calling.

"Eminence. Please wait."

He turned. A young priest was hustling across the cobblestones his way.

"Forgive me." The acolyte came toward him and stopped. "I went to your office and was informed you had left."

"I have business elsewhere."

The young man was winded. "I understand, but the Holy Father would like to see you."

The pope? "About what?"

"I do not know, Eminence. But I was sent to find you."

"Thank you for the message. I will contact his office and arrange a meeting at His Holiness' convenience."

He turned to leave.

"Eminence," the priest said. "He wants to see you now."

CHAPTER 10

ROME, ITALY
5:45 P.M.

STEFANO CROSSED HIMSELF AND STARTED HIS PRAYER.

He'd been hailed a hero at the end of the match, the goal regarded as somewhat miraculous. One hop, then up and in. And maybe it had been. He was the only Catholic priest among the four Calcio Storico teams.

A status he liked.

The Greens' victory would be toasted until the wee hours of tomorrow morning, but a summons from Rome had required that he travel south immediately. The instruction had come by secure text.

Return. Home Church. 6:00 p.m.

Since he'd specifically taken three days' leave for the tournament, the summons had been both unexpected and troubling.

The Basilica di Santa Maria Maggiore sat outside the Vatican borders, technically part of Italy but owned by the Holy See, possessing the same immunity and political status as a foreign embassy. Its canopied high altar was reserved for use by the pope alone. A cardinal was always in charge of the site, overseeing assistant priests, a chapter of canons, along with Redemptorist, Dominican, and Franciscan friars.

He was kneeling in one of the empty pews, the building closed to visitors for the day. The solitude was welcomed. He had to come down off the high from the match. The euphoria, the crowds cheering, his teammates congratulating was in many ways like a drug, stimulating, but also distracting. That was over now. It had to be forgotten. Back to work.

Quiet always helped with his thoughts.

As did St. Pius V.

Pope at a time in the sixteenth century when Protestantism first swept England, Scotland, Germany, Holland, and France. Talk about challenges. But he was a tough Dominican friar. A former grand inquisitor who standardized the Bible, formed the Holy League, and defeated the Ottoman Empire. He even had the audacity to forbid horse racing in St. Peter's Square, which the people loved. In day-to-day life he was highly ascetic and wore a hair shirt beneath his white robe, that color becoming a standard for all the popes who came after. The church canonized him in 1712. Fourteen years before that his body had been placed within a sarcophagus here in the basilica. A flap of gilded bronze, showing the effigy of the pope in shallow relief, could be swung open, revealing the remains, behind glass, adorned in papal robes. And here it had rested for over three hundred years.

Stefano lifted his head and stared at the sarcophagus.

Today the gilded flap was down, concealing the body.

Pius V also left another mark. One that had endured right up to the present. As in any other nation, security within the Vatican had always been essential. Since the early 1500s the Swiss Guard had been its public face. But the most secret agency within the Holy See had been specifically chartered by Pius V. Its purpose? To end the life of Protestant Elizabeth I and support her cousin, the Catholic Mary, Queen of Scots, for the English throne. Though Pius failed in that mission, what he created had served popes through schisms, revolutions, dictators, persecutions, attacks, world wars, even assassination attempts. First called the Supreme Congregation for the Holy Inquisition of Heretical Error, then the much shorter Holy Alliance. In the twentieth century the name was changed to simply *L'Entitá*, the Entity.

Its motto?

With the Cross and the Sword.

Never once had the Holy See ever acknowledged its existence, but it was the oldest and one of the best intelligence agencies in the world. A model of secrecy and efficiency.

And he was a part of it.

"Pardon me, Father," a voice said behind him.

He turned his head but stayed on his knees.

Sergio Cardinal Ascolani stood in the center aisle.

Stefano immediately rose to his feet and smoothed out the folds in his black cassock. Not only was Ascolani the Vatican's secretary of state, he was also the head of the Entity. Unusual, to say the least, for one man to occupy two high posts, but the current pope had seen no problem with such dual responsibilities.

"I appreciate your promptness to my summons," Ascolani said, stepping into a row of pews and sitting. Stefano stayed standing, knowing his place.

"I watched the match," Ascolani said.

He knew it had been televised across Italy.

"What a goal. That was quite a bold move."

"I got a lucky bounce."

"*Luck is where opportunity meets preparation.* And, you, Father Giumenta, are always prepared."

He appreciated the compliment.

"I am sorry you missed the celebratory dinner. I know how you love such things."

He did. But, "I have enjoyed them before, and there will be others. I am curious, though, as to why the sudden summons. I was scheduled to be off for the next few days."

"Eric Casaburi has finally surfaced."

Really? They'd been watching for several months, ever since it was learned that Casaburi had cultivated a source within the Vatican. And an odd one at that. Jason Cardinal Richter. Who'd been making inquiries across the Curia about Casaburi and his new-right National Freedom Party. Apparently gauging their popularity for any tacit political support the church might be able to offer. Thankfully, the covert monitoring of phone lines and cell phones was not illegal within Vatican City. The situation had elevated once Richter's possible involvement with the fraud trial was revealed by one of the co-defendants. Interestingly, the Swiss Guard had not reported that situation. Instead, more spies within the guard had alerted them. Friction between the two security agencies was not uncommon. One was domestic, the other foreign, though that line blurred on an almost daily basis. Richter was now under close Entity observation.

"Did Casaburi meet with Cardinal Richter?" he asked.

Ascolani nodded. "I had the room wired. All was recorded."

Efficient. As always. And another example of that blurred line.

Nine years ago Stefano had been working out of the Archdiocese of Boston when he was reassigned to Rome's Pontificia Accademia Ecclesiastica, where priests were trained as apostolic nuncios. The academy itself towered above the Piazza della Minerva in what seemed to be just another former Roman palace. He graduated the course and became part of what was considered to be one of the world's elite corps of diplomats. He served three years around the world as a deputy papal representative. There he learned that the principal gatherers of intelligence for the Holy See were the apostolic nuncios, similar to ambassadors deployed by every nation-state. The only difference was that the Holy See, unlike other nations, did not make its intelligence officers known to the host countries. Why? Because the Entity did not officially exist and the Vatican did not employ intelligence officers. Stefano had caught the eye of his superiors, who recalled him to Rome and placed him in charge of the Entity's Gruppo Intervento Rapido, the rapid intervention group, the people who handled the jobs that others could not, or did not want to.

Like Eric Casaburi.

"I was able to hear the entire conversation," Ascolani said. "Casaburi first asked nicely for the church's help then, once rejected, applied pressure."

"How did Richter react?"

"To his credit, Jason said no. Quite decisively, too."

He was impressed. "I did not see that coming."

"Neither did I. And yet there were four hundred thousand euros in cash hidden inside a German residence that Richter controls."

"So the information proved correct?"

"Apparently so."

He'd known that the Swiss Guard had asked the Americans to assist them in verifying whether Richter might be dirty. Again, not a word of that had been passed up the chain of command to the Entity. That omission had drawn Ascolani's attention.

"My source within the Swiss Guard," Ascolani said, "sent me a photo the American asset took in Germany. A satchel full of euros hidden inside a priest hole, booby-trapped with a dye pack."

All of which was interesting, but surely not why he'd been summoned.

"Another matter was raised during the conversation between Richter and Casaburi. A mention of something I thought I would never hear."

He was eager for an explanation, but none came. Instead the face, with its sallow, pockmarked skin stretched over thin features, maintained a glacial control. He'd come to know that Ascolani was a man of patrician tastes and earthly language, who delighted in intrigue. Also tight-lipped. So he would only be told what he needed to be told.

His boss stood from the pew. "Before we have a much more detailed conversation on that other matter, there is a task I must complete. Please stay in Rome, readily available. I will be in touch shortly."

Ascolani walked off.

He could not help himself and had to say, "You seem troubled, Eminence."

The older man stopped in the aisle but did not turn back.

"I am."

CHAPTER 11

Florence, Italy

Eric stepped out onto the platform. He sensed no one watching, no eyes turning abruptly his way, no hurried movements, no one acting suspiciously. He was known, for sure, but not enough to forfeit his anonymity among millions of Italians. Mainly he kept a watch for the media, but absent them he could still move about with relative impunity.

He'd taken one of Trenitalia's fast Red Arrow trains, splurging for its executive class that offered comfortable leather seats and complimentary steward service. The journey north to Florence had been fast. About ninety minutes, far preferable to a four-hour car drive. He'd needed to get here quick. He only had until Friday to gather his ammunition.

People were right. Florence was indeed one of the world's most handsome cities, wearing its age with an obvious dignity. It sat on an open plain filling both sides of the River Arno, surrounded by rings of higher ground adorned by nature and art. Little is known of its ancient history. Originally a mere suburb of an Etruscan hill town, its fate changed in Roman times thanks to a commanding location. Its most dramatic transformation began in the fifteenth century with the rise of the Medici. For the next three hundred years, they covered the city with monuments, churches, and palaces created and decorated by the greatest minds of the time. Petrarch, Boccaccio, Raphael, Michelangelo, Galileo. It became the cradle of the Renaissance. The Athens of the West. Its growth and prosperity due mainly to trade, woolen cloth the main export. He'd always liked what one observer had written. *We must dearly love Florence, for she is the mother of all those who live by thought. We must study her without ceasing, for she offers us an inexhaustible source of instruction.*

That she did.

He found a taxi and was driven into the heart of the city.

Evening had arrived and the cafés were alive with patrons, the streets bustling with tourists enjoying the end of another summer day. He walked toward the town center, the air becoming denser, the route twisting between endless rows of multistory buildings jammed together like soldiers on parade.

He entered the Piazza della Signoria and stared up at the Palazzo Vecchio. Once the political center of Florence and Tuscany. Fortress-like in appearance. Erected in a time of danger when Florence was divided by factions, assailed by conspiracies, and threatened by popular tumult. The home of the Signoria, who once lorded over the city. Its representatives held office for only two months, living in the palace together, each in their own quarters, ready to transact the public's business at any hour of the day or night. Every time he visited the piazza he thought about 1497, the last day of the annual carnival. Dominican friar Savonarola, a religious fanatic who'd managed to gain control of the city, erected a pyramid consisting of masquerade costumes, masks, wigs, rouge pots, musical instruments, dice boxes, books of poetry, parchments, illuminated manuscripts, works of art, and paintings, especially those that represented feminine beauty. The pile was set afire and the Signoria appeared on the palace's balcony, watching, the smoky air echoing song, the pealing of bells, and the sound of trumpets.

The famed Bonfire of the Vanities.

A year after that another pile stood in the piazza when Friar Savonarola and two of his companions were burned at the stake for treason.

What irony.

But the citizens of Florence had never been able to tolerate oppression for long.

The bells in the palazzo's tower rang for 6:00 P.M. In times of trouble those same bells had once called the men of Florence to arms. The sound, like the lowing of a cow, could be heard in every part of the city.

He slowed his step and kept walking until he found La Giostra, located between the Duomo and the Piazza di Santa Croce, his favorite Florentine restaurant. People stood outside studying the enticing selections on the menu displayed behind glass. The restaurant served only sixteen tables scattered beneath a low barrel ceiling supported by brick arches, low lit from twinkling amber lights, like Christmas all year long. It was constantly crowded and reservations were tough to get, but the owners always made room for him. So he'd called ahead and asked that a table for two be held. His guest was waiting, already enjoying some pear ravioli.

"Some wine would make that taste even better," he said, approaching the table and taking a seat.

"Then by all means, order us some."

He'd not come to eat, but knew this man would require stroking. He was one of the foremost experts on DNA analysis in Italy, teaching at the Università degli Studi di Milano and operating a testing lab that had an international reputation. He was also a vocal conservative who'd liked that the secretary of the fastest rising new-right party had taken an interest in him. Two years ago this expert had established a DNA link between himself and Gregorio Cappello. They were definitely related—to a probability of 99.99 percent. He'd known that when the time came to apply pressure the Vatican would want verified proof of his lineage. Recent evidence, too. So he'd held off until now to have the final test run. The one that would establish a definitive link between Gregorio Cappello and the Medicis.

"We have two hours until the appointment," he said to his guest. "So let us enjoy the food and wine."

He caught the waiter's attention and placed a drink order.

The first DNA matching request had been innocuous. A family thing, was what he'd told this man. A connection to a lost ancestor in the Cappello line. But this next test? That was something altogether different. Richter had been correct earlier. History noted that the Medici family ended in two steps. The first was in 1737 when the last male heir, Gian Gastone, died. The family had always been patriarchal but, with no male heirs, everything passed to Gian's sister, Anna Maria Luisa. But she died in 1743, leaving no heirs.

Or so the story went.

His grandmother had laid out the rest. How Cappello was a direct ancestor. Now it was up to him to prove her tale true.

So he took a few minutes and explained. When finished, he said, "If your tests are conclusive, I want you to announce the results to the world. It will be *your* triumph. The return of the Medicis, proven by you."

Not an altruistic gesture by any means. He needed the credibility that this academician would give the finding to hammer his point home to both the Vatican and the world that the Medicis had returned.

The media would love it.

The waiter returned with two glasses of a dark 2018 Sassicaia. His favorite. It was aged in French oak barriques for two years, then spent another six months stored in bottles before being sold. Loaded with the sweet flavors of wild berries tempered by a smoky tobacco-like taste. Perfection. He offered a toast. "To a successful endeavor."

They clinked glasses.

And he enjoyed a satisfying sip.

But he wondered.

Would the test confirm what his grandmother had told him? What his family had secretly believed for centuries? For so long he'd relied on faith.

But that would not be enough here.

It had to be real.

CHAPTER 12

JASON WAS LED ACROSS THE VATICAN, BUT NOT TO THE PAPAL PALACE. Instead, he was taken into the gardens. Forty-four hectares across a sloping landscape that eight hundred years of constant attention had molded into a paradise. It started out as a common medieval garden enclosed by walls and filled with symbols primarily tied to the Virgin Mary. But it had morphed into something extraordinary with manicured lawns, caves, kiosks, statues, and fountains.

He followed the priest down one of the crisscrossing avenues beneath a canopy of umbrella pines, cedars, cypresses, and Egyptian palms. He was perplexed. The pope was not much of an outdoorsman. Papal visits to the garden had been few and far between. Especially on a warm June evening. It was also well known that the pope enjoyed dinner. His favorite meal of the day. Always early and never alone. This pontiff liked people, and garnering an invite to his table was a big deal, one Jason had managed to snare a few times. He'd at first thought this another dining opportunity, but now he was not so sure.

They rounded a corner on the paved path and passed through one of the most attractive and shady areas, a place littered with gurgling fountains and marble benches. The air hung heavy with the cloying scent of honeysuckle. Down a short incline they approached the Fountain of the Eagle. He knew that, like all of the gardens' fountains, its water came from a lake forty kilometers away. Waiting for him was not the pope, but Sergio Cardinal Ascolani, the Vatican's secretary of state, second only to the pontiff in importance.

And no friend of his.

Quite the contrary, in fact.

The young priest left them alone.

"Come, Jason," Ascolani said in English. "Closer, please. We need to talk."

"I was informed the Holy Father wanted to see me."

"A small deception on my part, as I knew you would not come if I had been the one asking."

He should leave. Now. But he was curious. Though Ascolani held a higher position in the Curia, cardinals were, by definition, equal brothers in Christ. No one more important than the other. Which had, for centuries, bred nothing but conflict.

"We have two problems," Ascolani said.

"We?"

A finger was pointed his way. "More accurately, *you* have two problems."

He already knew what one of those was. "You know about Eric Casaburi's visit?"

"I do. And the church will have no part of him."

"I told him that. In no uncertain terms."

"What I do not understand is why you had anything to do with him in the first place? He and his party are neo-fascists with grandiose ideas."

"That 60 percent of Italy agrees with."

A smirk came to the Italian's face. "That is not how we measure our support."

"You cannot be serious. That is exactly how we measure support. We always have. We back winners. We have no use for losers. The National Freedom Party's chances of gaining control are quite good."

"They still need to win thirty-eight seats in parliament for that to happen. Those are elections we can affect. We will affect them. They will lose."

"Which I told Casaburi."

"What baffles me is why he chose you to talk with."

"Since you know of the meeting, you surely know of his mention of a *Pignus Christi*."

"I do. That is a fantasy."

"I said to him the same thing. It is irrelevant. Apparently, he came to me because of my connection to the Vatican Bank. I told him there were others far more politically connected than I."

"You sell yourself short, Jason."

"I spoke the truth."

"Yet he still came to you."

He heard the question in the words. "I do not see the problem here. He came to me. I made inquiries. I said no. He went away."

"A man like Eric Casaburi does not go away."

He shrugged. "What do you want, Sergio?"

"The truth would be welcomed."

"I told you what happened."

His nemesis' face registered nothing, the eyes staring noncommittal, enigmatic, giving zero indication as to thoughts. A talent that had surely come from the womb. He took a moment and noticed the sun setting past the western wall, its faint red glow bleeding color from the tall cedars. "You said there were two problems."

"You are banned from the Holy Father," Ascolani said.

"You don't tell me what to do."

"On this I do. You have been implicated in the ongoing fraud trial."

Had he heard right? "Implicated? How?"

"One of the defendants has offered a sworn statement that you were involved with the questionable real estate transactions and the embezzlement. You were paid moneys."

"That's absurd."

"Then why was a satchel full of four hundred thousand euros found at the diocese's Dillenburg residence?"

He gave a refined chuckle. "You're making that up, right?"

"No, Jason. I am not. It has been independently confirmed by an American intelligence operative, working with the Swiss Guard. I have pictures." He started to say something, but Ascolani waved him off. "Please, no denials or explanations. Save those for the tribunal. You will shortly be charged with fraud, theft, and bribery."

His heart seemed to catch in his throat. "Where was this money found?"

"Inside the old priest hole. Which was equipped with modern upgrades. Was that your doing?"

"The house was remodeled a few years ago, and I had the priest hole upgraded and preserved. It has historical significance."

"It apparently made for a good hiding place. The money is there."

"Sergio, if that is true then I am being set up."

An outstretched hand forbade further arguing. "You will have your opportunity to make a defense. In the meantime your access to the pope has been revoked. An action, I might add, that the Holy Father himself approved."

"He knows about this?" Then it hit him. "Of course he does. You'd be the first to poison his mind."

"I merely related that the confidential information provided to the tribunal had proven accurate. And I showed him the picture."

"I want to see it."

"It will be provided to your lawyer. I am formally notifying you that, effective immediately, you have also been suspended from all of your Curial duties. That suspension will remain in effect until this matter is resolved. Of course, it goes without saying that, if convicted, you will lose your cardinal's hat."

The decree came in a voice that carried an undertone of amused indulgence. "Won't you be happy."

"You have also been reassigned," Ascolani said. "You are to report to Munich and stay at the Holnstein Palace until further notice. Cardinal Schultz says you are welcome there."

The Holnstein was the official residence of the archbishop of Munich. Hanz Georg Schultz was a dear friend.

"Why can't I stay here, or in Cologne at my residence?"

"You know the answer. This will not stay secret. We do not want you having anything to do with the diocese, and I certainly do not want you here in the Vatican. Better for you to be isolated. Away. Cardinal Schultz has assured me he will keep a close eye on you."

Maybe not so good a friend after all.

He started to speak, but the older man lifted a hand to halt the protestation that he was about to make.

"No matter how I might personally feel about you," Ascolani said. "For the good of the church I hope all of this is explainable."

He said nothing. Shock was taking hold. This could not be happening.

"Is there anything else you need to say?" Ascolani asked.

"Like what?"

"Would you like me to hear your confession? Forgiveness from the Lord may help."

"No, thank you."

"As you wish. Go with God."

And his enemy walked off.

What in the world was happening?

He'd had no involvement whatsoever in those shady real estate dealings. He was as surprised as everyone else when it all came to light. And money found in Dillenburg? How? His salary was modest, to say the least. He had no more than a few thousand euros saved in the bank. Four hundred thousand euros? Found there? In cash? And there were pictures? As he'd said, somebody was setting him up.

But who?

And why?

CHAPTER 13

7:40 P.M.

COTTON DROVE ACROSS THE RHINE RIVER AND ENTERED THE HEART of old Cologne. He'd visited the German city before, a place of churches and ancient museums and universities—once a Roman fortification, later the seat of archbishops and cardinals. Both had left indelible marks on the landscape.

Outside the car window he spied the towering twin spires of the cathedral, massive even from half a mile away. He used the structure as a beacon and began a trek through a series of one-way streets. The oxidized copper roof cast the titanic structure in a pale-green halo, adding an appropriate touch of omnipresence, the building squatting like a massive four-legged creature, the bell towers ears, transepts paws, the creature silently studying its territory, assuring in all directions it remained inviolate.

He'd taken his time driving the seventy miles west from Dillenburg, but stayed contemplative, considering the consequences of all that had happened. No one had followed him. His instructions had been to meet a contact in Cologne at 8:00 P.M. after the sneak and peek for a face-to-face debrief. He assumed a recorded statement would be taken to serve as evidence to the tribunal. Then his task would be complete. Perhaps he could catch a late train north to Copenhagen and be home by midnight.

He navigated his way through the maze of streets and found a public parking lot. Then he crossed the open square that fanned out around the Dom, staring up at the towering façade. He'd visited the National Cathedral in Washington and churches all around the world, but they were nothing like this. Its main façade was all handcrafted, loaded with finial turrets, crockets, spires, intricate stone filigree, and stepped windows. It had stayed in a constant state of building and repair for the past fifteen hundred years. He knew the popular local saying. *When the cathedral is completed, the world will end.*

He followed a group of tourists chatting incessantly in French through the central portal in the west façade, the tympanum filled with scenes from the Old Testament. The jamb statutes portrayed biblical figures, the theme one of salvation. He hoped it was a good omen as he passed underneath. A soft melody from a pipe organ drifted across the interior. His eyes were immediately drawn up to the vaulted nave. The Gothic choir loomed at the far end, the ornate high altar beyond. Towering stained-glass windows lined the outer walls, their colorful images darkened by the ever-dimming sun outside.

He walked through the vestibule, down the center aisle between parallel rows of oak pews. A few worshipers knelt in contemplative prayer. Not many people around. Maybe fifty or so. At a side altar hundreds of tiny candles flickered, and he watched while a couple of veiled dowagers lit two more and crossed themselves. Atop the music was the echo of heels off stone. Occasionally, a photo flash pierced the semi-darkness.

The rows of pews ended before the altar.

He turned right and entered the south transept, following the ambulatory east to the far end. The golden reliquary sarcophagus stood to his left sparkling under floodlights behind a plexiglass shield. Supposedly, the remains of the Three Magi had been brought to Cologne in the twelfth century and had rested there ever since. He stood at the extreme east end of the massive church, away from the majority of visitors, at the crest of the ambulatory's semicircle, easy to see from either side if anybody approached.

He checked his watch. Nearly 8:00 P.M.

Right on time.

So where was his contact?

Stephanie had texted a picture of who to expect, so he was on the lookout for the right face. An elderly couple rounded the curve, strolling arm and arm admiring the chapels, chatting in German. Five minutes passed. Then ten. Something was off. Not right. Like what he'd felt in Dillenburg. He had no dog in this fight. None at all. He was asked to take a look, snap some pictures, then make a report. That's all.

But he was still on edge.

A woman appeared from one of the side chapels.

She hesitated at the iron gate, looking both ways before emerging. Tall. Lean-limbed. Pageboy hairstyle. Snug denim jeans and a casual check shirt. His alarm bell triggered louder and he moved toward the iron gate. The woman kept going. Away. Toward the front of the massive church. Never looking back. He glanced inside the dim chapel at the wall paintings and its darkened stained-glass windows. In one corner a body lay supine. A face he recognized. From Stephanie's email. The man he'd come to meet. He hustled over and saw a knife wound to the chest. He knelt down and checked for a pulse.

None.

Then everything just escalated.

A form sprang from his left, wielding a knife.

Long, wide, serrated.

The man pivoted off the balls of his feet, the knife sweeping in a circular motion of intense readiness. Cotton reacted and rolled to his right, away from the attacker, and came to his feet, swinging around to slam his right foot into the hand with the knife.

But it did not release.

Thankfully, this was not his first rodeo. So he swung with his right fist and pounded the man's temple, which had the desired effect, stunning the senses and causing the guy to stagger back. He wrapped his right arm around the neck in a vise grip, then transmitted the full weight of his body through a knee into the abdomen. Ribs cracked. A grunt signaled pain. The hand with the knife moved up and out.

Not good.

The arc could be trouble.

Make the call. Do it.

Releasing his grip on the throat he clamped onto the guy's arm and brought the hand down and in, puncturing his attacker's chest with the blade.

Breath swooshed from lungs.

Muscles relaxed.

A small rivulet of blood seeped from the corner of the mouth, and all resistance ceased as the body went limp.

Dammit. He needed this guy alive.

"Oh, my God," a woman said loudly in English.

He glanced up. The same woman from earlier stood out in the ambulatory.

"You killed him," she yelled, her voice echoing across the nave. "He killed him."

Then she ran.

He headed after her.

People were reacting to her words, emerging from the pews and into the side aisle. The clap of their feet echoed off the towering ceiling. Across the nave he spotted the woman. She saw him and reached beneath her jacket.

A gun appeared.

She leveled it his way.

He dove to the ground between the pews, flattening himself and crawling beneath them.

A loud pop filled the nave.

Above him a round whined by, smacking off stone. Voices rose, people panicked, all now heading for the exit in a rush.

He rose up.

The woman to his right had disappeared.

He darted her way, crossed in front of the main altar, and headed for a side door. He glanced back to see two policemen in uniforms run past the altar toward the chapel with the bodies.

He came to the exit doors.

Which opened.

He fled the church, out into the warm evening. He turned left and made his way back toward the front of the cathedral, keeping close to the building and using the crowd for protection. The woman from the chapel was hustling away, down a set of stairs to street level, where she crossed traffic and headed for the sidewalk on the other side.

Time to go. Now.

CHAPTER 14

THOMAS STEPPED FROM THE CAB.

He'd taken a private jet charter from Salisbury to Cologne. He maintained a running account with NetJets Europe under one of his many aliases, which granted him the freedom to move about, unnoticed, at will. On the short flight he'd thought about the manner and form of Jason Richter's suicide. That task he could not farm out. He'd have to handle it himself. The envelope Bartolomé had left with him contained background information, along with a notation that Richter had been suspended from his duties and sent back to Munich. Immediately. With an address where the cardinal could be found.

Floodlights encased the Dom, bathing the ancient stone in a warm chalk-white glow. He avoided the Domplaz and headed west, deeper into the old city. The streets gradually quieted. Past the cathedral zone the sidewalks were nearly deserted. Amber lights periodically cast a lambent glow into an ever-dimming evening. Cars hunched close to the curb on both sides of every street, a few decorated with yellow summons, revealing the length of their illegal presence. At a museum he turned right, then walked two more blocks before multistory apartment buildings and more parked cars signaled the entrance to a residential zone. Protective shutters were drawn tight on most of the windows, cracks of light indicating the presence of people inside.

He'd taken the roundabout walk to ensure that no one was following him.

Caution was never a waste of time.

His phone vibrated in his pocket.

He retrieved the unit and saw it was an incoming text.

Problem. Headed to debarkation.

He entered Cologne's central train station, which sat within sight of the cathedral. Nearly 8:30 P.M. and the station buzzed with activity. A high-vaulted metal-and-glass roof echoed the chatter and occasional laughter of passengers who hustled through the beautiful concourse. People sat in rows of seats, waiting, more queued up to purchase tickets. He glanced up at the big board and watched as the white lettering flickered and clattered to update the display. The train to Munich left in thirty minutes. He'd headed straight to the station after the text. Originally he was to meet up with his two operatives, and they would leave town together.

But something was wrong.

Across the terminal he caught sight of one of his acolytes. She'd been hired, along with one other, and sent to Dillenburg to make sure the police caught the American operative inside the church's residence, along with discovering the cache of cash that was hidden there. All part of his original instructions. The idea was for the money to be verified as there, then a whole lot of attention drawn to the entire situation, especially the American involvement. He got it. No sense framing someone if nobody knew it happened. But where was the second operative? Her partner.

One word kept resonating through his brain from the text.

Problem.

COTTON HEADED AFTER THE WOMAN, CROSSING THE STREET and blending into the people on the other sidewalk. What was happening? A dead Swiss Guard contact. A man with a knife. Then a woman with a gun. Somebody knew his business. Even worse, somebody knew the Vatican's business. If the idea was to keep a low profile, that ship had now sailed.

The woman kept moving, paralleling the Dom's northern façade, heading straight for the train station, which sat in sight of the cathedral. He stayed back but kept pace. Plenty of folks were out for the evening. Nothing unusual for Northern Europe in summer, which stayed cold and dismal most of the time. Behind him, more uniforms were rushing to the cathedral. Sirens wailed. Lights flashed. Police were converging. Two dead bodies had that effect.

He quickened his pace and closed the gap between him and his fleeing target to about a hundred feet, careful that she not see him.

He was in bird dog mode. On the hunt.

She disappeared inside the terminal, never looking back.

He started to trot and made up the distance, staying outside. Inside, a shiny terrazzo floor was complemented by the splendid glass roof that ran the length of the station. He'd been here before and knew all of the entrances and exits were at street level, the track platforms on the upper level. Passageways beneath the railway lines provided access to and from the trains. He also knew that Cologne was not a terminal station, the trains merely pausing here on their way to other destinations.

The inside was like a mall with a variety of shops and eateries. Plenty of places to disappear into. But he spotted the woman in line for a ticket. An electronic sign above her indicated it was for Munich, leaving in less than thirty minutes.

Three people were ahead of her.

He slipped inside and eased toward one of the shops, waiting for her to complete her purchase. When she did and left, he hustled over and bought himself a ticket. He wasn't sure where this was headed, but he wasn't going to lose sight of her.

THOMAS STOOD ON THE UPPER LEVEL, STARING DOWN AT THE TICKET counters. He'd already bought his ticket and watched as his female operative did the same, then headed for the escalators. He retreated and waited for her to arrive. She spotted him and started over, but he waved her off.

Instead, he simply pointed to the right.

Time to head for Munich.

COTTON RETREATED TO THE SHOP, WHICH ALLOWED HIM AN ANGLED view up to the second level. The woman stepped off the escalator and turned left, walking for a bit before the upper railing, then disappearing into the upper terminal. He hurried up the escalator and came off, catching sight of his target. He stayed back, using the bustle all around him for protection. She was fifty feet ahead, headed for the Munich train. He found his phone and sent a text to Stephanie, which expressed the gravity of the situation.

This has become a lot more complicated.

CHAPTER 15

JASON WAS IN A PANIC.

His religious life was spartan, his tastes simple save for well-prepared food and some good wine. True, he could be at times pedantic, a little cynical, and he disdained illogical tradition. He'd told himself more than once to mind his tongue. But for him the great new sin of modern times was the unwillingness of people to become involved. The sin of omission. He loved the glory of the church. The sunlight slanting through stained glass laying down fields of fractured color. An organ and chorus together echoing off the vaulted ceilings. And the triumphant hallelujahs.

It all made sense to him.

He'd waited in the evening warmth, watching as Ascolani waddled his way out of the Vatican Gardens, not sure what to do next. He knew the petty humiliation was designed to sting, to slowly sap away all courage and strength, replaced with a helplessness that hopefully led to capitulation. But he also knew the enemy here was more than Ascolani. The Curia was like a malignant serpent that slithered in darkness and drew strength from the confusion of its opponents. That hydra had many heads, and when one was severed, two more grew back. The only way to slay the monster was to face it squarely, resist the paralyzing dread, and aim straight for its heart. Nothing else would work.

So he needed to get moving.

To do something.

He fled the gardens and kept his pace slow and steady, showing not a hint of the apprehension that coursed through him. He knew cameras were everywhere. Not often was he scared. He could recall only one time before in his life. When he knelt before the bishop to take Holy Orders and become a priest. His calling came in his early teens, when he heard the Lord say, *Give me your life and trust me as to what I am going to do with it.* He'd not hesitated, offering himself completely, but telling no one. His father's sudden death when he was seventeen made him frustrated with God. Why was that good man taken? What was the point? There'd been catechism in school, but not much. Never was he an altar boy or privy to any of the church's inner workings. He was twenty and in college when, out of nowhere, he heard a voice say, *Be a priest.*

So he applied for and was accepted to the seminary at Sankt Georgen School. There he was exposed to different cultures and ideas, all of which opened his eyes to view the church as a universal entity. He also learned that religious service could take many forms, and his seemed to be in administration. From the day he lay before the bishop and accepted Holy Orders he started a steady rise up the ladder to now being a cardinal, part of the select committee that oversaw the Vatican Bank.

Or at least that was the case until a few minutes ago.

Now he was suspended and exiled.

He kept walking, leaving the confines of the secured areas behind the basilica and heading for St. Peter's Square.

In its simplest form the Catholic Church was a global community of believers founded by Jesus Christ over two thousand years ago. There were more than one billion Catholics, from countless diverse cultural backgrounds, all united by the same central religious creed. They sprang from the first group of Christians that ever existed, from which all other Christian groups emerged. But at its heart the Catholic Church had always been an institution with a unique leadership structure. Servant-leaders. Priests. Following the example of Jesus. At the service of those whom they led. Men, like himself, who'd answered the call and undergone Holy Orders. Becoming a priest was then, and remained, a special privilege. Christ picked his twelve apostles. So the church selected its own servants. But sadly, it was not exempt from having bad apples. They came in all forms. Some incompetent. Others arrogant and vain. Some downright evil. He was not any of those. He'd been a good priest and cardinal.

Why was this happening?

Was it his outspokenness?

He'd been warned to tone down the rhetoric. But he'd thought himself immune to retribution thanks to his friendship with the pope, who'd privately encouraged him to speak out. He supposed now, thinking on it, a comment made a few weeks back may have placed him on Ascolani's radar. *"The church should be as brave and outspoken about women as it has been about so many other subjects."* He'd been talking to the Curia, who were expert at thwarting change. But for him, reality was clear. The church could no longer operate without women actively being a part. They were the future. But men like Sergio Ascolani were not interested in change. They liked the status quo.

The only way to slay the monster is to face it squarely, resist the paralyzing dread, and aim straight for its heart.

So he had no choice.

Go straight for the heart.

CHAPTER 16

STEFANO FINISHED HIS DINNER, A TENDER FILET OF SPANISH BEEF with some pasta. He was careful about what he ate and worked hard to maintain a lean physique. He stood tall but not overly so, with square shoulders, sinewy arms and hands, and a face sharp-featured, the eyes capable of being both piercingly astute and as naïve as those of an innocent, depending on the situation. He was nearing forty and considered himself in his prime. For the past few months he'd been training hard for the Calcio with daily workouts. Those fifty-minute games, running on a soft carpet of sand, took a toll on the body. But he was in terrific shape, no ordinary priest. Not at all. He was a working intelligence officer who'd been dispatched to hot spots across the globe. Now he was entangled with something that struck close to the heart of the Holy See. The ongoing fraud trial had tested everyone's nerves. Sure, there'd been scandals before. Plenty. But never had the Vatican publicly charged and tried the offenders for the world to see. Every member of the Curia was following the unfolding events. Especially Cardinal Ascolani, who'd taken a personal interest in the entire manner.

He knew all about the crusty Italian.

Ascolani was old school. Born south of Turin in the Piedmont to a rural family. His father had been both a tailor and a Christian

Democrat in parliament, his mother a respected schoolteacher. He'd studied in Rome, obtaining a doctorate in theology, then trained as a diplomat at the Pontifical Ecclesiastical Academy. He had a special talent. Languages were easy for him. Ascolani spoke eight fluently. Which made him ideal for the diplomatic service. He finished his pastoral work in Italy before being moved overseas, serving in South America, Asia, and Africa. The current pope elevated him to secretary of state the day after the last conclave ended. Why? Pundits said it was payback for his help. Not unusual. Especially considering that Ascolani had been in the running for the papal tiara himself. But nonetheless odd since the new pope and Ascolani had never been considered friends. In fact, the new pontiff passed over several close associates to give the coveted second-in-command position to Ascolani.

Stefano paid his bill and left the restaurant, walking back to Vatican City. Ascolani had told him to stay close, and he'd followed that order. He crossed the narrow streets, squeezing between parked cars and finally entering St. Peter's Square. A car passed by, its windows tinted dark, bearing the distinctive license plate of the Vatican state. Not many people out tonight enjoying the fountains and obelisks. He passed through the security checkpoint and reentered the restricted areas. Ascolani had sent another secure text telling him to come immediately to his official residence, which had necessitated the skipping of dessert. Which he'd not liked. Sweets were a soft spot and that restaurant made some terrific gelato.

Ascolani's residence sat atop the Palazzina della Zecca, near the center of the Vatican. The building itself served as a hotel for visitors, along with accommodating several cardinals in residence. Stefano had visited before. The apartment seemed more something that a Forbes-list billionaire would enjoy than a home for a prelate pledged to austerity. Ascolani assumed control of the space right after his appointment, merging two flats into one, and had been steadily renovating ever since. About five hundred square meters, three times larger than the pope's residence and a hundred times more opulent. The furniture was all imported pale wood—sleek, elegant, and modern. Ascolani's spin on the project, and its expense, was that the apartment would henceforth serve as the official secretary of state's residence. A place where holders of that office could impress and persuade emissaries. A stretch? Without a doubt. But no one had questioned the move. Not even the pope. Three nuns took care of all of the domestic work, and the interior was also furnished with an impressive array of antiques and other collectibles from the Vatican Museums' extensive collection.

A Swiss Guardsman allowed him onto the private elevator, which took him straight to the top of the building. The car opened into a marble foyer that led to the front door, which Ascolani opened, inviting him inside and offering a seat. His boss was out of uniform. No black cassock or red robes. Just pants and an untucked shirt, slippers on his feet. The casualness reflected the level of trust being placed in him.

"This has been an eventful day," Ascolani said. "More so than I ever imagined this morning when I woke. Cardinal Richter has been suspended and ordered to Munich until the trial is over. We, though, have an extremely delicate situation developing. We are going to have that much more detailed conversation now. One that, as you observed earlier, is troubling me."

His host poured two generous measures of whiskey into tumblers and offered one to him.

"If you would indulge me," Ascolani said. "I need to tell you a story that will help place things in context."

In 1542 the growing Protestant Reformation made Catholic authorities more suspect than ever of new ideas. Eliminating heretics became complicated by the politics of Protestant powers, especially those in Northern Europe. The Catholic Church could no longer do as it pleased, especially in lands that had officially adopted Protestantism. So Pope Paul III established the Congregation of the Holy Office of the Inquisition to maintain and defend the integrity of the faith from all enemies. A Dominican named Miguel Ghislieri was summoned to Rome and charged with collecting information the Inquisition might need. Ghislieri lived a simple life in poverty and moved about on foot. His irreproachable conduct and uncompromising attitude were well known. Within a year over twelve hundred people were judged by Inquisitorial courts, more than two hundred of them being tortured, found guilty, and executed. In 1551 Ghislieri was promoted to head of the Inquisition. He quickly set about reorganizing the office and assembling a network of spies. Little to nothing happened in Rome, or within the Vatican, without him knowing. In 1557 Ghislieri was made a cardinal. By then he possessed so much confidential information on so many that no one challenged him.

Not even popes.

His "black monks" wreaked havoc.

But when Paul IV died suddenly in 1559, the cardinals became emboldened, hunting down Ghislieri's spies and killing them all. The masses even attacked the palace where the Inquisition held its trials. Cardinal Ghislieri barely escaped with his life. Peace returned on Christmas Day 1559 when Cardinal Giovanni Angelo de' Medici was elected pope as Pius IV. He was intent on purging all that had occurred through the Inquisition, so his first order of business was to send Ghislieri into exile and dissolve his network of black monks. Ghislieri took refuge in a Carthusian monastery, Santa Maria di Castello, and stayed there for six years until Pius IV died in 1565.

On January 7, 1566, Ghislieri was elected pope.

He chose the name Pius V.

By then everyone had grown terrified of the Protestant Reformation and wanted a pope who could take on the movement. Ghislieri's experience at heading the Inquisition made him perfect for the job. He promptly created the Holy Alliance, the first official papal intelligence service, and turned it loose on the world. Pius V reigned for only six years, dying in 1572.

His war on Protestantism failed.

But the Holy Alliance lived on.

* * *

Ascolani reached for a pack of cigarettes on a side table and slipped one between his lips. He lit it and exhaled the smoke quickly, as if ridding himself of something unpleasant. "An odd name, wouldn't you say? The Entity. I have no idea how that came about. Of course, since we never officially acknowledge it even exists, I suppose we could call it whatever we desire."

Stefano was wondering why he was here. Most of what Ascolani had just said he knew. But he also knew to keep quiet and listen.

"I need you to find something for me," Ascolani said.

Okay. Progress.

"When Giovanni Angelo de' Medici was elected as Pius IV and banished Cardinal Ghislieri into exile, Ghislieri took with him all of the records of the Inquisition."

He'd not known that.

Ascolani finished the cigarette and stubbed out the butt in a crystal ashtray, while exhaling a stream of blue smoke. "It has long been thought that Ghislieri took other documents, unrelated to the Inquisition, with him too. Especially those that a Medici pope might find important." The older man assumed a deliberately casual and unconcerned pose. "Are you loyal, Father Giumenta? To the church? The pope? Me?"

He noticed the drop in tone, and the omission of *God*. Definitely an odd question. But add it to the list when dealing with this man, whom he regarded with a mixture of apprehension and admiration.

"I don't think my loyalty to any of those you mentioned has ever been questioned."

"We are about to embark on something that has far-reaching implications. Much farther than Eric Casaburi and his current political ambitions, though they remain a growing concern. Thankfully, though, the mission I am about to assign to you should resolve both matters."

"I am at your disposal."

"Yes, you are. So listen carefully."

CHAPTER 17

COTTON APPROACHED THE TRAIN AND SIGHTED DOWN THE LENGTH of cars. A scattering of passengers had already boarded, more coming on.

The woman had to be aboard.

The doors hissed open and he stepped inside, the train throbbing, waiting anxiously to leave. A clanking of mechanical joints signaled an imminent departure. The German railway was famous for being on time. Today seemed no exception. The doors closed and the train moved without a sound, gliding from the station. No bells or whistles or announcements. Just moving. Slow at first, then gathering speed.

He sat down opposite a young couple, their eyes half closed, their heads together, hands touching lightly. They smiled, not looking at each other, obviously drawing strength from the other's presence. He thought of Cassiopeia. He hadn't seen her in a couple of weeks. He'd asked her to come along, but she'd been needed in France at her rebuilding site. What an effort. Erecting a thirteenth-century castle from the ground up using only the tools and materials of the era. She was passionate about the project and told him she needed to make up time from some recent setbacks. He admired her dedication. She was a smart, sassy, brave woman who'd saved his hide more than once. And he loved her.

As she did him.

He angled his head and stared down the long corridor of swaying cars through the windows at each end.

The woman was here.

He just needed to find her.

THOMAS SAT ALONE, HIS HIRED HELP IN THE NEXT CAR.

His new instructions were to proceed to Munich and await the arrival of Cardinal Richter, then orchestrate the man's suicide. He'd accomplished his first task, making sure there was money to find inside the Dillenburg residence and that the local police were involved to corral the American. The killing of the Swiss Guard contact in Cologne had also been part of his original mission. Why was that necessary? Not his place to ask. Nor did he care. What concerned him was the *problem* the text mentioned.

The plan was to travel overnight to Munich and deal with Richter, who was scheduled to arrive there tomorrow evening. The envelope he'd been provided earlier at Stonehenge contained details about the Munich residence and Richter's most commonly known traits and habits. All of that information would prove vital in the coming days as an appropriate "suicide" was enacted. How? When? No need to think about that now.

A little rest would be welcomed.

He was about to lay his head back and relax for a few hours when he caught sight of someone in the car ahead.

Standing up.

A man.

With a face he recognized.

COTTON STOOD FROM HIS SEAT AND DECIDED TO MAKE HIS WAY closer to the woman. She was somewhere in the cars ahead. He needed to be close, but not too close. She knew his face. And he needed to see where this led. What he was doing was way outside his mission parameters. But there seemed no choice. Things had not played out according to plan.

He worked his way down the aisle, passed through the connecting door between cars, and kept going through the next car. The seats were about half full with an assortment of singles and doubles.

Through the next car and still no target.

Then he spotted her in the following car. The conductor was checking tickets, so he took a seat, but kept watch through the glass panels.

Nowhere for her to go.

So don't rush it.

THOMAS WATCHED AS COTTON MALONE RETOOK ANOTHER SEAT two cars ahead. What was he doing here? He should be under arrest in Dillenburg. He'd been told about Malone and provided a bio and photograph. The man was a trained intelligence officer who once worked for the United States Justice Department. Retired now. Living in Denmark. Owner of a rare-book shop who apparently still freelanced on occasion.

A professional.

The plan had been simple.

Plant the money, confirm its presence officially, then have the American arrested for trespassing, drawing lots of attention. He assumed the media would have been involved next. Now Malone was here. On the train. In pursuit of his associate?

Was that the *problem*?

Malone was not supposed to be anywhere near Cologne. Was he himself likewise compromised? No. Malone had walked right past him and never blinked. But Malone clearly knew about the woman. What had happened in the Cologne Cathedral?

He needed to know.

Acolytes could be easily hired. He had a running list of names who all worked for a price. Nothing was out of bounds, and the loss of one would not matter in the least.

This trail had to go cold.

Now.

CHAPTER 18

9:40 P.M.

Eric enjoyed the stroll across Florence from the restaurant to the Church of San Lorenzo. For over three hundred years it had been favored by the Medicis as their family church, where they were christened, married, and buried. Gathered here were the threads of a checkered history from over three centuries between the tomb of Giovanni in the Old Sacristy, the first Medici, and that of Anna Maria Luisa, the last, in the crypt below. A family that spawned four popes, countless dukes, two French queens, and an assortment of cardinals.

Florence had been *their* city, and the family name still met you at every corner, their shields and images everywhere. An amazing legacy for latecomers to banking, but they were masters of parlaying, intermarrying with crowned heads, and interjecting themselves into a prominent role in European history. Most of the other Florentine bankers were forgotten. Not them, though. Their secret? Historians would say it was their ability to always have the right man in the right spot at the right time. Then making sure the opposition did not do the same thing. Which served the Medici well, as they effectively controlled Tuscany for three centuries.

The basilica and the chapels at San Lorenzo were now popular museums, closed for the day. Thankfully he had long known the current curator, a personal friend, who was thrilled to be close to a member of parliament and the secretary of a rising political party. The same was true of his DNA expert, who now accompanied him on the walk. They avoided the main entrance and rounded to the far side of the building. Its façade was austere rough stone, crossed by deep horizontal lines whose purpose would have been to support a marble facing that was never applied. There'd been lots of talk of finishing the exterior to Michelangelo's medieval specifications, but no one had, as yet, raised the money to make that happen.

In the beginning the Medici were careful, assiduous men of business, prudent and generous, defenders of the poor against tyranny. Then they became farsighted capable statesmen, burdened with public affairs, raising the power and prosperity of Florence and advocating the arts and learning. Finally they morphed into crowned heads, dukes of the most important territory in Italy.

The family's motto?

Semper. Always.

What set them apart? They were consistently superior in mind and spirit.

Like himself.

But he was also a realist.

A populist thrived only off what was said. Not what was done. Like the Medici of the past he and his colleagues promoted the idea that they alone represented *the people* in their struggle against a corrupt and indifferent establishment. They alone understood disenchantment. Fear. A desire for alternatives. Critics said they advocated demagoguery and authoritarianism like Mussolini, offering overly simplistic answers to complex issues, presented in a flamboyantly emotional manner. Okay. What was so wrong there? Opponents called it political opportunism. Trying only to please voters and ease their minds without considering rational, carefully thought-out solutions. Maybe so. But it worked.

He'd carefully studied other populists. Latin American leaders like Juan Perón in Argentina and Hugo Chávez in Venezuela.

But there'd also been a more recent emergence of the movement in Spain, Greece, and Brazil. Even the United States had seen its share, where the message was aided by a constitutional freedom of speech. Viktor Orbán's Civic Party recently won a majority of seats in the Hungarian national assembly. True, Orbán's close ties with Moscow raised concerns, but his core voters were persuaded by his iron-fisted rhetoric that mending ties with the European Union might lead Hungary into war. A good lesson learned there.

Brazil taught the opposite. Jair Bolsonaro won the country's presidential election in 2018. He openly expressed admiration for the brutal military dictatorship that once ruled Brazil. But Bolsonaro became arrogant, ignoring the nation's aggressive press and strongly independent judiciary. He failed to accomplish anything meaningful regarding taxes or Social Security. He also underplayed the recent pandemic, assuring Brazilians that the illness was no more than *a little flu*. He opposed lockdowns in favor of keeping the economy open, disparaged masks, and voiced doubts regarding vaccines. Not surprisingly, the death rate in Brazil soared to the fifth highest in the world and Bolsonaro lost his bid for reelection.

So populism came with limits.

He spotted the curator, who waited at the church doors.

"Everyone is gone," the man said as they approached. "The building is empty and secure."

"Cameras?"

"Off for the next hour."

Perfect. He stepped close and laid a hand on the older man's shoulder. "I appreciate that. Tonight, we change history."

"It would be incredible if the royal Medici returned."

He'd said enough to gain trust. "We have the one link established. Now we need to complete the chain."

He knew, of course, that his own bloodline worked its way all the way back to Gregorio Cappello. But who were Cappello's parents? That was the question for the night, or at least half of it.

They'd come to find Gregorio Cappello's mother, who held the distinction of being the last royal Medici.

Anna Maria Luisa was born in 1667, the middle child of three to Cosimo III, Grand Duke of Tuscany. The family succession seemed secure with three healthy heirs, two of whom were male. But in reality, the Medicis' time was running out, the family vitality gone sour and drying up. At age twenty-four Anna married Johann Wilhelm, the Elector Palatine of the Rhine, and moved to Germany. By all accounts their twenty-five-year marriage was a good one, but it remained childless.

Grace and fascination hung round her every move, and whether she was grave or happy, silent or speaking, quiet or in motion she was always attractive.

He liked that description of her.

Along with *while without any particular regularity of features she concentrated within herself the varied influence of every feminine beauty.*

Sounded like quite a lady.

When her husband died in 1716 Anna's world fell apart, and though he left her amply provided for in his will, the Holy Roman emperor, Charles III, denied her that wealth. So in 1717, she left Germany and returned to Florence. There, she took up residence in the royal palace with her father. Her older brother, Ferdinando, had already died and her younger brother, Gian Gastone, was an inept alcoholic. But when her father died in 1723 Gian became grand duke. Brother and sister did not get along and for fourteen years Anna languished in isolation, watching her brother's steady decline. She was seventy years old when Gian Gastone, the last legitimate male royal Medici, died in 1737.

Childless.

Anna died in 1743. Childless.

Or so history noted.

He could still hear his grandmother's words.

"She had a baby when she was fifty-three years old, telling no one but her chambermaid, who kept all of her secrets. That child

was given away and grew up not a Medici. But the blood is there. It remains in you and me, Eric."

"How could that ever be proved," he asked her.

"God will show a way. When He does, take it."

Indeed.

God had shown a way.

CHAPTER 19

Cotton settled into a new seat, one car behind the woman. He wasn't exactly sure what to do next. Involve the police? But that would only magnify his failure to honor the Vatican's request to keep things close. The better tactic was to sit tight and see where she led him. He could then make a thorough report, which hopefully would end his involvement.

He was tired. Long day. Not to mention the gymnastics from earlier getting off that roof. He was beginning to feel his age. Staring down fifty came with challenges. Just another reason he'd opted out from the Magellan Billet early. Along with going out on top and all that crap.

But getting shot?

That was never a good career path.

The bullet tore into his left shoulder.

He fought to ignore the pain and focused on the plaza. People rushed in all directions. Horns blared. Tires squealed. Marines guarding the nearby American embassy reacted to the chaos but were too far away to help. Bodies were strewn about. How many? Eight? Ten? No. More. A young man and woman lay at contorted angles on a nearby patch of oily asphalt, the man's eyes frozen open, alight with shock, the woman, face down, gushing blood. He'd spotted two gunmen and immediately shot them both, but never saw the third, who'd clipped him with a single round and was now trying to flee, using panicked bystanders for cover.

The wound hurt.

Fear struck his face like a wave of fire.

His legs went limp as he fought to raise his right arm. The Beretta seemed to weigh tons, not ounces. Pain jarred his senses. He sucked deep breaths of sulfur-laced air and finally forced his finger to work the trigger.

Mexico City. His last official Magellan Billet assignment. People died that day. One of whom was almost him. It was a few months later that he retired.

A big change.

And not really.

He was still being shot at. Only now as favors to friends instead of getting paid for the risk. What irony.

Would he have it any other way?

Not really.

THOMAS KEPT AN EYE ON WHAT WAS HAPPENING IN THE NEXT CAR, catching glimpses as Malone halted his advance. Normally, he never encountered an opponent of Malone's caliber. The targets he usually dealt with were soft. Mainly troublemakers who had never really been in a firefight before. People who had no idea that someone wanted them dead. He could easily stay a step ahead of them, using their anger and violence against them. But an experienced government agent? That was another matter. The smart play was to leave Malone alone and deal with the easier problem.

He checked his watch.

The train was scheduled for a quick stop at Koblenz in less than thirty minutes.

That would work.

COTTON LAID HIS HEAD BACK ON THE SEAT AND DECIDED A QUICK rest of the eyes would be great. Nobody was going anywhere. A lighted sign at the end of the car indicated that a stop at Koblenz was coming in twenty minutes. He'd have to be alert then, just in case the woman decided to leave. In the meantime a few minutes of quiet seemed welcomed.

His life was in a good place. The bookshop was doing great. More than enough income to offset costs and make a profit. He was blessed with a great group of employees. His love life was likewise good. He and Cassiopeia seemed bonded. His relationship with his son, Gary, was also solid. The boy was still in high school and was still talking about following in his father's, and grandfather's, footsteps and joining the navy. College was not really his thing and he wanted to serve and make a difference. His ex-wife, Pam, was not happy with that decision but was smart enough not to press her opposition. Gary had to make up his own mind.

Just one thing was an issue.

And he'd only learned about it recently.

He opened the envelope and shuffled through the papers. A lot there. Mainly field reports from an investigative agency that apparently had located a woman, some of which he skimmed through. There were three color images showing a lean figure in a simple red dress, her face sharp-featured and attractive. At the bottom of the papers he found an order of adoption, issued by a Texas court. The petitioner was Susan Baldwin, noted as the natural mother. The adoptive parents' names were also there, with Suzy relinquishing all her parental rights. The order also provided that the petitioner had sworn, under oath, that she did not know the identity of the natural father. A copy of the new birth certificate was there showing the adoptive parents now as mother and father, vested with all the rights as if they'd produced the child themselves.

But the last sheet grabbed his attention. The original Texas birth certificate. Listing Suzy as the mother and the father as unknown. And the date of birth? He did the math. Seven months after Suzy left Pensacola. An uncomfortable question forced its way into his thoughts.

Could it be?

Long ago, while still in the navy, before his time with the Magellan Billet, he'd had an affair with Suzy Baldwin. Nothing about that was he proud of, and he never repeated that mistake again. But recently he'd come to learn that he might have a daughter from that relationship who would be approaching twenty years old. The problem? Suzy Baldwin was dead and the truth died with her.

But maybe not.

He had enough information to go find the young woman. The question that kept crowding his mind was, should he? Wrestling with that difficult inquiry had caused his insides to wither and shrink, leaving pangs of regret and plenty of confusion. Everything about the situation seemed blurred by uncertainty. He sometimes questioned himself for pursuing the problems of others, like here, especially when he had plenty of troubles of his own that required attention.

But that ghost had lain dormant for a long time.

Better to leave it alone?

The train slowed.

They were coming into Koblenz.

THOMAS FOUND HIS PHONE AND SENT A TEXT.

Come to the lavatory one car behind. Now, before we stop.

He watched through the glass panel in the rear door and into the next car. His female acolyte stood and walked toward him, sliding open the doors, leaving the car, and entering here, disappearing into the lavatory. He surveyed the people around him.

Less than ten. All comfortable in their seats. He reached into his shoulder bag and found his gun. Keeping the weapon inside the bag, he attached a sound suppressor to the end of the short barrel. This was risky. No question. But it had to be done.

He stood, his senses sharpened, with one hand inside his bag, the other cradling it, and walked to the end of the car. The lavatory door was closed. He lightly tapped the panel.

Which opened.

He stepped inside.

"What was the problem?" he asked.

"We planted the money and the police came for the American. We took down the Swiss Guard contact, as you wanted, but the American showed up unexpectedly in Cologne."

"Your partner?"

She shook her head. "They fought and he was stabbed to death."

Then Malone had followed her. Right here. Yes, this was a problem. "Why did you not shoot him?"

"Too many people around. I would have been caught. Definitely seen."

Incompetence.

He hated it.

He brought the gun out and fired one round into her skull.

The rumble of the train helped mask the soft pop of the well-placed sound-suppressed shot. The bullet exploded into the forehead, leaving a jagged red pulpy opening from which gray matter trailed. The head jerked back, a hand moved upward, blood splattered the wall like a work of modern art. The body lurched backward, but he caught it in time so there was no noise.

He helped her settle atop the toilet.

Lifeless eyes stared back.

He left, engaging the OCCUPIED notice and closing the door.

The train was beginning to slow more.

He needed to hurry.

He slid open the exit door and moved to the next car. Through the glass panel at the other end he peered ahead and saw no sign of Malone. About a dozen people filled the seats ahead of him. Several were asleep. No one seemed to be readying themselves to leave. He stepped down the aisle and entered the space between the cars where a door leading off the train awaited. A red light indicated it was still locked, but the light changed to green once the train came to a full stop.

He opened the panel and stepped off the train.

CHAPTER 20

Stefano had listened to everything Cardinal Ascolani said, amazed at what he was hearing. He'd been read in on something huge, which showed the trust the secretary of state, and head of the Entity, had in him as head of the Gruppo Intervento Rapido.

Currently, the Entity employed about six hundred operatives around the world, and about five times that number in unpaid informants among the priests, nuns, and countless lay and clerical workers. The church possessed a massive global reach. Out of 195 countries the Holy See maintained diplomatic relations with 183. That was more than even the United States recognized. There were 120 apostolic nuncios, each one an ambassador that required supporting. Eighty-nine nations maintained Vatican embassies in Rome, which all required monitoring. Operatives were scattered throughout them all.

"Cardinal Richter has been relieved of his duties," Ascolani said. *"He's been ordered to Munich to stay at the archbishop's residence. I want you to monitor his trip tomorrow, without him knowing you are watching. Make sure he arrives there, then contact me."*

Surveillance videos showed that Richter left the Vatican Gardens and headed straight for the Apostolic Archive. Once it was known as the Vatican Secret Archive—*secret* connoting "private" as opposed to "sinister"—but a previous pope had bestowed a less mysterious label.

First task?

Ascolani had been clear.

"Find out why Richter was there."

He left the apartment and followed a road that led to the Court of the Belvedere. The archives were housed there next to the Vatican library. Three successive Swiss Guards checked his credentials before he reached the stairway that led up into the building. No one questioned his presence, as his Entity credentials contained the highest security clearance.

Inside were fifty-three miles of shelving laden with books, manuscripts, registers, and documents. The central repository of the Holy See. Everything there belonged to the current pope, and the ownership would be passed to his successor. This functioning organ of the church detailing two thousand years of struggle and accomplishment was closed to outsiders until the late nineteenth century. Today the main archive and the library could be accessed with permission from the prefect. Other areas remained highly classified, still denied to outsiders, including everything after 1958. Those materials could only be viewed by permission of the pope. Seventy-five years have to pass after a pope's reign before the records of that reign are opened. The repository remained staffed twenty-four hours a day, albeit with fewer people at night. He headed for the prefect's office, where a young priest sat behind a desk.

"Is Cardinal Richter still here?" he asked in Italian.

"And you are?"

He knew the clerks liked to flex their muscles, which was easy considering how many access restrictions the archive possessed. The Entity had eyes and ears inside the archives, and he wondered if this priest was among those. So he produced his credentials, which the young man barely noticed. "I am Father Giumenta and I need an answer to my question."

"He was here. But is now gone."

He waited, knowing this clerk knew what he wanted.

"He spent some time in the bunker, with the indexes," the man finally said.

"Show me."

"I'm alone here at the moment."

Which meant he did not want to leave the desk.

"And I will need the prefect's approval," the priest added.

"By all means. And while you do that, I will check with Cardinal Ascolani and see what he says about... your needs."

On the make-an-enemy pole the secretary of state outranked any prefect.

The priest stood. "Follow me."

They walked into the main archive, then through a series of security doors and down a staircase. The underground bunker was two stories, fireproof and secure, with constant temperature and humidity control. He'd been down here before. Everything inside the bunker was classified, requiring papal authority to access through the prefect. So he was curious, "How did Cardinal Richter get down here?"

"He called the prefect, who granted access."

Interesting.

They reached the bottom of the stairs, and the priest tapped a keypad that opened a steel door. Beyond were racks of metal shelving upon which lay sleeves, bound manuscripts, and plastic containers, each labeled and containing precious documents. He knew that, of late, everything related to the church's sexual abuse scandal was stored here. So for the prefect to allow Richter inside, unsupervised, was a big deal.

"What am I looking at?" he asked.

"You wanted to see what the cardinal saw. This is it."

Another locked steel cage door separated a small entrance foyer from the stacks themselves.

"Cardinal Richter did not go beyond here?"

"The indexes are over there," the priest said, pointing at a desktop terminal atop a small desk. "They catalog what is on the shelves, all sequentially numbered. Everything is grouped by pontificates running from the eighth century to the present. It has taken decades to create those digital indexes, but about 40 percent of the collection is now on the computer."

This man's obliqueness was wearing thin.

"Did Cardinal Richter use the computer?" he asked.

"You do realize that we are required to respect our patrons' privacy?"

"Answer the question."

The young priest stepped over to the desktop, tapped the keyboard, and studied the screen. A curious look came to the young man's face. "It seems the cardinal was interested in a cache of documents from the early sixteenth century associated with Pope Julius II."

"Is that unusual?"

"It's not something we see a lot of investigation into. We have precious few records from that time."

He recalled what Ascolani had said. When Giovanni Angelo de' Medici was elected as Pius IV and banished Cardinal Ghislieri into exile, Ghislieri took church records with him.

He told the clerk what he knew.

"Starting in the first century popes kept their papers with them at all times," the clerk said. "No systematic collection of papal records existed until the late twelfth century. When printing came along in the fifteenth century, popes began to acquire books, creating the largest library in Italy. Now there are literally millions of documents in the collection."

He let the guy talk, hoping there was a point to be made.

"The archives have been subjected to a lot of purging," the priest said. "Most of the collection from the eleventh to the thirteenth centuries disappeared through carelessness. During the Great Schism more vanished during the move to Avignon. When German troops sacked Rome in 1527 they looted the library, melted the lead seals down to bullets, tore up the parchments and used them as litter for the horses. After Napoleon's looting over a third of the materials never came back from Paris. So our records are incomplete, at best. We have no way of knowing what was here and what was taken."

"Did Richter ask any questions?"

A nod signaled yes. He waited.

"He asked if I knew anything about a *Pignus Christi* associated with Julius II and the Medicis."

"And your reply?"

"No more than I have read in the history books."

He was curious. "And what is that?"

"Supposedly Julius II borrowed money. But from who? And how? Nobody knows. Many popes borrowed money."

He sensed that was all he was going to get. So he made clear, "Your discretion in this matter is expected."

A hesitation. Finally, a nod of understanding.

He signaled for them to leave.

But this visit had only generated more questions.

Without answers.

CHAPTER 21

Eric entered the Basilica of San Lorenzo.

It sat at the center of the main market district. A focal point since the fifteenth century. Here, not long after its completion, in 1562, the first great Medici mourning happened when Cosimo the Great's favorite son, Giovanni, died, followed twelve years later by the funeral of Cosimo himself. In 1578 it hosted the marriage of a young Lorenzo the Magnificent to Clarice Orsini, and the whole city gave itself up to feasting and delight. A few years later, after the brutal murder of Lorenzo's brother, Giuliano, a huge black catafalque surrounded by tall candles and the weeping crowd of mourners attested to Florence's collective grief and opposition to the famed Pazzi Conspiracy. A parade of weddings and funerals came through in the 16th, 17th, and into the 18th centuries, all ending with the funeral of Anna Maria Luisa, the last of the Medicis to be buried here.

The plain severe style of the church, with its columns of gray *pietra serena*, had a calming, peaceful effect. There were three parts to the basilica. The Old Sacristy where the early Medici lay at rest. The New Sacristy, like a Roman hall, abundant with windows and pillars. And the Chapel of the Princes, with its amazing array of colored marble. In the two former, the sarcophagi contained remains. But in the chapel, all of the tombs were below in the crypt, the sarcophagi there only as monuments. He knew the church itself stood on a height, the floor of the mausoleum below that of the church, making the crypt aboveground level with the Piazza di Madonna. That helped keep water out. Long ago, there was no entrance from the piazza, and the crypt could only be accessed by a staircase leading down from the mausoleum floor. It had foolishly been thought a safe place to keep the coffins free from thieves who might plunder them for jewels.

And there they remained for about a hundred years, until 1791. To further protect the coffins they were then moved to a lower, subterranean crypt of the exact size as the one above. But during that removal, or in the sixty years thereafter, owing to the want of guards, thieves searched the remains. The Medici grand dukes had a reluctance to be crowned with the regalia of their predecessors, so each duke was buried with his crown and scepter.

Which worked like an invitation.

And thieves took their toll.

Finally, in 1857, an official examination, sanctioned by Pope Pius IX, was commissioned. Forty-nine coffins were opened and examined. Only two of the grand dukes were found to still have their crown and scepter. Other remains were likewise devoid of valuables. Each of the workmen was assigned two sentries to ensure that none of the remaining jewels were stolen. The condition of the bodies, along with their dress and ornaments, was minutely detailed in an official report. Interestingly, the bodies of the Medici cardinals were untouched by thieves. It seemed even criminals feared hell. Once the examination concluded the coffins were closed and arranged in the lower crypt in the same location as they'd occupied above, each placed immediately under its tombstone in the upper crypt.

Then the entrance to the lower crypt was walled up.

He and his expert followed the curator through the basilica and the chapel and now stood in the upper crypt. Hundreds of people visited here every day. The lights were dim. The gift shop and book kiosk were closed for the day. In the center of the crypt, buried in his black armor, lay Lodovico de' Medici, an Italian *condottiero*, leader of the Black Bands, who served in combat for Popes Leo X and Clement VII, his third cousins. He died young, at age twenty-eight, from battle wounds. His wife, Maria, lay beside him. Eric read the words on the tombstone.

COGNOMENTO INVICTUS. Invincible.

He loved the Medici audacity.

It had served them well.

Around him, in the various bays, lay markers for Medici descendants from ten generations. The tomb he sought was located near one of the center pillars. He walked over, closer, to the one for Anna Maria Luisa de' Medici, who died February 18, 1743.

When her grave was first opened in 1857 the body was found wrapped in a silk sheet, under which was a handsome dress of violet-colored velvet. On her head perched the electoral crown of the Palatine, fixed by a long silver pin. According to some accounts she died a slow, painful death, supposedly suffering from syphilis. In 1966 Florence had been severely flooded, the tombs of the Medici swamped in water and mud. Many had feared the bodies had been irreparably damaged. But in 2013 Anna Maria's skeleton was found to be mostly intact when it was exhumed, part of a research collaboration between the University of Florence and the Reiss Engelhorn Museum in Mannheim, Germany. The DNA expert standing beside him had been part of that exhumation. Her body had been examined for a week before being reburied. Bone samples were then tested that suggested syphilis may not have killed her.

Which was important.

A message from the grave?

Maybe.

A piece of her bone had been retained for future testing. But neither he nor his expert had access to it. And trying to gain such would only raise questions. So he'd come tonight for another sample.

"Lead the way," he said to the curator.

And they walked toward the iron gate and the stone stairs that led below.

CHAPTER 22

COTTON HAD WATCHED AS THE WOMAN ROSE FROM HER SEAT IN THE next car. She'd headed his way but not passed through into his car, which meant she entered the lavatory. Another man had also gone that way. Smallish, with pale skin stretched across a puffy face, the effect augmented by thinning hair, a smooth brow, and high-boned cheeks. He'd stayed a few moments, then left, heading back forward into the next car. Had he used one of the lavatories? Or was there something else at play?

The train was slowing quickly, entering the station at Koblenz.

The woman still had not emerged.

Something was wrong.

He rose and headed for the next car, passing through the open connector and stopping before the lavatory door, which indicated it was occupied. He glanced around and saw no one coming his way. A few people were moving toward the exit at the other end, in the direction the other man had gone.

The train was almost stopped.

He tested the latch, which moved.

He twisted further and opened the lavatory door. Inside the small space the woman sat slumped on the toilet with a bullet to the head. He stepped farther inside, closed the door, and searched her pockets. He found a wallet, some keys, an automatic pistol, and two spare magazines.

He pocketed it all and left.

His mind flashed back to the other man whom he'd seen come toward the lavatory. He was blessed with an eidetic memory, a gift from his father's side of the family. Not photographic, as some would say. More the ability to retain an amazing amount of detail. He searched his memory for what he could recall and etched the face of the killer into his mind.

He stepped down the center aisle and headed toward the other end of the car. The train was now stopped, and the PA system announced that they were in Koblenz. Apparently someone had come to the conclusion that the woman was a liability. Which only added to the ever-growing list of complications. He exited the car into the connector where a portal led off the train and onto the platform. Was the killer still on board?

Doubtful.

He studied the few people on the platform, some leaving, others entering, and no one flagged suspicious.

No sign of the man either.

The body would be found. Then all hell would break loose. People on the train would be detained and questioned. He didn't have the time for that. The Koblenz station had four platforms and ten tracks. A busy place. He decided to stay here and regroup. He'd come to learn that people always left trails. So whoever took down that woman would resurface.

Eventually.

He stepped from the platform and entered the terminal building, finding a spot where few were around, and called Stephanie Nelle. He described all that had happened, including the identity of the dead woman.

"I see what you mean," she said. "This is a mess."

"Four hundred thousand euros are there," he said. "Then the police just miraculously show up? That house was not alarmed. Somebody is going to a lot of trouble to implicate Richter and us."

"They clearly knew you were coming."

"Which means the leak is high up in the Vatican, or inside the Swiss Guard."

"I can make some inquiries with the Entity," she said.

"No. Let's not do that. We have no idea who's pulling the strings here. I'd rather have an open field right now. Bad enough they knew all about what we were doing. Let's keep them in the dark."

"I thought you had no dog in this fight? What changed?"

"Let's just say I'm getting more curious in my old age. Where do you think I can find Cardinal Richter?"

"That's an easy one. I was told he's been suspended from duty and sent to Munich."

Really? "Which is where the train was headed. Now, that does tickle the curiosity bone. Is Richter still in Rome?"

"Until tomorrow."

"He needs to stay there. I have a feeling he's next on the target list. Whoever took out that woman may have their sights set on him."

"We're way off the rails here," she said.

And he caught the strained, edgy tone of her voice. She was right. An intelligence officer was simply a collector of information, trained to be intrigued, seeing connections where others did not. But there were times when they became much more. Players. Part of the unfolding events. Involved. Game changers. Every operation he'd ever been part of came to a crisis point. When that happened there were two choices. Get out or keep going. Many times the *keep going* meant placing your trust in something senseless, taking a risk, and hoping for the best. He once lived for those moments. And nothing had changed. His reputation was that of a maverick that always got the job done.

No sense stopping now.

"They asked for our help," he said. "So we're going to give it to them. I need to know all about that dead woman."

"Already on it."

"And one more thing."

"I know. You need to get to Rome. Fast."

CHAPTER 23

JASON LEARNED NOTHING IN THE VATICAN ARCHIVES.

He wasn't sure what he'd been expecting. A specific reference to some Pledge of Christ given to the Medici family? Highly unlikely. Any such document would have been long since discovered and surely destroyed. Why keep it? No good reason existed in his mind.

He'd taken a chance asking the clerk about the pledge, but he had no choice. It would not be long before the entire Curia knew of his suspension and began the whispers that had destroyed many a career. Ascolani would make sure that fact was widely known. He estimated he had until morning before that happened, so he needed to make the best of the next few hours.

The time was approaching 10:00 P.M.

He had many friends within the Curia, but one of his closest was Charles Cardinal Stamm, an Irishman, the man once in charge of the Entity. He'd served for decades, reappointed by pope after pope until the current pontiff, when he'd been asked to retire. The talk had been that Ascolani had championed that effort, wanting the Entity for himself. But as with every other rumor, nobody knew for sure. Even so, Ascolani most definitely ended up in charge of the Entity.

Jason had left Vatican City and made a quick stop at his apartment to change clothes, losing the clerical garb and donning plain pants, a pullover shirt, and casual shoes. Things he normally wore either at home or on the weekends. He then walked the streets of Rome toward an apartment building about three kilometers away, one of many the Holy See owned across the city. The apartments inside provided affordable housing for various cardinals, bishops, and priests who worked in the Vatican. Stamm had been allowed to keep his residence, most likely as an offering so he'd stay quiet in retirement—an offering that could just as easily be taken away.

He'd called ahead and Stamm was waiting up for him. His old friend was a tiny man, rail-thin, pinched in the cheeks, with a pockmarked face and a hooked nose. The hair was a trademark close-cropped frizz of silver. His age? Hard to say. But based on longevity it had to be approaching ninety. He'd been known for wearing only a trace of a scarlet bib below a white clerical collar just above the top button of a plain black cassock. No signet ring. A simple brass pectoral cross the only sign of his high office. Scarlet was reserved solely for mandated occasions. True to the nature of the Entity, Stamm had always kept an extremely low profile. But his prickly humor, boundless vigor, and suspicious nature had not made him a favorite within the Curia. For all his faults, though, Stamm was noted as calm and precise, his words always ringing with reason. He possessed a legion of friends, but also a large quantity of enemies.

Ascolani chief among them.

They sat, the entire apartment the picture of austerity. Nothing flashy or extravagant. More what you'd find at a secondhand store.

He explained all that had happened.

"Quite a day you have had," Stamm said.

"An understatement."

The cardinal chuckled. "I know what you mean. I had one of those days myself a few years ago when I was unceremoniously let go. You are being herded, Jason, along a predetermined path, like a rat in a maze."

"By who?"

"There is a host of likely suspects, but one shines above all others."

He knew. Ascolani. "Why? I am no threat to him."

Stamm sat back in his chair, head angled to the ceiling. "But the *Pignus Christi* is."

"Is there something to it?"

"No one has actually ever seen one. Supposedly, they were common in the early days, just after Constantine sanctioned Christianity and made it the empire's religion. It was all those bishops and early popes had to offer to get anything. A promise before their God. But its use faded away as the church's secular power and wealth grew. No need to make any sacred promises. The church came to be able to do whatever it wanted, whenever it wanted, however it wanted, without repercussions."

"Is it true what Casaburi said about the Medicis loaning ten million florins to Julius II?"

"It is certainly possible. The Warrior Pope spent a lot of money, and the Medicis had the funds to lend."

"What does it matter any longer?"

Stamm pointed a thin, gaunt finger his way. "It matters a great deal. The pope swore before God that a promise would be kept. He placed that promise in writing, under papal seal. To breach that would be a mortal sin."

"Since when do popes care about committing mortal sins?"

"I agree. They had no problem denying that some of our priests were pedophiles. Lie after lie after lie. The church cannot afford another blow like that to its credibility, no matter how ancient the threat may be."

"You're saying that if such a document exists, we would honor it?"

"The pope would have no choice. Either that or openly breach the promise. Either one is bad. I suspect an ecclesiastical court might even uphold the validity of that pledge."

"Why would Ascolani care about this?"

"He fashions himself as a savior. I suspect this would be another grand gesture on his part. Saving the Holy See, and all that. It is no secret that the current Holy Father's mind is not his own. And I mean no offense. I know he is your friend. But Ascolani controls the information flow, so he controls him. Totally. That is why Ascolani wanted the Entity. He can now feed the pope whatever information he wants. He is the gatekeeper and, from what I am told, the pope's personal secretary is close to the secretary of state."

He'd heard the same thing.

"Ascolani is nothing but trouble," Stamm said. "I tried to warn the pope when he asked for my resignation, but he would not listen. The Secretariat of State demands a more moderate personality, somebody who is a diplomat as well as an administrator. Who inspires trust, not controversy. And under no circumstances should that same man head the Entity."

"I have to find that document," he said to Stamm.

"No, Jason. *We* have to find that document."

He realized that a man like Charles Stamm would not take rejection lightly. By all accounts he'd run the Entity masterfully for nearly five decades. Other popes had bowed to his expertise. This one had rejected it. The difference? Ascolani.

"You hold a grudge?"

"I do." Stamm sat silent for a moment. Finally, he said, "Your meeting with Eric Casaburi was monitored. So Ascolani knows that a Pledge of Christ was mentioned. He will dispatch assets to investigate. He will not be able to resist."

"I am not going to Munich."

"I certainly hope not. But once you do not go, you are a marked man. You have intentionally ignored a direct papal order. They will come to arrest you, and charge you with bribery. Munich was a way to get you out of sight and avoid that. Your conversation with the clerk in the archives will also alert them that you have taken an interest in the Pledge of Christ."

A mistake on his part, for sure. But at the time, he felt it the only play.

"The good thing is that Ascolani will not assume you would come here," Stamm said. "For a while, after I resigned, I was watched continuously. But that stopped about a year ago."

"Is there that much paranoia?"

"A man like Sergio Ascolani has many enemies. The Entity has now become his personal information and protection force."

Not necessarily what he wanted to hear.

"I have a confession," Stamm said. "I was aware of the allegations made against you. The head of the Swiss Guard is an old friend. When the trial prosecutors asked for verification on the information they received, he called me and I connected them with a woman I know in the United States Justice Department, who provided him one of her retired operatives. He's the one who took the photograph of the money in the priest hole. I worked with both of them, right before the last conclave, on a matter out of Malta. His name is Cotton Malone."

"Why didn't you tell me before now?"

"I could not. But I also believed that if any money was found, it had to be planted. I was hoping you would come this way and ask for help."

He appreciated the confidence and felt better with this old warrior on his side.

"As Cardinal Ascolani is about to find out," Stamm said, "I am not dead yet."

CHAPTER 24

ERIC SETTLED INTO THE SMALL SETTEE INSIDE HIS SUITE AT THE ST. Regis. Florence was blessed with a multitude of hotels, most modest, some fine, but a few, like the St. Regis, were exceptional. The nightly rates were not any bargain, but management offered a political rate that made the luxury affordable. His suite faced the River Arno and consisted of a bedroom, two baths, and a roomy sitting area.

Where he could think.

His expert had assured him that he'd been able to extract enough viable samples that at least one of them should yield to DNA testing. Thankfully DNA did not lie. Absolute to greater than a 99 percent accuracy. Which hopefully would reveal one more line of Medici that sprang from Anna Maria and ended with himself.

But there was something else.

Of equal importance.

Francesco della Rovere was elected pope in 1471 and took the name Sixtus IV. He was both wealthy and powerful. A man accustomed to having his way. For Girolamo Riario, who may have been Sixtus' son, he wanted to buy Imola, a small town in Romagna, with the aim of establishing a new papal state in that area. Imola lay on the trade route between Florence and Venice. Lorenzo de' Medici had arranged in May 1473 to buy the town from the Duke of Milan for one hundred thousand ducats, but the duke reneged on the deal and agreed to sell it instead to Sixtus for forty thousand ducats. The purchase was to have been financed by the Medici bank, but Lorenzo refused, not wanting a papal enemy so close to Florence. Sixtus, in retaliation, closed the church's accounts with the Medici and transferred them to the Pazzi family bank, which financed the purchase.

By 1478 friction between the Medici and the papacy was high. So a plan was concocted to assassinate Lorenzo and his brother, Giuliano de' Medici. Sixtus was approached for his support and in a carefully worded statement made clear that while in the terms of his holy office he was unable to sanction killing, it would be of great benefit to the papacy to have the Medici removed from their position of power in Florence. Not a ringing endorsement, but enough for the conspirators to move forward.

The attack took place on the morning of Sunday, April 26, 1478, during High Mass at the Duomo of Florence. Murder within a church was typical for the Renaissance. It offered the easiest way to get to a well-guarded family at an unguarded moment. Lorenzo was assaulted by two of Jacopo Pazzi's men, but managed to escape to the sacristy with only a wound. Giuliano was killed by Bernardo Bandini dei Baroncelli and Francesco de' Pazzi, stabbed sixteen times. A number of Jacopo Pazzi's men stormed the Palazzo Vecchio and attempted to take control of the signoria, but failed. The Florentines did not rise up against the Medici as the Pazzi had hoped. Just the opposite occurred. Many of the conspirators were captured that day and hanged, including the archbishop of Pisa, who'd been part of the plot.

More than thirty all total were hanged. Jacopo de' Pazzi, head of the plot and the Pazzi family, escaped from Florence but was caught and brought back. He was tortured, then hanged. He was buried at Santa Croce, the Pazzi family church, but the body was dug up and thrown into a ditch, then dragged through the streets and propped up at the door of Palazzo Pazzi, where the rotting head was used as a door knocker. From there it was thrown into the River Arno. Children fished it out and hung it from a willow tree, flogged it, and then threw it back into the river.

Between April 26, the day of the attack, and October 20, 1478, eighty people were executed. Three more executions occurred on June 6, 1481. The Pazzi were banished from Florence, their lands and property confiscated. Their name and coat of arms were perpetually suppressed. All buildings and streets designated in their honor were renamed. Their family shield, with its twin dolphins, was obliterated. Anyone named Pazzi had to take a new surname. Anyone married to a Pazzi was barred from public office.

The family was all but erased.

Eric knew the stories.

The Pazzi were supposedly founded by Pazzo di Ranieri, the first man over the walls at the First Crusade during the Siege of Jerusalem in 1099. He returned to Florence with flints supposedly from the Holy Sepulcher, which the family safeguarded and used each year to rekindle the Easter fire for the city. But another tale said the Pazzis came from ancient Rome and were one of the first to settle by the River Arno and colonize Florence.

Nobody knew if either story was true.

But the Pazzis did become one of the leading noble families and gained power and wealth through banking, placing them in direct competition with the Medicis. They also managed to wrestle control of the papacy's finances from the Medicis. The Pazzis were alarmed by the absolute authority the Medicis wielded over Florence, a sentiment shared by others. The plot to kill Lorenzo and his brother was designed to end that control. But it exploded into failure, the participants too bound to their own ideas and not able to see reality.

A majority of Florence was loyal to the Medici.

In the end the failed Pazzi Conspiracy served only to strengthen the Medicis' control over Florence, as they used the opportunity to rid themselves of their most dangerous enemies. They ruled, barely challenged, for centuries, controlling all offices and appointments, their bank woven into the city's existence. The Pazzis never recovered.

And the Medicis never stopped hating them.

Except one.

CHAPTER 25

ROME, ITALY
TUESDAY, JULY 1
2:40 A.M.

COTTON WALKED THE NEARLY DESERTED STREETS, HEADING FOR THE address he'd been provided. Stephanie had again supplied him with fast transportation from Koblenz by authorizing a quick charter flight. He'd reconned the train station on the off chance that the other man he'd seen might surface, but no such luck. Whoever took out that woman was a pro, moving in fast, getting the job done, then disappearing. He was still perplexed as to why. Best guess? His appearance on the train had something to do with it. Which meant the man knew his identity. There was clearly a leak within the Swiss Guard that had alerted outsiders to every single thing they were doing. But who? And why? Stephanie had assured him that she would pass everything along to the right people within the Vatican. His concern now was Cardinal Richter, a man who may indeed have a target on his back.

But from who? And why?

He'd landed at a small commercial airport just outside of Rome. A private car service had been waiting and had taken him into the city. Thankfully, he'd managed a power nap on the flight and was now rested, ready to go. There'd even been some food. His destination, though, was a bit of a surprise. An acquaintance. Someone he'd dealt with a little while back. The former head of the Entity, Charles Cardinal Stamm.

Stephanie had told him that the current pope had made a change at the head of Vatican intelligence. Stamm had served many and was way past the age of eighty, which disqualified him from actively participating in any future conclaves. Forced to retire? That had to have been brutal for a guy accustomed to being in charge.

"Apparently, Richter and Stamm are old friends," Stephanie said. "Richter went straight to him. Cardinal Stamm is the one who gave my name to the Swiss Guard, so he's aware of what's happening. But he now tells me there is more to the story."

"Care to share?"

"Stamm asked that he be the one to tell you."

He found the address and the wooden apartment door, its peeling blue paint casting a tired look. It was answered not by Stamm but by a younger man. Late fifties. Thick, tawny hair. Square, tensed jaw. Blue eyes. Compressed lips. And a faint, almost weak smile from either exhaustion or anxiety.

"Jason Richter," the man said in English, extending a hand, which he shook. Richter was dressed in street clothes, nothing at all suggesting that he was a prince of the church. "You must be Cotton Malone. I have heard all about you."

He smiled. "Just cruel and vicious lies put out by my enemies to discredit me."

"Chas said you would say something like that."

He caught the familiar "*Chas,*" which was what Stamm's friends called him, himself included. "And where is the cardinal?"

"Right in here," Stamm called out.

Together, he and Richter walked back to a cozy den, dimly lit, where Stamm sat in a high-backed upholstered chair. The cardinal looked the same as at their previous dealings and, like Richter, was dressed casually. Nothing pretentious about him. Much like the Entity itself, which worked under an umbrella of total deniability, never venturing far from the shadows but always getting the job done.

Stamm motioned for him to sit. "We meet again. Under equally difficult circumstances."

He and Richter sat in their own chairs.

"Though this time," Stamm said, "I am no longer head of the Entity. The pope thought it was time for me to take a rest."

"Maybe it was?"

"I could say the same for you."

Touché. "Okay, point made."

"Did you really see a bag full of cash in the Dillenburg residence?" Richter asked.

"I'm afraid so. Booby-trapped with a dye pack. Somebody went to a lot of trouble."

He found his phone and showed them the images. "Those were sent to the Swiss Guard hours ago."

Richter faced Stamm. "Ascolani mentioned there were pictures."

"The Swiss Guard is keeping him informed," Stamm said. "Like the chickens telling the fox everything that's happening in the coop. But it is hard for them to accept that he is no friend of theirs."

"Who is Ascolani?" Cotton asked.

"The current Vatican secretary of state," Richter said, "and head of the Entity. A bit of a megalomaniac. He thinks he possesses capabilities and strengths exceeding those of all others. He and I have never cared for each other."

"So you're a known enemy to him?"

Richter nodded. "He's always been resentful of my relationship with the pope. Who apparently has now turned on me."

"We cannot be harsh on the pope," Stamm said. "He's an absolute ruler, blessed with a stamp of infallibility, unhampered by any checks and balances. He lives and works within a protective bubble, one the secretary of state can greatly influence. Our current pontiff is not the most learned of men. Spiritual? Yes. Devoted? Absolutely. But he is ignorant of politics." Stamm motioned toward Richter. "Tell him about the pledge."

And he listened as the cardinal explained what Eric Casaburi, an Italian politician, had revealed. When Richter finished, he asked, "Is it real?"

"Oh, yes," Stamm said. "Most real. I learned during my time

with the Entity that there are many things the church would prefer to remain lost and forgotten. Part of my job was to make sure they stayed gone. This is one of those things, though I can understand how it became a non-concern. The pledge was supposedly given around 1512. The Medici died out in 1743. During their existence no one came forward to claim the debt. Then, after 1743, the royal Medici were gone."

"So Casaburi has to be a real Medici heir?" Cotton asked.

"Correct. But Casaburi is no fool. He would not bring forth this claim unless he can prove that he is legitimate. Today, DNA testing would be irrefutable."

He'd seen his share of the incredible. And probably Stamm had too. So this could not be taken lightly. He studied the spymaster, imagining what this man had been privy to. Certainly the intelligence resources of the Vatican were not comparable in funding or cutting-edge technology to those of the CIA or the SVR, but what was lacking in money was more than made up for in human resources. The Entity had eyes and ears everywhere, and it would be a fatal mistake to underestimate its reach and capabilities. The fabled Nazi hunter Simon Wiesenthal once observed that *the best and most effective espionage service in the world belonged to the Vatican.*

"I think we have a two-front problem," Stamm said. "The first involves the discrediting of Jason. Why is this happening? Who will benefit from that? The second is the ambition of Eric Casaburi and his National Freedom Party." Stamm raised two fingers and moved them closer, then apart. "Two parallel issues. About to converge."

"To what end?" Richter asked.

Stamm lowered his hands. "That is what you two must discover."

He decided to level with Stamm and told them both about what had happened in Cologne and on the train. Stephanie had left the decision on that openness to him.

"That is troublesome," Stamm said. "Those murders seem targeted at whatever is happening to Jason. I am sorry, old friend, but you have been selected as the patsy. I would assume your death was next on the list."

"My thought exactly," Cotton said.

"But luck favors the fortunate," Stamm said. "And Eric Casaburi may have revealed something far more powerful than anything Cardinal Ascolani imagined. Make no mistake, he will go after that pledge."

"But where?" Richter asked.

"It does not exist within the Vatican," Stamm said. "Of that I am sure. But there is one other place where it may be."

He and Richter listened as Stamm told them about the Dominican friar Miguel Ghislieri who, in 1551, was promoted to head of the Inquisition. He was eventually banished from Rome and barely escaped with his life, taking refuge in a monastery. There he stayed for six years until January 7, 1566, when Ghislieri was elected pope.

"He chose the name Pius V," Stamm said. "It was he who started the Entity, empowering it from the beginning with an autonomy that still exists today. During my tenure that freedom was used with caution. My fear is that Ascolani has modified that restraint."

Cotton was beginning to connect the dots. "You're afraid he will use the Pledge of Christ for his own benefit."

"It would be a powerful weapon. The sacred promise of a pope, in writing, upon the name of the Lord. The church could only deny that to its own detriment. He would want to find and destroy the pledge. An act the other cardinals might find important enough to elevate him to pope."

"Now it makes sense," Richter muttered.

Stamm appraised the younger cardinal with oily eyes. "I was wondering if you knew."

Richter nodded.

"Can we not do this?" Cotton asked. "What is it?"

"The pope is contemplating quitting," Richter said. "He wants to retire and enjoy his final years without the pressures of the Vatican. He and I have privately discussed it."

"Ascolani most certainly knows," Stamm said. "So he is making a play. A big one. In secret. Before the gathering storm clouds appear. And Eric Casaburi just gave him an unexpected gift."

"So let's find that document first," Cotton said. "And take the wind out of his sails."

Stamm nodded. "Precisely. But I am afraid it will not be easy."

He did not like the sound of that.

"When Ghislieri fled Rome in 1559, he took with him a great many records," Stamm said. "We have long known that. Documents from the more recent popes, Julius II being one of those, included. Julius II is the one who supposedly offered the pledge to the Medicis. My guess is that, if the church's copy still exists, it is within those papers. But those have long been secreted away in a Tuscan monastery. Santa Maria di Castello. I learned of the cache decades ago. That is where you must look."

"How do we get in?" Cotton asked.

"That is the hard part. The Carthusian Order controls the site. They will never allow you in voluntarily. They will not even allow the Vatican in. But there is one person who might be able to open the way. A friend of mine, who lives in Siena."

"You said it won't be easy," Cotton said. "What's the problem?"

"She's an opportunist. Not to be trusted."

CHAPTER 26

STEFANO HAD LEFT THE ARCHIVES AND HEADED STRAIGHT FOR Cardinal Richter's Rome apartment, the address provided by the Entity's main command. It seemed the best place to start his search. Central operations was located in a building toward the rear of the Vatican, near the outer wall, beyond the gardens, close to an array of satellite dishes.

Richter lived in one of the many apartment buildings that the Holy See owned across Rome. Part of the countless investments the Vatican Bank made with church money. Most of the occupants paid market-price rent, but cardinals working in the Curia were granted a subsidy and paid little to nothing. Clergy like himself lived much more modestly. He'd been assigned a room within the rectory for the Archbasilica of the Most Holy Savior at the Lateran across town. He owned little more than a few clothes and a laptop. He stayed constantly on the move, shifting from one assignment to the next. The room at the rectory was just a place to sleep when he was in Rome. Everything else he required was provided, including a specially made mobile phone for secure communications. His meager salary was appreciated and he'd managed to bank almost all of it, as the Entity covered travel expenses and the rectory fed him. He liked the freedom he enjoyed. Connected to nowhere in particular. Unbound by material things. His focus entirely on getting the job done.

He would like to stay attached to the Entity and rise through its ranks. Most who were selected were either promoted or fired. Few ever left on their own. Surely there was a place for him there, and he intended to do his job to the best of his ability and find that place.

Arriving at Richter's apartment building he discovered that the cardinal was there. Excellent. His hunch played out. So he'd maintained surveillance, prepared to stay all night if need be. But Richter had emerged from the building dressed in street clothes and headed off in a hurry. Thankfully the cardinal had decided to walk to wherever he was headed.

He'd followed.

Ascolani had made clear that this was not an assignment that would involve the Gruppo Intervento Rapido. A dozen men worked under Stefano in the rapid intervention group.

"At present, this job is for you alone," Ascolani said. *"But that could change."*

Which meant he had to be ready to pivot.

Richter hustled through Rome's maze of intersecting streets, never hesitating, taking each turn with confidence. He was headed somewhere familiar.

And fast.

The euphoria from the win earlier in Florence had faded. Calcio Storico had been an important part of his life since he was a teenager. But he was nearing the end of his time to participate. It was definitely a young man's game, and he was approaching middle age. His body could take only so much pounding. He'd always returned home in June to play in the annual matches. Something he looked forward to. He'd been part of winning and losing teams. Definitely winning was better. As a kid he'd dreamed of making the final goal, with the match on the line, the crowds cheering him on.

Today he'd done just that.

A one-bouncer. But enough.

He'd miss those matches.

He grabbed his bearings. Richter was a kilometer or so away from the Vatican, deep into Rome central.

Where were they headed?

His parents had no idea what he did for the church. They thought him assigned to the Curia, working in the secretary of state's office as a junior administrator. He used the secrecy of the office as an excuse not to discuss any particulars, which they'd seemed to understand. His extended absences were chalked up to the work of the church. They were clearly proud of him on two levels. First, he was a priest, a servant of the Lord. And second, he was part of the Curia, something special, working for the pope. He wanted to tell them the truth, and maybe someday he could.

But not now.

The neighborhood around him was definitely familiar. He'd visited here before. Was Richter headed there? Possible. But other cardinals lived in this area too. Richter turned a corner then headed straight for one of the apartment buildings and stepped inside.

"Have you ever considered serving the church in a different capacity?"

He knew what to say. "I am at its disposal."

"Your bishop tells me that you are a resourceful individual, one he has come to depend upon."

"I have done what he asked of me."

"Modest, too, I see."

"Vanity has never been something I suffered from."

"Good. Because the service the church will now ask of you requires neither vanity nor ego. Only discretion. Absolute and total discretion."

That man changed his life.

Charles Cardinal "Chas" Stamm.

Who recruited him for the Entity.

Richter had entered the building where Stamm lived. Coincidence?

No way. He found his phone and placed a call, reporting to Ascolani what he'd observed.

"It seems our wayward cardinal has sought out an ally," Ascolani said.

"Others live in the building."

"That is true. But at this hour? And on this night? After all that has happened? No. He has gone to Stamm."

He waited for instructions.

"Stay there," Ascolani said to him. "Alert me to any change. Then we will decide what to do next."

CHAPTER 27

ERIC WAS HAVING TROUBLE SLEEPING.

He'd been born and raised about an hour outside of the city, in an ancient hilltop town, one of many scattered across Tuscany. His grandmother would tell him a giant carved the town straight from the rock, and to see it was to believe that story. Less than five hundred full-time inhabitants. Lots of blooming flowers, laundry hanging from lines, street names like Via dell'Amore and Via del Bacio. Its main claim to fame? Sheep cheese. High quality, made from an especially aromatic milk thanks to the succulent pastures in the nearby valleys. Its pungent smell remained in his nostrils, even after all the years that had passed since he left.

Earlier, he'd followed the curator and his DNA expert as they made their way down to the lower crypt in the Medici Chapel, off limits to tourists and any other visitors, to the coffin holding the remains of Anna Maria. There she'd rested for nearly three centuries. But not peacefully. Far from it with all the so-called scientific investigations. With regard to Anna he'd always found it curious that she'd been buried wearing the crown of the German Palatinate, for her husband, rather than the traditional Medici death crown. That had been a relatively unimportant piece of information to those performing the examination of her remains.

But to him? It spoke volumes as another message from the grave. True, Anna had been first and foremost a Medici, conscious of her birthright, proud of her family heritage. But she'd been resentful when she was denied the opportunity to succeed her father as grand duchess. Especially considering the ineptness and unpopularity of her brother. After Gian Gastone died she was still denied, as the duchy was confiscated by the Holy Roman emperor and given to Francis of Lorraine, effectively ending Medici rule. She'd been relegated to being the widow of Wilhelm, Elector Palatine of the Rhine, daughter of the late Cosimo III, sister of the departed Gian Gastone.

Which meant nothing.

But fate worked in her favor.

Her brothers left no legitimate heirs. Which meant that after Gian Gastone died, everything the Medici possessed became hers. Paintings, statues, bronzes, gems, cameos, busts, books, antiquities, suits of armor, furniture, reliquaries, clothing, land, money, anything and everything dating back three centuries. The fact that the duchy itself had been lost did not affect the vast holdings of family wealth. Prior to her death Anna Maria made a momentous decision. In her will she left all of it to Tuscany on the condition that *it be maintained as ornamentation of the State for public use and to attract the curiosity of foreigners, never to be removed or transported outside of the Capitol and the Grand Ducal State.*

The famous Family Pact.

A final Medici bow to dignity and greatness.

In the years after 1743 Medici possessions flowed into the galleries and museums of Florence. Anna's final act was one of great generosity. An astonishing gift that laid the groundwork for modern-day Florence. Yet few knew her name. No statue of her adorned any of the city's open spaces. No gallery or museum displayed her name above its doors. No bust or picture of her was placed in honor on any walls. Only a sculpture in the Medici Chapel above her grave. Hundreds of thousands pass through Florence every year without ever hearing her name. Yet none of what those people came to see would be there but for her.

Was he related to Anna Maria?

He had to know.

They'd opened Anna's tomb, the bones reverently arranged anatomically by the latest investigators from a few years ago. Everything else that had been there in the 1857 exhumation was gone, decayed over time or ruined by the 1966 great flood. His expert had extracted several samples. He was bolstered by the fact that viable DNA had been found in her bones during the last exhumation.

Find it once. Find it again.

He knew he now faced several vexing issues.

First, he had to establish a verifiable DNA link to the Medici, through Gregorio Cappello and Anna Maria. If what his grandmother had told him was true, Gregorio Cappello and Anna Maria were mother and son. Which meant the historical accounts of Anna Maria being childless were wrong. But a DNA accuracy of 99.9 percent would rewrite that history. Since he'd already verified his DNA link to Gregorio, along with what his grandmother had always said, that would make him a royal Medici.

Check that off the list.

Second, he had to establish a DNA link from the paternal side.

Then the third part. The hardest of them all. Proving that Anna Maria and her baby's father were legally married. Only then would he be a legitimate royal Medici heir.

Could he do it? In three days?

He was about to find out.

CHAPTER 28

JASON WAS WIRED.

Fatigue was nowhere to be found.

It was well after midnight and Cardinal Stamm had retired to his bedroom. Cotton Malone was still there, and he was glad. He did not want to face this alone, and Stamm had vouched for the American.

"He was one of the best intelligence officers the U.S. ever sent out," Stamm said. *"He knows what he is doing."*

Quite a compliment from the Vatican's former spymaster, who had been one of the best himself.

"Chas speaks highly of you," he said to Malone.

"He seems to like you too."

"He and I have always enjoyed each other's company. Neither one of us ever tried to fool the other."

Malone chuckled. "That does make for a good friendship. Me and my former boss were similar."

"Sure you would not like a drink?"

"I'll stick with water. I never acquired the taste for alcohol as a young man."

He raised his glass, which contained a generous splash of Irish whiskey. "I cannot say the same. And, I might add, Chas has some top-shelf selections." He enjoyed a sip. "This is serious. Right?"

"Four hundred thousand euros in cash, hidden inside a building you control? Then to get one of the co-defendants to implicate you and plant the seed?"

"That co-defendant is a monsignor from the Secretariat of State. Easy to see how he suddenly had a pang of conscience and confessed."

"All of which takes planning and nerve," Malone said. "Those same people may also want you dead. Killers were on their way to Munich."

It was important that Malone saw him as pragmatic and reasonable. A victim. Not a criminal.

"I am curious," Malone said. "Why target you? There's more here than you being a friend to the pope."

"I suspect Cardinal Ascolani is consolidating his power and eliminating any and all threats."

"Does he think you papabile?"

The unofficial term described a Catholic man thought a likely, or possible, candidate to be elected pope. Most times the cardinals choose from among themselves a clearly papabile candidate. Occasionally, though, they veer away and take a chance, electing a man outside the norm. John XXIII, John Paul I, John Paul II, and Francis were notable recent examples. Yet the old saying was true. *He who enters the conclave as pope leaves it as a cardinal.* A warning that no one should be too sure of themselves.

"I am anything but papabile. There have been but two German popes. But I do have influence with other cardinals. I can be persuasive. Ascolani is trying to neutralize that threat."

"He knows you would never support him?"

"No question. He does."

"I'm curious," Malone said. "Why is a five-hundred-year-old I-owe-you important? What would it matter?"

He motioned with his drink. "That is where the church's reputation comes into play. *If a man makes a vow to the Lord, or takes an oath to bind himself with a binding obligation, he shall not violate his word. He shall do according to all that proceeds out of his mouth.* Numbers 30:2 is quite clear. Could it be dishonored? Sure. But not without consequences."

"Ascolani knows about the pledge?"

"Oh, yes. I knew Casaburi coming to me would raise questions, and I assumed the head of the Entity would be interested."

"So you played to the microphones?"

He nodded. "Exactly. And all was fine until Casaburi mentioned that pledge."

"And you think obtaining it will give *you* leverage?"

"It will definitely give me something to use against Ascolani. Which explains my interest. What is yours? Chas says you are retired and own a rare-book shop in Copenhagen. Why are you here?"

"I've been asked to find out what is going on. And a Swiss Guardsman is dead. My job is to sort it all out."

"This seems a matter for the Vatican, not the United States."

"Lucky for you we're nosy."

He smiled. "Indeed. Lucky for me."

The whiskey was settling inside him, working its way through his bones. It felt good. Comforting. He was finally tiring. But he could not go to his apartment. It was surely being watched. Stamm had invited him to use the guest room, which was sounding better and better by the moment.

"You know, the first financial manager of church property was St. Lawrence, a deacon of Pope Sixtus II," he said. "He suffered martyrdom in the third century. Rather than obey an order to reveal the church's wealth during persecution under Emperor Valerian, he was roasted to death on a gridiron. Before that happened he gathered poor and sick Christians and told the emperor that they were the church's treasure. Things have really changed."

Malone just sat there. Listening.

"The Prefecture for the Economic Affairs of the Holy See, the supreme financial control authority, is forbidden from even looking into the bank's affairs. How is that possible? It is all up to a committee of cardinals to exercise vigilance over the bank. Highly sensitive information confined to a small number of people who are, I might add, highly unqualified."

"You sound disgusted."

"I am. For so long there was an unwritten rule within the bank to keep no documentation. Incredible. As a token of appreciation for that restraint an envelope with cash was attached to any information someone was allowed to see. *For your personal charities,* a note would say. That meant 'publish no balance sheets, disclose no assets or liabilities, ask no questions.' No wonder bankers all over the world wanted to do business with us. The people in the bank are polite, reserved, and taciturn, but criminals nonetheless."

"That's a strong statement."

"Yes, it is. But the truth. The whole place is riddled with corruption. The last thing the Holy See wants is for some medieval pledge to surface that obligates the church to pay hundreds of billions. What baffles me, though, is that the Medicis are gone and have been for a long time. But Casaburi seems quite sure that he is a legitimate Medici heir."

"Why bring it up if he is not?"

He tipped his glass at Malone. "Exactly. That bluff could be easily called." And downed the rest of the whiskey.

His life had changed radically over the course of the past twenty-four hours. He was nearly sixty years old, relatively young for a cardinal, part of the so-called new majority that the current pope had cultivated with a calculated handing out of red hats. All of them were good, learned men, which the church desperately needed. But he'd found that many cardinals possessed an escape hatch for their consciences, taking public positions that they did not privately agree with so as to avoid popular criticism.

Not him.

He'd been outspoken on economic reform, openly criticizing the culture of greed in modern capitalism. His stand on gay rights had drawn a lot of attention. How awful for people to be judged solely by their sexual orientation. One particular quote of his had drawn a lot of interest. *If a same-sex couple are faithful, care for one another, and intend to stay together for life, do we really think God would say, "None of that interests me. I only care about their sexual orientation."* For him everyone was loved by God, as a part of His creation, and no one should be discriminated against. Ever. He had repeatedly questioned why the church could not offer the sacrament of matrimony to everybody, equally.

He'd stayed on the good side of his colleagues with his opposition to abortion and embryonic stem cell research, and his outspokenness against physician-assisted suicide. Though, if the truth be told, he was unsure why any of those were bad. Nothing was black and white. Everything seemed shades of gray.

Doctrine was clear to him. It remained the same, but the church's understanding of it changed over time. It had to. Times changed. Thoughts changed. Morality changed. But truth never changed, only a greater understanding of it came as we grew older. He was not arrogant enough to think, as some of his fellow cardinals did, that the church owned the truth. No. The truth owned us. It was something we encountered, not something we possessed. So he was not afraid of what was to come.

Truth would prevail.

But himself?

That was up in the air.

"You and I will go to Siena," he finally said to Malone. "We will find this Pledge of Christ, if it still exists, and then we will clear my name and deal with Sergio Ascolani."

"It may not be that easy."

"I am sure it will not. But I have no choice."

CHAPTER 29

SIENA, ITALY
10:40 A.M.

COTTON DROVE A JEEP RENEGADE THAT CARDINAL STAMM HAD obtained for him and Richter. He'd managed a few hours' sleep, along with a shower and shave. A change of clothes had been provided by Stamm, as a younger man arrived at the apartment with an array of pants and shirts that both he and Richter had utilized. There'd even been food. A breakfast of cornettos and frittatas, along with coffee and juice. He'd never been a big coffee drinker, another one of those unacquired tastes from his youth. Thankfully, the orange juice had been plentiful and delicious.

They'd driven north on the A1 autostrada, a toll road, but the car came with a Telepass that allowed them to pass right through the booths. Stamm had thought of everything. But he'd expected no less. About two hours north of Rome they'd left the autostrada for SS715, the Italian answer to rural divided highways, and headed west.

No tolls here. But more traffic.

The rolling landscape between Florence and Rome, a tangle of orchards, vineyards, and forests, came with an eclectic variety of towns, villages, and hamlets. Each also came with its own charm and story. Siena ranked as one of the most picturesque. A high-piled collection of rosy brick and gray travertine buildings that straggled along the crest of three Tuscan ridges. Its ancient walls, great town hall with a soaring campanile, narrow, hilly, winding streets, and sunlit piazzas all harked back to the Middle Ages. But it also hosted a university, an academy of music, trade, and industry, and a busy agricultural market. Home to about fifty thousand. He knew the legend about its creation, when a soldier named Camulio was sent by Romulus, the founder of Rome, to capture his nephews. Instead of obeying, Camulio stayed and built a town with a grand central portal. Over the centuries that gate, which led north toward Florence, became heavily defended.

The Porta Camollia.

He told Richter what he knew.

"You have a good grasp of history," the cardinal said. "Many have no idea of that story."

He smiled. "You'd be surprised how much I can recall."

He also knew that Siena had a conflicted history. It took the sides of emperors while its rival, Florence, supported popes. For centuries the two cities fought for control of the countryside. Siena rose to be a thirteenth-century center of banking and commercial power, perched right above the Via Francigena, the great medieval highway on the way to Rome. And it made the most of the locale, considering there was neither a river nor a harbor.

"The Porta Camollia is still there," Richter said. "Three arches, and on the outer one is the Medici coat of arms. The inscription was placed there in the sixteenth century to record the entry of Ferdinand de' Medici into Siena, when he took control of the town. Along with *Cor magis tibi sena pandit.* A heart that is bigger than this gate. A bit of tongue in cheek there. Siena had been a proud republic for over four hundred years. But not after that."

That was the problem with enemies.

Sometimes they won.

"The rub for this town came because the Spanish king Philip II owed huge sums to the House of Medici," Richter said. "To repay that debt he ceded Siena and its entire territory to Florence, which led to the creation of the Grand Duchy of Tuscany, ruled by the Medici. Ferdinand came here in 1558 to personally accept the investiture. He heeded Machiavelli's advice to *hold and occupy the people with feasts and spectacles.* So he encouraged the *contradas* to compete, focusing their anger internally on one another and not at Florence."

"And tried-and-true Sienese to this day still hate the Medici, right?"

"That they do. Those bad feelings run deep. But there was a silver lining to all that. Siena is now one of the best-preserved medieval cities in the world. And that is mainly thanks to the economic stagnation that happened after its secession to Florence. Not a lot of development occurred. It just stayed the same. Bad for that time, but good for the tourists today."

Stamm had briefed them before they left Rome. They were going to meet an old friend of his and Sienese resident whose family roots traced straight back to the time of Medici rule.

Camilla Baines.

She was connected to at least three of Siena's oldest families, the Chigi, Borghese, and Sozzini. Particularly to the Sozzini, who were noted as bankers, merchants, jurists, and scholars. Some even called them the most famous legal dynasty of the Italian Renaissance, once receiving a confirmation of nobility from the Holy Roman emperor. A long time ago Sozzini served as members of the Grand Council, as diplomats, judges, and other officials. In this patriarchal family, the male line of heirs died out before Italy was unified in 1861. But the family survived. Farming was now their main investment, and they owned huge swaths of Tuscan land. But over the past few decades they'd branched out into biotechnology. Several of their vaccine manufacturing facilities were located nearby.

"A few years back," Stamm said, *"they cashed out, selling to GlaxoSmithKline for an enormous amount of money. Camilla brokered that deal. She is quite wealthy. A savvy businesswoman."*

Good to know.

Stamm had also warned them that Siena would be hectic, as the

Palio happened tomorrow. One of the world's oldest, oddest, and most chaotic horse races. It officially started in 1310 when Siena's General Council declared a race every year on August 16 in honor of the Virgin Mary, though versions of the race had existed long before that. Now there were two, another tomorrow on July 2. It had evolved into a spectacle that brought the Sienese to tears of joy and despair. Three times around the Piazzo del Campo in the center of town. About a thousand meters in less than eighty seconds. The prize? A *pallium*, a length of precious silk fabric with images upon it. Once those had been only of the Madonna. Now it could be anything. A work of art, stylistic, even modern. A contest each year determined which artist would create it. Once done the *pallium* became a sacred object, deeply coveted, paraded through the streets, blessed by the bishop, sought by every *contrada* in Siena as their reward for winning the Palio.

Half an hour ago a text had come from Stamm to Cotton's phone informing them that Camilla Baines was not in Siena but outside of town, at a farm she owned. Stamm had provided directions and called ahead to make the necessary introductions, so she was expecting them.

Cotton left the main highway and turned south on one of the *strade regionale*. The narrow, paved road twisted a path up into the hills bordered by more ridged vineyards, orchards, and oak forests. Occasionally lines of olive trees made an attractive diagonal pattern against stripes of red plow. A bright sun trimmed the few thin clouds overhead in a pink border. They passed a road crew removing the remnants of a recent rockfall. Finally they came to a gated entrance where a dirt road led inside, past a fence, toward an array of low brick buildings. The pasture in between was fenced on either side. Horses strolled about, grazing on thick emerald grass.

After learning about Camilla Baines Cotton had done some homework, trying to get a better feel for both her and the lay of the land.

Siena was divided into eighteen urban wards known as *contradas*. Originally, they evolved from the times when the trades were all grouped together within their own defined space. Then they became districts that supplied troops to defend Siena. Both purposes faded away and the *contradas* lost their administrative and military functions, becoming more bastions of local patriotism, held together by tradition and the pride of their residents. Each had its own defined territory within the Sienese walls that came with an administrative center, museum, chapel, public square, and fountain. They also had their own songs, mottos, symbolic plant or animal, racing colors, and patron saints. The leaders were selected by vote and could be either male or female. They prided themselves in being classless. All members, *contradaioli*, were equal, whether rich or poor. They possessed their own government, constitution, and culture, like a mini city-state, headed by an elected *priore*. A *capitano* was also elected, who assumed operational command of the *contrada* each year during the few days of the Palio.

Contrada members paid dues, like a local tax, to offset expenses. Membership was determined by birth, blood, or choice. You could marry outside your *contrada*, but during the Palio those couples parted ways for a few days and generally celebrated with their own. There were four types of *contrada* relationships. Ally, friend, no relation, or enemy. Most *contradas* had a nemesis *contrada* that was their avowed opponent. Most also had open allies. Those extremes had a tendency to shift from one Palio to the next. Each was named after an animal, object, or symbol. Eagle, Caterpillar, Snail, Little Owl, Dragon, Giraffe, Crested Porcupine, Unicorn, She-Wolf, Seashell, Goose, Wave, Panther, Forest, Tortoise, Golden Oak, Tower, and Valley of the Ram.

Camilla Baines served as *capitano* for Golden Oak.

One of only two women to ever hold such a high post.

"It is a little odd," Richter said. "The Palio is tomorrow and Golden Oak is in the race, which means Camilla Baines should be a busy woman."

He understood. "Yet she made time to see us. That means one of two things. Either she's extremely curious or she wants something."

He drove through the gate.

The land on either side was clothed with more orchards, olive trees, and cypresses. The tires churned up dust in his rearview mirrors as he gunned the car along the dirt track.

"My vote," Richter said, "is she wants something."

CHAPTER 30

STEFANO WORKED HIS WAY THROUGH A CROWD INFECTED WITH Palio fever. A mass celebration of municipal pride. He liked how one observer described it. *A burlesque, with a touch of cruelty, that tens of thousands of people enjoy.* It reminded him of the Calcio Storico, when Florentines behaved the same way every year for a ball game.

He'd stayed on station outside Charles Stamm's apartment all night, until Cardinal Richter and another man emerged around 8:00 A.M. Thankfully, he'd thought ahead and had a car and driver dispatched from the Vatican, waiting nearby if needed. He'd also snapped some pictures of the second man. Tall, broad-shouldered, sandy-blond hair. He'd forwarded those to Entity headquarters, and an identification came back fast.

Harold Earl "Cotton" Malone.

Ex-military. United States Navy commander. Trained fighter pilot. Obtained a law degree from Georgetown Law School. Worked for a short time as a navy litigator, then transferred to the Magellan Billet, a covert arm of the United States Justice Department. He received eight commendations for meritorious service in his twelve years there, all of which were refused. He suffered three serious injuries while on assignments, and a fourth came in Mexico City during the assassination of a public prosecutor. Malone brought down three of the assailants but sustained a severe gunshot wound. After that incident he retired from the military and quit the Justice Department, moving to Copenhagen, Denmark, where he owned a rare-book shop.

But he still freelanced for the United States.

Malone's presence raised two questions. Had Stamm involved him? Or was there another player on the board?

Richter and Malone had driven off and Stefano had sent the car at his disposal to follow discreetly. Ascolani had ordered him to keep Richter in their sights. Okay. Done. He'd moved in another direction, after receiving a short text from Ascolani. Come to Siena. Which he'd also done. He'd texted his boss on arrival and a reply had come fast. Upper gallery of Cathedral of St. Mary of the Assumption. At your convenience.

Which he knew meant now.

He continued to make his way toward the cathedral, the buildings and balconies draped with colorful banners. Every nook and cranny of Siena vibrated with the tingle of the celebration. There would be games in the streets, concerts, and baptisms of all those born during the previous year. So much to see, even more to feel. The famous parade was happening. All eighteen *contradas* participated, though only ten of those would race tomorrow. It had to be that way as the track could not accommodate them all. So a procedure had evolved. The eight who did not run in the previous race were automatically included. The remaining two were drawn by lot from the other ten. Here, though, in the streets, there was plenty of room for all.

Each *contrada* fielded drummers, men-at-arms, horsemen, and flag wavers who performed with flawless agility. In the lead were the trumpeters dressed in medieval black-and-white tights and red tunics. Next came the standard-bearers marching in formation, followed by the flags of the mercers, apothecaries, painters, blacksmiths, and stonemasons. Then came the Capitano del Popolo astride a solid charger adorned in armor, with a page walking ahead bearing a sword and shield. He was the ceremonial head of the Palio. Strangely, no one appeared out of place or embarrassed by the odd regalia. Just the opposite, as the people of Siena seemed to walk with grace and ease into the fifteenth century.

Representatives of the *contradas* then appeared. One after the other. Last rode each *contrada's* jockey upon a parade horse, the actual horse for the race at the end with only a cloth flung over its back.

Color abounded. Which he knew was important. White for glory. Red for strength. Blue for peace. Yellow for nobility. Each *contrada* utilized a unique mix of the four colors, their territory across Siena marked by their flags angling from the buildings. Those individual color schemes were also incorporated into scarves the people wore around their necks, given to them when they were children but donned only twice a year. It was considered bad luck to wash the scarves, so they all bore the dirt and grime from past Palios.

He stopped for a moment.

One of the *contradas* drew level to where he stood. The men were dressed in tunics of yellow with black and blue edging, their hose yellow, the calf of each leg encircled by two blue bands.

Eagles.

The roll of a drum moved the air.

Several of them then faced one another and cast the flags they carried up thirty feet, catching them shaft-first. As if that were too easy they cast them up again, then turned their backs on the falling flags, catching them backward as they came down. Then they twirled them beneath their legs and tossed them back and forth like flaming torches, one to the other, while the crowd roared its approval. The *alzata*. A talent unique to Siena, which harked back to when a banner on the battlefield was every soldier's reference point. Lose the banner and they lost the fight. So its bearers learned to keep it high, which eventually developed into an art form.

The pageantry would go on for another two hours.

No time for him to stay and watch.

He hustled along, elbowing his way through the thick throngs.

The cathedral sat on the highest point in town, on the site where a temple to Minerva once stood. Started in 1229 the Sienese wanted to build the grandest church in the world, but it eventually became only a fraction of what it was supposed to be. Outside was a magnificent striped marble façade, topped by a huge dome and a massive bell tower that could be seen from all over the city.

Why was it never completed?

History noted that a devastating outburst of black plague killed a huge percentage of the population and made it tough to find workers. But constantly battling its archenemy Florence had been the main factor, draining resources. He'd often thought that if Siena had won the Battle of Marciano and never fallen to their Florentine rivals, they may have possibly built one of the greatest cities in all of Italy.

But perhaps they had still managed to do just that.

He crossed the street and climbed the stone steps to the cathedral's main doors. The parade was headed this way and would culminate out in front. Before all that arrived he paid his admission fee and entered. He could have shown his Vatican identification, which would have granted him free entrance, but he knew not to draw attention to himself.

Inside, the crowded nave was striking with its zebra-striped black-and-white walls, the colors in the Siena coat of arms. A forest of clustered columns reached to ceiling vaults painted a deep blue and sprinkled with golden stars.

He turned right and headed for an open portal, stepping over a chain that said NO ADMITTANCE and climbing a steep set of stone risers. At the top, before a stone balustrade, stood Cardinal Ascolani, dressed in nondescript street clothes, admiring the people below.

He walked over.

"I have always found this cathedral so intriguing," Ascolani said in a low voice. "Such an array of color and style. But the busts are my favorite."

Projecting from above the arches around the nave were the terra-cotta heads of the first 172 popes.

Ascolani pointed. "The head labeled Hadrian I. See how young and unlike the others he appears?"

He agreed. There were physical differences.

"Some say that is really Pope Joan. Hadrian lived at the time when a woman might have managed to disguise herself and become pope."

"That is a legend," he had to say.

"Is it? For me it is more a mystery."

And he saw that Ascolani liked the dichotomy.

"Your men following Cardinal Richter say he and the American are at a horse farm, outside of town."

News to him, as no report had come his way.

"It is owned by Camilla Baines. Do you know her?" Ascolani asked.

He shook his head.

"A rich and powerful woman," Ascolani said. "She's the *capitano* for the Golden Oak *contrada*. Interestingly, she is there and not here, in town, in the parade, leading her *contrada*."

Which was tradition, he knew.

"They drove straight there," Ascolani said, his attention still on the crowds below. "Stamm sent them. No question. We need to know why."

He waited for more.

"Do you recall what I said about Miguel Ghislieri, when he was sent into exile in 1559. Banished by Pius IV."

He nodded.

"Nobody knows how many records Ghislieri took with him."

He recalled what the priest in the archives had said.

"Inventories were sparse."

"Those records almost certainly dealt with the popes of his time. Especially the controversial ones. Clement VII. Leo X. Both Medicis, by the way. And of course, Julius II. If the church's copy of that pledge still exists, it will be within those lost papers."

Ascolani turned to face him.

"Those records have long been secreted away by the Carthusians. Few know that fact. But Charles Stamm is one who does."

"How does Camilla Baines fit into this?"

Ascolani smiled. "That is where this becomes really interesting. That monastery has minimal contact with the outside world. But Carthusians have to survive in the modern world, and Camilla Baines' family has long been their most ardent supporter. If anyone can gain access to what may be hidden away in that monastery, she is that person."

"You think Richter and Malone will go to the monastery?"

"It is not all that far away. So we are going to find out."

"And if they do go there?"

"We will be there too."

CHAPTER 31

FLORENCE, ITALY
1:15 P.M.

ERIC WALKED ACROSS THE PIAZZA DI SANTA CROCE AND HEADED for the basilica. Workers were busy disassembling the grandstands and ball court that each year dominated the plaza. The yearly games were over. The Greens had won. Truth be known he'd always been partial to the Blues. He envied those who played Calcio Storico. He'd never had the physique to compete, though he'd come to learn that it favored not only the strong but also the clever.

The Basilica di Santa Croce anchored the west side of the piazza. A minor basilica, but it had long ranked as the largest Franciscan church in the world. Its current claim to fame was as the burial spot for Michelangelo, Galileo, and Machiavelli. Quite a funerary roster. But where San Lorenzo served as the Medicis' chapel, the Pazzi family had always favored this church, erecting a chapel of their own that sat on the southern flank of the cloister. A masterpiece of Renaissance architecture. Built by Andrea Pazzi, head of the family in the fifteenth century, whose wealth at the time was second only to the Medici.

He'd never been especially close to his own parents. Neither considered him much of anything, both of them more interested in his brother, whom they'd harbored high hopes for. Why? He'd never understood. The man amounted to nothing more than a manual laborer working the marble quarries, dying over a decade ago from alcohol abuse with no wife or children. He, on the other hand, had gone to university, which he paid for himself, and graduated. He recalled the pressure he'd felt there to conform, the feelings of being left out. But he survived and eventually entered politics. Now his party might be on the verge of dominating the Italian government. Most likely he would play a key role in that move and hold a high position in an incoming administration. Of course his mother and father would never know any of that, as both had been dead a long time.

Only his grandmother had ever shown him interest. Though that attention had been tempered with her anger. She was a bitter, resentful woman whose husband had been jailed in the aftermath of the last great war, dying in prison as a devout postwar follower of Mussolini. He'd long listened to her stories, thinking them fantasy. But not anymore. They were far from that. In fact they might be the key to winning the upcoming elections.

He entered the cloister and walked to the end of the graveled path.

Not many people around today.

He stopped, then stepped inside the Pazzi Chapel. Where the adjacent Gothic basilica was adorned with stained glass, frescoed walls, pointed arches, and a trussed wooden ceiling, the chapel was the opposite, steeped in the humanism of Greek and Roman culture. He'd always admired its utter simplicity. The perfect combination of rectangles, squares, circles, and semicircles. All of the supporting elements—the arches, entablature, and pilasters—were highlighted by gray *serena* limestone, which stood out against the lighter white walls. Shallow arches became barrel vaults, and the overhead dome cast a sense of weightlessness. It took its name from the Pazzi who commissioned it as a funerary place, but it once also served an everyday function as the monks' chapter house. The stone bench around the outer walls a leftover from those days.

"It is a special place," his grandmother said. *"There is a message there. A powerful one. Of unity."*

When he was a boy the two of them had visited Santa Croce and the Pazzi Chapel several times, but she'd never fully explained anything, offering only riddles. As an adult he'd come to understand what she'd alluded to. And what might have been only a footnote to history was now of immense importance.

He stopped before the altar and stared upward into the dome at the fresco, painted like the night sky, all the stars in place, the constellations ordered as they appeared over Florence on July 4, 1442. Only half of it had survived the over five hundred years since its creation.

Yes. There was a message here.

He studied the rest of the chapel.

Parliament was in its summer recess. He'd told everyone that he was taking a few days off. Many others were doing the same thing. Legislative sessions would resume September 1. Elections would come two months after that, the campaign season also opening September 1. Unlike in America, campaigning here was forbidden except in the sixty days prior to the election. It was imperative he be ready. His party had to achieve a meaningful majority in order to persuade the president of Italy to name their leader prime minister.

For that they needed the Catholic Church. And to get that he had to finish what he'd started. He'd come here for strength. Time to take a drive into the Tuscan countryside.

Back home.

And face reality.

CHAPTER 32

SIENA, ITALY

COTTON SIZED UP CAMILLA BAINES.

She was maybe mid-sixties, with a narrow waist and an elaborate styling of reddish-gold hair that made her small and delicate features look even smaller. Her dark eyes shone with eager expectancy, and her demeanor was one of calm. She stood with both arms propped against a wooden fence that encircled a long riding track. A rider and horse were navigating the dirt at full speed, making a turn at the far end. She'd briefly greeted them, then turned her attention back to the track. He and Richter joined her at the fence.

"This is my farm," she said to them in English. "A hundred years ago it was an orphanage. This track was once a lake. Now it makes for a good place to train horses."

He agreed. The site was spectacular. And private too, as only tall forest lay beyond the meadows they'd passed earlier. Chain saws roared like lions in the distance.

"The Palio runs tomorrow," she said, "and there are decisions to be made. Have either one of you ever seen the race?"

"I have not had the pleasure," Richter said.

"And you, Signore Malone?"

"I have. One time."

"Then you understand its beauty, the poetry, its majesty."

"I understand it's a free-for-all, a drama full of duplicity, where deceit is not only part of the race but expected."

She smiled. "You do know the Palio."

Across the track the horse and rider kept barreling along at full gallop, making the turn, preparing for the final straightaway. The jockey was leaned forward, riding bareback.

"That can't be your horse for the race out there," he said to her.

He knew that today the cavalcade would be happening inside Siena, where the *contradas* would be out in full force with their medieval displays. Part of that involved revealing their respective horse and jockey.

"You are correct," she said. "That is neither our horse nor our jockey. Rules require otherwise."

As much as the Palio seemed a race without rules, there were in fact many that governed its existence. One hundred and five to be exact, if he recalled correctly.

"Three days ago," she said, "during the *enthrone* the vets presented this year's array of horses. They then ran around the piazza three times, just like in the race, to show their suitability, then the *capitani* chose the ten best from the group. Lots were drawn and each *contrada* was assigned a horse at random. Sometimes you get a good ride. A strong mount. And there is joy. Sometimes, though, you find a hack, a *brenna,* and there is sadness."

"What did Golden Oak draw?" he asked her.

Horse and rider raced by at full speed, hooves pounding, and kept going, leaving a swirl of dust in their wake.

"I am afraid we have a *brenna,*" she said.

Which meant Golden Oak had little chance to win.

"We also have an even worse problem," she said. "Our jockey is a dishonest man."

Traditionally, the jockeys were not locals. Instead, they were mercenaries who trained all year for the chance to ride. Hired from far away, usually Sardinia, their allegiance was only to how much money they could make, regardless of its source. And they were well paid, sometimes in the millions of euros, which could tax the *contradas'* financial resources.

But winning was everything.

"There is an old saying," she said. "*For the piazza three things are needed. Heart, guts, and a killer instinct.* But another saying tempers that. *Without poverty, there was no incentive.* Shifting alliances make the Palio special. Betrayal is common and guile is prized. Many times it is not about winning, but rather preventing someone else from winning. Yet the deceit is still annoying."

The horse and rider were making the far turn again.

Now at a light gallop.

"The Palio is not about how fast a horse runs," she said. "More on how smart one runs. The horse is, in many ways, more important than the jockey. In the Palio it is the first horse across the finish line that wins, rider atop or not. For us, we informed our jockey what we wanted him to do. He told us he could do it."

He was beginning to understand. "Who do you want *not* to win?"

"The Porcupines. They have won two of the last four Palios. We want that to end."

The horse and rider rounded the final turn and again headed for the home stretch, moving faster now.

"You gain *contrada* membership by birth, blood, or choice," she said. "Once done, you cannot change that. Nor can you move from one to the other. We are part of our *contrada*. So my loyalty is clear." She paused. "What did Cardinal Stamm tell you about me?"

Richter said, "That you have long been the power and force within Golden Oak."

The horse raced by and gradually came to a stop. The jockey turned toward Camilla and she gave him a wave, indicating he should head for the stable.

For the first time she turned and faced them. "Did he now?"

Richter nodded. "He also said that you have a close relationship with the Carthusians at Santa Maria di Castello."

Cotton appreciated the fact that Richter had omitted the reference Stamm had made to being an opportunist and untrustworthy.

"My father and the monks were quite close, and I have maintained that relationship."

"Can you get us in?" Richter asked.

"I might be able to."

Cotton wondered about her posturing. She surely already knew all of this since Camilla Baines did not appear to be a person who enjoyed surprises.

"My vote," Richter had said on the drive north, *"is she wants something."*

He agreed.

"What do you want?" he asked.

CHAPTER 33

THOMAS LOCATED THE KEY EXACTLY WHERE HE'D BEEN DIRECTED to look. Late last night, after fleeing the train in Koblenz, he was redirected from Munich to Siena. So he flew to Rome, rented a car, and drove the two hours north, finding one of the many palazzos that bordered the Piazzo del Campo. This one was in the Renaissance style, constructed, according to a bronze plaque outside, in 1460. Three stories. Large, rambling, its stone-and-brick façade overlaid with a rough coat of gray cement. Stone animals topped the cornice. Iron beasts held unlit torches. Rows of mullioned windows, topped by triangular pediments, dotted all four sides, one of which faced the piazzo. Each floor was a longitudinal series of successive rooms, one into another. He admired the Old World feel of the ornate parquet floors, timbered ceilings, gray-green walls, and tiled stoves. Some of the walls were decorated with frescoes displaying geometrical motifs, birds, and heraldic devices. Up high a painted arched loggia offered trompe l'oeil views over lush gardens.

He carried his travel bag upstairs to the main bedchamber, a comfortable, airy room with blue-gray walls and a white ceiling. The still air carried the musty scent of age. He laid his bag down and stepped to the windows, each a high, iron-bound rectangle with casement doors of leaded glass. He released the latch and pushed the panes outward. Below stretched the Piazza del Campo, across the way sunlight and shadow etched on the pink brick of the Mangia tower and the Palazzo Pubblico. Once it was the tallest tower in all of Italy. Buildings completely encircled the piazza up four and five stories. Mostly opulent palazzos built by the Sienese wealthy. Many of the homes remained, but a lot had been converted to cafés and boutique hotels. People were moving in every direction across the cobblestones. Workers were busy readying everything for tomorrow's race. The D-shaped piazza was ringed by a dirt track, created especially for the event. He noticed the turns. Two seemed treacherous, one nearly a right angle, the other a sharp bend at the end of a slope. Both were equipped with padded crash barriers. A feeling of anticipation vibrated in the air, which seemed intensified by the tolling of the Mangia bell for noon. He glanced upward and caught the figure of a man ringing the bell, his tiny swaying figure outlined against the clear sky.

He never questioned orders. He simply obeyed. A good and loyal servant. How had he been first located? Impossible to know. But a few years ago a priest had appeared in London who knew an awful lot about him.

"You are a man of extraordinary talent," he'd been told.

"I have never heard what I do explained that way. Especially from a servant of God."

"The church has long been in need of services like yours."

Which was correct.

Centuries ago protection came from armies that popes personally commanded, fighting alongside their soldiers. That eventually evolved into popes employing men to lead their armies and fight for them. When the church was threatened by what it regarded as heresy from Cathars, Muslims, and Jews, it created the Inquisition. Holy men, anointed by the pope, mainly Dominicans and Franciscans, who traveled from town to town, ridding them of heresy through torture and murder.

Millions were killed.

"Here is something we learned long ago," the priest said to him. *"First, when the faith is in question, there is to be no delay. Rigorous measures must be resorted to with all speed. Second, no consideration is shown to prince or prelate, however high his station. Third, extreme severity must be exercised against those who shield themselves. And fourth, never show tolerance toward any enemy or heretic. Those principles were first uttered in 1542. They apply today, just as they applied then."*

The modern church faced threats from all sides, especially in the most dangerous parts of the world. Today the largest percentage of Catholics were Hispanic, living in places with either little to no government or an openly oppressive one. Hot spots. Where prayer was not always the answer. An organization so vast as the Roman Catholic Church could not exist without enemies. His job? To deal with those enemies, as requested. No longer were there inquisitors appointed by popes. Those were abolished long ago.

Now there was only one.

Twenty-four hours ago he'd been directed to Munich with a kill order on Cardinal Jason Richter. That had been rescinded. What had changed? What now? He felt like the inquisitors of old. Come to town in the search for righteousness.

Doing God's work.

He stepped away from the window and knelt beside a large poster bed, his intertwined hands lying atop a dull white embroidered spread.

He was here. Ready.

Time to pray.

CHAPTER 34

STEFANO GREW UP IN A FLORENCE NEIGHBORHOOD WHERE TO SURVIVE you had to be tough. And smart. He'd mastered both, which eventually made him a great calcio player. The game was violent. No question. But you had to choose your battles. Speckled across it all had been his faith, which eventually called him to God. Never had he struggled with that decision. He was nineteen when he first realized. Thankfully, his family had been supportive, making sure he went to university then entered the seminary. They were all there at Holy Orders when the bishop addressed the congregation.

"My dear sons, before you enter the priesthood, you must declare before God your intention to undertake this office. Do you resolve, with the help of the Holy Spirit, to discharge without fail the office of priesthood in the presbyteral rank, as worthy fellow workers, with the Order of Bishops, in caring for the Lord's flock?"

He'd gladly said he would.

As a priest he could celebrate mass, offer communion, hear confessions, give absolution, perform baptisms, serve as the church's witness at the sacrament of Holy Matrimony, and administer the anointing of the sick. He was a minister of religion. Head of a parish working within established rules. But as an intelligence officer?

There he could do pretty much whatever he wanted. In fact, innovation was the name of the game. It's what got you noticed. As did paying attention. Cardinal Ascolani had come out into the field. Which was highly unusual for the head of the Entity. Not only that, but Ascolani had come to Siena not as a prince of the church with an official presence, but anonymously. All of which was both intriguing and concerning.

On the way north from Rome he'd called a friend who lived in Siena. Ascolani had dismissed him from the cathedral and told him to stay nearby, ready. So he used the opportunity to hustle across town and check in with his friend.

He entered La Soldano.

Its owner, Daniele Calabritto, was a big, muscular slab of a man with a balding head, thick jaw, and shoulders like cliffs. What really set him apart, though, were the bracelets that wrapped both arms, more than he'd ever seen any one person wear. Maybe seventy or more. Stacked tight from wrists to elbows. Unusual, to say the least. Daniele had told him that it started when he was a teenager with one silver bracelet bought at a festival. He'd liked it so much that he'd bought more. Over time one after another was added, none removed, each coming with a story of where and how it had been acquired. Many of them were from Africa, where his old friend spent a lot of time. For as long as Stefano had known Daniele, which stretched back more than a decade, those forearms had been sheathed in clinking metal.

As always, Daniele was working the tables, greeting diners, taking selfies, making people feel right at home. More of his trademark. People came to La Soldano for both the food and its owner.

The Palio was a time of celebration, when local eateries and bars catered to visitors. The Café Soldano was noted as a place locals loved to frequent. Small, intimate, with spotless napery and gleaming silverware. Getting a reservation had to be done weeks in advance.

He caught his friend's eye, but Daniele never lost a beat, continuing to entertain his patrons. More servers wove among the crowded tables, the murmur of conversation everywhere. Stefano knew the drill and drifted toward the restrooms, slipping through a curtain blocking an open doorway. A short corridor led to a closed door. There, inside a small office, he waited until Daniele arrived.

"Stefano," his friend said. "I watched on the television as you scored that goal. A thing of beauty. *Magnifico.*"

Daniele shook his hand with a grip like steel.

"I was sweating that bounce," he said. "Hoping I had given it just enough to get there."

"We all held our breath."

"The good Lord was looking out for me."

"Have you eaten?" Daniele asked. "I need to feed you."

"That would be great. But were you able to take care of what I asked?"

"Of course. Of course."

He knew Daniele commanded an army of loyalists. He'd been born into the Istrices. The Porcupines. Who were unique among the *contradas* in that the Knights of Malta granted them the special title of sovereign, since the knights' local headquarters had been located within the Porcupines' neighborhood since the fourteenth century. Daniele was a long-standing member of the governing council. The Porcupines' sworn enemy had always been the She-Wolf, due to enduring conflicts over neighborhood borders that no amount of negotiation had been able to resolve. Keeping each other from winning the Palio had evolved into an obsession and was reflected in the Porcupines' motto. *I prick only in defense.* So for the Porcupines, intel on the She-Wolf was considered vital, and Stefano knew that Daniele was the one who provided that information from eyes and ears on the ground. A sort of *contrada* Entity. With Ascolani here, in secret, Stefano had decided that some of those eyes and ears were needed to ensure the cardinal's safety. Earlier, he'd offered to personally accompany his boss around town, but Ascolani had politely refused. Thankfully, Daniele had made sure two of his men were outside the cathedral, ready to go.

And they'd followed discreetly.

"I received a text a little while ago. The cardinal walked straight toward the campo and the Palazzo Tempi. It faces the square on the west side. One of the older palaces. Has the coats of arms of the Piccolomini and Bandinelli on its walls outside. It was totally renovated a few years ago."

"Who owns it?"

"One of the land trusts holds title. That's not unusual here. Those buildings are expensive to maintain, and the city requires they stay pristine. So people pool their money and own things together. That particular one, though, stays empty most of the time."

"Is Ascolani still there?"

Daniele nodded. "My men are waiting outside, front and back."

He was hungry. But he was more curious.

"Tell me exactly where it is."

He navigated the labyrinth of Siena's narrow cobbled streets and stepped into the campo, admiring one of Italy's greatest public spaces. A shell-shaped piazza set in a sloping hollow where three hills of the city met. To prepare for the Palio the outer portion of the square had been turned into a racetrack. The gray flagstones all around covered with thick layers of volcanic *tufo,* trucked in, packed tight, ten meters wide, its central open core separated from the track by a chest-high fence. Centuries ago the pre-race trials were more dangerous than the race itself, since the dirt was not brought in until the day of the race. Many a horse had been killed or maimed. Today the track's depth and firmness were carefully gauged.

Tens of thousands would be crowded into the center tomorrow, the horses racing around them. Today there were only workers busy with last-minute preparations and tourists taking a final opportunity to examine the track. In a few hours there would be a closing trial run, the sixth, the *provacci,* called by many the sham trial. Run at night when the suspense mounted to an almost religious intensity, providing the last opportunity for horse and jockey to become accustomed to the surroundings. All ten would line up at the start and leave together, but only a few would make it all the way around three times. Most would stop their run long before finishing one lap. The point? To not tire the animal? Sure. No jockey would be crazy enough to run out his mount so close to the race. But the main idea was not to give away what the horse may or may not be capable of doing.

Hence the label *sham*.

Growing up in Florence he'd attended many Palios. He'd often stood inside the center, crushed shoulder-to-shoulder with sixty thousand other people, unable to see much except the jockeys' heads atop their mounts. The best views came from the palazzos that ringed the campo with their hundreds of windows. Some came free to the owners and their invited guests. Others were hotel rooms with a view. The vast majority were rented out to visitors, who occupied the private palazzos during the day before and the day of the race for huge fees. He'd watched one Palio years ago from a third-story window near the starting gate. The view had been extraordinary, casting the race in a whole new light.

Daniele had said that the Palazzo Tempi, which Cardinal Ascolani now occupied, was located on the campo's west side. The majority of the buildings there dated to the thirteenth and fourteenth centuries, all made from one particular type of a brick in a distinctive reddish-brown color.

Burnt Siena.

A long row of bleachers lined the ground beneath most of the buildings. Invited guests from the various *contradas* would fill those seats tomorrow, each decked out in their respective colors. Above them he determined the Palazzo Tempi's location and zeroed in on the windows where one set hung open.

He stood near the fountain that occupied the highest point of the sloping piazza among a few hundred other people. Movement past the open window caused him to seek refuge among a clump of tourists who were busy snapping photos. He did not want to be seen. Within the darkened rectangle he caught sight of a face he knew. Ascolani. Staring out. Beside the cardinal another man appeared. Shorter, pale-skinned, middle-aged, thinning hair. Ascolani was speaking to the other man, pointing outward. Stefano felt awkward spying on his superior. But he considered it merely looking after the second in command of the Holy See, making sure he was safe.

Still, he wondered about the other man.

Who was he?

CHAPTER 35

THOMAS HAD NEVER BEFORE MET HIS VATICAN BENEFACTOR. ALWAYS contact was through Bartolomé. But last night, when he'd been ordered to Siena, Bartolomé had informed him that further instructions would come once there.

And not from him.

They would be delivered personally by someone else.

He'd been waiting inside the palazzo for nearly two hours, the window open, sitting back and away, out of sight, taking in the sounds from outside. He'd prayed some more and enjoyed the solitude. On the far wall of the bedchamber hung an oil painting, its detail dulled by time. Four figures with wings circling Christ. The four Evangelists. Man, Bull, Lion, and Eagle. Symbols for Incarnation, Passion, Resurrection, and Ascension. Then there was the carved crucifix. A figure at rest. Not a dying man, but a surviving God. Fitting for here. And his own life. Something a priest once said came to mind.

Itself to itself.

How true.

He'd been forced to act on the train, taking out the woman. Surely, the body had been discovered. But what had the American, Malone, done, if anything? Hopefully he'd gone back to wherever he'd come from.

A knock broke the quiet.

From downstairs.

He left the bedchamber and navigated the rooms, finding the wooden staircase and descending to ground level. He opened the front door to see an older man, dressed casually, standing outside in the entrance alcove off the street past the closed iron gate.

"It is a pleasure to finally meet you," the man said in English, the voice carrying a firm, self-confident ring. "I am Sergio Cardinal Ascolani."

The name meant nothing to him.

"Your employer," the cardinal said. "May I come inside?"

He gestured and closed the door after the man entered.

"I am head of the Entity."

Thomas bowed his head in respect and noticed that the man wore no cross or ring—nothing that marked a status as a prince of the church.

"Forgive me," he said. "I have no idea that you are who you say you are."

"I understand your concern. Perhaps this might help alleviate your fears."

And for the next several minutes the man recounted one past assignment after another, each one right on target and correct. When finished, the man who called himself Ascolani said, "Is that sufficient?"

He nodded.

"You were there and did what you did on my orders. Have you had an opportunity to explore the palazzo?"

"It is an impressive place."

"I have sometimes stayed here myself. There is a wonderful view of the campo from the main bedchamber."

"I have been enjoying that."

Ascolani motioned toward the stairs. "Shall we?"

He led the way back up to the third floor. Once they arrived Ascolani approached the open window and stared out. Thomas stayed back near the entrance door, out of sight.

An old habit.

Finally, the cardinal retreated from the window. "I never thought I would meet you face-to-face. I have always directed you through another, and you have always done exactly as I asked. I respect that. But I have always wondered. Did you ever find it odd that the church asked you to kill?"

"It is not for me to question."

"For this one time. Question."

"I assume that you had a good reason for wanting that done. The church has long had enemies."

"You are correct. In fact, today might be the most threatening time in our history. We are under attack from every side, every corner. Especially from oppressive governments that want to control their populations. Membership is down. Doctrine is threatened. Prelates are rebellious. My task is to protect us from any and all danger."

"Is Cardinal Richter a threat?"

He noticed a hesitation in the elder man's face.

"Forgive me," he said. "But you asked me to question."

"That I did. And yes, the cardinal is a threat of the highest order. I was hoping we could merely expose Richter as a thief, discredit and humiliate him. But that is no longer enough. So I ordered you to eliminate him with a supposed suicide."

"What has changed?"

"Cardinal Richter is not in Munich. He is here. Along with the American agent Malone. Whatever you did in Dillenburg was not enough."

Now he knew what happened with Malone.

"He was supposed to be arrested," Ascolani said. "Along with Richter. But Malone has now connected with Richter, who has joined with my predecessor, Cardinal Stamm, to clear his name. The situation has become much more complicated."

"Not for me." And he meant every word.

Ascolani smiled, though the face radiated about as much feeling as a tombstone. "Confidence. It can be both a blessing... and a curse."

He offered a slight bow as a concession to his vanity.

"From this point forward you will take all your instructions from me personally." Ascolani reached into his pocket and removed a cell phone. "We will communicate through this device only."

He accepted the phone and nodded.

The cardinal walked back to the open window and motioned for him to join.

He hesitated.

"It is okay," Ascolani said.

So he stepped close.

"Have you ever seen the Palio?"

He shook his head.

"It is a grand spectacle. A demonstration of liberty and self-expression. The track down there is itself a metaphor, a boundless loop around which people press and horses run. The sacred and the profane both dwell in the Palio. As does danger. Jockeys and horses have died. Tomorrow all that open space will be filled with people. I want you here. Ready. At the very least you will have an excellent vantage point from which to watch the race. Are you a practicing Catholic?"

"My faith is strong."

"Do you take confession?"

"I do. With some qualifications."

"I thought that might be the case. It is hard to be entirely honest with a stranger, regardless of priest confidentiality. And I appreciate your discretion. I truly do. Would you like me to hear your *full* confession? There would be no reason to be hesitant with me."

No, there would not. "I would like that."

"Then kneel, and I will absolve you of all sin."

CHAPTER 36

Cotton was wondering just what exactly he'd managed to drop himself into. Nothing good, for sure. Here he was in the middle of Tuscany, on a horse farm, with a cardinal cast in the shadow of corruption and a woman, noted as an *"opportunist,"* who definitely seemed a few steps ahead of them. That last part was the most troublesome, since Camilla Baines knew exactly what she wanted.

They'd retreated to the stable, a rambling building of olden stone that housed a number of animals, the air filled with the scents of sweat, oil, and hay. Camilla spoke with the jockey for a few moments outside before returning inside and motioning that they should walk to the far end.

"Signore Malone, you asked what I want. I have a problem."

Finally, she was getting to the point.

"We Golden Oakers have a long history. We were part of the original decree, from 1730, that established the eighteen wards of Siena. We have claimed the Palio forty-three times, which is nearly a record. Among the other *contradas* we have both allies and enemies."

"Who are your enemies?" Richter asked.

"We have two. The Dragons and the Porcupines, though the latter is because of our ally, the She-Wolf, who hate the Porcupines."

"Sounds like a complicated situation," Richter noted.

Camilla grinned. "Similar to having four hundred thousand euros hidden in your diocese residence? That seems worse than complicated."

"I see Chas briefed you," Richter said.

"He explained your situation. He also thought you were being framed."

"What do you think?" Cotton asked.

She shrugged. "Cardinal Stamm has great instincts. So I trust his judgment. If I did not, we would not be talking to each other. With regard to you, Signore Malone, the cardinal thinks you are a most competent individual. He says you were most helpful to him a while back with a serious problem."

Yes, he had been.

Which was now paying dividends.

Camilla Baines reminded him of his mother. Both were eminently practical women, good listeners, careful planners, and focused on what they wanted. For his mother that had meant raising her son, alone, after his father died when he was ten. Killed when his navy submarine was lost at sea. She'd stepped right in and filled the void as best she could. She still lived on her family's onion farm in central Georgia, running it as her father, his beloved grandfather, had done before her. He'd learned many valuable lessons from his mother, but one seemed apt here. *Keep your mouth shut and your ears open and you'll learn a lot.* His mother had also had a low bullshit tolerance level. Same as, he believed, Camilla Baines.

"The jockey we contracted with," she said, "is not working out. We hire them, then watch them day and night. They are not allowed to speak to anyone or use the phone. We isolate them to keep any double-dealing to a minimum. This one, though, has proven especially resourceful and self-serving."

"Isn't that just part of the Palio?" Cotton asked.

"To a point. *Contradas* are forbidden from entering into any agreements that help another to win the race. But they do not forbid us from making agreements that ensure another *loses* the race."

He caught Richter's eye and saw that he agreed.

This was it.

"I am the Golden Oak's *capitano.* I am supposed to represent strength, dignity, courage. I have to be a strategist. Capable, alert, daring. Diplomatic, too. The *capitano* selects the jockey and sets the strategy for the race."

She was taking her time. Working her way to the meat of the coconut.

"The Palio is a race of chance and fate," she said. "The ten *contradas* who participate are chosen by random lots. The horses are assigned randomly. How the horses line up at the starting line is also determined by luck of the draw. That is the chance part. But how those various elements are utilized? That is the fate part. But I made a mistake. The jockey I chose took our money to stop the Porcupines, then made a separate deal with them to do just the opposite. Thankfully, we discovered his deceit."

"What did you do to him?" Richter asked.

"Nothing yet. But he will eventually be using what we paid him for medical bills."

He was impressed. Especially since she'd spoken without a hint of emotion or regret. Just part of doing business.

"I need a jockey," she said. "Do you ride, Signore Malone?"

He nodded. "I grew up on a farm. My grandfather had horses. He taught me. But not bareback."

He knew the Palio never used saddles. Just a bridle.

"I am sure you can adjust," she said.

"Why not just use a more experienced jockey?" Richter asked. "Like the man who was riding earlier? Or another who has participated in the Palio before?"

"Because I have been burned once. I do not have the time to be burned twice. I want someone who cannot be bribed. Someone where only I can provide what they want. You, Signore Malone, meet all those criteria."

That actually made sense, in an odd sort of way. "You want me to make sure the Porcupines lose."

She nodded. "And I don't care what you have to do. The rules that govern the race forbid jockeys from hitting or attacking each other with arms, fists, or bodies. To break those rules leads to disqualification and a ban from the Palio for life. But that penalty means nothing to you."

"Or to you," he added.

"Not in the least. I want results and I am willing to pay for them."

"But we do not want money," Richter said. "You know that."

"Cardinal Stamm told me what you want. I have a close relationship with the Carthusians."

"How much money do you give them?" Cotton asked.

"Enough that they would not tell me no. I also own all the land surrounding the monastery. I allow them free use for what they need."

"And if Malone rides the race and does what you want, you can get us inside the monastery?" Richter asked. "We can see what they have stored there?"

She nodded. "I will make that happen. Can you deliver for me?"

Nothing about this seemed good. The Palio, for all its spectacle, was a dangerous race. Especially for the untrained. People could, and did, get hurt. As did some of the horses. The other nine jockeys would be seasoned pros who knew what they were doing. Especially when it came to deals. Most of those would involve getting a head start, or no obstruction during the race, or maybe some parrying of an adversary or squeezing him at the turns to slow him down. Camilla Baines just wanted her enemy stopped and could not have cared less how that was accomplished. But surely the Porcupines would be equally intent on affecting Golden Oak. That meant a free-for-all. Atop horses running about thirty miles an hour along a rough, treacherous track.

Bareback.

None of which mattered.

Since he knew what to say.

"Sure. I can get it done."

CHAPTER 37

ERIC NAVIGATED THE NARROW TWO-LANED ROAD THAT WOUND A path through Tuscan forests, high meadows, and pastureland. He'd left Florence and driven north in a borrowed car with a spongy suspension and modest power. The great dome of Florence, with the expanse of red-gray roofs huddled around it, was visible in the distance. From this perspective he could appreciate how close the city was held by the protecting embrace of the hills that ringed it.

The time had come to make the pilgrimage.

The first nineteen years of his life had been spent among the northern hills with flocks of sheep and wild goats. There were plenty of good memories. The kind of experiences the young in body and mind reveled in creating. His parents were decent people, but the grandmother who'd essentially raised him struggled with grief and anger. She had few friends and no family that could tolerate her abrasiveness. Only him. He'd always ignored her shortcomings and clung to her until old enough to know better. They had a falling-out two decades ago, their interaction after that minimal at best. But he'd not abandoned her. Instead, he made sure she was properly cared for, whether she appreciated the gesture or not.

He downshifted and began an uphill climb among the olive trees and vineyards. He loved the clear, clean landscape. A seemingly perfect blend of tranquility and beauty. The grapevines were thick with ripening fruit, readying themselves for picking soon. As a teenager, like most everyone else, he'd worked the vineyards. A low stone wall ran along the road, its rough coping covered in thorny vines.

He passed a chapel surrounded by tall firs, along with the jagged pinnacles of two castle ruins. They were once owned, in the time of the Medici, by a nobleman and freebooter. Stories of family fortunes and misfortunes, their loves and hates, formed the history of this region. His grandmother loved to tell him stories. Her life seemed firmly rooted in the past, the present more a nuisance. As a child he'd loved her stories. But as an adult he came to find them annoying. He'd matured into a pragmatist. A realist. That's what made him a good populist, and he wore that label with pride, since what was wrong with telling people what they wanted to hear.

The winding road passed more farmland lined with chestnut, oak, and copper beechwoods. Whole towns with towers appeared from afar. Higher up, firs climbed dense and dark to the crest of the mountains. In the fall there would be a resplendent mass of color, bold and bright, that he could still see in his mind.

"In 1512 the Medici saved the pope," his grandmother said. "We loaned Julius II ten million florins. He gave them his solemn promise, in writing, to pay that money back."

"Did he pay it back?" he asked with a twelve-year-old's inquisitiveness.

The woman spit to the ground. "Not a florin. He died and the next pope, a Medici, had no desire to repay the loan. A few years later the Medici were granted the duchy of Tuscany to rule. Pope Pius V himself did that. But the Medici were smart. They attached a condition. So long as their duchy existed, untouched, the debt would be ignored. But take it away and they would call the debt. Their rule of the duchy lasted until 1737 when the last male Medici of the royal line died."

"Did the pope pay the debt then?"

"Not a florin. Two hundred years had passed. The world had changed. But the Medici never called the debt."

Later, while at college, he'd read some historical accounts and spoken to a few historians. It was true that Julius II and the head of the Medici clan did meet in 1512. But what they discussed remained a mystery. Julius II died in 1513. A Medici became the next pope as Leo X. Another Medici, Clement VII, became pope in 1523. The title Duke of the Florentine Republic was bestowed by Clement on the Medici in 1532. Then, in 1569, the title of Grand Duke of Tuscany was created. Pius V came himself to crown Cosimo de' Medici as Cosimo I. For the next three centuries the grand duchy managed to absorb practically the entire Tuscan region, until its own eventual annexation into the Kingdom of Italy. Never was the debt mentioned anywhere. It seemed to fade away. Becoming unimportant.

"Those bastards in Rome," his grandmother said, "still owe on the promise Julius II made. They are bound by it, as we are all bound to God. It was a Pledge of Christ."

"Can anyone make them pay?"

"Maybe you might be able to do that one day."

Perhaps he could.

But to do that he had to connect a lot of dots.

True, he'd made a start, and the dots were beginning to form a picture. But many remained unattached, loose ends that would have to be closed. The one thing that he could not allow to happen was to be made a fool. The National Freedom Party was counting on him. He'd assured its leaders that he could deliver the Vatican. He'd taken enough risk going to see Richter. But he had to rattle that cage. Time was running out. And besides, he'd established his DNA connection to Gregorio Cappello, and was about to complete that with a direct link to Anna Maria herself.

That made him Medici. Halfway there.

Now he needed his grandmother to help.

Would she?

Hard to say.

But he had to find out.

CHAPTER 38

ERIC MOTORED INTO VARALLO.

An Old World place, for sure, enclosed by low bastioned walls topped by grass. A medley of crowded houses and shops stood within, most broad and squat, their stone a warm yellow merged with bricks fighting hard to resist the assault of time. At its center spread the Piazza San Martino with a Romanesque church anchoring the northern side.

Inside the church was a most celebrated relic, the Volto Santo, enclosed within an elaborate tabernacle. An ornamented wooden cross with the face of Christ painted upon it in a strange representation that suggested a Byzantine origin. The myth accounting for its existence stated that, after its creation in 782, a bishop found it by way of a vision. He then placed it on a ship and abandoned it to the sea. Cast hither and thither in the waves, the ship finally ran aground on the western Italian shore, where the bishop of Varallo was visiting on a holiday. He decided to bring it back home, but the people of the village where he was visiting objected. To appease them he placed the cross in a cart driven by two white oxen and, as it had been abandoned to the sea, it was now given to the world. The oxen walked off on their own, pulling the cart. Legend said the cart ended up in Varallo, so the relic was kept there.

Was a word of it true? Nobody knew.

But it was a great story.

Which taught him two lessons.

People wanted to hear good things, and the better the story the better their listening.

He navigated the narrow streets and found a row of three-story red-brick façades, their front doors set back behind iron railings. His grandmother lived in the center one, which had once belonged to his parents. He parked the car and knocked on the door, which was answered by a woman dressed in a nurse's uniform. He paid for the constant care, which was not cheap, but the old woman had long since lost the ability to care for herself. He'd called ahead and alerted the nurse that he was coming. She'd warned him that this might not be the best time for a visit, as the past few days had been trying.

But he had no choice.

"How is she?" he asked, stepping inside.

"Agitated. Uneven."

"So, normal. Where is she?"

The nurse motioned to the front parlor where, as a boy, he'd played. "She's in there enjoying the sun."

He gave her twenty euros. "Why don't you have lunch. We need to speak alone. Give me an hour."

The woman accepted the money, nodded, then left.

He steeled himself and entered the room. A heavy mahogany table with turned legs displayed his mother's bric-a-brac mementos, along with photographs in tarnished silver frames, one of his father in an army uniform. A bookcase carved with leaves and branches was overflowing with volumes. A chair, his father's favorite, upholstered in faded plush with horsehair in bunches at the worn corners sat empty. The warm, still air smelled of stewed tomatoes.

His grandmother was nearly a hundred years old. Nobody really knew her exact age, as she'd always lied about her year of birth. She'd managed to outlive her husband and son. Only he and she remained of the Casaburi family. Paradoxically, she'd always had a naturally friendly face with a snub nose and high bright cheeks. But time had taken its toll. Now she was a shriveled, shrunken shell, a bony creature, the face a mass of crinkles, the lips thin, the teeth nearly gone. Her hair, once dark and thick, now hung sparse and gray. But the eyes. They remained black like a crow. Deep and dark. Ever inquiring. Surveying everything with the curiosity of a cat in a new house. She sat facing the window in another chair from his parents' time, the curtains opened to each side, staring out at the bright afternoon. Never did she leave the house. Her entire world was within these walls. He told himself to be careful.

Prod but do not push.

"Nonna," he said in a low voice.

She turned his way.

Recognition was not immediate. She seemed to be struggling to find the memories. Finally she grasped reality and asked, "What do you want?"

He caught the contempt in her question. No *how are you, good to see you, go to hell.* Nothing. Typical. But he was in no mood to humor her.

"I see you on television," she said. "You are some sort of important man now."

"I am an elected minister in parliament, the secretary of a national party on the rise. And if our party leader becomes the next prime minister, I will be a high government minister."

She scoffed at his prediction. "You are a minor, insignificant man who does not realize his true importance."

Which ran straight to the heart of their last conversation, years ago, when he'd rebuffed her insistence that he was of royal blood.

"You live in a fantasy world," he'd said.

"You have no idea."

"I am tired of all the stories and your riddles. Who cares if we are Medici? It means nothing."

Which he'd meant at the time. But that was before he sensed what might be possible. Everything he planned hinged on what happened next. This woman knew things. Cardinal Richter's rejection of his proposal for the church to help in the election had forced his hand. He now had to call the Vatican's bluff. But to do that—

"I need you tell me about Anna Maria."

"You never cared for any of that," she said. "Never once."

"I was young and ignorant."

And that was true.

"I was also wrong," he said.

"You made fun of me," she said. "Like your father did. You laughed at me. I remember. I remember it all. You think I do not?"

Soften her up. Be conciliatory. "I am sorry for that. Truly I am. You told me once that God would show us a way to prove what you said. And He did. Through DNA. I tested the remains of Gregorio Cappello from the cemetery in the mountains. I also tested the remains of Anna Maria. They are related. A positive match. They were mother and son. You were right."

A lie. But a workable one. He was still waiting on the test results. Which should come anytime. But he had faith that all would be good.

"Gregorio was her son," his grandmother spit out. "He was Medici."

"My DNA matches theirs," he said. "I am Medici. Through you. Which means you are Medici."

She seemed to consider that concession for a moment, liking it, before saying, "I am the last one alive who knows."

"You must tell me, before."

A curious look came to her wizened face. "Before what?"

"Before you forget."

She went silent for a moment and returned her attention to the window and the sunshine. He'd known this was not going to be easy. But she was right. She was the last one.

"Nonna, please listen to me. It is not enough that we are Medici. To collect the debt, to make the pope pay, we must be a legitimate royal Medici heir. Illegitimacy gets us nothing. Clearly, Anna

Maria became pregnant and birthed a child. But who was the father? And were they married? That is what matters now. You never explained that part of the story."

"It is a wondrous tale," she said. "A grand love story."

She paused.

"Without a happy ending."

CHAPTER 39

JASON STOOD PROPPED AGAINST THE FENCE AND WATCHED AS COTTON Malone rounded the dirt track one more time atop the horse.

Camilla Baines stood beside him.

Late afternoon had arrived and the sun was heading down, painting the stable and the track in a golden tan. He was trying to stay composed, but his emotions swayed toward panic. His entire life and career were on the line, everything he ever worked for, ever wanted, at dire risk. Like on a roller coaster that he had no way of stopping. You just kept racing ahead, one drop, one curve after the next.

"He rides that horse with confidence," she said.

He agreed.

Malone had hopped right onto the back of the stallion and grabbed the reins. The first lap around the track had been a slow trot, Malone apparently testing the animal, getting comfortable riding bareback. The next was a full trot. Now he was up to a solid run.

"I have never ridden a horse before," he said. "I grew up in a large German city. Our visits to the countryside were confined to a hike, swim, or fishing. No horses."

"He seems to be trying to get a feel for the animal," she said.

"Is that difficult?"

She shrugged. "Not with a horse. They can sense the rider. Know when he or she is confident or scared. Horses like confident. It reduces the amount of thinking they have to do."

Malone rounded the far turn and the horse sped up.

They thundered past for another lap.

"Cardinal Richter," she said, "may I offer some personal advice?"

"I can use all of that I can get."

"In the Palio deceit and deception are part of the experience. They are expected, the idea being to make it hard for your enemies to win. No one is immune. No one is a saint. Neither is anyone the devil. We are all simply trying to uphold the tradition of the race."

"Yet you want to win."

"Of course. But the luck of the draw with the horse sets your course. We try to have ten solid contenders, but that is not always possible. And once you have a horse that is surely not going to win, everything changes."

"You have a loser?"

"Our groom says we do, and he is the expert."

Malone was now moving the horse at a full run, his body angled down, head high.

"He knows to balance his weight on the horse," she said. "He's remembering what to do."

He was waiting for the advice, so he asked, "You think I am in trouble, don't you?"

"I think, like us, you have a horse who cannot win. Which means you have to make sure your enemy does not win. Priests? Cardinals? Bishops? Those I know about. Many are worthy of the Palio."

He smiled. "Such a diplomatic way to insult them."

Malone made the last turn. The horse's hooves pounded the ground as they raced by.

"I meant no insult," she said. "Just a fact."

"Sadly, it is true."

"I have read about the trial going on inside the Vatican. Now you are being implicated in that corruption?"

"I am. But it is a lie."

"Still a problem, though."

On that she was right. Truth seemed to matter not anymore. Only perception. The bullet points at the beginning, as opposed to reading the whole article. Nobody read the whole article anymore. He was being systematically framed. Set up to be brought down. As an example? Maybe. To send a message to the other cardinals? Surely. Nothing was more dangerous than a cardinal who wanted to be pope. Especially a cardinal with the power of the Secretariat of State and the Entity behind him. They needed to get inside that monastery and see if anything meaningful was there. Long shot? Perhaps. After all, five hundred years had passed.

But they had to find out.

Malone slowed the horse and brought them both around to the fence.

"Can you do it?" Camilla asked.

Malone nodded. "Good thing, though, I don't have to win."

"You rode hard," Richter said. "It will be different tomorrow with the crowd and the other horses."

"Just make sure the Porcupine horse does not win," she said. "That's all I ask."

But Jason wondered. Was it?

Cardinal Stamm was right.

Everything about Camilla Baines signaled one thing and one thing only.

Trouble.

COTTON GENTLY STROKED THE HORSE'S NECK.

This was not the mount he would ride in the race. That animal was with the *contrada's* groom back in Siena, who'd kept a constant vigil, day and night, ever since the horse had been selected three days ago. The idea was that the animal remain inviolate, protected, not subject to any mischief or mayhem. Each *contrada* had its own veterinarian too. Everything was kept close and in house. The horse he'd just tried, he'd been told, had run in two previous Palios. So it was an excellent trainer.

Camilla had explained that horses were specifically bred for the Palio. No thoroughbreds. Too feisty. Only mixed breeds, trained on tracks similar to Siena's campo, chosen for their ability not to be spooked by the crowds and thus incur fewer injuries. The only rule? Breeders must reside in Sienese territory or have a substantial attachment to the Palio.

Whatever that meant.

He'd never ridden a horse that fast before, especially bareback. It was like the ones on the merry-go-round when he was a kid. Hard. Slippery. In constant motion. His parents had been there then, holding on to him. No such luck now. Definitely a unique experience. Going thirty miles an hour, gripping a bridle, with only your legs holding on. Luckily, a horse knew what to do. All a good rider did was give the animal the freedom it needed to do its thing. Could he ride in the race and all of the chaos associated with it? Horses constantly bumping into one another. Jockeys hitting the ground. Some being trampled. Horses collapsing in hard falls. Some seriously injured.

Survival of the fittest.

But if he was nothing else, he was fit.

"Does it matter how I do it?" he asked Camilla.

"Not in the least. Just make sure the jockey goes down, and also make sure the riderless horse does not make it to the finish line first."

He caught Richter's gaze and read the cardinal's thoughts. And he agreed. This was insanity. Definitely not what he'd signed on for.

Thirty years ago, when he was a teenager in middle Georgia, before the navy, he believed that the world would treat him fairly if he removed his cap in church, always spoke the truth, and said *sir* or *ma'am* to everyone. Boy he was wrong. Fairness had to be earned. Which generally involved paying a price of some kind. Here, though, there was something about the abstract challenge he faced that was buoying. How many times in his life would an opportunity like this come by? Not many. So no matter how foolish it might be, he was going to do it.

"You ready?" Richter asked.

"As I'll ever be."

CHAPTER 40

Anna Maria Luisa de' Medici was trying to enjoy the evening. Dinner had been hosted by her father, Grand Duke Cosimo III, the sixth from the House of Medici to rule Tuscany. He had occupied the throne for fifty years, the longest of anyone before him. The party at the royal palace had been organized to mark that glorious occasion, and the local nobility had turned out. Even her father, who rarely smiled in public, seemed pleased. Most had left after the meal ended, but her father had asked twelve of the noblemen to stay. Tuscany was in the midst of an economic depression with the downturn deepening. Compounding this was her brother, her father's named successor, Gian Gastone, who was spending money at a rapid pace in Bohemia, racking up massive debts. Even worse, there were no grandchildren. Her older brother had died childless and Gian despised his wife. They lived totally separate lives in separate countries. Children for them was out of the question. Her own marriage to Johann Wilhelm, Elector Palatine, had been a long and good one. They spent twenty-five happy years together before he died. Early in their marriage she even became pregnant, but miscarried. In the end their marriage had seen no Medici heirs birthed either.

A royal family without heirs was a dangerous thing.

The vultures would descend from all over Europe to take Tuscany.

She knew there would be no place for her at the discussions about to happen. Men only. So she took her leave and left the palace. A lovely summer evening enveloped Florence. Many were out enjoying the warm air. A welcome respite from the bitter north winds that raked across the city each winter, sometimes bringing snow.

She walked at a leisurely pace, heading away from the palace and across the River Arno, turning right toward the Church of Santa Croce. The piazza in front of the building was busy with people, including children playing on the cobbles. She'd chosen a simple black dress, keeping with her official status as being in mourning, and had come alone so as not to draw any attention. Just a few weeks ago the annual Calcio Storico matches had been played right here in the piazza. She loved the violent spectacle, steeped in history, which was so utterly Florentine.

Her widowhood was in its fourth year. And she was tired of it. Grief did not become her. She was lonely. She missed having a husband. The only true relationship she had here in Florence was with her father. She and her brother despised each other, and the rest of the family viewed her as a threat, an interloper, who had returned after years of being gone, wanting it all for herself.

But it was her birthright.

After her father, she and her brother were the last two royal Medicis.

Life had been kind to her. She was still blessed with a fair complexion, eyes large and expressive, teeth white as ivory. She loved the outdoors, walking, hunting, horseback riding, and dancing. Especially the dancing. She was educated, refined, aware of her status, and she should be the one to succeed her father as grand duchess, not her vulgar and incompetent brother. He would do nothing but make a mess of things. Gian did not have the capacity to govern Tuscany. She knew that. Her father knew that. But Medici tradition demanded that the duchy only go to male heirs.

Her father had tried to change that but to no avail. It seemed that Florence had become accustomed to the fact that male succession was sometimes based on nothingness.

She entered the church and found the family chapel. Though San Lorenzo was their main house of worship, the Medici had long maintained a presence at Santa Croce with a modest chapel dedicated to St. Cosmas and St. Damian, the family's patron saints.

She liked coming here.

No one else was around.

Which she also liked.

After a few minutes she left the chapel and walked out into the open cloister. Above, in the rectangle of ink-blue sky, a brilliance of stars lifted her heart. At the far end stood the lesser-known Pazzi Chapel, an outward sign of the once disgraced family's climb back to influence in the late fifteenth century. She had no desire to return to the palace, so she walked down the graveled path between two stretches of summer grass and entered through an open portal. Her eyes were immediately drawn upward to the spherical dome and its dark oculus. During the day light poured through but now, at night, it stared back black. The twelve windows along the dome ribs were likewise lifeless. The chapel's overall emptiness could lead someone to dismiss the space as unimportant.

But that would be a mistake.

As it was the space itself that was the star.

The Pazzi had long been rehabilitated, their property restored. Their attempt to kill Lorenzo de Medici and their murder of his brother Giuliano had neither been forgiven nor forgotten, it was just that three centuries had dulled the anguish. The family still existed, though scattered, its wealth coming from land, farms, receivables, and business capital. Nothing like it once had been, but nonetheless substantial. She'd always admired their coat of arms, which depicted crescents, battlemented towns, and, of all things, twin dolphins on a blue field with nine crosses. They continued to trade on the legend of how the family was rewarded during the First Crusade with sacred flints. The annual Easter procession that featured them had once again become part of Florence's yearly routine. Medici and Pazzi never mingled, but neither did they war with each other.

They just stayed apart.

She approached the altar, which filled a tall niche in one wall. The two stained-glass windows above were dull without the sun. In the dome above was a fresco, painted in the fifteenth century, depicting the constellations present in the night sky over Florence on July 4, 1442. Interestingly, an identical fresco was present inside the Medici's Church of San Lorenzo. Both created by the same artist at relatively the same time. She'd always wondered how two families who hated each other tolerated having the same thing, especially considering the Pazzi purge that happened after the sinister plot failed.

"It is magnificent, is it not?"

A male voice. Behind her. Speaking in the local Florentine vernacular.

Which startled her.

She turned.

Before her stood a man about her age. Tall, like herself, with a stiff military-like bearing. He was brawny of the chest, a touch sunburned on his face, a beard and mustache neatly trimmed. A mass of auburn hair covered his head and fell to his ears. Marks of what appeared to be left over from the ravages of smallpox dotted his cheeks and chin but did not detract from his handsomeness.

"And you are?" she politely asked.

"Raffaello de' Pazzi."

Eric listened in amazement.

"That was the beginning," his grandmother said. "When they first met. Within a few weeks they were lovers."

"A Medici and a Pazzi?"

"They were, and quite happy with each other."

He was skeptical. "How could you possibly know that?"

"Anna recorded many of her thoughts and feelings."

Really? "You have never mentioned that fact before."

She shrugged. "It was not necessary. It should have been enough that I told you."

Don't argue with her. "I agree. It should have been. But I would love to read her thoughts. Do you have Anna's writings?"

"Of course. My father gave them to me."

"Can I see them?"

A puzzled look came to her wizened face. "Why would I do that? You have shown no interest in this. Why now?"

He had no time to explain anymore. "During my entire childhood, into the time I was out of university, all I heard was how we are Medici and that we can never forget that. How the family is owed a debt that Rome never paid. How history has it all wrong. On and on you went. Yes, I thought it all a fantasy. Unimportant. Who cares. But now I believe you. If you meant all that you said, then it is time we do something."

"You just want the money," she spit out.

"No, I do not. Nothing is to be gained by bankrupting the Vatican. But I do want the church to feel the pressure from that long-overdue debt, and the world to know it exists." The first part was true, the second a lie. "Is that not what you want too?"

She pointed another crooked finger. "The pope should pay. He owes us."

"Yes, he does. And we, you and I, can make him pay." He shifted gears. He had to know more. "What happened between Anna Maria and Raffaello de' Pazzi?"

"They fell in love. But that was dangerous. Even in the eighteenth century, three hundred years after the attempt on Lorenzo the Magnificent's life and the killing of his brother, Pazzi and Medici kept their distance. Her father, Cosimo III, never would have approved of the relationship. Nor would her brother."

He had questions. "Why would Anna, a Medici, even consider such a thing? And was she not still in mourning for her husband?

Would it not have been improper for her to have had an intimate relationship with anyone?"

She tapped her chest. "She followed her heart."

He waited for more.

"She was lonely. Her father was old and would die within three years of her meeting the Pazzi. She hated her brother and knew that once he was grand duke, her life would never be the same."

Eric knew his history. Cosimo III died in 1723. Six days before his death he issued a proclamation commanding that Tuscany remain independent and that Anna should succeed to the throne after her brother, Gian, died. Ultimately, the monarchs of Europe failed to respect his wishes, and her brother, for years, made her life miserable. Finally, she abandoned her apartment in the royal palace and left Florence. When her brother drew his last breath in 1737, the great powers of Europe gave Tuscany to the Duke of Lorraine.

Anna Maria was totally ignored.

"She became with child by Raffaello de' Pazzi," his grandmother said. "A total surprise since her only other pregnancy miscarried. Having a child was not something she expected. She was in her fifties. To have a child at that age then, or now, was dangerous. Even worse, Raffaello de' Pazzi died in a carriage accident before the child was born. Some said it was no accident, though. Anna Maria believed he was murdered."

That information surprised him. "She wrote that down?"

She nodded. "All of her thoughts and fears."

Anna Maria died in 1743. History made no mention of a child born to her in the years before her death. Just the opposite, in fact. Her last will and testament was remarkable. She'd inherited all that the Medici owned, including art, land, buildings, cash, contracts, jewelry, and other valuables. Priceless things. She cemented her place in history with the *Patto di Famiglia,* the Family Pact, which ensured that everything the Medici acquired over nearly three centuries of political ascendancy stayed in Tuscany, provided that nothing was ever removed from Florence. And nothing ever was. All the art, architecture, and grandeur that was modern Florence owed its existence to her.

"You took me to where Gregorio Cappello is buried," he said. "You told me that he was a royal Medici. I am a royal Medici. It is not a story anymore. It is fact. But the father, Nonna. Raffaello de' Pazzi. He is now the key. I need to be connected to him, and I need to know if he and Anna Maria legally married?"

"Of course they married. She would not have had it any other way."

"She wrote that down too?"

His grandmother nodded.

"So why not leave her child, a legitimate Medici, everything? Why give it all to Florence? Why allow the royal line to become extinct?"

"She had her reasons. Good ones too."

Another non-answer. But intriguing. For another discussion. Right now he wanted to know, "Where is the Pazzi buried?"

"I have no idea."

Not good.

He should be able to find that out now that he had a name and time frame. But this woman was the only one who knew where to find the other piece of the puzzle.

"Where are Anna Maria's writings?"

CHAPTER 41

Stefano remained perplexed with both Cardinal Ascolani's presence here in Siena and his visit to the Palazzo Tempi. He'd gone back to La Soldano and spoken with Daniele, who informed him that an American and Cardinal Richter had spent most of the day with Camilla Baines at her horse farm.

"During the Palio we watch her day and night," Daniele said. "She is the Golden Oakers' capitano. *A slippery one, too. Always up to something. The Porcupines and the Golden Oaks do not care for each other. Even worse, Golden Oak has a bad horse who cannot win. So they were paying their jockey to stop us from winning. We made a side deal with that jockey and paid him more to leave us alone."*

"The way of the Palio, right?"

"All part of the spectacle. That American I mentioned rode one of their horses bareback earlier at her track. She would not have done that, without a reason."

"Which is?"

"We think she may have found out what we've done and is preparing to make a change in jockey."

"With the American on their horse?"

"We are not sure. But it is a possibility."

"And what worries you is that he cannot be bought."

"Exactly."

He was still at the café when a text came from Ascolani ordering him to head back to the cathedral, which remained open late today because of all the festivities related to tomorrow's race.

So he hustled that way.

He entered through a side door, paying the admission fee once again, and found Ascolani at the far end of the nave near the octagonal pulpit.

A thirteenth-century marvel.

Eight granite-and-marble columns supported sculpted scenes that dramatically narrated the life of Christ. Ascolani stood among the visitors, still dressed casually, admiring the opulence. To their right hung this year's *pallium,* the silk banner draped before one of the towering black-and-white-striped pillars, where it had been brought earlier for the archbishop's blessing. Tomorrow it would be moved to the campo, behind the judge's stand, where it would wait to be claimed by the winning *contrada* of this year's race.

"This pulpit is one of the great wonders in Christendom," Ascolani said in a low voice. "All in Carrara marble. The detail is astonishing. Such a richness of motion and narrative. See the central column. It is adorned with the figures of arts and crafts. *Grammar,* with a little boy reading a book placed on his knees. *Dialectia,* whose withered face is plunged in deep thought. *Rhetoric,* pointing out a word in a book. *Philosophy,* arrayed in sumptuous clothes with an illuminating torch in her hands." Ascolani motioned. "*Arithmetic,* counting upon her fingers. *Music,* playing on a cithera. *Astronomy,* bearing the astrolabe." His boss paused. "Amazing representations."

People were moving all about, most there to admire this year's banner. He noticed that many crossed themselves and were brought to tears in its presence. Odd, considering it was but a work of art upon silk, this year's leaning toward the traditional with an image of the Madonna of Provenzano.

"There are things you must now know," Ascolani said. "Pope

Julius II and Giuliano de' Medici met right here, inside this pulpit, in late spring 1512. The head of the Medici clan and the head of Christendom."

His boss then explained the deal the two men had made. The Medici were not going to simply take the pope's word for repayment, especially considering that Julius was nearing the end of his life. So the pope issued a Pledge of Christ.

Ascolani motioned and they walked away, toward a nearby empty corner. More people were still streaming into the cathedral.

Ascolani stood quiet and still. "Julius died in 1513, only a few months after making the pledge. A Medici was elected the next pope, as Leo X. The church had no way then to repay such a large debt, so the balance just accrued. Giuliano de' Medici, though, had troubles of his own. He gave up his leadership of the Medici family and married a French noblewoman in 1513. He was given the title Duke of Nemours, and the French were grooming him for the throne of Naples. But he died prematurely in 1516. All Florence mourned him."

"Would not the family have known about the debt?" he asked.

"Of course. But here is where fate played a part."

Ascolani explained that the Medici controlled the Vatican from 1513 to 1534 through two popes. Neither had any interest in calling in the pledge, as both actively drained the Vatican of its wealth with their patronage of the arts and other extravagances. Their reigns also coincided with the Protestant Reformation and the infamous sack of Rome by the troops of Charles V in 1527. It was Clement VII, a Medici, who ultimately convinced the Holy Roman emperor, Charles V, to make Florence a republic once again, with the Medici as its ruler. But in 1569 that was changed to a duchy, and Pius V crowned Cosimo I grand duke.

But that had come at a price.

"Pius told Cosimo that to get the duchy and the title, the Medici would have to forbear on calling in the pledge," Ascolani said. "A brilliant move that neutralized the financial threat in one swift blow. But the pledge was not destroyed. There the Medici were smart. They insisted it remain in existence to ensure that no one took back the duchy or the title that had been given to them. If that happened they would call in the debt. It was as if they both had loaded guns pointed at each other."

"How do we know this," Stefano asked.

"I have spoken to our most senior historians, and they related to me all the details. In our history the *Pignus Christi* has only been issued six times. Five of those were honored. This is the only one outstanding. This particular one, though known within the church, has not been an issue. It died when the Medici died out in 1743. No more legitimate Medici. No more pledge."

He wanted to know, "Do we have the document?"

Ascolani shook his head. "Not in the Vatican. I had a search done. It rests, if at all, with the Carthusians, inside Santa Maria di Castello with all those stolen records from the sixteenth century. That is where Cardinal Ghislieri went in exile and where he stayed for six years until becoming Pope Pius V."

"The current pope cannot order them to open their doors?"

"He would never. They are a cloistered sect. And besides, the Holy Father knows nothing of this situation. I have kept this close. The fewer who know the better. Only you and I know the full situation."

He appreciated the degree of trust the cardinal was placing in him. He wanted to ask about the Palazzo Tempi and the man in the window, but he knew better. So he offered only a nod, acknowledging the situation as explained.

Ascolani motioned to the people. "The archbishop has yet to discover I am here, and I would like to keep it that way. This is a highly confidential matter. Entity business."

He understood.

"Something, though, has changed," Ascolani said. "Eric Casaburi knows something we do not. He went to Cardinal Richter and specifically mentioned the Medici and the pledge. That is most disturbing, and we are going to find out the full extent of the situation. But first I want you to keep a close watch on the American agent, Malone, and Cardinal Richter. We must know what they are planning. Use some of your team, if need be. But remember, the fewer who are involved the better."

Interesting how life dealt its opportunities. Twenty-four hours ago he was the hero of Florence in the Calcio Storico, the entire country watching him on television, his childhood neighborhood singing his praises. Now he was in the middle of something that no one could know a thing about. He was accustomed to discretion and secrecy. But he could not shake the strange feeling that swept through him.

Something was not right here.

CHAPTER 42

8:30 P.M.

COTTON WALKED THE STREETS OF SIENA, THE WAY LIT BY LIGHTS AND lanterns. People were everywhere, the excitement evident. Camilla had told him that all across the city each *contrada* would be holding a celebratory dinner. Like the pep rallies he remembered from high school before each football game. A way for the *contrada* to gather and hear emotional speeches from their *capitano* and jockey, further building enthusiasm for the race tomorrow. Some of the *contradas* held their celebrations right in the streets of their neighborhood. He'd passed one where tables, some fifty-plus feet long, lined the cobblestones, following the street's hilly contour up and down. Golden Oak gathered in the plaza before their church. He found the area loaded with people singing and cheering.

The sun was gone, the evening warm but pleasant. More long tables were here in rows, overflowing with bottles of Chianti, baskets of bread and plates waiting to be filled with pasta, meat, and vegetables. He caught the inviting waft from their stewing. Revelers filled nearly every seat, all Golden Oakers, born and bred. The atmosphere was exciting yet serious, with flags and banners hung everywhere and lots of chanting. Just after he arrived they all stood reverently and sang the *contrada's* anthem. One huge family, all united behind one thought.

Win tomorrow.

But that was not what Camilla Baines had in mind.

"Just make sure the Porcupines lose. However you do that, I do not care."

"And what about our entrance into Santa Maria di Castello?"

"You will not be disappointed."

"You've already spoken with the monks?"

"Of course. You will have access."

That he'd liked to hear.

Especially considering the risks he was taking.

At the head table, elevated above the others on a long dais, Camilla sat beside the current jockey, who was dressed in the black and gold livery colors for Golden Oak. The remaining chairs at the table were filled, he assumed, with *contrada* officials. Camilla was busy talking to the jockey, carrying on with the others, everything seemingly fine, no one aware that she would be firing the Sardinian tomorrow morning. The jockey himself seemed oblivious to the fact that his duplicity had been discovered.

All part of the Palio, though.

"Mockery and irony are always present," Camilla said. *"The Palio mirrors life with all its ups and downs, lies and truths, good and bad. I do not fault our jockey for making his side deal. So he cannot fault me for reacting to it."*

Camilla had explained that Palio rules allowed a *contrada* to change jockeys up till 10:30 A.M. tomorrow, when they had to finally declare a name. Once done there could be no further substitutions, even if the jockey was injured, became sick, or was unable to ride. If that happened the *contrada* simply forfeited their spot in the race.

He was not going to stay and eat. Instead he would find dinner at one of the many cafés across town. Camilla had provided him and Richter rooms for the night at her palazzo, a spacious residence far away from the campo.

Stephanie had texted him information on the dead woman from the train. She was a career criminal with a long arrest record. The dead man from the Dom in Cologne possessed a similar résumé. So they were hired help. Engaged most likely by the other man from the train, who'd ended his association with her through a bullet to the head.

Then there was the murdered Swiss Guardsman.

Another matter entirely.

He stood at the end of one of the many streets that drained into the crowded plaza, all of them closed to traffic, pedestrian-only tonight. He was about to leave when a face caught his attention. Across, on the far side, with a thousand-plus people in between chowing down.

Pale skin stretched across a bony face. Thinning hair. Smooth brow. Hollow, high-boned cheeks.

The killer from the train.

STEFANO STOOD AMONG THE STREAM OF PEOPLE MOVING IN AND OUT of the Golden Oak dinner. He'd made his way here because of the man from the Palazzo Tempi. The men Daniele had loaned to him to watch the residence had reported that the stranger was on the move.

So he'd made his way over from La Soldano where he'd been eating his dinner, finding his target. He'd even managed to snap a few photographs. He needed an identification but could not risk going through the Entity, not with Ascolani's connection to this individual. His boss would not appreciate his curiosity. If Ascolani had wanted him to know about the man, he would have told him. Whoever he was, he was clearly on a mission. It might be nothing. Something none of his business. But he'd been a field operative long enough to know when things felt off. Daniele had said that he had *contrada* contacts within the local *carabinieri* who might be able to provide an identification from a photo. Now he had several. Good ones too. So there'd be no harm in checking this out.

He watched as the man turned and dissolved back into the crowd beyond the dinner in the open plaza. Daniele's two men would keep an eye on him.

His phone vibrated with a call.

From Daniele.

He answered and retreated back, settling close to the stone wall of a closed shop.

"Something is definitely happening within Golden Oak," Daniele said. "Camilla Baines is going to change out jockeys for the American, Malone."

"You do have a good intel network on her."

"We have learned from experience not to take an eye off her."

"That seems unusual. To change jockeys this late."

"It is. And it presents us with a problem. We were counting on that jockey."

He wondered if any of that had prompted his presence here. Ascolani had been stingy on the details, though heavy on the history lesson. So all he could do was roll with the punches and see where things led.

"Keep me posted."

He ended the call and stepped back to the end of the street, where the plaza started. Okay, he knew what Malone was doing.

So where was Cardinal Richter?

CHAPTER 43

JASON STEPPED FROM THE CAR.

The vehicle had been waiting for him where a caller from earlier had instructed him to go. An older priest had been behind the wheel and they'd left Siena, heading south toward Rome. After about fifty kilometers they veered off the main highway and took one of the narrow local routes into the darkened countryside. Finally, the path turned to dirt for the final few kilometers, broad at its start but narrowing as they climbed.

He was deep into the Val d'Orcia, a region of Tuscany that extended from the hills south of Siena down to Monte Amiata. A landscape of cultivated hills broken by gullies and picturesque towns and villages. Its wines were considered some of the best in Italy, the entire region a World Heritage Site. The journey ended at Castiglion del Bosco, a luxury hotel located in the heart of the Val d'Orcia. He knew the place. Unique in that its buildings were once a small village, all converted into elegant guest suites, a cooking school, and two restaurants, along with all the other amenities expected at a five-star resort. He'd actually stayed here for one night a few years ago.

He was directed past the registration building and down a set of stone steps to what was once the village's main street. Lanterns lit the cobbles with a flickering amber glow. Towering cedars reached up into the sky at the end of the path, more steps leading upward to the top of a hill dissolving into the night. Before that, tables and chairs dotted an outdoor restaurant, all unoccupied save for one.

He approached and smiled.

Chas Stamm was still in command.

"I was unaware that a retired cardinal could afford a room here," he said. "What do they go for? Several thousand euros a night?"

His friend was nursing a glass of wine and what appeared to be a cheese pizza.

Stamm motioned. "At least that. Sit. I ordered this food for you."

He accepted the offer and helped himself to a slice, which was hot, fresh, and delicious, fire-oven-baked.

"Wine?" Stamm asked, lifting the bottle on the table.

He nodded.

"It's a local red. Quite good," Stamm said, filling the glass with a generous pour. "And expensive."

"You know the management here?" he asked.

Stamm nodded. "They have always been quite accommodating for me."

He kept enjoying the pizza.

Stamm set the wine bottle down. "Not far from this place is the Badia Ardenga, a handsome abbey, built around A.D. 1000. Have you ever seen it?"

He shook his head.

"Emperors and popes once visited there. There is a story that, in 1313, the German emperor Henry VII and his army went to the abbey to take communion. Taking advantage of the opportunity, the monks supposedly poisoned the Eucharist and killed him."

He finished the slice and reached for another. "And the point of that lovely story?"

"Careful what you eat."

He ignored the jab and kept chewing.

"When Henry died," Stamm said, "the town of Pisa built a monumental tomb inside their cathedral for him. Sadly, it did not last long. For political reasons it was dismantled, its stone reused elsewhere. But the body stayed in the ground."

He sipped some of the wine. Yes, it was good.

"In 1921 Henry's tomb was opened and examined. It was studied again in 2013, seven hundred years after his death. The bones were examined by X-ray diffraction, infrared spectroscopy, and scanning electron microscopy to study medieval postmortem practices."

He decided to bite on the bait. "Did they determine he was poisoned?"

Stamm shrugged. "There was no way to confirm or deny. History says he died of malaria. But I like the story of the murderous monks better."

Two pieces of pizza were plenty, but the wine he would continue to savor. "There has to be a good reason why you have come here from Rome, summoned me from Siena, then related this fascinating story."

"Along with Henry VII other bones have been freed from their graves and studied," Stamm said.

He waited for more.

"I received a call earlier from a close friend, a bishop assigned to the Basilica of San Lorenzo in Florence. Last night Eric Casaburi made his way into the Medici crypt and opened the grave of Anna Maria Luisa de' Medici. He came with a renowned DNA expert who extracted a sample for testing."

He instantly recalled what Casaburi had told him.

"You have DNA evidence of your ancestry?"

"I do, and DNA evidence does not lie."

"You will have to prove all of that."

"I will."

"Anna Maria was the last legitimate royal Medici heir," Stamm said. "Or at least that is what history notes."

"Casaburi is obviously trying to establish a connection to her."

"Clearly. Which is both disturbing and fascinating. He is currently in the village of Varallo, where he grew up," Stamm said. "His parents are dead, but his grandmother is still alive. She lives there in his childhood home. All her life she spoke of being a Medici. No one ever paid her any mind."

"And you would have dismissed all that as fantasy too. Until tonight."

Stamm lifted his own wineglass and gestured. "Precisely."

"Are you watching Casaburi?"

Stamm finished his wine. "Quite closely."

"More wine," Jason said, motioning that he would pour.

His friend waved the offer off. "Lucky for you there are lots of people still loyal to me."

"You have your own private Entity?"

"Something like that."

He was grateful for his friend's foresight and efforts. It was good to have him on his side.

Stamm reached down and brought up a small cardboard box, sealed with tape. "Please give this to Malone. He asked for it."

"Do I want to know what that is?"

The older man shrugged. "I do not see why you should. I hear that Malone will be riding in the Palio tomorrow."

He nodded. "I am glad it is him and not me."

"It is important he do as Camilla wants."

"He gets that." But he was still bothered by another point. "Do you think Casaburi is actually a Medici?"

"Many Medici were left after Anna Maria died in 1743, from the two other branches of the family. But they were not of the royal line. That went extinct. Casaburi came to you and specifically mentioned the Pledge of Christ and the fact that only a legitimate Medici could call the debt. I am assuming he was not bluffing and knows more than we do. He would not have risked going into that tomb unless he was reasonably sure. But it seems the real question for Eric Casaburi is not whether he is Medici. There are countless of those around from those other two branches. No. He has to prove that he is a *legitimate* royal Medici heir."

"How could he do that?"

Stamm smiled. "We are about to find out."

CHAPTER 44

Because of the great obstacles that life has placed before me, I must do by writing what I have not allowed myself to do face-to-face. The extreme sadness at the bitter loss of my dear husband made me feel overwhelmed. It is only with difficulty that I can still breathe. Love was not something I thought obtainable for a second time, but he brought me the greatest of joy. I did not believe at the time of his death, nor so do I believe such now, that his demise happened by chance. Instead it is my belief that he was assassinated. That belief is bolstered by the fact that my brother was aware of my marriage. I was told this by someone close to him. He holds me responsible for the miserable marriage he has long endured. Of course that ignores his excessive drinking, overindulgences, and the many vices that plague his existence. The death of my husband cut through my heart and soul. There was in this world no good equal to him. Beginning from his infancy, by those who raised him and who saw signs in him that foretold of his invincible and great mind, he did everything gloriously until the end.

So why then did I decide not to keep and raise our son as my own. First and foremost was the vengeful nature of my brother. Never would he have allowed me that happiness. Then there is the current hostile political world in which we live. I dared to love a Pazzi. Even worse, I birthed a son, half Medici, half Pazzi. His safety, his life, is most important. So I sought out a suitable family who may be willing to raise my child as their own. I have no words to express how greatly indebted to you both I am for taking the responsibility for that I cannot assume. This failure on my part is the greatest disappointment of my life, but there is simply no other choice. It is to the benefit of our duchy, my family, and to the private worth and health of my son that he be raised in obscurity. God has placed many burdens upon my shoulders. To be born a Medici is not only a blessing but a curse. Once we were proud and distinguished, possessed of power and influence. Now we are but an illusion. A shadow without form that only lingers through the bright light of others. It is better that I do not pass on to him those burdens. Please know that my son was conceived in the deepest of love and in the eyes of God. My dear Raffaello and I were married by the bishop at Santa Croce, in secret. We deeply cared for one another and, if not for his untimely demise, things would have been different. We would have raised our son together. My father had wanted me to succeed my brother and rule the duchy. But others had differing ideas. If that had occurred things may have been different for both myself and my son, yet that was not allowed to happen. By the grace of God the sole decision of whether this family continues or not has fallen to me. I could claim my son, reveal my marriage, and make him heir to the Medici throne. But I have chosen another path, one that ensures the end will come. My son being surely of an easy and kind nature, I pray that he be sent along his governance route with a life that is full and happy. Sadly, he would have never found peace in the world in which I exist.

I am told you are both the finest of people, the most loyal of subjects, and the most devoted to God. So many happy memories fill my heart. My husband was the best of men, and bringing his son into the world was my great honor. Such a shame that he never lived to see his son. I shall leave the vendettas to my enemies, as they will surely deserve their sins. My most fervent wish is that none of them will ever find their way to you. My son, your son, deserves a life free of greed, arrogance, pettiness, and hate. Please kiss him on my behalf and may the Lord keep you and him forever safe and happy.

Eric was amazed.

The writing was penned in the Florentine style and signed in the formal hand of Anna Maria Luisa de' Medici, precisely how she signed all of her documents. It would not be difficult to have the handwriting authenticated. The archives at the Pitti Palace in Florence contained a multitude of Medici writings. He'd visited there before and seen correspondence signed by Anna Maria.

He'd found the writing exactly where his grandmother had said, inside an oak chest, the hinges and catch a dull brass that barely showed against the rich color of the scarred wood. The chest had sat in his grandmother's room for many years, but he'd never looked inside. The letter had been tucked into a plastic sleeve, the sheet of vellum dark and fragile, the ink fading.

It seemed to confirm that a marriage occurred *by the bishop at Santa Croce, in secret*. That was far more than Anna Maria merely *saying* that a marriage occurred. The records for the basilica would have to be searched, and hopefully ones that far back still existed. He wondered why no one else had discovered any entry before, as the Medici had been extensively studied for centuries. But Santa Croce was not noted as one of their domains. Quite the contrary. Santa Croce was far more associated with the Pazzis.

He had so many questions.

How had his grandmother managed to obtain such a valuable historical document? Its provenance had to be impeccable. What he was about to do would invite the closest of scrutiny. Nothing could be open to question. The ultimate conclusion had to be unmistakable.

"Eric."

His grandmother calling out. He'd thought her down for the night. He stood and walked into her room. Her frail body lay beneath a blanket, the room unlit.

"Did you read it?" she asked.

"I did. Several times."

"She carried great pain. But she was strong."

"Were you being truthful earlier when you said you did not know where Raffaello de' Pazzi is buried?"

No answer.

So he decided to return to the subject he'd not fully explored earlier. In order to convince the church and the world of his family lineage, he would have to be able to answer all of the questions. At the top of that list would be an explanation as to why Anna Maria bequeathed all the Medici wealth to Florence when she supposedly had a legitimate male heir. So he posed that inquiry to his grandmother.

"She was fed up. Sick and tired of dukes, kings, popes, and emperors. Her father wanted her to be grand duchess, but no one would honor that wish. Men just took it all from her. When Raffaello de' Pazzi died she was devastated. Two husbands she'd lost. And she firmly believed that Raffaello was murdered by her brother. So she made a hard choice and decided to not reveal her marriage or the child. Instead, she gave the boy away so he could grow up in peace. Then years later she gave everything the Medici owned away too."

"A bit cold and hard, wasn't it?"

"Not for her time. Women had little power or say. And Medici and Pazzi never mingled. They kept their distance. She broke a family rule and loved a Pazzi. But she was a rebel. She had spirit. Who knows what she would have done if Raffaello had not been killed."

"But once her father and brother were gone, she inherited everything. She was the last Medici standing. Why not reclaim her son and give it to him?"

"By then the world had tired of Medicis. Emperors and popes wanted them gone. There was no way she would be able to retain the duchy. Her son was a man when she died. Twenty years old. But she did not forget him."

That was intriguing. "What do you mean?"

"The only loose end was the pledge. That she did leave for her son to find and collect."

"She had the pledge?"

"She hid it away."

He'd grossly misjudged his grandmother, now realizing that she had not been imagining things. But he wanted to know, "Why did not you, my father, your father, or his father, go after the pledge?"

"None of them ever grasped the significance. I was the first one in our family to be able to read. Your father never cared for the stories. He thought them nonsense. So I stopped telling them to him. You, though, were different. You listened. For a while."

"I am listening now."

"Also, there was no way then to prove we were Medici. So what good would it have done to produce the pledge? You are the first of Gregorio Cappello's heirs to be able to prove that our bloodline is true."

But there were still two problems. "I have to locate the pledge."

"Go back and look in the chest. There is a false bottom."

He fled the bedroom and re-found the oak chest.

Inside were clothes, photographs, and a few other family items. Anna Maria's note had been lying among those memories. He removed everything and carefully examined the interior. The three panels of the bottom seemed solid, but the left one slid a few millimeters, enough that it could be lifted free revealing a compartment beneath. Inside was a flat ornate wooden box with writing etched into the top. MEMORARE NOVISSIMA QUOD SUM ERITIS MIHI HODIE TIBI CRAS. He found his phone and typed the words into a translating site, which revealed the message. "Remember about the ultimate matters. Who I am, you will be. What I will face today, you will face tomorrow."

Interesting words.

He lifted the lid and saw eight small leather-bound books. He removed one, opening it to see page after page of writing in the same feminine script from Anna Maria's note to the adoptive parents. Diaries? Maybe. He removed the volumes and walked back to his grandmother.

"Anna Maria wrote her important thoughts down," she said. "She wanted her son to know who and what she was. All you seek is there."

Proof enough?

He had to admit.

It could be.

CHAPTER 45

SIENA, ITALY
WEDNESDAY, JULY 2
6:45 P.M.

COTTON FOLLOWED THE OTHER JOCKEYS INSIDE THE PALAZZO Pubblico. He'd spent the day with the Golden Oak's horse, trying to develop something of a rapport with the animal.

"There are three types of horses," his grandfather said. *"A gelding, a neutered male. Real cooperative and friendly. A stallion. A fearless male who can do almost anything. Then there are mares. Everything has to be a suggestion to her, since she will do whatever she wants. But the most difficult of all is the chestnut mare. A hardheaded animal, bred to be cantankerous. A real powerhouse."*

Golden Oak drew a chestnut mare with the unlikely name of Leone.

The groomer had recommended he talk to the animal in Italian and call her by name. Luckily, thanks to his eidetic memory, languages were easy for him, Italian being one of several he spoke. So he'd talked to Leone and was rewarded by a flare of the nostrils and a desire to smell her new friend.

"A horse's way of saying hello."

Last night he'd roamed the streets and tried for over an hour to locate the man from the train, but to no avail. He'd then attempted to make contact with Richter, but the cardinal had left a message that he would be back later, saying, Going to see our guardian angel. He hadn't heard from Richter since then other than a text that said he was back in Siena and had something for him.

Earlier, inside town hall, far from the clamor of the day, the mayor, captains, and jockeys all met to go over the race rules. Each jockey was then registered. Camilla had shocked everyone when she announced their jockey would be replaced. Most of the *capitanos* had been puzzled. And for good reason. During the morning's sixth, and final, trial heat the Sardinian had ridden Leone. But he'd noticed that the Porcupines had not seemed surprised at the change.

As if they'd known it was coming.

There'd been more pomp and circumstance through the day.

At 3:00 P.M. the city bells had tolled and he'd been present in the Golden Oak chapel for the blessing of the horse. Richter had explained that animals were generally not allowed within a Catholic church, but the Vatican waived that rule for the Palio. The church itself was specially outfitted with no pews, few stairs, and large wooden doors so a horse could easily move in and out. Interestingly, the horse was blessed before the jockey, which showed which of the two was more important. After the service he'd participated in another parade through the city center, which eventually made its way to the Duomo for a spectacular flag-throwing performance.

That had definitely been a first for him.

From there he joined the other jockeys and made his way to the campo, where each was given a special riding crop. A *nerbo*. Made from a stretched, dried ox penis. Unusual to say the least. He'd inquired as to why such a thing had ever been created, but Camilla had no idea, telling him, *"It is just the way it has always been."*

"You can use that on the other jockey," Camilla said in a whisper. "Rules say that is about all you can do with it. It is never used on the horse. But of course, those rules do not apply to you."

He got the message. Do whatever.

She motioned. "They are drawing the ten lots now that will

determine how the horses line up for the first start. That happens in secret. Your position on the starting line is important. Remember, somebody always false-starts on the first attempt. That way we all know the order for the next start. Between those two starts is when the deals are made. What happens then is another unpredictable element to the race. Sadly, a jockey's loyalty is never guaranteed, no matter what they are paid."

"That include me?"

She smiled. "It depends on how bad you want inside Santa Maria di Castello."

Good point.

"I have confidence in you," she said. "But keep an eye on the Porcupine. He will be buying allies to get you."

That advice did little to quell the anxiety swirling in his gut. But he was here to make sure someone else lost, and lose they would.

"Time to mount your horses," a man announced.

"Good luck," Camilla said to him and she offered her hand to shake.

Which he did.

Then he donned his metal helmet, snapped the chin strap in place, and headed outside where Leone waited with the other horses, the Golden Oak groomer holding the reins. Cotton took a moment and brought the back of his hand close to the horse's nose to allow her to savor the scent. He felt the warmth of the mare's breath. Cotton returned the favor and breathed onto the animal.

"You ready?" he whispered to Leone. "It's you and me now."

He stroked the animal. This had to be stressful, since the horse had developed an attachment to the other jockey. Now a new rider, out of nowhere? The groomer offered a treat. Some gummy bears and Skittles, which Leone lapped up from an open palm. One by one they all mounted their horses and entered the campo, gathering behind the starting rope. The crowd erupted in cheers as each *contrada* emerged. What would Stephanie Nelle say about all this? And Cassiopeia? Neither woman would be pleased. This was a bit above and beyond the call of duty.

But he was in it now. Time to get the job done.

Clarions played in a single cadence.

The great bell atop the Mangia tower began to clang.

Then all the bells in Siena joined in.

The multitudes of people inside the campo roared their approval. This had to be what it felt like to be on the field for the Super Bowl or World Series. Another procession of medieval-garbed Sienese had ended with the prize banner being escorted to the judge's stand, where it was raised high for all to see. The mayor and the ten *capitani,* Camilla Baines among them, stood before it. The bell in the Torre del Mangia stopped ringing, as did all the others across town. Sunlight was fading, the campo half lit, half in shadow. All ten horses and jockeys made their way to a point a few yards behind the starting rope.

Silence reigned.

Impressive.

Tens of thousands of people holding their breath.

Waiting.

He and the others maintained what the locals called the dance of the jockeys, circling behind the starting line, thick as thieves. The horses pranced, nostrils quivering. He noticed that no jockey spoke to another. Not the time for deals.

Not yet, anyway.

Earlier, Camilla had explained how ten *barberi,* small balls painted in the colors of each *contrada,* were inserted into a long-necked flask, shaken, then turned upside down, where the balls lined up. That order was recorded on a piece of paper, which was sealed in a white envelope and delivered by a policeman to the mayor. All eyes seemed to be on it as the mayor held it high, then ripped it open.

Nine horses would be called to enter the starting line according to the order of the balls. The tenth, the *rincorsa,* runner-in, would tease the others, moving forward, falling back, then finally rushing past the rope signaling the start of the race. He'd realized there was a chance he might be the *rincorsa.* So he'd watched YouTube videos of past races to get an idea of what that might entail. But one out of ten seemed like good odds that would not happen.

He gently stroked Leone's neck. The horse's ears swept back, signaling she was listening. His grandfather taught him about the ears. Like radar antennas. Wherever they pointed dictated what the horse was hearing. So pay attention to those ears.

A hush swept over the campo.

Everyone was focused on what was about to happen.

One by one a *contrada's* name was called out and the corresponding horse and rider assumed their place before the starting rope. Golden Oak was called sixth, which placed him in the middle of the pack. The Porcupines came eighth, two horses over. Camilla had told him that the inside and outside spots were the best for winning, and the middle was where all the mischief occurred. So he was in the right spot. The Dragons were assigned as *rincorsa*. There was lots of nudging, pushing, searching. Hooves pawed the ground. Leone threw her head up in the air, like a giraffe, a signal that she was irritated with all the motion. Cotton stroked the animal's neck, trying to calm her. They had to be a team, riding in rhythm, the more relaxed the better.

But he got it.

The air reeked of excitement and fear.

The race was about to begin.

CHAPTER 46

Thomas was ready.

When he'd returned last night from dinner a cylindrical canvas case had been waiting for him. Clearly, someone other than him had access to the palazzo. Inside had been a black Stealth Recon Scout rifle, about three-quarters of a meter long. Bolt action. Hand-loaded with full-metal-jacketed .243-caliber Winchesters. Good choice. Barely seventy-five grains of propellant so the round stayed subsonic, eliminating the noise of crossing the sound barrier. This one came with a lightweight vertical foregrip and a built-in bipod that emerged with the press of a button, the grip light and durable. Of particular importance was a high-pressure sound suppressor that easily screwed onto the end of the barrel.

A solid and effective weapon.

He'd wandered the streets last night, visiting a few of the many celebrations that had been occurring. The entire town seemed electric with excitement. Around midnight a call to the phone Ascolani had left with him disturbed his meditation.

"I assume you are familiar with the item left for you," the cardinal said.

"I am."

"I have learned that the American from the train will be riding

in the race tomorrow, wearing the black and gold of Golden Oak. You know the face, correct?"

"I do."

"He will begin the race, but please make sure he does not make it to the end."

"I understand."

"Afterward, leave the gift and head for the Church of Santa Margherita. It is near the outer wall. A red Peugeot will be parked in a lot outside the wall. The keys are in a magnetic box above the right rear driver's-side tire. Take the car to Florence, check into a hotel, and await further instructions."

He'd moved a small table back from the open window, far enough that no one could see the rifle, unless they were directly across the campo and level with him—which was not possible, as the Mangia tower occupied most of the space in the opposite line of sight. The firing angle was perfect to catch Malone in either the second leg of the lap or into the third, just before a treacherous right-angle turn. After that, the crowd would be between him and the target. He wondered about the openness of this kill. Why take the risk? Perhaps Ascolani wanted to send a message. To Cardinal Richter? Maybe. But a kill amid all the chaos and confusion of the scene below would go relatively unnoticed until the race was over. Which should allow for ample opportunity to escape.

Everyone's attention was on the horses as they were called one by one to the starting rope. Finally, on the sixth name came Golden Oak. He leveled the rifle in his grip and took measure of his target through the scope.

Malone filled the crosshairs.

A round to the chest would be an easy kill.

JASON STOOD ON THE MAIN DAIS AMONG THE *CAPITANI* AND SIENA'S mayor. An envelope had been delivered, and the Capitano del Popolo was now announcing the order of the horses for the starting line. Camilla had insisted he come with her to this place of honor, but he'd made a point to stay back and dissolve with others who'd likewise been afforded the privilege. Malone was on the track, in the sixth spot from the inside, fourth from the outside, the horses all a seeming bundle of nerves and jitters. No formal starting gates here as you would see at any other formalized horse race. Just nine horses and riders jammed together behind a thick rope, weighted to fall fast to the ground. The tenth, the Dragon's horse and jockey, loitered about ten meters behind the pack.

Camilla came back to where he stood. "We have a good position. The Porcupine is close. Let us hope Signore Malone is successful."

They both turned their attention back to the track. The hush from the crowd continued as the Dragon continued to tease the other nine jockeys, seemingly bursting forward then stopping just short. After another faux surge one of the horses hopped past the starting rope.

A couple more followed.

A firecracker exploded, signaling a false start.

The crowd relaxed.

"Now we get down to business," Camilla said. "The next one is for real."

THOMAS EXTENDED THE TELESCOPING BUTT STOCK, THEN TOUCHED A button that transformed the rifle's foregrip into a miniature bipod, which he carefully balanced atop the wooden table he'd located about two meters back from the open window. Ascolani had called earlier and explained what would happen. So he'd used the opportunity of the false start to acquire a feel for the rifle. How it moved from side to side. How the scope focused. He played with the angles, knowing that he would have only a few seconds to make any adjustments and take the shot. He'd have to account for not only the distance but also the elevation and the constant movement of the target. And those adjustments would have to be made in a matter of milliseconds.

He practiced his marksmanship regularly at shooting ranges outside of London. He moved among several, never frequenting one more than the other. It was important he stay anonymous and never be noticed by anyone. His entire existence was dependent on being a ghost.

Malone was pacing his horse in a circle with the other nine, awaiting a recall back to the starting line. He again centered the American between the crosshairs, estimating the shot to be less than a hundred meters. Ascolani had been clear. It had to happen during the race. Once the horses left the gate they would be running toward him, on his side of the track, reducing the shot to fifty meters or so. The tricky part would be the unpredictable movement across the track and the constant changing of positions.

So he set a plan.

On the first lap he would take measure and practice centering the target. He'd take the shot on the second lap. If he missed, there was always the third and final trip around.

JASON NOTED THE TENSION THAT HUNG HEAVY IN THE AIR. APPARently all of the Palio aficionados knew what was about to happen, the excitement seemingly coming from watching the drama play out.

Like a piece of art acted out on a grand public stage.

Horse and jockey.

Contrada versus *contrada*. Siena celebrating itself. Adding to that was the fact that this whole thing was extremely dangerous. Cotton Malone had guts. No question. This was not his fight, yet here he was right in the middle, getting the job done. But he supposed intelligence operatives did whatever it took.

Or at least the good ones did.

The horses were again back behind the starting rope, pacing in a circular formation. This time, though, there was definitely talking among the jockeys. Deals were being made. Alliances formed.

Loyalties bought. The order was once again announced, each *contrada's* name called one by one.

He took a moment to survey the crowd.

Shade fell across the campo in the golden light of sunset, half lit, half in shadow. People were everywhere. Every millimeter of the center filled. Hundreds more occupied bleachers that had been erected around the outer perimeter. Windows all around framed out spectators. To his left, about fifty meters away, was a group wearing white, red, blue, and black. The Porcupines. On their feet. Among them, his eye caught a face. An older man not wearing the *contrada* colors.

But intensely watching the horses.

Cardinal Ascolani.

CHAPTER 47

ERIC HAD STAYED UP INTO THE EARLY HOURS OF THE MORNING READ-ing Anna Maria's diaries. They were in places affectionate, full of lively incident, but also packed with compassion and insight. Sadly, almost none of the Medici family writings had survived. Most disappeared long ago. Some of the bank ledgers still existed, as did scattered correspondence, and the poetry of Lorenzo the Magnificent had long been published, but few of their personal thoughts committed to words had made it into the modern world. When the royal line extinguished in 1743 so had their memory. If not for Anna Maria's extraordinary gift of the Medici art and possessions to Florence the family could have easily faded away to nothing.

Like the Pazzis.

But they had not.

His reading of the diaries revealed that Anna Maria was a deeply conflicted woman. She'd birthed a child at age fifty-three, which in the eighteenth century was more often than not a death sentence.

Yet she'd taken the chance.

I lapsed into exceeding sharp pain in great extremity, so that the midwife did believe I should be delivered soon. But it fell out contrary, for the child stayed in the birth with his feet first and in this condition continued till Thursday morning between two and three a clock. By then I was upon the bed, bearing my child with such exquisite torment, as if each limb were divided from the other. Being speechless and breathless I was, by the infinite providence of God, in great mercy, delivered. I trust in the mercy of the Lord. He requiring no more than He gives and, in His infinite grace, He spared me from death, my soul was miraculously delivered.

But that joy had been quickly enveloped by a harsh reality.

She'd secretly married a Pazzi without the permission of her brother, the Duke of Tuscany. Her husband had died, leaving her alone without any visible means of support, except what her father provided. True, Cosimo III adored his daughter. But eighteenth-century Italy was a man's world. There were no equal rights, MeToo movement, or political correctness. Occasionally a woman could rise to power. Elizabeth I of England, along with Catherine the Great of Russia, showed that it was possible. But a lot of things had to align just right for that to happen. None of which fell Anna Maria's way.

Her father died and her brother became grand duke.

Unfortunately, years earlier Anna Maria had been involved with engineering her brother's marriage to a German princess. Gian despised his wife and blamed Anna Maria for his misery. That, combined with his resentment over how their father had felt about her, eventually made the situation intolerable.

My brother has a body that is unpleasantly formed, whose breath seriously stinks, and has the worst constitution imaginable. He burns with arrogance and anger. He sends me fiery letters that voice his distaste and disgust for his only sister. He drinks and eats to excess and grave extravagance. We are so different. I have learned that the simpler you live the more you will be esteemed by others. My brother thinks the opposite. I have always tried to maintain the dignity of the Medici in public. My brother will be the ruin of Tuscany but there is nothing that can be done about it. He is destined to rule, but will most likely find an early death.

History noted that just after her father died in 1723, Anna abandoned the Medici royal palace and moved to a family villa outside of Florence. She lived there until her brother died in 1737. Could she have carried on a secret love affair and birthed a child without anyone knowing?

Apparently so.

But he was still perplexed. Why give the child away?

His grandmother had been correct, however.

The diaries provided the answer.

I have twice visited with His Holiness Our Pope, Clement XII, who was most considerate, and I made him aware of my private regrets and desires. His Holiness's response, being a citizen of Florence, was both wise and comforting. He agreed that my esteemed family has come to its natural end. At my departure from this life those who remain, not of the royal line, will surely dissolve themselves into nothing. For so long I have marked my time, waiting until matters take shape. My loving husband has been gone for sixteen years. My primary concern was then, and remains, the safety and well-being of my son. Because he now prospers as a vital young man, I am able to reduce my sorrow somewhat. Even now, these so many years later, he seems close and will always be remembered. He is called Gregorio Cappello. His first name means watchful, vigilant. I like that. Perhaps my thoughts might one day make their way to him. If so, I want him to know that I tried to temper the situation. As any mother would I want my spirit to endure, to be a good and faithful servant. But above all I do not want my son to hate me.

* * *

The reference to Medici murder was not fleeting.

In 1576 Isabella de' Medici, daughter of Cosimo I, found herself trapped in a loveless marriage. Her husband humiliated her openly with a mistress. In response she made the mistake of taking a lover. So her husband strangled her to death and promptly married his mistress. Historians say that the husband acted under the instructions of Isabella's brother, Grand Duke Francesco I de' Medici, as her growing influence and popularity began to rival Francesco's power. With the birth of Isabella's son, concerns of a potential coup further spurred Francesco to act. Then an ironic twist occurred. Eleven years later, Francesco and his wife, Bianca Cappello, died within hours of each other. Malaria was the named cause, but many believed it to be acute arsenic poisoning. The culprit? Francesco's brother, Cardinal Ferdinando de' Medici, who was in danger of being excluded from the succession if Francesco's own illegitimate son was legitimized and inherited the title of grand duke.

No question. What went around came around.

So Anna Maria's concerns about violence were understandable.

Thankfully, each entry bore a date. What he'd just read was dated March 1741. Two years before she died. By then her son would have been a young man. Was he aware of his adoption? Or had the secret of his birth parents been maintained? He gravitated to the latter since the diaries mentioned nothing about any direct contact.

They did, though, speak of grief.

Being alone has toughened me, which was all the more tender in that not an hour, not a moment, not an instant has elapsed that I do not think of my beloved. Men take greater satisfaction in the powers of their own eyes than in their fame proclaimed by others. But my late husband was held in the highest esteem. I take pride and assign pre-eminence to the valor and wisdom in which he was abounded. It is true that pain is greater in the one who has greater knowledge than in the one who is least aware. I could have died myself as I saw his body breathe its last breath. Only the consolation of his eternal memory has sustained me in life. His wisdom and virtue are the jewels of my widowhood and have many times worked to dry my tears. It nourishes me to hear what great people said about him. "A force of nature has died." "A paragon of ancient loyalty has expired." "A true heart of Tuscany is gone." What better boast could one who has been torn from human affairs have than the fond recollection of others. I still recall what was said at his funeral, when one man proclaimed, "Here he is, just buried, and pride rises up to heaven terrifying the most courageous." No truer words could have been spoken. I have long ago consented to the Divine Will, without piercing my heart further, by lending an ear to the harmony of praise.

She clearly loved Raffaello de' Pazzi. Entries continued to speak of him in nothing but glowing terms. One in particular was reflective.

Since childhood I have admired the ceiling fresco in the Old Sacristy of San Lorenzo. It is a representation of the sky, with the constellations visible over Florence the night of July 4, 1442. An identical starry vault fresco exists over the altar in the Pazzi Chapel at Santa Croce. The great Brunelleschi created both, before the infamy that some misguided Pazzis brought to their family. Yet my family allowed them both to remain. Lorenzo could have destroyed them, but he did not. I found his actions instructive, and perhaps a sign that the Medici hate knew its bounds and that forgiveness was not something out of the question. After all, Lorenzo's precious sister was married to a Pazzi, and was allowed to remain in her marriage, though living in exile. I too chose to love a Pazzi and I too went into a self-imposed exile. My husband was fond of saying, Into the wolf's mouth. May the wolf die. Such good wishes were always easy to come from his lips.

She was right.

After the attempt on his life Lorenzo hung every Pazzi he could link to the murder of his brother. He showed no mercy. None. But his sister Bianca's Pazzi husband was not hung. Instead he was sent into exile and Bianca went with him, both dying away from Florence. All Pazzi women were forbidden to marry anyone. Many fled Tuscany. But he exempted his sister's daughters from that decree.

Which showed something.

Eric knew Anna Maria died February 18, 1743. The last entry was dated nine days before.

And seemed most critical.

I write this to my son with a frankness that is necessary. My illness has progressed and I am not long for this world. Writing this seems superfluous because, as my son, I could not have any greater love, benevolence, or reverence for you. May God grant you a long and prosperous life so all may enjoy your sweet success. To those good people who raised you I thank them with all the abundance of my heart. You have been liberated from the burden of my troubled past and for that I am happy. As my life grew older and the burden of what I was bequeathed from my father and brother became more evident I made two decisions. The first concerned the beauty and art my family has amassed over the centuries. It now all belongs to me and I decided that it would stay in Florence, for the benefit of the Florentines, in perpetuity. That seemed the right course to take. All of that was done to the greater good. But for you, my son, one thing remains. Something our family acquired long ago and only you, or your children or their children, can claim. If these words ever find their way to you, know that I have made this decision as a way to say, once again, how sorry I am for not being a part of your life. All that was Medici is gone, save for one sacred pledge given by Pope Julius II to Giuliano de' Medici in 1512. Ten million gold florins, loaned to the Pope, with repayment sworn before God to the Medici, their heirs and assigns. You, my son, are Medici. Your mother and father were duly married. You are the last remaining royal Medici heir, as will be your children after you. The pledge was secured with two writings, one for Rome, the other for our family. I leave that pledge to you alone. It does not belong to the people of Florence. Instead, it rests safely under a watchful eye and this verse will lead the way.

Know the darkened world
has long missed the night and day, which
while the shade still hung before his eyes,
shone like a guide unto steps afar.
Ne'er will the sweet and heavenly tones resound, silent be the harmonies of his sweet lyre,
only in Raffaello's bright
world can it be found.
Auguror Eveniat

The last two words were interesting. *Auguror Eveniat.* He used the phone to translate them. I wish it will come.

He'd read all nine volumes. There had been a lot of insight, but the most pressing inquiries remained unanswered. Number one? How had all this remained secret for centuries? His family had clearly harbored the diaries. Why not reveal them? Expose them to academicians? Tell the world. His grandmother blamed it on indifference and illiteracy.

Was that the answer?

He'd slept in his former room, the one he'd occupied up to the time he left for university. A shower and shave had also been possible after he walked to a nearby store for some toiletries. His grandmother had slept soundly through the night, with the nurse there, on duty. They needed one more conversation. Perhaps the last one they would ever have. His patience with the past had reached an end. Only the future remained important. And it had become that much brighter thanks to a text from Florence. Confirmation. You are genetically connected to Anna Maria Luisa at a probability of 99%.

Good news.

Now for the rest.

He found his grandmother again in the parlor, sitting quietly, staring out the window.

"I read them all," he said.

"Then you know the depth of her pain, and the joy of her gift."

"Why did you keep those diaries hidden? Why did your father and his before him do the same?"

"No one cared what we knew or what he had."

"But the pledge? The promise to pay the debt. What about that?"

"That document is gone. It has been five hundred years."

That he did not want to hear.

But it did answer the question. His family had simply not possessed the drive or ability to do anything meaningful. And without DNA technology their claim to be a royal Medici would have fallen on deaf ears. He was the first of his family to have all the necessary tools.

"Nonna." He thought the more intimate name might soften the bitter nerves. "I have four problems. The first is establishing that there was a legal marriage between Anna Maria and Raffaello de' Pazzi. The second is locating Pazzi's grave. The third is proving a genetic connection between Pazzi and me. The final dilemma is finding the Medici copy of the Pledge of Christ."

"It does not exist."

"How do you know that?"

She said nothing.

But she'd been right on one thing. They *were* Medici.

It rests safely under a watchful eye and this verse will lead the way.

Those words had to mean something, along with what came after.

Know the darkened world has long missed the night and day, which while the shade still hung before his eyes, shone like a guide unto steps afar. Ne'er will the sweet and heavenly tones resound, silent be the harmonies of his sweet lyre, only in Raffaello's bright world can it be found.

What had Anna Maria meant?

Then it hit him.

Only in Raffaello's bright world can it be found.

Of course. Now he knew.

CHAPTER 48

COTTON HAD WATCHED AS THE PORCUPINE JOCKEY WHISPERED WITH two others, the conversations short, but nods of the heads had signaled the *partitit,* an agreement.

"It is critical you pay attention to who the Porcupine approaches," Camilla said. *"They will be your enemy."*

He'd also studied all the *contrada* colors and now knew that the trouble would come from the Tortoises and Panthers. The two flanked him on either side at the starting rope, one in the fifth position the other in the seventh. Coincidence? Hardly. The Porcupines had waited for the starting order to be revealed, then chosen their allies wisely. No telling how much money had passed on a promise. The Porcupine was two horses over toward the inside in the fourth position. Nothing about the glare the bearded jockey threw his way signaled friendly.

Nine horses pranced anxiously at the starting rope. The tenth horse, from the Dragons, remained behind them, ready to start the race with a dash toward the starting line. The *rincorsa* was apparently reveling in his power position since he'd already teased a start twice only to stop short and retreat behind the pack. Cotton's two minders on either side were keeping their mounts close to his, which Leone clearly did not appreciate. One kept shifting on his hooves, returning every bump into him one for one.

Horses generally shied away from a fight, fleeing problems, not embracing them. Cotton stroked Leone's neck, calming her, but noticed that the ears were constantly shifting. Pointed forward meant the focus was on the horses. Ears back? She was listening to her rider. Pinned straight down? That meant she was pissed. And all of that was compounded by a fun fact he learned from his grandfather. Horses could not focus directly ahead. Only at the periphery. Leone would have to turn her head to see, and she was doing just that, agitated at the horses to her right and left, ears straight down.

Watch out.

The crowd was becoming impatient with the Dragon's flirtations with the starting rope. They wanted the race to start.

So did he.

"You two need to stay out of this," he said in Italian to the jockeys on either side. "It will not end well. I don't give a damn about rules."

Neither replied.

But both stepped up their assaults on Leone with their own mounts.

He turned his head around and saw the Dragon jockey, the face set in hard determination. The man squeezed his calves into the horse and clicked for them both to race forward. The horse leaped ahead and this time there was no retreat.

The rope dropped.

He and the other jockeys spurred their mounts and all ten horses shot forward in a cloud of dust, hooves thundering, horse ears pointed ahead. He leaned his body forward and spurred Leone to run faster. He was careful not to lean too far, as that could cause the horse to stumble. Balance was the name of the game. The Tortoise and Panther jockeys kept their mounts close, not allowing him to escape their embrace. All the other horses bunched as they approached the first turn.

The Porcupine in the lead.

And moving away.

THOMAS FOLLOWED MALONE IN THE RIFLE SCOPE, PRACTICING KEEPING the American in the crosshairs. He could take the shot now.

But did not.

Instead he followed his target and simulated pulling the trigger, getting a feel for things.

Ready for the second lap.

COTTON GRIPPED THE REINS, HOLDING TIGHT AS THE HORSES MADE the second turn, known as San Martino, a descending curve. He was careful not to grip his thighs too tight, as that would signal for Leone to slow down. He needed the opposite. More speed. He could feel Leon's heartbeat pounding through his calves.

Stay relaxed.

Leone's generous gallop kept steady.

The Porcupine was slipping away.

But the Panthers and Tortoise were staying right with him. The Tortoise jockey reached across and smacked him on the right shoulder with his crop.

Which hurt.

Another blow.

This time to the side of his face.

Really?

He yanked on the reins and brought Leone into contact with the Tortoise's horse. The other jockey seemed undaunted and tossed over a few more blows with the crop.

Enough of that.

He pulled on the reins and popped his thighs against Leone. The horse responded and increased her gait. They pulled away from his two minders and headed for the Porcupine.

JASON'S ATTENTION ALTERNATED BETWEEN THE RACE AND ASCOLANI, who stood stolid among the Porcupines. Everyone else was cheering the riders along at a furious pace, arms waving, voices loud. But the cardinal remained dispassionate, like a statue. As did Camilla, who stood beside Jason, with the other *capitani* standing in front of them.

"I told him to wait until lap two," she whispered. "Then make a move."

The roar from the crowd was deafening, everyone's attention on the race as the horses entered the third turn.

The most treacherous.

It had a name too, as Camilla had informed him. Casato. Which ascended slightly at a nearly right angle. Tough to navigate at a full run for a horse and rider. A lot of injuries and some deaths had occurred there. So many that the outer wall was cushioned to break any fall. He'd not liked the sound of that when she'd explained the race to him and Malone. Now, watching a thunderous pack of horses and riders make the sharp swing, he could see just how tricky that turn could be.

But they all made it around, the horses now on a straight part of the track that went down, then up to the final turn toward the finish line.

He kept an eye on Ascolani.

Who was glancing back over his left shoulder, away from the action, toward the buildings that lined the campo.

What was that devil thinking?

CHAPTER 49

Eric finally left Varallo and drove back out into the Tuscan countryside. Earlier, the morning had broken gray and misty, a warm steady drizzle enveloping the world. He'd talked more to his grandmother, then worked on his laptop. Amazingly, he was able to find out where Raffaello de' Pazzi was buried. After the family's banishment from Florence in 1478, with the failed conspiracy to murder Lorenzo de' Medici, the Pazzis scattered throughout Italy. But when the Medici themselves were banished in 1494, some of the family had been allowed back to Florence.

But it was never the same.

Especially after the Medici returned in 1513 and even more so in 1569 when the Grand Duchy of Tuscany was established with them in charge. Most Pazzi stayed away, living where they'd settled after 1478, outside of Florence.

Raffael de' Pazzi no exception.

Apparently, his line of the family centered themselves on land about a hundred kilometers east of Florence. Far enough away to be out of sight, but near enough not to become out of mind. There they built villas and established lavish estates, none of which existed any longer. The land had long passed from the family and into a multitude of private hands, the Pazzi all but gone. But according to the internet there was a family burial plot in the village of Panzitta, which was about fifty kilometers north of Varallo. He'd wondered about the closeness of the name Pazzi to Panzitta, but had found nothing online to show a connection, except that all of the land surrounding the town was once owned by Pazzis. Nowadays Panzitta was a sleepy place, home to about a thousand people that catered to the nearby wineries.

He motored into Panzitta and noted the time. 7:10 P.M.

The village, nestled in a shallow pass atop a hillcrest, seemed another of the endless procession of Italian places that were built up, torn down, then built again, without much ever changing. He avoided the main plaza and parked off to one side. The few shops were all closed for the day, but he could hear people and gaiety from inside a small café. The sun was setting, the day waning, the air cool. Panzitta seemed a typical walled city with one main street, a central plaza, and a church that was too large for the smallness of the village. Romanesque in style with a plain stone exterior and a row of tall green cypresses rising in front.

He approached the church and pushed open the heavy wooden doors, both with scrolled iron grilles over leaded-glass panels. Inside was a simple but elegant design with faded frescoed walls. The central nave was supported by arches resting on columns and capitals, all stripped of plaster and ornaments. The floor was rough patterned marble, slick from centuries of use. He noticed a chapel to the left of the nave devoted to the Madonna. The tabernacle at the far end behind the altar was flanked on either side with figures of saints. His research earlier detailed that the Pazzi had a burial crypt beneath this church, there since the sixteenth century. An unimportant place that held the remains of relatively unimportant people.

Until now.

The church was empty, the still air laced with the scent of stale incense. He needed to fully investigate this place before engaging his DNA expert. The maternal line had been proven. Now he had to establish the paternal side.

He walked deeper into the nave and found the stairs down to the crypt. An iron grille barred the way, but the gate hung open. He descended the stone steps. Above, in the arch, was the carved image of the Pazzi coat of arms. Easy to spot with the two unusual sea creatures. Beneath, an inscription was carved into the stone.

ISTI SVNT VIRI SANCTI
FACTI AMICI DEI

The crypt was unlit, but he found a switch that activated a series of concealed incandescent fixtures that dissolved the darkness and revealed a multitude of tombs. The walls were a familiar gray *pietra serena* stone against white plaster with a barrel-vaulted ceiling.

All well maintained.

He counted. Twenty-three. The dates carved into the stone varied from the nineteenth to the sixteenth century. Everything was quiet and still. Spooky. How easy it would be to surrender to the peace and antiquity of this sanctuary of old bones.

But he had work to do.

He started to closely examine the tombs and found the one for Raffaello de' Pazzi who, as noted, died in 1725. He did the mental math off Anna Maria's year of birth and determined that she was fifty-eight when Raffael died. Did the accident happen before or after the birth? She then lived another eighteen years after his death. He gently caressed the limestone exterior, his fingers tracing the lettering. In French. *VOILA UN HOMME*. Here is a man.

"May I help you?"

He turned.

Standing at the base of the stairs was a young priest dressed in a black clerical robe complete with white collar. He'd not heard the man approach.

"What does the Latin inscription above the entrance say?"

"These are saint men who made friends with God."

"A bit bold, would you not say?"

The priest shrugged. "The Pazzi were never known for being modest. Are you a Pazzi?"

He considered the inquiry for a moment and decided to be honest. "I am not sure. I might be."

"We have many people who come here thinking they may be Pazzi."

Now he was curious. "And what do you do about that?"

A smile came to the young face. "Come. I will show you."

CHAPTER 50

Cotton spurred Leone forward as they passed the starting point and began lap two. He noticed the horse's ears were swept back, ready to listen to what he might have to say, so he obliged.

"Keep going," he called out in Italian, over the thunder of hoofbeats.

He had to trust Leone, since the horse knew this racetrack better than he did. His two antagonists stayed with him. He dug his knees into Leone, keeping his body moving in rhythm with the horse. The Tortoise and Panther jockeys worked in unison to impede his progress, bumping into him at regular intervals, swiping him with their crops. Suddenly, one of the jockeys ahead of him flew off his mount, landing atop the crowd in the center of the campo, disappearing into the bodies. The riderless horse broke into a long, loping gait and continued with the pack, momentarily accelerating without the weight of the jockey.

The Panther horse smacked into Leone's left side.

Enough. He slammed back. The jockey reacted and crashed down his right arm onto Cotton's shoulders.

"No jockey can interfere with the reins of another," Camilla said. *"But if that happens, the one interfered with can defend himself. Without penalty."*

He released his left hand from the reins and elbowed the jockey. The man seemed unfazed and returned blows with his crop. Cotton brought his left arm up, hand tight-fisted, pivoted upward and over, cold-cocking the Panther jockey with a solid cross, knocking the man from the horse.

One down.

THOMAS READIED HIS SHOT.

He'd followed Malone through the telescopic scope, from the starting point to the second turn, then around the third and fourth turns, back to a straightaway for the starting line. But the jostling and maneuvering of the horses was making things difficult. Ascolani had told him that the race happened at a frantic pace, and the man had been correct. He gently gripped the rifle that lay atop the table on its bipod. He liked how the weight had been shifted to the rear, creating a central balancing point. He'd already adjusted the cheek rest and raised the pads to more securely nestle the weapon into his shoulder. He had five rounds in the magazine, the threaded muzzle fitted with the high-pressure suppressor.

Plenty of ammunition.

The pack passed the starting point and made the first turn, now right below him, headed for the more treacherous second.

Back in his sights.

Close.

Perfect targets.

COTTON NOTICED THAT LEONE'S EARS WERE PRICKED FORWARD, THE horse now focused on the other animals. The pack had thinned, with several riders falling behind along with the riderless horse. He was surrounded by four other riders, the Porcupine just ahead of him.

They were in the second lap.

A lot was happening. Fast.

The second turn was again approaching. The Tortoise horse ran parallel on his left, toward the outside. Another horse and jockey to his right, near the inner rail. The Porcupine was still in front. He caught a sadistic smile on the Tortoise jockey's face right before the two horses collided. The other jockey reared up atop the horse and smashed his left boot into Cotton. Apparently, the Tortoises were unconcerned with disqualification, as that kick certainly qualified as "interference with the reins."

But he appreciated the aggressiveness.

Now he could defend himself.

"Keep us straight," he said to Leone.

He knew horses realized trouble long before their rider. So he was counting on the animal's intuition. He swung one leg up and readied for a kick. The Tortoise saw it coming and slowed his horse, bolting upright and readying his own kick.

Then the Tortoise jockey jerked back still gripping the reins. An almost unnatural move. Even for the Palio. The spine curved inward and Cotton heard a grunt of pain. There was a moment when the body froze in its pose, then the Tortoise's jockey let go of the reins and collapsed off the horse, smacking the track hard, before being trampled by another horse, which lost its footing and tumbled to the ground, hard, with its rider.

They entered the turn and Leone took them smoothly around, slowing slightly as they swung right.

THOMAS REALIZED INSTANTLY THAT HE'D MISSED.

The jockey of the horse beside Malone had unexpectedly come upright and blocked the bullet. He quickly readjusted his aim and brought Malone back centered in the scope's crosshairs. The horses were now past the third turn on the far side of the campo, a ton of people between him and them, only the jockeys' bobbing heads visible. He was three stories up, the angles were all wrong, and the small targets were moving fast.

He removed his eye from the scope and stared out the window.

He watched as the four remaining horses passed in front of the Palazzo Pubblico, disappearing below the crowd as they negotiated a dip in the track. Back up they headed for the final turn toward the starting gate. The jockey he'd shot had been removed from the track by men who rushed out to get him. It would not take long for them to discover the bullet hole.

The pack passed the starting line and began the final lap.

Shortly, Malone would be dead.

CHAPTER 51

ERIC HESITATED BEFORE FOLLOWING THE PRIEST, SAYING, "I CAME only to pay my respects."

"You said you might be Pazzi. Why do you think that?"

"My grandmother always believed we were half Pazzi."

"Such a noble family. Unfortunately, defined in history by one horrible mistake."

"Plotting to kill Lorenzo and Giuliano de' Medici was more than a horrible mistake," he told the priest. "It was stupidity."

"And the Pazzi paid for that. Dearly."

Indeed they had.

The family head Jacopo di Pazzi, Francesco di Pazzi, two of Francesco's brothers, a nephew, and seven first cousins were all hanged. Then the family lost everything. But all that changed in 1494 when the Medici themselves were exiled. Four days after that happened all of the Pazzi descendants, including their offspring, were exonerated and welcomed back to Florence, their right to hold public office restored. Not long after that legislation was passed proclaiming that the Pazzi, in trying to kill Lorenzo and Giuliano, had acted *out of zeal for the liberty of the people and city of Florence* and had been *unjustly condemned.* The family was allowed to sue to recover their land and belongings, their prominence somewhat restored.

Historians agreed that Lorenzo de' Medici was indeed something of a tyrant. Guilty of a multitude of sins that included the hijacking of Florentine foreign affairs, manipulation of government debt, tampering with the courts, purloining of public moneys, filling key offices with cronies, and debasement of the coinage. His form of Florentine government depended on compliance and cooperation, whether freely given, bought, or coerced. Didn't matter which. Granted, the oppressive political system had existed long before Lorenzo, but he made the most of what he inherited. So it seemed easy to say the Pazzi may have been justified, since political assassination was the norm for change in the fifteenth century.

He pointed at the tomb. "Can you tell me about this man?"

The priest nodded. "Raffaello de' Pazzi. An interesting individual."

He waited for more.

"A nobleman and politician," the priest said. "One of eight children, he grew up to own and manage several estates nearby. He married twice. Both wives died."

"Do you know the wives' names?"

He'd asked the question a bit too quickly and hoped the priest would not pry.

"I do not. But they both died young, that I do know. One in childbirth, the other from cholera."

He knew from the etchings on the tomb that Pazzi died at age fifty-five. So he asked, "Did he marry a third time?"

The priest shook his head. "Not that I am aware of. But that means nothing, since records from that time are few and far between."

Not an encouraging thought.

"Raffaello died tragically," the priest said. "In a carriage accident."

He recalled what Anna Maria had written. "No indication that he was intentionally killed?"

"None I am aware of. But I am no historian."

"Has this tomb remained inviolate since his death?"

"To our knowledge, for the past hundred years or so, yes. But it was opened before that. The wax seals placed there in the early 20th century, around its lid, are still intact."

He stepped close and examined the wax, which was indeed free of cracks. If it had been violated, that had to have occurred a long time ago.

"May I ask," the priest said. "What is your interest?"

He shrugged. "As I said, I might be half Pazzi."

"I am aware of who you are," the priest said.

Really?

"You are the secretary for the National Freedom Party. I consider myself one of its followers."

Interesting. "Then you know we are on the verge of controlling parliament. Our party leader will be the next prime minister."

"And you?"

"I will be a government minister. Interior. Education. Culture. One of those. Which means I will be on the council of ministers."

"How exciting."

"We will set national policy. And there will be changes."

The priest nodded. "I read the newspapers, watch television, listen to the commentators. This country needs a change."

"Then I ask your help in finding out if I am a Pazzi. Knowing who you are is always important. I have struggled with my identity for a long time. I want to know, for certain, from where I came."

Half true, at least.

Anna Maria had specifically pointed the way here. That could not have been for mere sentimental reasons. There had to be more. "You said a few moments ago that there was something you wanted to show me."

"There is. And it may help with your quandary. Please, follow me."

CHAPTER 52

Siena, Italy

Stefano had positioned himself where he could watch both the race and the Palazzo Tempi. The window was again open, but no one had appeared within the dark rectangle.

All quiet there.

But not on the track.

Ten horses started. Now only four remained with riders. Jockeys had been vaulted off their mounts, a couple seriously injured and carried off the track. Daniele had arranged for him to view the race from one of the other palazzos that ringed the campo, this one owned by a wealthy Tortoise. His was just down from the starting line, on the second floor, with a good view of the track over the crowd but not the best angle for the open window in the Palazzo Tempi. Several others were there with him, all crowded before the open windows. The American, Malone, was riding the Golden Oak's horse, and was still in the race. He'd not been able to spot Cardinal Richter but he had located Ascolani among the Porcupines in their designated bleachers.

The horses rounded the final turn and passed beneath him, headed back toward the finish line, ready for the third and final lap.

He'd watched as Malone had been confronted by both the Panthers and Tortoises, fending off one, then the other had fallen off his horse. The open window in the Palazzo Tempi continued to intrigue him. Thankfully, he had two of Daniele's men staked out on the front door, keeping an eye on the comings and goings.

Instantly available by phone.

COTTON COULD NOT GET THE LOOK FROM THE TORTOISE JOCKEY'S face out of his mind, especially the eyes. Their gazes had met for only an instant, but long enough for him to clearly see not the determination that had been there before, but fear. Pain. Surprise. Then the jockey had collapsed off the horse. The man's sudden reaction, jerking sharply upward, his spine arched inward, was odd for someone riding a horse, as you always tried to stay forward and low. But he could not focus on that. He was in the final lap and the Porcupine was within reach. He spurred Leone forward and closed the gap. Time was running out. The last lap would take less than thirty seconds to complete.

He had to make a move.

Another animal lost its footing and slammed into the track, tossing its rider aside. The horse whelped in pain and Cotton maneuvered Leone around the chaos. Only four horses were left, one of which had no rider. But the pilotless animal was slowing, dropping back, leaving only three to finish the race. They were now in a straightaway, heading away from the starting line, toward the first turn. Suddenly, Leone let out a low whelp and slowed. Cotton felt the horse favoring her front right leg.

Something was wrong.

They kept slowing to a bumpy trot.

The other two horses with riders, including the Porcupine, pulled away. He had to do something. Fast. He stole a quick glance behind and spotted the Giraffe's riderless horse about ten feet behind. He angled Leone so they were close to the animal as it passed. Leone was hurt. No question.

And the Porcupine was getting away.

"Come on, Leone. We have to do this."

The horse seemed to respond and mustered a last burst of energy that caused another whelp of pain. The riderless horse came parallel.

Now.

He leaped from Leone, grabbing the mane of the other horse, searching for the reins. The crowd let out a collective sound of shock. His body slid off the sweaty animal and his feet brushed the track, boots skidding along. He clung to the mane, then found the reins and pulled himself up, settling on the new mount.

The nostrils blew out a burst of exhale with excitement.

Cheering began at his success.

Leone, seemingly sensing her race was over, had fallen back. The horse beneath him seemed nervous, unsure about the new rider.

But they had no time to get acquainted.

"Let's go," he told the animal in Italian.

And he pressed his legs together, signaling for speed.

THOMAS HAD PATIENTLY WAITED AS THE RACE HAD TURNED PROgressively chaotic. Several horses had gone down, along with their riders. In other cases only the riders had been eliminated, one of whom had been from his errant gunshot. Malone was now right beneath him, but his horse was slowing, as if hurt. The angle for the shot was not right, as he was too far back from the open window to make any meaningful adjustment. To fire now would require him to lift the weapon from the table and approach closer to the window.

But that could risk detection.

And that was the one thing Ascolani had been emphatic about.

Draw no attention.

He raised his head and watched as Malone leaped from one horse to another. Now the American was spurring his mount forward, gaining ground on the remaining two horses. Only a matter of seconds before they all found the second turn and the best angle for the shot returned. He pressed his eye to the rifle scope and waited. He knew from the first two laps that there would be about five seconds when the horses would be in a short straightaway, headed for the third turn.

His opportunity.

COTTON SWUNG TO THE OUTSIDE, THEN BACK INSIDE. THE HORSE'S giant strides swallowed up the track. They were making up time, closing the gap. He took the second turn faster than he should, taking advantage of the horses slowing around the sharp loop. They came out of the turn and he found himself clumped with the other two riders, the Porcupine one horse over.

No way to get to him. No way to stop him from winning. He had no choice. Only one alternative remained.

Just win the damn race.

THOMAS FIRED.

And missed.

He readjusted and fired again.

Another miss.

Both rounds had found the dirt in the track. Malone was zig-zagging. Lots of unpredictable movement. He'd tried to anticipate where next, but failed. The horses were now around the third turn, again on the far side of the campo, out of reach. No more good opportunities would come for another try. Ascolani would not be pleased. But this entire endeavor had been questionable from the start.

Be smart.

He removed the rifle from the tabletop and broke the weapon

down, replacing it back into the case. He zipped the top shut and left it on the bed, per Ascolani's instructions.

He then closed and locked the window.

Time to leave.

COTTON'S EYES PRICKED FORWARD TO THE TRACK AHEAD, WHICH was pitted with hoof marks from the first two passes. He was hoping he had an advantage since this horse had been running jockeyless for at least a lap, maybe more. Which might prove helpful for some added stamina. He kicked his heels into the horse, spurring the animal on. He also pushed the reins forward, which sent a signal to go faster. He had no connection with this animal, unlike Leone, but he leaned in close and tried some vocal encouragement.

"Come on. Run. Fast. Run," he said in Italian, close to the ears, running one hand up and down the neck, the other clinging to the reins.

The horse responded, legs pounding the ground, and their speed increased. They rounded the final turn and thundered into the home stretch. About fifty yards to go. It was still not possible to take the Porcupine out. The only way to deliver on what he'd promised was to win the race outright. He and the other two horses were clumped together, moving in unison. He was on the inside, riding near the rails that separated the track from the crowd. The horse's powerful legs swept over the track, each step as sure-footed as the one before. Hysteria swept the crowd. Arms were raised, voices shouting, all in unison.

Thirty yards.

The Porcupine was to his left and just a few feet ahead, another horse behind him. Cotton kept pumping his thighs into his mount, urging more speed.

They swept past the Porcupine, into the lead.

He tightened his grip on the reins.

Ten yards.
The noise was deafening.
Five yards.
He leaned further forward and urged the horse to its limits.
Two yards.
Victory.

CHAPTER 53

ERIC WALKED WITH THE PRIEST.

They left the crypt and climbed back to ground level, exiting by a side door into the summer evening. A paved path led through a small garden to another building, which the priest unlocked with a key from his cassock.

"Over the centuries some of the tombs have been periodically opened and inspected," the priest said as he flicked a wall switch and the room lit up. "When that happened, these are the things that were found."

The room was filled with glass cases that displayed a variety of artifacts. Nothing overtly formal about the presentation, but its presence was unexpected. He stepped around the room and took a quick survey of the various artifacts. Lots of jewelry, clothing fragments, lace, combs, ornaments, a brush with no bristles. No gold. Silver. Or anything else of obvious value.

"We have never advertised the fact that we have this," the priest said. "Academicians know about it, and it has been mentioned in some historical texts. But the Pazzis are not the Medicis. So their graves were not littered with wealth."

He smiled. "No, they were not. Which, I suppose, was always the bane of their existence."

"Sadly, that is correct. The family seems defined solely by what a few criminals did nearly six hundred years ago."

"And the irony of it all was that what they tried to do had the opposite effect," he said. "The killing of Giuliano de' Medici and the attempted murder of Lorenzo de' Medici only created more Medici power."

Which was true.

And the old adage also seemed relevant. *History is written by the victors.* A dramatic account of the Pazzi attack, *Pactianae Coniurationis Commentarium,* was quickly published in 1478 that nearly sanctified the Medici. But that was unrealistic. The fifteenth and sixteenth centuries were brutal in Italy. Murder and mayhem common. War nearly an everyday occurrence. It was the time of Machiavelli. Eric's hero. Who wrote his favorite text. *The Prince.*

For Machiavelli people acquired power in five ways.

By conquest, virtue, fortune, crimes, or popular selection.

True, an election would be involved in the National Freedom Party's rise to power, but that ascension would come about only through skill and resource. According to Machiavelli, those who relied on virtue had a hard time rising to the top. Once there, though, they could easily become secure in their position. Why? Simple. They crushed their opponents along the way, which earned the fear and respect of everyone else. The virtuous were usually strong and self-sufficient, making few compromises with their allies.

Reforming an existing political order was one of the most difficult things to do. People were naturally resistant to change, and those who benefited from the old order definitely resisted that change. Those who stood to benefit from the new order were less enthusiastic in their support, as it was impossible to satisfy everyone's expectations. Inevitably, somebody would be disappointed. Which meant, according to Machiavelli, that a smart prince must have the means to force people's continued support, even when they had second thoughts, otherwise power would be lost.

Hence why he had to recruit the Roman Catholic Church.

"There may be something of interest to you," the young priest said.

His mind came back to the present.

And he was led to one of the cases.

"There, the second shelf, and a copper plate. It has writing etched into it."

He'd seen something similar before. When they'd opened Anna Maria's tomb there'd been not only a crown but a large gold medallion, one side showing her likeness and name, the other a sun irradiating the world with the words *DIFFUSO LUMINE*. Behind her head, engraved on a copper plate, was a Latin inscription of forty-four lines describing her good deeds and high character, the sorrow she'd borne in seeing all of her family die before her, and the fortitude with which she'd endured her disappointments and sorrows. Medici graves were full of such self-serving epitaphs. Apparently the Pazzi were no different, as here was another.

"We know this came from Raffaello de' Pazzi's grave," the priest said.

He studied the words.

VIRTUTES GENERIS MIEIS MORIBUS ACCUMULAVI. PROGENIEM GENUI FACTA PATRIS PETIEI. MAIORUM NUI LAUDEM UT SIBEI ME ESSE CREATUM. LAETENTUR STIRPEM NOBILITAVIT HONOR.

"Can you read it?" he asked. "I do not know Latin."

"It says, 'By my good conduct I heaped virtues on the virtues of my clan. I begat a family and sought to equal the exploits of my father. I upheld the praise of my ancestors, so that they are glad that I was created of their line. My honors have ennobled my stock.' "

He wondered who composed the epitaph. Anna Maria? Unlikely, considering the covert situation of their marriage and child. But whoever composed it obviously felt strongly about the man.

He noticed there were a few more of the copper plates in other cases.

"It was a funeral tradition," the priest said, "to place the copper plates inside the graves. These were removed long ago. What makes this one, from Raffaello de' Pazzi's grave, unique is that there is writing on the back. None of the others have that."

He was intrigued. "Can I see?"

The priest nodded and opened the glass case, carefully turning the copper plate and its stand to reveal more Latin.

"It's an odd paragraph," the priest said. "One that no one here has ever been able to understand."

"Could you translate it for me?"

" 'Ne'er will the sweet and heavenly tones resound, Silent be the one nature feared, and when he was dying, feared herself to die. Forever silent be his harmonies, only in his third son's bright world be justice found. *Auguror eveniat.*' "

CHAPTER 54

JASON WAS AMAZED.

Malone had won the race atop the Giraffe horse. According to the rules the Giraffes were the winners as their horse crossed first, and the bleachers where their supporters had watched the race erupted in elation as they emptied onto the track. Pandemonium reigned. People leaped the barriers that had blocked off the center of the campo, racing toward where Malone and horse had stopped. All of the other horses and jockeys were likewise being engulfed. Bells rang out in a peal of triumph.

"He did a good job," Camilla said to him. "The Giraffes will be thrilled. They have not won the Palio in many years."

"It is truly the oddest horse race in the world."

She smiled. "It is uniquely Sienese."

The others had fled the dais and plunged into the mayhem. The Giraffes were rushing the judge's stand shouting *"Dàccalo"*—give it to us. The Capitano del Popolo was lowering the pallium down to the Giraffe *capitano.*

"They will parade it through the streets to the Basilica of Provenzano for the blessing," Camilla said. "After that the festivities begin. They will go on all night and into tomorrow."

"Their jockey ended up on the ground."

"But their horse won, and that is all that matters."

Jason searched the crowd for Malone. He was somewhere among the tens of thousands of clamoring people. He'd also lost sight of Ascolani. Camilla reached into her pocket and removed her phone. She studied the screen for a moment, then motioned that he should read it.

The Tortoise jockey removed on the second lap was shot in the back. He's dead.

He was shocked.

"I suppose this has something to do with you?" she asked.

THOMAS LEFT THE PALAZZO AND DISSOLVED INTO THE WAVES OF people filling the streets. All those thousands who'd filled the campo were now flooding out. He'd left the rifle in its case and was now implementing the escape plan he'd developed last night.

After a quick meal at a nondescript café he'd walked the streets, finding a couple of the celebratory dinners being held across the city beneath lights and lanterns on streets doubling as dining rooms. He'd then mapped out the quickest route to the Church of Santa Margherita, along with a more circuitous way. Just in case. He did not like the masses of excited bodies all around him. Impossible to know if anyone was more than casually interested in him. In his line of work it paid to always be sure, so he decided to take the circuitous route.

His instructions were to use the train to head to Florence and await further orders. Leave the rental car where it was parked. He was not comfortable dealing directly with his employer. He preferred the layers of insulation. Change was not something he'd ever been comfortable experiencing. True, he never lived by habit. His line of work dictated a certain amount of unpredictability. Never do the same thing over and over. That would get you caught. But there were some things that should remain the same.

Like lines of authority.

He kept moving through the crowd.

STEFANO HAD BEEN IMPRESSED WITH THE AMERICAN, MALONE, changing horses at a full run and crossing the finish line first. Unfortunately, it had been for the Giraffes, not the Golden Oaks. There'd been a lot of contact among the jockeys during the race and he wondered if there'd be some disqualifications. Direct contact was generally forbidden, but there were exceptions. He'd also kept an eye on the Palazzo Tempi and its open window. But nothing unusual had occurred except that it had been closed just after the race ended.

He decided to head that way.

His phone vibrated in his pocket. A text. That told him a man had left the palazzo and was heading away on foot. He replied, asking them to stay close and keep him informed. An opportunity had presented itself so he headed straight for the Palazzo Tempi and found the front doors locked. On the off chance someone might be there, he banged the iron knocker several times.

No reply.

The two men watching the palazzo had reported no one in there except for the one man, who was now gone. No way to force the doors open. Too many people around for that anyway. So he headed around to one side of the building where a narrow alley separated the buildings and led toward the campo, blocked off at the far end to prevent anyone from entering. Windows lined the walls up three stories. Most were closed, but two on the first floor and one on the ground floor hung open. He approached the lower one and carefully peered inside to see a small furnished parlor. He gripped the stone sill and hauled himself up and in.

You had to be bold to get results.

That was what one of his instructors had taught him.

And he was definitely bold.

He walked carefully, his ears attuned to everything around

him. Noise from the crowds leaked in through the open windows. He found the staircase and climbed to the upper floor. He passed through a small wood-paneled room. Two windows at the opposite end opened out to the campo. Both closed. He stepped toward them and glanced left, where an open door led to a large bedchamber.

This was the one.

Both of the casement windows were closed.

The room was immaculate and everything about it seemed normal except for a canvas case on the bed. He stepped over and estimated it was about a meter long, cylinder-shaped. He reached down and unzippered the top. Inside was a disassembled rifle. He recognized the weapon. Not something amateurs would use. He glanced at the window, then noticed marks on the parquet floor that led from a point near the center to a table against the wall. It had been dragged over, then back. He'd already noticed that the rifle had an attached bipod. To rest on the table?

He stepped to the window and turned the latch, opening it just enough to peek out at the campo, which was still emptying of people. The view was expansive. The horses and jockeys were all gone. The banner too.

The Palio was over.

He closed and locked the window.

His mind raced with questions.

He heard a noise from below. The front doors. Their hinges squeaking as the heavy panels moved. The doors opened, then closed. Footfalls pounded on the wooden staircase.

Climbing.

He had to hide.

So he stepped over to a door that opened to a small walk-in closet. He slipped inside but left the door cracked so he could see past.

The footfalls stopped.

Then more steps through the small anteroom, coming his way. He stood rock-still and saw a man enter the bedchamber. No. Not just a man. A priest. In black garb. Pants. Jacket. White collar.

Maybe mid-thirties. Thinning brown hair above the ears. The man moved straight to the bed and shouldered the soft case.

Then he left.

Stefano waited, listening as the footfalls retreated.

The front door opened and closed.

He fled the closet and headed off in pursuit.

CHAPTER 55

COTTON KNEW HE HAD TO GET AWAY FROM THE CAMPO. CAMILLA had warned him that once the race was over there would be jubilation from the winner, but a lot of consternation from the losers. And there'd be nine losing *contradas*. A lot of bad feelings. Especially considering what happened during the race. The Panthers and Tortoises would not be happy.

Not in the least.

So he'd slipped off the horse and elbowed his way off the track. If he'd waited another few seconds he might not have escaped. He was wearing the black-and-gold livery of Golden Oak, which was like a neon sign providing a target for his enemies. It was not unusual for jockeys to be beaten after the race. In centuries past some had even been killed. Passions ran ultra-high for the weeks leading up to the race, and then during the race itself, so losing could sometimes take a violent tone.

His clothes were at the Golden Oak's headquarters, along with his cell phone and the gun that Richter had brought to him from Cardinal Stamm. He'd asked for the weapon and Stamm had delivered it sealed in a small box, along with some spare magazines. He needed to find Richter, then have Camilla Baines live up to her side of the bargain. Cassiopeia would not be happy with anything he'd been doing. Not one thing. He needed to call her. She was surely wondering what was happening. Their last call had been a short one. She was busy. He was busy. But she'd repeated what they always said to each other.

Don't be stupid.

And what he'd just done seemed the precise definition of stupid.

Now he was hustling for life and limb.

None of the flags angling from the buildings around him were black and gold. But he had a great sense of direction and he remembered the walk over, trying to emulate it on the way back. He also needed to report to Stephanie. She had to be wondering what he was doing. Maybe she watched the race? It had been televised live all across Italy.

She would not be happy either.

But she'd also want him to get the job done.

He and Stephanie had a long relationship. She took a chance on him when he was a young JAG lawyer. She brought him into the Magellan Billet and hammered him into a trusted field operative, demanding nothing short of the best. Along the way the Magellan Billet became a first-rate intelligence agency. Under former president Danny Daniels it had been the go-to agency for the toughest assignments. Not so much under Daniels' successor, Warner Fox. In fact, there'd been lots of friction, even a temporary suspension of duties for Stephanie for a few weeks, but all seemed okay now. She was back at the helm. In charge. Getting things done.

She was why he was here.

And the last thing he wanted to do was disappoint her.

JASON WALKED WITH CAMILLA BAINES AS THEY LEFT THE CAMPO. The streets were alive with Giraffes ecstatic at their unexpected victory. Camilla had already told him that the only disqualification would go to Malone for switching horses, which was not allowed, but the finish would stand as it unfolded with the Giraffe horse the winner. Malone's violation would not be passed on to the horse. Camilla could not have cared less. All that mattered was that the Porcupines had lost.

He followed her into a building about a hundred meters from where he'd watched the race. Jockeys filled the room. Their faces bathed in sweat, the colorful livery smeared with dirt, grime, and blood. Looks of concern filled their faces. Camilla had told him these men were all mercenaries, available to the highest bidder. Not given to emotion. Yet these men were clearly upset.

Camilla spoke to an older man then motioned for him to follow her. They entered another smaller room where a man lay still atop a table. Two other men stood beside it. Blood heavily stained the clothing. Camilla spoke to them in Italian. Unfortunately, he did not understand the language, which the Italian cardinals within the Curia many times used to their advantage. She motioned for him to come closer.

"This is the Tortoise jockey who fell from his horse during the second lap," she told him.

One of the men pointed at the body, and he saw a blood-soaked hole in the livery.

"He was shot," Camilla said. "The bullet went right through him."

He was shocked. The body lay supine, arms at the sides.

"Many things have happened to jockeys through the centuries," she said. "But none has ever been shot during the race."

One thought raced through his brain.

He stared at Camilla and she seemed to read his thoughts.

Was the bullet meant for Malone?

She shrugged, then said, "That is the question of the moment."

COTTON TURNED A CORNER.

He estimated he was just a few blocks away from the Golden Oak headquarters. The flags angling from the buildings were red and blue with white stripes. He also saw the panther, which informed him which *contrada* he was traversing. Not good. Considering what had just happened. Down the street he noticed how the flags changed to black and gold, signaling more friendly territory. People packed the route ahead. Slow going. Suddenly he was grabbed from behind and shoved to the right into a narrow alley. Three men waited there. Two more were behind him. All smooth-skinned, swarthy, skin tightly drawn over fine-boned faces. But it was the eyes, hard and cold, that betrayed their intent. All wore scarves with the Panther colors.

One of the men pointed a finger and said in Italian, "We owe you a beating."

He feigned not being able to understand and said, "No Italian."

Five to one. Not good odds. He knew in the weeks leading up to the Palio there were many icy relations between friends and competing *contradas*. Fisticuffs were common. But to prevent serious injury, the unstated rule was that everyone used only their open hands. These guys looked like they couldn't give a damn about that rule.

This was going to hurt.

CHAPTER 56

STEFANO BURST OUT OF THE PALAZZO TEMPI AND CAUGHT SIGHT OF the priest with the canvas case walking away. He was trying to assess the situation, thinking like an intelligence operative. He'd never known exactly why he'd been invited to join the agency, but he knew what the Entity looked for in its people. Excellent physical and psychological health. Check. Plenty of energy. Check. Street sense and a good intuition. Check. Copes well with stress. Check. Prepared to work wherever needed. Check. Inquisitive and action-oriented. Check.

He would add to that list.

Not afraid to use investigative skills. And able to develop a clear and concise picture of a situation. Which was exactly what he was doing. Of course, there were other parts of his training that were in conflict. Like the ability to follow his superior's commands and work as part of a team. On those two he was pushing the envelope. But a high-powered rifle? What in the world. Then a priest comes and hauls it off?

Unusual, to say the least.

His target was marching quickly through the streets. Not a moment's hesitation. Each turn taken with confidence. More of his training came to mind. *Don't run unless you are being chased.*

Walk slow. Head down. Use your ears not your eyes. Hear the pursuit. Never see it.

His job?

Make sure he was not seen or heard.

They were headed northward along a spiderweb of streets that formed Siena's tracery, away from the campo, the crowds beginning to thin. He could hear the shouts and drums of a victory procession from somewhere else in the city as the Giraffes celebrated, which should go on all night. Silence would reign in all of the other *contradas*.

They were headed toward the Stadio Artemio Franchi. The concrete stadium had been around since the 1930s and had played host to a multitude of entertainment and sporting events. More important, it sat outside the city walls where cars parked. Was this priest leaving? If so, he had no way of following. His men with the car left yesterday after tailing Malone from the horse farm to Siena. He'd been relying on Daniele's people ever since, and they'd done a great job.

He entered the Piazza San Domenico.

It was busy with tourist traffic from buses that parked near the stadium and used the many sides streets to venture deeper into Siena. Large clots of pedestrians seemed to paralyze one another. Two small green spaces, both with grass and Cyprus pines, broke the pavement around him. The priest walked fifty meters ahead and did not veer right toward the stadium. Instead, he headed straight for the red-brick Basilica of San Domenico that anchored a hill on the west side of the piazza.

Stefano stepped up his pace and closed the gap.

The church was famous thanks to the dismembered, mummified head of St. Catherine. Thousands came each year to see it. Add to that list a priest with a rifle, who now entered the basilica.

Stefano ran forward but stopped at the main doors, allowing a small group of visitors to head in first. He joined and used them for cover. Inside was a large aisleless nave first built by Dominicans in the thirteenth century. The walls were plain and oddly devoid of decoration.

Where was the priest?

His eyes raked the interior. Nothing.

To his immediate right, up a few short risers, opened the Chapel of Miracles. The priest with the rifle stepped up. Stefano shifted to his right toward a wooden pew that fronted a stone wall. The chapel sat recessed around a corner, behind three wide arches. From his angle he was invisible to anyone inside the chapel. He eased his way down the pew until he came to its end. He risked a peek around the corner and spotted Cardinal Ascolani standing before another wooden pew and greeting the courier-priest.

So much for the benefit of the doubt.

Ascolani and the priest spoke, then the priest handed off the rifle case to another priest who approached from the right. The first priest gave Ascolani a bow, then turned to leave. Stefano turned in the pew and shielded his face as the man passed. The other priest with the rifle case descended the risers and walked off down the nave, deeper into the basilica. He risked another glance back into the chapel and saw that Ascolani had taken a seat in the pew.

His phone vibrated in his pocket.

He checked the display.

A text. From the men following the man from the palazzo. He is in the train station buying a ticket for Florence.

He tapped in a reply.

Buy one too and stay with him.

Then another text appeared.

From Ascolani.

Please come to the Basilica of San Domenico immediately. I am in the Chapel of Miracles.

Eric immediately noticed a connection with what Anna Maria had penned in her diary—

Know the darkened world has long missed the night and day, which while the shade still hung before his eyes, shone like a guide unto steps

> afar. Ne'er will the sweet and heavenly tones resound, silent be the harmonies of his sweet lyre, only in Raffaello's bright world can it be found.

Then on the copper plate from the Pazzi grave had been—

> Ne'er will the sweet and heavenly tones resound, Silent be the one nature feared, and when he was dying, feared herself to die. Forever silent be his harmonies, only in his third son's bright world be justice found.

Both ended with *Auguror eveniat.*

I wish it will come.

And the diction and syntax of both writings seemed to suggest that the same person had composed them. It actually made sense that Anna Maria would create an epitaph to be included within her husband's grave. She had to be sending a message. She'd told her son that *the pledge was secured with two writings, one for Rome, the other for our family. I leave that pledge to you alone. It does not belong to the people of Florence. Instead, it rests safely under a watchful eye, and this verse will lead the way.*

Definitely a message.

He'd brought Anna Maria's writings with him. Those would stay within his exclusive control. Now he had to obtain what he'd come for.

"I must ask something of you," he said.

The young priest faced him.

"It is a matter of great importance that I be allowed to open the tomb of Raffaello de' Pazzi."

"Whatever for?"

"I need a DNA sample to confirm my blood connection to him."

The time was approaching 10:00 P.M. Late. Which he was hoping would work in his favor. He'd called his expert on the drive earlier, and the man said he could be there within an hour, no matter what the time.

But it all hinged on gaining access.

"I have discovered that Raffaello de' Pazzi married Anna Maria Luisa de' Medici. They had a child. A boy. Who is my distant ancestor."

"Why is it so important that you discover this connection?"

A fair question. No way he could tell this priest the truth. So he said, "I have wondered about this all my life. Recently, I was granted access to Anna Maria's grave, and the DNA sample I obtained proved she is my ancestor, on the maternal side."

"Is that not unusual? To allow a Medici grave to be opened outside of an official inquiry?"

"Most unusual. But who said this was not official."

He was hoping the lie might work.

"I would have to speak with the bishop," the young man said.

"Do you? Really? It would be better if this stays between us." He could see that the young man was considering his proposal. So he pressed. "It would take only a few minutes and be minimally invasive. I can have my expert here before midnight. We can be done and gone fast."

Hesitation remained.

"This crypt is not on the national registry, is it?" he asked.

"It is not. It remains a private burial site under the church's control."

"Then you can give permission for the inspection."

"Perhaps so. But I will still need to check with the bishop."

CHAPTER 57

THOMAS ENTERED SIENA'S TRAIN STATION.

Small, two-story, with five platforms. There was a ticket office, restrooms, a café, a small shop, and a pharmacy. It sat about two kilometers away from the Piazza del Campo, outside the city walls. People were still flowing out of Siena, headed home after the race, many from the train station. Thousands more, though, remained for the celebrations. Surely, Ascolani was aware that Malone had survived the race. The cardinal had not looked like someone who missed much of anything. He wondered what was next. Where was this headed?

The station was not crowded and the line for tickets short. He waited until his turn and bought a seat on the train to Florence leaving in forty minutes. Everything had to appear perfectly normal. Nothing out of the ordinary. The police were surely going to be involved once a shooting was discovered. Television cameras had encircled the campo, so there would be plenty of footage to review, not counting the endless amount of video the spectators themselves generated. Still, with all the movement and position shifting on the track, it would be next to impossible to determine where the shot had come from. So many windows had been opened to the race. Hundreds. Doubtful the bullet had lodged in the jockey, but if so that too would be useless as he assumed Ascolani would take care that the rifle was never seen again.

He decided to grab a quick bite to eat in the café while he waited for the train's arrival. Truth be told he was no fan of Italian cuisine. Too much pâté and garlic for his taste. He liked simple foods and was thrilled to see an ordinary hamburger on the menu. He ordered and settled into a seat.

His phone vibrated.

An incoming text.

Directorium Inquisitorum. Stand by in Siena. Do not leave. Back to you shortly.

The first two words were code to ensure that it was Ascolani sending the message. The cardinal had chosen the title of a famous fourteenth-century text that had been used as a manual of operation for medieval inquisitors. Fitting, he supposed. His reply likewise contained a code word.

Eymerich. Message received.

The book's author. Precautions were always appreciated.

There'd been a change in plans.

Okay.

A young man brought his hamburger, along with a soft drink in a bottle.

He had plenty of time.

So he ate slowly.

STEFANO HAD TO DEAL WITH TWO ISSUES.

The first was the man at the train station, so he slipped out of the Basilica of San Domenico, without Ascolani seeing him, and hustled toward one of the two green spaces that fringed the piazza before the church. There, behind one of the tall cypresses, he called the two men who were following the man from the Palazzo Tempi. He still was unsure what had happened at the palazzo, why a rifle was there, and if it had even been used.

"He's eating a hamburger," the man said.

"When does the train arrive?"

"Twenty minutes."

"Can you get somebody else there fast, who can go onto the train?"

"We can do even better. It's a direct ride to Florence. I can have somebody waiting there when he arrives."

"Do it. When does the train get there?"

"9:34 P.M."

About two hours from now. "Make sure he gets on that train. Keep me posted. I do not want to lose that man. You understand?"

"Perfectly."

He ended the call.

The second issue was Ascolani himself.

His boss was clearly in the middle of something way beyond the scope and scale of the Entity. Weapons were never sanctioned for use by any Entity operative. Not ever. They were an intelligence-gathering unit. Nothing more. Guns never factored into their operations. True, he was no stranger to weapons. The rifle he'd found inside the palazzo was a high-tech precision weapon, used by trained snipers for long shots. Like out an open third-story window to a crowded piazza.

But who was the target?

He checked his watch.

Twenty minutes had passed since Ascolani's text.

He'd give it another ten.

He casually entered the basilica.

It was nearing 8:00 P.M., but the nave was still open owing to it being race day. Too many people were in town to have the doors locked. He stepped inside, walked confidently past the pew he'd occupied earlier, and stepped up into the Chapel of Miracles. Ascolani sat in the same pew against the outer wall, head bent, hands folded in his lap, no one paying him the slightest attention. Stefano approached and took a seat beside his boss.

They both sat in silence for a few moments.

"It is right here," Ascolani said, "that Catherine first donned the habit of the Third Order of St. Dominic, consecrating her entire existence to God. Here too she would withdraw in prayer, fall into bouts of ecstasy, and lean right there on that octagonal pillar and talk to Christ."

Frescoes adorned the chapel walls, all of St. Catherine at various times in her life. One, he knew, was particularly important as it was created in the fourteenth century, when Catherine was still alive, so it might represent what she actually looked like. Which was rare for a medieval saint.

"Did you watch the race?" Ascolani asked.

"I did."

"The Porcupines lost, which means the American, Malone, fulfilled his promise to Golden Oak."

"Which was?"

"I told you about Camilla Baines. She wanted the Porcupines to lose. That happened. Now she will take Malone and Cardinal Richter to Santa Maria di Castello."

"What is it you want me to do?"

Ascolani stood. "Come with me."

CHAPTER 58

Cotton was no stranger to a fight. He'd been in many. Some he won, others not so much. These guys had come to teach him a lesson. The colorful scarves around their necks identified them as Panthers. Apparently, retribution came fast in the Palio. He'd never been one to shy away from a fight, so he readied himself to take the blows.

"We don't think so," a voice called out in Italian.

Five new guys had arrived in the alley who bore the black-and-gold scarves of Golden Oak.

Okay. The odds just got better.

The five Panthers seemed to consider their situation and decided that discretion was most definitely the better part of valor. They brushed past him with contempt in their eyes and disappeared farther down the alley.

"*Grazie,*" he said to the Golden Oakers.

One of the men motioned and said in English, "We take you to our place."

He was not about to argue.

So he nodded and followed them.

JASON STOOD OFF TO THE SIDE WHILE CAMILLA SPOKE TO THREE other men. Their conversation seemed intense. She was agitated. But who could blame her. A jockey was dead. Three others were seriously injured, one severely trampled. A lot of hurting. Some was to be expected. But not the gunshot. Apparently, that had never happened before.

Camilla finished talking and stepped over to him. The body remained in the other room behind a locked door.

"Those three are the *capitani* for the Porcupines, Tortoises, and Panthers. They are, to say the least, concerned. They are blaming me for what happened, saying our jockey broke the rules. They even think I had that man shot. The Tortoises have called the police, who should be here shortly."

"We need to find Malone?"

"I am told he's nearly back at our headquarters."

"This whole situation is escalating. Two people have now been murdered."

She looked puzzled.

"A few days ago a Swiss Guardsman was killed in Cologne, Germany."

"No one said a word about that before—"

"You agreed to help us?"

She nodded.

"Would that have changed your mind?"

"Perhaps. A jockey is dead. That may have been avoidable."

"Really? Yesterday you did not seem to mind what was done, so long as the Porcupines lost."

"We must go," she said, ignoring his insult. "I promised access to the monastery, and I always keep my word."

COTTON ENTERED THE HEADQUARTERS FOR GOLDEN OAK. THE PLACE seemed to double as an assembly hall and museum. The *contrada's* chapel was attached to one end. Winning banners from Palios dating back to the early twentieth century had been hung with reverence inside glass cases. Quite a few. Golden Oak seemed to have enjoyed a great deal of past success.

The building also came with a locker room where people could change and clean up. He'd used it before the race and now entered again, ditching his sweaty livery. He then took a quick shower and re-donned his own clothes. He checked his phone, and a text from Richter said he and Camilla were headed his way. He took the moment to send a text to Stephanie informing her that he was making progress. She would know that meant he was working the situation and did not require any assistance. No need to bore her with details. She wanted results and that was what she was going to get. He left the locker room and headed into the assembly hall. But not before tucking the Beretta that Stamm had supplied under his shirttail and pocketing the spare magazines. Not quite Magellan Billet issue, but it would do.

The doors at the other end opened.

Richter and Camilla Baines entered.

He listened as they explained what had happened during the race.

"I saw when that jockey took the bullet," he said. "That round was meant for me."

"Somebody is trying to kill you? Over me?" Richter asked.

"I assume whoever it is does not want you having my help."

"Why not just take me out?"

"Good question. You might have been next."

"How lucky for me."

Cotton faced Camilla. "When can we get inside the monastery?"

"We leave in half an hour."

Good to hear. No need to put anything off. Like the Cable Guy would say. *Let's get 'er done.*

"The police are dealing with the shooting," she told them. "I will be kept informed. And by the way, you were officially disqualified, though the horse you were on at the end is the official winner."

"The Giraffes should be happy," he said.

"To say the least. They have not won a race in a long time."

He checked his watch. 8:20 P.M. "It's getting late to visit a monastery."

"On the contrary. The late hour is exactly what we need. But there is something you both must know before we get there."

CHAPTER 59

THOMAS STEPPED FROM THE PLATFORM AND ENTERED THE TRAIN bound for Florence. He had no intention of staying aboard. His plan was to use the train to see if anyone may be following. The idea was to keep his actions both casual and expected, like eating a hamburger and enjoying a soft drink. Nothing had seemed unusual during his dinner. People had come and gone from the station, no one loitering. No one had followed him to the train either. The car before him was sparsely occupied. Less than a dozen people spread out among the seats. Not many people were traveling tonight. He walked through the car and entered the next, which contained even fewer people. He kept moving until he came to the last car, where he found the exit door and stepped back out onto the platform.

Which was also devoid of people.

A bell rang.

And the train began to ease its way from the station.

His phone vibrated.

He checked and found an incoming text tagged with the same coded identification.

Along with new instructions.

ERIC LEFT PANZITTA.

He'd decided not to attempt to force, coerce, or bribe the young priest. Let the bishop be contacted. That might actually work in his favor, sending more messages back to Rome. He was 99 percent certain that any DNA test would link him to Raffaello de' Pazzi. There really was no other logical conclusion. So at this point, the more attention the better.

Especially within the church itself.

He was also convinced that Anna Maria and Raffaello were married, and a check of the archives for the Basilica of Santa Croce might reveal definitive proof of a mid-eighteenth-century marriage, reinforcing what Anna Maria herself had written. But given the nature of this particular marriage, and its volatile political consequences, no record may have been entered. Which could present a problem. But he would have to take a look. Thankfully, access to Santa Croce's archives would not be an issue. They were open to all. From the diaries he knew when the two first met and when Raffaello had died. So the marriage had to have happened during that interval.

At this point, then, he had one thing left to determine. Where was the Medici copy of the Pledge of Christ?

Anna Maria had specifically pointed the way to her husband's grave, where she left a message. *Ne'er will the sweet and heavenly tones resound, Silent be the one nature feared, and when he was dying, feared herself to die. Forever silent be his harmonies, only in his third son's bright world be justice found.*

A puzzle? Clearly.

But where did it lead?

He had to find out.

STEFANO KEPT SILENT.

Everything about this situation seemed wrong. He was not some novice priest or rookie recruit who stood in awe of anyone and everyone who wore a red hat. Cardinals were to be admired, for sure. Most were good, decent men who worked hard and tried to do what was best. Most people did not know that cardinals had two jobs. First they were either high-ranking Vatican officials or the bishop or archbishop of a large diocese. Their day job. Being named cardinal added a whole other layer of more responsibility. A second job. One that connected them directly to the pope. They became bishops with special rights and privileges, the most prominent of which was their right to participate in a conclave to elect a new pope. Every cardinal, upon receiving the red hat, chose a motto, opening a window into their spirituality and priorities. The sayings were varied and usually intensely personal. Ascolani's was particularly unique. *Virtus in infirmitate.*

Power in weakness.

Perhaps irony was the point since Ascolani was anything but weak. Though he'd come to learn that the Italian loved for others to underestimate him.

But again, Stefano was no initiate.

And a lesson he'd learned early on in his Entity training kept repeating through his brain.

One night he and three other recruits were out late, enjoying themselves, and had not studied for a written test scheduled the next day. In the morning one of them thought of a plan. So they all went to the cardinal-instructor, an older man from Africa who'd worked with the Entity for decades, and said they had gone to a wedding the night before and, on their way back, the tire of their car burst and they had been up all night, in no condition now to take the test. The cardinal was understanding and offered them a retest in three days' time. When that day came the cardinal told them that it would be a special retest, with each of them occupying a separate classroom alone. They all agreed, since they had each prepared for the test by now and were ready. But this special exam came with only two questions. (1) Your name? (2) Which tire burst? Four options were offered. Front driver's. Front passenger's. Back driver's. Back passenger's.

He learned two things that day.

Take responsibility, and always tell the truth.

Sergio Cardinal Ascolani certainly had learned the first lesson, but not the second. He was lying. No question.

They had left Siena by car. Stefano was driving them through the dark Tuscan countryside to God-knows-where. Ascolani had not offered any explanation, nor had he asked for one. He'd received a text from the two men following the man from the Palazzo Tempi saying that he'd boarded the train for Florence. But an hour later another text had come that said the man had not departed at the end of the trip. In fact, he was not on the train at all.

They'd lost him.

"You have stayed quiet," Ascolani said.

"There is nothing to be said until you explain to me what we are doing."

"That is what I like about you. Never crossing the line. Always respectful of authority."

If Ascolani knew what he'd done over the past day, he might not be so generous with his praise. But he wondered. Was he being humored? Rocked to sleep? He wanted to ask about the man from the palazzo and the rifle, but knew better. He'd thought he was a step ahead on that count, but that was no longer the case. He should report what he suspected to Rome. But that presented a problem. His chain of command ran to the head of the Entity, then to the Secretariat of State. Unfortunately that was the same person. The only other place to make a report above that was to the pope himself. But he'd never get anywhere near the pontiff.

So he tried, "Where are we going in the middle of the night?"

"Santa Maria di Castello. To see the Carthusians."

"I thought you said that their records are closed to all, including the Vatican."

"They are. But I have found that people will bend their beliefs when it is in their best interests."

This man was the king of obtuseness.

"And you plan to show them it is in their best interest to share what they have?" he asked.

"In a manner of speaking."

"And if they do not see the wisdom of that move?"

Ascolani chuckled. "That would be a big mistake on their part."

CHAPTER 60

COTTON STARED OUT THE CAR WINDOW AND ADMIRED SANTA MARIA di Castello. The monastery looked like a medieval fortress, gray, walled, tower-crowned, isolated, and inviolate, seated nobly atop a hill overlooking a darkened wooded valley. Floodlights bathed the outer walls in a rich amber glow. He, Richter, and Camilla had left Siena with Cotton driving the car Stamm had provided to them yesterday. He was following her directions, heading toward the northeast, deeper into Tuscany.

They wound their way up on a road that clung to the hilltops and clamored along the narrow necks connecting them. Finally, they came to an open gate that formed a boundary between the monastery and the outside world and drove through. No other vehicles were there. Lights in the buildings were all off, the facility apparently closed for the night. A cowled figure in a white robe stood in the dark, illuminated only by the car's headlights.

They parked and exited.

Camilla approached the monk and spoke in a whispered tone, then walked over to where he and Richter stood. Cotton was still rattled and sore from the horse race, adrenaline coursing through him, keeping him on edge.

"We can have access now," she said.

She'd explained to them along the way that the prior had not sanctioned their visit.

"So we're trespassing?" he'd asked.

"We are... arriving uninvited," she said.

She'd also explained more of her connection.

The Chartreuse liqueur produced by Carthusian monks for more than three centuries had always been surrounded by a veil of mystery. Only two friars were entrusted with the recipe, which was inscribed on a seventeenth-century manuscript that was kept locked away. Over time the monks developed what would become their core product—a digestif known as Green Chartreuse. Yellow Chartreuse came later, lower in alcohol, sweeter in taste. The monks eventually developed a host of other alcoholic beverages, the sales of which had long provided a steady income to the Carthusian Order. About a million bottles a year, with annual sales of around twenty million euros. Half of the liqueur was exported, especially to the United States, the rest sold in Europe.

Which was where Camilla came in.

She facilitated those exports, along with providing huge swaths of farmland for the plants needed in production.

"Are we in trouble being here?" Richter had asked her.

"Only if we get caught."

JASON NEVER THOUGHT HE WOULD FIND HIMSELF INSIDE A CARTHUSIAN monastery. There were two in Italy. One north of Pisa, the other south of Milan. The Carthusians were a bit of an anomaly. They had long retained a unique form of liturgy known as the Carthusian Rite, and they had been resistant to the changes that had enveloped the rest of the modern Catholic Church. Rome had always left them alone. They were founded in the eleventh century, their motto part of their maxim, *Stat crux dum volvitur orbis,* the cross is steady while the world turns.

Their monasteries were generally small communities of hermits with a number of individual living cells built around a large cloister. The focus of Carthusian life was contemplation with an emphasis on solitude, silence, and humility. It took seven years for a brother to pronounce his final vows. The Carthusians were one of the best-run and best-funded monastic orders in the world, with charterhouses on three continents. Until yesterday he'd not been familiar with this site, which had stayed isolated and protected. Smaller too. Normally the charterhouses were huge complexes. Here, the main church stood across the courtyard, facing east as required. Beyond that living quarters would be arranged around the cloister. Next to the church would be the refectory, a typically elongated rectangle furnished with tables and benches. Close to the refectory would be the kitchen and storerooms. He knew there were no guesthouses. No need, as the Carthusians did not allow visitors. Which begged the question. How were they here?

"This place is only a repository?" he asked Camilla.

She nodded. "A distillery is located at the larger charterhouse near the Adriatic coast. They have other distilleries across Europe. This location is where their records and documents are preserved. Some say, but no one knows for sure, that the recipes for their famed liqueurs are locked away right here."

"It's that important to them?" Malone asked.

"So important that they have never copyrighted or trademarked their liqueurs, for having to reveal their secrets."

The monk stood silent in the dark, like a shadow.

Camilla motioned toward him. "He and I enjoy a close working relationship. We understand each other. But the prior and I are not as close. Thankfully, he is eighty kilometers away at the main charterhouse, near Pisa."

"And what would happen if he discovers our trespass?" Jason asked.

"I assure you, that would not be good."

COTTON HAD BUILT A CAREER AROUND NOT WAITING FOR THE RIGHT opportunity. Instead, he preferred to create it. But he'd never forgotten what his grandfather taught him as a teenager. He'd been asked to join the high school baseball team but had turned the coach down. His mother had not liked that decision at all and made her displeasure known to him.

His grandfather told him a story.

"There was a young man who wanted to marry a farmer's beautiful daughter. So he did what every good young man should do and went to the farmer to ask permission. The farmer looked him over and said, 'Son, go stand out in that field and I'm going to release three bulls, one at a time. If you can catch the tail of any one of the three, you can marry my daughter.' That sounded easy, so the young man stood in the pasture. The barn door opened and out ran the biggest, meanest-looking bull he'd ever seen. He decided that one of the next bulls had to be a better choice, so he ran over to the side and let the bull pass through the pasture and out the back gate. The barn door opened again. And wow, another big, fierce bull, pawing the ground, grunting, slinging slobber, came rushing out. Whatever the third bull was like, it had to be better than this one. So he ran to the fence and let the second bull pass through the pasture and out the back gate. The door opened a third time, and a smile came across the young man's face. The third bull was small and scrawny. This was the one. So the bull came running by and he jumped at the exact moment to grab the tail, then realized somethin'. The bull had no tail."

He'd gotten the point of the story.

Never let a good opportunity pass you by, as they seldom came knocking twice. Lost opportunities were only a gateway to regret. Which, more than anything else, explained why he'd ridden a horse in the Palio. What he was doing here, in the middle of the night, at an ancient monastery violating an assortment of centuries-old rules also seemed the precise definition of opportunity.

And he had no intention of allowing it to pass by.

But he was no fool either.

Not in the least.

CHAPTER 61

THOMAS SAT IN HIS RENTAL CAR, PARKED IN THE TREES, NEAR A PAVED overlook that rose high above a black landscape. He was to the southeast of Florence, northeast of Siena, within sight, according to the map on his phone, of a place called Santa Maria di Castello. A medieval fortress-like monastery, isolated and inviolate, seated nobly on a hill overlooking a dark valley with a Tuscan forest and vineyards. He was not a drinker at all. Part of that aversion came from his father, who'd loved to drink and then abuse his wife and sons. Drunkenness had been an everyday thing during his childhood, something he vowed never to repeat. So he avoided both drugs and alcohol.

He'd fled the train station in Siena and returned to his rental car. More instructions as to where to go came by text. No one had followed him. He was alone. Was he electronically tagged? Was his phone being tracked? Both were possibilities. Yet unlikely. He was so careful. What happened earlier at the palazzo during the Palio was perhaps the greatest risk he'd ever taken. He'd managed to leave Siena unseen, so perhaps there'd been no harm. But here he was, out in the woods, at night, alone, wondering what was next.

Headlights appeared from down the road, rounding a bend.

The vehicle drove his way, slowing as it approached, finally stopping at the overlook. A door opened and a man emerged, who opened the rear driver's-side door and removed a case identical to the one he'd earlier left on the bed in the palazzo. Was it the same one?

The man walked over and handed him the case.

"There is ammunition inside," the courier said, before returning to his car and driving off.

The phone Ascolani had given him vibrated with a text.

Stand by at your location. More instructions are coming. In the meantime, assemble your toy.

STEFANO AND CARDINAL ASCOLANI DROVE FROM SIENA TO THE VILlage of San Gimignano, one of the most recognizable and iconic destinations in Tuscany. Many called it the medieval Manhattan, thanks to the thirteen stone towers that loomed over the town and shaped its skyline. It sat on the ridge of a hill encircled by three walls with eight entrances, all dating from the twelfth and thirteenth centuries. The main streets crossed from north to south bisecting four open squares, all lined with shops and cafés that catered to the thousands of tourists who visited every year. No one was around at this hour, all of the buildings closed and dark. They stopped in the Piazza del Duomo and Ascolani climbed out.

He followed.

He was still waiting on an identification of the man from the Palazzo Tempi. Daniele's police sources were working on it.

Two more cars motored in and came to a stop.

Headlights extinguished.

The passenger-side door of the lead vehicle opened and a man emerged, who walked over to them. He was tall and lean, his features illuminated from the headlights all belonging to age. Gaunt cheeks. Coarsened hair. Tired eyes.

"Eminence," the newcomer said. "I came. As requested."

"I appreciate that, Prior. But it is for your benefit we are here. At this moment your repository at Santa Maria di Castello is being violated by outsiders."

"That cannot be possible. The lay brothers there would never allow that."

"I assure you, I would not have made contact with you if this were not the case. And it is not your lay brothers. Just one lay brother who is allowing the intrusion to Signora Camilla Baines. I believe you know who she is."

The prior hesitated a moment, then walked back to the car on the driver's side. The window lowered and there was a short conversation. A few more moments passed, then he returned to them.

"Forgive me, Eminence, but I am having that information verified. I am also wondering why you did not tell me this earlier, when you called."

"I prefer face-to-face," Ascolani said. "And frankly, so we are clear, I do not have to explain myself."

"And so we are clear, I am not subject to your authority or control."

"Really? Then you do not fully understand the extent of my reach. Your superior, the order's prior-general in France, and I are quite close. I may not be able to order you about, but he can. Should we call him?"

"Do whatever you want. You will anyway."

"I came here to help, not hinder."

"And what is your interest in this?"

"That is Entity business."

The door to the other car opened and the driver called out, "No one answers."

"Keep trying," the prior said.

Stefan knew that, like all monastic orders, the Carthusians strove for ascesis, work, poverty, chastity, obedience, prayer, and humility. But they also fiercely protected their solitude through limiting visitors and carrying out no outside apostolate work. No radio or television. The monks spent most of their time in their individual cells. Which was a misnomer. More like a little house. Two stories with a workshop and garden. Quite nice, actually. They could not leave their cells without permission, except on occasions expressly stipulated by the order's rule. Only the prior received news and made known to the monks what they ought to know. Carthusians withdrew from the world *to worship God, to praise Him, to contemplate Him, to be conquered by Him, and to give themselves to Him in the name of all.*

The internal hierarchy was simple. There were both fathers and lay brothers. Fathers were all priests or destined to be priests. The lay brothers were not, but they still bound themselves to the order, responsible for the smooth running of the charterhouses, performing all of the essential chores.

"Are there no fathers at Santa Maria?" Ascolani asked.

"All lay brothers, which might explain the situation. The lay brothers are not as disciplined. Signora Baines provides us with land and valuable services. She has always been respectful of our ways. I suggest we head there. Immediately."

"I could not agree more," Ascolani said.

The prior turned and headed back to his car, where he climbed inside. Engines revved in the two vehicles, but neither moved. Though the older man had made clear that he was not going to be ordered about, he also had not seemed eager to make an enemy of Ascolani. Especially considering that he'd been alerted to a heretofore unknown danger. Ingratitude would only compound the situation.

Ascolani motioned and they returned to their own car. Stefano cranked the engine and they drove off, leading the three-car procession.

"Eminence," Stefano said. "Why did you not just call the Carthusian charterhouse and tell the prior the situation? Allow them to handle it. Why was it necessary we come here?"

"Because, Father Giumenta, we need to give our intruders time to locate what may or may not be there."

He was beginning to understand. "The Carthusians would never allow you to look."

"Correct. They would accept the information we provided, then shut us out, dealing with it internally. Camilla Baines has access, so why not use that reality. It will take us nearly an hour to get to Santa Maria. More than enough time for her, and her two accomplices, to have a thorough look."

"And what happens if they find something and leave before we arrive?"

"Not to worry. I have that covered."

CHAPTER 62

COTTON FOLLOWED THE WHITE-ROBED FIGURE INTO THE MONASTERY.

They came in through the church's main doors, which were shut and, interestingly, not locked behind them by the lay brother. Richter dipped a finger into one of the stoups for holy water and crossed himself. The cardinal then genuflected toward the tabernacle at the far end, illuminated by a few dim night-lights. A bank of votive candles sat unlit off to the right.

Cotton spotted a stairway through an arch that disappeared downward. The nave before him was three-aisled and pillared with five bays. Thin and tall, classic Romanesque, with a touch of Gothic. No ornamentation. No statuary. Just plain stone and empty niches. The white-cowled brother did not say a word and kept walking down the aisle. Beneath his feet Cotton noticed that they were walking atop gravestones embedded into the floor. Surely brothers from long past. His senses were on high alert. He was deep in the unknown.

Enemy territory? No way to know.

But definitely uncharted.

The far west wall of the nave was pierced by clerestory windows that allowed in some of the moonlight from outside. He imagined what those colorful portals would look like when the sun streamed through onto the wooden choir stalls beneath. They came to the end of the nave and turned right before the main altar and headed for another door that the brother unlocked and motioned for them to pass through. There they found themselves back out into the night within the cloister. That door too was not relocked.

Interesting.

Did it mean anything?

Hard to say.

Cloisters were covered walkways that surrounded a central courtyard and connected all of the important rooms. For a Carthusian charterhouse the central space was oversized, full of gardens that could be seen in the ambient light washing through the passage. Arches lined the outer side of a wide corridor, a series of doors on the interior side, vaults arched overhead. They proceeded down across the rough stone floor to another door that was opened without a key. Inside stretched a long room with more vaults held aloft by squatty, unadorned columns that stretched in two rows. Once a low-vaulted hall, probably divided into smaller spaces by screens. Maybe a scriptorium? The room was filled with rows of shelving grouped in stacks of two, one after another, each enclosed within a glass cocoon. A soft hum signaled some sort of air quality control. Apparently the Carthusians stored their records with great care. Fluorescent fixtures hung from the vaults and illuminated each enclosure, which were numbered starting with 101.

"We have several rooms like this," the robed brother said, speaking for the first time in English. "Here are the records we possess from the sixteenth century."

Which seemed like a lot.

Something he'd once read came to mind. *The pomp of a palace may seem hollow and vain for it be the dwelling of one man. But no building can be too magnified for the hundreds of immortal spirits that dwelled inside a library.*

How true.

The brother said, "When Cardinal Ghislieri was sent into exile, he came here and stayed for six years until the Medici pope Pius IV died in 1565. In January 1566 Ghislieri was elected pope and became Pius V. He then returned to Rome, but left all the documents he brought with him years earlier here. Here they have remained. Unimportant."

Richter stepped further into the room and approached one of the glass enclosures. A sealed door allowed access on the short side. "How long have they been protected like this?"

"We upgraded decades ago. Each of the enclosures is temperature- and humidity-controlled. Some are fed by pure nitrogen to slow the decay process."

"This is not cheap to operate," Cotton said.

"Nothing worth it ever is," the brother said.

He agreed.

The robed man pointed toward a table at the far end. "What you seek is there."

THOMAS HELD THE RIFLE.

He'd reassembled it from its case and added a fresh magazine with plenty of rounds. He tested the scope and saw that a night-vision version had been substituted. Across the way from his perch, maybe half a kilometer in the distance, was the fortress-like compound of Santa Maria di Castello, its walls lit to the night. He leveled the weapon and sighted the main gate through the scope. No cars had come his way on the road. The last text he'd received had instructed him to park in the trees and stay out of sight. The night air was warm, the Tuscan countryside quiet as a cemetery.

He laid the rifle upright against a tree trunk and knelt on the hard ground. Prayer always seemed to calm him. Having his confession heard by Cardinal Ascolani had brought a measure of calm he'd not felt in a long time. He'd been honest and recounted all of the evils he'd participated in during the past few years, including multiple murders. Ascolani had sat dispassionate, unfazed by any of it, then delivered absolution and assigned a penance of four Hail Marys and two Our Fathers. Which he'd said.

He intertwined his hands, bowed his head, and said the prayers again.

A double penance.

What could it hurt?

The church taught that there was no sin, no matter how serious, that could not be forgiven. He assumed that to imply otherwise was a challenge to God's omnipotence, His mercy more powerful than any human ability to do evil. But people also had free will, along with the freedom to accept or reject divine mercy. But for sin to be forgiven, you had to admit your faults. He'd always found the parable of the Prodigal Son helpful. A son rejects his father, then squanders his inheritance. Once done, he returns home, admits to his arrogance, and begs his father's forgiveness. The father does not chastise the son or resent him. Instead, he welcomes the son back home, proving that no sin was greater than God's mercy, so long as we acknowledge that and seek forgiveness.

Not even murder.

A sound disturbed the silence.

Car engines.

He crossed himself, stood, and retrieved the rifle, staying among the trees out of sight. From the direction he'd come two sets of headlights appeared in the distance. He waited as the vehicles wound their way upward and roared past him, continuing down the road. He stepped out from the trees and watched as the headlights raked the asphalt and closed the gap to the lighted gate that led into the old monastery.

Then both cars disappeared inside.

CHAPTER 63

Jason could not help making comparisons between this storage facility and the famed Vatican archives. Both harbored caches of precious, one-of-a-kind documents dating back centuries. Both utilized high tech to minimize the effects of time, temperature, and moisture. Both kept their treasures to themselves.

"You are aware of what we are after?" he asked the lay brother.

"I explained earlier today what Cardinal Stamm told me," Camilla said, "and asked them to make a search."

"And you are just now telling us this?" Malone asked.

She shrugged. "I did not see the need. Unless something was found."

Which apparently had happened.

"Cardinal Ghislieri removed a great deal of documents from the Vatican in 1559," the lay brother said. "He was angry and disillusioned. He'd headed the Inquisition for many years and amassed a great deal of enemies. We have long studied what he left with us, and he definitely was looking for things that could be used against the Holy See."

"When he took all that, he never thought he would be pope," Jason said. "But what happened when he was chosen? Why did he not have the documents brought back to the Vatican?"

"We have no idea. All we know is that they never were removed from here."

"It could have been that Pius V kept some private insurance for himself," Malone said. "He had control of these documents, and he kept it that way."

"That was our assessment too," the lay brother said. "Then, once Pius died in 1572, they were forgotten by Rome."

"But not by the Carthusians," Jason noted. "You seem to have taken your caretaker duties quite seriously."

"This location holds most of the historical records for the Carthusian Order, along with our accounting ledgers dating back centuries. We pride ourselves on good record keeping."

That he could believe.

It had been Bruno of Cologne, a highly respected eleventh-century scholar, wearied of the political aspects of his role as canon of a cathedral, who led six followers into the Chartreuse Mountains outside of Grenoble, France. There, Bruno and his companions built small log cabins in a semicircle in an Alpine valley four thousand feet above sea level, which became the first charterhouse, later known as La Grande Chartreuse. There were now twenty-one Carthusian monasteries around the world, each perceiving itself as a *desert,* where God drew His people to speak to their hearts. Carthusians lived stripped of comforts and consolations. Isolation was their mantra. Yet here was a lay brother voluntarily interacting with outsiders.

Doing the unthinkable.

"Why are you doing this?" Jason asked the man.

"I am not a father of the order," the man said. "I am not bound by their vows. But I have pledged to devote my life in their service. To operate this facility and accomplish my tasks requires resources. Signora Baines has been most helpful in providing those. She asked for this favor, so I granted it."

A straightforward answer to a simple question. So he asked another. "You said what we want is on that table. What is it?"

"The stories in the history books are true. A loan was made

in 1512 to the Holy See by the Medicis. Ten million gold florins. Secured by a Pledge of Christ."

COTTON MADE HIS WAY ACROSS THE REPOSITORY TOWARD THE TABLE. Sitting atop the pitted wood was a piece of vellum, brown and brittle, about a foot square. The lines of writing were written in a tight scrawl, the black ink faded but legible. It lay inside a stiff plastic sleeve, half an inch or so beneath an elevated sheet of glass that acted as a protector.

He studied the writing. Latin.

The others gathered around the table.

"Can you read it?" Cotton asked the lay brother.

The man nodded.

And they listened as he translated.

In the name of our Lord Jesus Christ let it be clear to all reading or hearing these presents that we, Julius II, Bishop of Rome, Vicar of Jesus Christ, Successor of the Prince of the Apostles, Supreme Pontiff of the Universal Church, Metropolitan Archbishop of the Roman Province, Servant of the Servants of God, has accepted ten million gold florins provided by God's humble servant, Giuliano de' Medici. Desiring to make this act appeasable to the Lord we bind ourselves and the Universal Church to return the full sum to Giuliano de' Medici, his heirs, successors, and assigns, no earlier than twenty years from this date. We are grateful to be served worthily and praiseworthily by our faithful one which, out of the abundance of piety which exceeds the merits of mere suppliants, we shall repay in a sum much greater than any he be capable of earning. To that end the said repayment shall be accompanied by a gift, to acknowledge and thank such extraordinary generosity, equal to ten percent of the outstanding balance for each year since the date noted herein. We offer this gift freely and voluntarily, with our sincere thanks, and know that the Universal Church will always and forever honor this pledge without challenge or protest. We trust in the mercy of Almighty God, and the merits and intercessions of the blessed saints, to ensure that this pledge survives for the present and eternal times until fully satisfied. We have caused the faith and testimony of each and every one of the forgoing promises to be made in the name of Christ and on behalf of Christ, in duplicate. On this we, Julius II, do solemnly swear upon our oath given before God, in this year of our Lord one thousand five hundred and twelve, on the sixteenth day of the month of July.

At the bottom, beneath the single paragraph, were the words *Fiat et Petut,* then beneath those a simple letter G.

He asked the lay brother about both.

"Julius was one of those rare popes who did not change his name. Julius, or Giulio in Italian, was his given name. At that time it was common to sign any document using the first initial. Here, the pope wrote in his own hand *Fiat et Petut,* let it be done according to Peter, then added the G. There are other documents from that time he signed identically."

There was also one other mark.

A strange one too.

He pointed and asked about its significance.

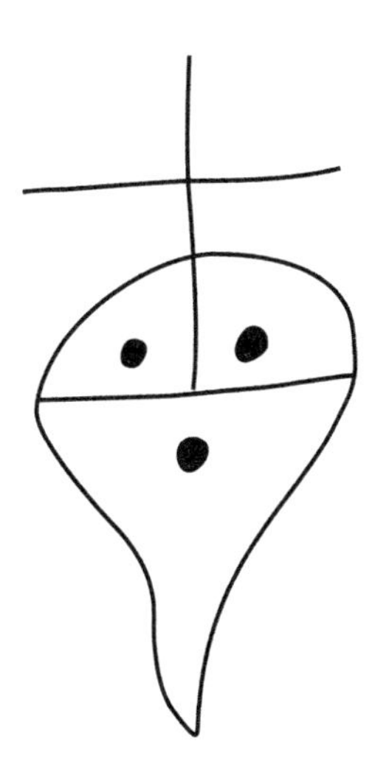

"It's the medieval mark of Banco Medici, used for authentication of their documents," the lay brother said.

"Which means this is authentic?" Richter asked.

"It does."

Which meant Cotton was looking at a five-hundred-year-old I-owe-you, payable *to Giuliano de' Medici, his heirs, successors, and assigns.*

"That debt remains unpaid?" Camilla asked.

"It does," Richter said. "It would amount to hundreds of billions of euros in today's currency thanks to that 10 percent 'gift' added to the balance for 513 years. It is a sum the church could never repay."

"Incredible," Camilla said.

"But meaningless," Cotton made clear, "unless you are an heir, successor, or assign of Giuliano de' Medici."

"Eric Casaburi thinks he is a descendant of Giuliano de' Medici," Richter said.

If that was true, what was heretofore a historical curiosity would become a binding legal document. Its terms were clear. *The Universal Church will always and forever honor this pledge without challenge or protest.* Cotton had not been a practicing lawyer for a long time. When Stephanie Nelle recruited him for the Magellan Billet, she'd liked the fact he had a law license, but during his dozen years on the government payroll there hadn't been many occasions to really use it. But that did not mean he'd forgotten what he'd been taught. The document lying on the table, safe under glass, was a promissory note, due on demand, to the bearer, provided that bearer was an heir, successor, or assign of Giuliano de' Medici.

He heard vibrating.

Camilla reached into her pant pocket and retrieved a phone, studied the screen for a moment, then slipped it back into her pocket. She nodded to the lay brother, who turned and walked back to the door, leaving the repository. Unlike the young man who wanted to marry the farmer's daughter and passed on two perfectly good bulls with tails, Cotton had no intention of allowing any opportunity to escape.

Much less two.

CHAPTER 64

THOMAS HAD WATCHED AS TWO CARS ENTERED SANTA MARIA DI Castello. He'd stayed at his post, as ordered, rifle nearby, back propped against the tree. There was a feeling of comfort here in the blackened woods, a velvet sky overhead, only the stars watching him. A three-quarters moon hung in a western sky that did little to dissolve the darkness.

He'd been at the church's disposal for the past nine years, working assignments around the world. Nigeria had been his first, where Christians were targeted by the Boko Haram insurgency, Fulani herders, and the local bandits. In the diocese of Minna a priest was burned to death and another injured. He'd been sent to extract a measure of retribution and had with the assassination of several key officials. He'd slipped in and out of the country, wreaking havoc, with none the wiser as to his identity.

In India, a Hindu nationalist government had curtailed the rights of all Christian faiths. Thousands of Catholics were being arrested and held without trial. Open harassment was common with more subtle pressures, including daily abuses at workplaces, schools, and public facilities. He'd been dispatched to apply some reverse pressure—five unexpected deaths—that helped persuade a few important officials that a change in policy might be in order.

In the Middle East and the Sahel region in Africa, due to jihadist insurgencies, Christians were in constant jeopardy. He'd helped there some, but the extent of the persecution was too much to effect any meaningful change. In Myanmar, thanks to a military coup, the ruling junta's army had been targeting churches, especially Catholic ones. He'd been sent to the diocese of Mandalay where the Tatmadaw burned down a historic church. After the arsonists were identified, and nothing was done to them, he killed three.

Many other places had required his attention and he'd visited Burkina Faso, Mozambique, Colombia, Comoros, and Nicaragua. Two passages from Corinthians were his mantra. *No believer should suffer alone* and *if one part suffers, every part suffers with it, if one part is honored every part rejoices with it.*

Amen.

A few minutes passed in silence.

More engines could be heard in the distance.

He turned.

Three more cars were coming down the road, headed for the monastery. They passed by at a high speed and kept going, also disappearing inside the gate in the wall.

Plenty of visitors tonight.

Still no further instructions.

So he stood.

And waited.

STEFANO CLIMBED FROM THE CAR WITH ASCOLANI.

The prior emerged with four more Carthusians from the other two vehicles. None of them wore white robes, as the fathers normally were required to do. All were dressed in street clothes.

Which was telling.

They were now inside the walls of Santa Maria di Castello. Ascolani had explained on the trip from San Gimignano how the Carthusians lived by an old maxim. *Cartusia sanctos facit, sed non patefacit.* The charterhouse makes saints, but does not make them known. Which clearly enunciated the low profile the order had always maintained. Ascolani also explained how Santa Maria was suppressed by Napoleon in 1809, closed off, but that it returned later in the nineteenth century. Its greatest challenge came in 1944 when German troops broke in to arrest thirty-two partisans and Jews being sheltered by the fathers. Some were able to escape, but six monks and six lay brothers were arrested, tortured, and killed by firing squad. None of which had even been widely known until the past decade. More of that low profile. By all accounts the Carthusians were men of honor who cared little for the outside world, other than to profit from it through their liqueurs. So what were they doing in the middle of this fray?

Three other cars were parked in the courtyard.

The prior marched off into the night. Not toward the church, but to another gate that was open. Before heading off with the rest of them, Stefano checked the hoods of the other three vehicles. Warm. Apparently, the information about an unauthorized intrusion was true. They walked a concrete path that led to another door, which the prior opened with a key from his pocket. Inside was an office equipped with three desks. No phones. No computers. But there were several wooden filling cabinets. One of the men reached for a light switch on the wall.

"No," the prior said. "Leave them off."

Windows filled the wall opposite the entrance door. Stefano assumed those looked out into the dimly lit cloister.

A pop disturbed the silence.

Muffled.

From outside.

Gunshot?

CHAPTER 65

Cotton had fully surveyed the cavernous workroom. Fourteen rows of shelving. Fourteen overhead fixtures within glass enclosures beneath. Two entry doors, the one they'd first come through and another, past the table where the pledge was displayed at the far end. Both lockable from the inside with iron latches. A bank of four switches protruded from a silver junction box attached to the stone wall, conduit running from it up to the vaulted ceiling then over to each of the light fixtures. These buildings were erected long before there was electricity or indoor plumbing, so their later occupants had to add those amenities however possible. One other nod to modernity was a fire alarm switch that had its own conduit running upward, disappearing into a hole in the stone. A fire extinguisher was attached to the wall both here and near the other door. Fire was most definitely a fear in an olden place like this.

Thankfully his bullshit radar had gone to full alert from nearly the first moment he met Camilla Baines. Stamm had warned them. So he'd taken those words to heart. Her proposal that a perfect stranger with no experience ride a horse in what many considered the most perilous race in the world seemed questionable at best, downright suspicious at worst. But what choice had he possessed? So he did his job and took a chance. But he'd also thought ahead and decided being unarmed was not the smartest of moves. The Beretta remained nestled close to his spine beneath his shirttail. He'd also caught the unspoken contact between the white-robed brother and Camilla. A familiarity, where their eyes did the talking.

The lay brother had left for a reason.

None of which would be good for him or Richter.

Camilla had drifted away from the table back toward the door at the other end of the room. He stepped close to Richter and whispered, "Get close to the door behind us. Be ready to open it and leave."

"When?"

"You'll know."

The door at the other end creaked open and four men entered. Faces he'd seen before. Part of the five who helped him out earlier in the alley. Golden Oakers. Surprise. Surprise.

"I will be taking that document," Camilla said.

"You think it's going to be that easy?" Cotton asked.

Camilla shrugged. "I do not see why not."

JASON HAD BEEN A PRIEST THE VAST MAJORITY OF HIS LIFE. HIS YOUTH in Germany had been comfortable and sheltered. He was one of three children to parents whose family had been expelled from East Prussia at the end of World War II. His father was a local teacher and his mother a librarian. During his high school years he lived in a Catholic student home. Had there been bullies? Absolutely. But he'd never engaged them. Instead, he'd used wits and words to wiggle out of things. He'd continued that practice after being ordained and definitely after acquiring a red hat and being brought to the Vatican. You needed a keen survival sense to work within the Curia, an instinct to know, according to the old American song, *when to hold 'em and when to fold 'em.*

He loved poker. Fun game. Where you needed to pay attention. Like here. Was Malone bluffing with a pair of twos or calling with a straight flush? The box Cardinal Stamm had him deliver to

Malone was no token of appreciation. Best guess? Knowing both Stamm and Malone? A gun. Had to be. And though he himself had never been in a physical fight, Cotton Malone definitely had experience. But four against one? Two, if he counted himself? Those were not good odds. And a pair of twos never, ever beat a straight flush. Malone had told him to stay close to the door and be prepared to move. Okay. He was ready.

"What's your interest in this?" Malone asked Camilla.

"I have learned that Eric Casaburi is in great need of that pledge."

"Stamm tell you that?"

"Never. That man is tight-lipped, careful with his words. But there are others in Rome who are not. I made some calls."

"I bet you did."

She's an opportunist. Not to be trusted.

That she was.

"Casaburi is quite the politician," Camilla said. "Some believe his party has an excellent chance of controlling the government after the coming elections. If that happens, he will definitely be a part of that new government."

"So you're trying to get in on the ground floor?"

"Something like that. I like what the National Freedom Party says. We need big changes. Italy is stalled with nothing. I am told Casaburi wants the church's help with his party's candidates being elected, which they refused. Maybe now they might reconsider."

"He knows this copy of the pledge exists?"

"He does now. I sent him a picture. My friend, the lay brother who allowed us inside, provided it to me earlier today."

Jason was curious. "Why wait? Why even bring us here?"

"She had to see it for herself first," Malone said. "To be sure it was real."

"Quite correct."

"She also wanted the privacy this place affords to deal with us?" he added.

"Doubly correct."

And she motioned.

The four men standing behind her advanced. Malone reached back and brought out the gun from beneath his shirt, aiming with his outstretched right arm, finger on the trigger, his thumb cocking the hammer back with a clear click.

Which halted the men's advance.

"Come now, Signore Malone, do you plan to shoot us all? Here, in this holy place."

"I'm actually not opposed to doing that. But there's no need."

And Malone swung the gun around and fired a round directly into the junction box for the overhead lights. Electrical sparks exploded in blue flash. Then the room was plunged into darkness.

"Let's go," Malone said.

Jason knew what to do and released the latch on the door. They both stepped out into the night. But before leaving Malone grabbed the pledge in its plastic sleeve and yanked the fire alarm switch downward.

A klaxon wailed.

STEFANO STOOD SILENT. BUT HE AGREED. WHAT THEY'D JUST HEARD was a gunshot.

"Sir," one of the men said, getting the prior's attention.

They all moved toward the window. Across the cloister, past the line of arches, two figures emerged from a door and rushed ahead, winking in and out as they traversed the dim cloister.

An alarm went off. Loud.

"Get them," the prior said.

The other three men exited out a second door from the office.

"What is happening here?" the prior muttered over the noise, still staring out the window.

"Apparently," Ascolani said, "you have some dissension in your ranks."

"How wonderful of you to note the obvious. The question is why."

CHAPTER 66

ERIC WAS HAVING TROUBLE SLEEPING.

He'd returned to his parents' house in Varallo, his grandmother and the nurse down for the night. He'd wanted to head back to Florence but he was tired, the hour was late, and Florence was another hour away. The day had been one of the most momentous of his life. He now knew who and what he was.

A Medici.

No. More than that.

A Medici in the royal line that traced all the way back to Cosimo de' Medici, Cosimo I, who traced his heritage back to Giovanni di Bicci de' Medici, the founder and originator of the Medici Bank. Cosimo I ruled for thirty-two years and was an ardent supporter of Pope Pius V who, in 1569, declared him the first Grand Duke of Tuscany. For the next 168 years a Medici sat on the throne. Francesco. Ferdinando. Cosimo II. Ferdinando II. Cosimo III. Gian Gastone. All Medici. Gian died without heirs, which ended the Medici hold on the duchy with Gian's sister, Anna Maria, hiding her legitimate, royal Medici heir.

Then there was the Pledge of Christ itself.

On the drive back from the Pazzi crypt he'd received a text from a woman named Camilla Baines, who lived in Siena. Being ever cautious, he'd asked for and received information on her. She was a known commodity. A successful entrepreneur who'd made a sizable fortune from the pharmaceutical industry. Not noted as overly political, she had supported several of the local candidates and had expressed support for the National Freedomers. Siena's district for parliament's lower house was one of the thirty-eight the party wanted to turn their way. Baines clearly was a woman in the know, as she'd been quite blunt in her message.

You are looking for a Pledge of Christ granted by Julius II to the Medici. I have it and the attached photograph proves that. We should talk.

Sure enough a high-resolution image was included that showed an olden document written in Latin. But Baines had included a translation to Italian that evidenced *Ten million gold florins provided by God's humble servant, Giuliano de' Medici* to the Universal Church, the way Catholics referred to themselves before the Protestant Reformation. Due no earlier than July 16, 1532, along with something else. No Christian in the sixteenth century, much less a pope, would ever acknowledge the payment of interest. That was a mortal sin. *To that end the said repayment shall be accompanied by a gift equal to ten percent of the outstanding balance for each year since the date noted herein. We offer this gift freely and voluntarily, with our sincere thanks, and know that the Universal Church will always and forever honor this pledge without challenge or protest.*

But who could collect?

Giuliano de' Medici, his heirs, successors and assigns.

He'd already checked. Giuliano, who lived from 1479 to 1516, was also in the direct line of succession from Cosimo I back to Giovanni di Bicci de' Medici.

Was there an end date for collection?

No.

We trust in the mercy of Almighty God, and the merits and intercessions of the blessed saints, to ensure that this pledge survives for the present and eternal times until fully satisfied.

Perfect.

Interestingly, the pledge spoke of duplication. There were two. *We have caused the faith and testimony of each and every one of the forgoing promises to be made in the name of Christ and on behalf of Christ, in duplicate.*

And he was staring at the church's copy, found, according to Baines, within a nearby Carthusian monastery. He'd made a quick calculation based on the gold content of ten million florins of the time, their worth today, along with the yearly gift compounded, and come out with hundreds of billions of euros.

All good.

Which helped temper the bad news that had also come his way.

He lay in the bed, his gaze locked on the ceiling.

His pollsters had sent an email earlier that indicated the National Freedom Party's 60 percent support had waned a bit, down 3 percentage points, especially in the south of Italy. Those thirty-eight seats in parliament were becoming more difficult to secure. They needed the party leaders back on the campaign trail, doing what they did best. Stirring up emotions. Cementing support. Raising money. Every day of the soon-to-start official campaign season had to count.

Italian politics had always been shrouded in mystery and scandal. Its political system had remained largely the same since 1947, but its electoral laws changed frequently. New parties emerged as quickly as they disappeared, and controversy and corruption were commonplace. So much so that the people had become anesthetized. Apathy was at an all-time high. General elections decided the composition of both the lower house, the Chamber of Deputies, and the upper house, the Senate. Every Italian over the age of eighteen was eligible to vote, but strangely the voters themselves did not select the most powerful person in government, the prime minister. Rather, he or she was chosen after the new parliament convened and a candidate had won both a confidence vote from the Deputies and the president's personal approval.

Governments collapsed with alarming frequency. There'd been

sixty-eight different ones in the seventy-nine years since the republic was formed in 1947. The nation's socioeconomic frailties, owing to a fragmented cultural heritage, a stark north–south divide, and overreliance on external financial support, exacerbated things. Even worse, the country's political landscape had grown more volatile in the past few years. Violence was not out of the question. Achieving a working majority government had risen to the level of a near impossibility. His party wanted to change all that. With 60 percent support they had a chance. What they could not afford was for the Catholic Church to stay neutral or, even worse, to back other candidates. To make sure that did not happen he needed to speak with Camilla Baines. But both calls he'd made to her had gone to voice mail.

The hour was late.

Nearing midnight.

He'd try again, first thing tomorrow.

CHAPTER 67

COTTON HOPED THE FIRE ALARM HAD THE DESIRED EFFECT AND roused everyone inside the monastery from their sleep. The more the better. He was counting on the lay brother who'd allowed them inside to be working alone, and that he could find some allies among the remaining residents.

He led the way as he and Richter hustled back toward the front of the complex, past the door where they'd first entered the vaulted storeroom. Their car was parked in front, outside the church in the main courtyard. Get there and they had a chance of outrunning any pursuers. Across the cloister he heard another door open. Through the dimness he spotted three men rush out, headed their way.

Fast.

Richter saw them too and asked, "What do we do?"

No question. "Into the church and let's get out of here. No time for pleasantries."

The iron lock clicked open on the first try and he shoved the leaden oak door inward, then closed it. No lock was on the inside. The three men would be there in a less than fifteen seconds. Friend or foe? No time to find out. They turned into the center aisle and headed for the main doors at the far end. The iron latch on the door behind them engaged. Was it the Golden Oakers? Or the others they'd seen? They would not make it out before company arrived. He searched the darkness and spotted the stairs he'd seen earlier to the right. A pallid glow strained from below.

He headed for them.

"Where are we going?" Richter asked, trying to catch his breath.

He pointed. "Down there."

They descended into the crypt, a cold cloud of worry filling him. An iron gate opened into a three-naved wide space. The ceiling was low-vaulted, a small rectangular altar niche to the right. Three medieval stone sarcophagi topped with immense slabs of carved granite lined the center. The only break in the darkness came from a tiny yellow light near the altar that illuminated only a few square feet. The rest of the space remained in shadows, the air stale, fetid, and noticeably chiller.

Footsteps bounded across the marble floor above.

His eyes, alert and watchful, shot to the top of the low vault not two feet from the crown of his head. He signaled for quiet and led Richter across the crypt into the far nave. He handed over the pledge, gripped the Beretta, and searched the darkness. In a small apse about twenty feet away he saw the image of an iron candelabrum. He crept over. The ornament stood about five feet tall, a solitary wax candle, about four inches thick, rising from the center. He grabbed the stem. Heavy. And brought both back with him to where Richter stood. He handed over the candle.

"Use it if you have to," he whispered.

He turned to leave but Richter grabbed him and mouthed, "Where are you going?"

"Over there. Stay here and keep still."

He slipped across, taking a position behind another of the pillars. He was armed and could shoot his way out, if need be. But no sense killing or maiming anybody tonight. Not unless absolutely necessary. Instead, he slipped the gun back at his spine against his belt and gripped the iron candelabrum.

Someone started down the steps to the crypt.

He peered around the edge, past the tombs, through the blackness. The tiny altar light offered little assistance, but he was glad for the cover. He was galvanized into action, his emotions alternating between calm and excitement, his body alive with a strange kind of energy that always clarified his thoughts.

Bad decisions.

That was what got you killed.

Like the one the man at the base of the stairs was making.

The silhouette crept in. He tightened his grip on the iron stem and cocked his arms back. He knew he had to get the man away from Richter, so he ground the sole of his right shoe into the grit on the floor. A quick glance around the pillar confirmed that the shadow was now moving toward him.

His muscles tensed.

He silently counted to five, clenched his teeth, then lunged, swinging the candelabrum. He caught the man square in the chest, sending the shadow back onto one of the Romanesque tombs. He tossed the iron aside and swung his fist hard into the man's face. His pursuer shot up and pounced. He was just about to punch again when the opaque shadow of the candle swooped out of the darkness and slammed into the nape of the man's neck. There was a groan, then the form doubled over. He kicked at the man's midsection and the assailant went down for good.

"Not bad," he whispered, realizing what Richter had done.

"It looked like you needed help."

Another set of footsteps bounded down and into the crypt. He shoved Richter behind the pillar and peered around the edge. The newcomer stopped his advance, taking up a position behind the farthest tomb, between them and the only way out.

The time for playing nice was over.

He reached back and found the Beretta. He needed to draw the other man out, make him move. Richter still clutched the candle. He reached over and took hold of it and focused across the nave. Yes. There was enough darkness there for the candle to be mistaken. He arched the wax cylinder across the open space between the pillars, flipping it end over end, hoping the diversion would attract attention.

And it did.

As the candle passed midway, the other man stepped out.

Cotton leveled the Beretta and sent a bullet into the man's thigh, which caused a groan of pain. He raced across, gun leveled. The assailant lay sprawled on the stone floor, bleeding, but he'd live.

"Let's go."

They cautiously climbed the steps back to ground level. No one there. The wounded man was crying out in Italian for help. Cotton motioned and they headed for the main doors, which he eased open. Richter carried the pledge and he held the Beretta. The outer courtyard was dark and quiet. Six cars were now there, including theirs.

A lot of people for a place that was off-limits to visitors.

They hustled to their vehicle, climbed in, and drove off.

CHAPTER 68

STEFANO SAW THE FACES OF THE CARTHUSIANS WHO'D FLED THE monastery office. Concerned. As was the prior who stood before one of the windows.

"This facility holds the recipes for all of our liqueurs," the prior said. "Those are precious secrets that many have tried to obtain. We have to protect them."

"This is not about your recipes," Ascolani said.

"Please enlighten me, Eminence. What is this about?"

"As I made clear, this is Entity business."

"Inside my charterhouse."

They watched as the two fleeing men disappeared through one of the cloister doors.

"They went into the church," the prior said.

Two of the Carthusians followed, the third headed for the door from which the other two had emerged. More people now exited from another door. One a woman. Inside a restricted monastery where females were never allowed? And quite the crowd. Six people, along with the other Carthusian. A downright party in the middle of the night.

The klaxon continued to wail.

"Holy mother of God," the prior muttered, then he fled the office.

Stefano moved to follow, but Ascolani grabbed his arm and shook his head.

"Let him go."

Ascolani turned and headed out the office's front door, away from the cloister. Stefano followed. They hustled down the path back to the entrance courtyard.

Two figures emerged from the church.

Darkness blocked faces but Stefano could see that one held a gun, the other something large and stiff, like a piece of cardboard. They climbed inside one of the cars, the engine cranked to life, and they sped through the gate.

"Who is that?" Stefano asked.

"The American, Malone, and Cardinal Richter."

Ascolani found his phone and tapped the screen.

THOMAS'S PHONE VIBRATED WITH A TEXT.

A car is emerging. Take it out. Use your toy.

Headlights burst from the open gate and turned left, heading for him. He grabbed the rifle and assumed a position where he could take a shot once the car cleared a curve about a quarter of a kilometer away. The weapon still had its high-powered sound suppressor attached to the end of the long barrel. He lay down prone on the pavement, balanced the rifle on its built-in bipod, and sighted through the nightscope. The headlights would be a problem, amplified by the night-vision capabilities, and potentially blinding. So he told himself to focus away from them. Down. On the tires.

He had eight rounds in the clip.

Should be plenty.

COTTON WORKED THE ACCELERATOR AND STEERED THEM OUT OF THE monastery, beyond the walls, and back on the highway.

They'd escaped with the pledge.

"Is the document okay?" he asked Richter.

"I think so. The plastic sleeve is thick, and I've tried to hold it carefully."

Good to hear.

"You did not seem surprised by what Camilla Baines did."

"I knew she'd make a move, and this seemed like the right time and place."

"So Cardinal Stamm provided you with some protection."

"Always pays to be prepared."

He took another curve in the road and kept speeding ahead, headlights probing the darkness.

Would they follow?

Damn right they would.

THOMAS WAITED AS THE CAR DREW CLOSER, STILL NOT IN SIGHT, BUT as it rounded the curve and found the straightaway that led to him, he prepared to fire. The headlights burst into the scope as momentary twin flashes that he avoided, focusing the crosshairs instead on the front driver's-side tire.

He pulled the trigger.

Missed.

Another shot.

The tire exploded.

He quickly shifted his aim to the passenger side and planted a third round into the second tire.

Good shooting.

All that practice paid off.

The car was now skidding out of control.

COTTON WAS MINDFUL THAT THE ROAD THEY WERE ON WAS ELEVATED with trees and steep slopes on either side. He was an experienced driver in pressure situations, so he relaxed his foot on the accelerator and kept a light touch on the wheel. He also managed to buckle his shoulder harness, as did Richter. The serpentine road sloped downward toward the valley, no lights anywhere. Darkness all around.

Up ahead something appeared in the road.

A person lying flat?

He heard a bang.

The front end veered left.

He could feel resistance and knew that a tire had blown. Then another lurch from the opposite side. A second tire gone? The steering wheel slipped from his hands and their momentum kept sending them forward in an uncontrolled slide that crossed the center line into the opposite lane. The driver's-side tires, or what was left of the front one, wobbled on the road's edge. He hit the brakes to slow their acceleration and tried to cut the wheel to the right.

Metal grated asphalt.

The brake pedal gave way to a spongey sensation signaling that the pads were not working. He tried the opposite. Jamming the accelerator to the floor, increasing speed, and working the front end as best he could to keep them on the road. But the car continued to drift left, the front rims screaming against the pavement. He strained to keep the vibrating steering wheel under control, but the car began to fishtail even more.

No guardrails anywhere.

"We're going over," he said to Richter.

The car veered, then vaulted over the embankment. They tore through scrub, bumping and weaving, sliding across the rocky scree between the trees. They hit one tree, then another, and the car tumbled. Over and over. The windshield shattered into spiderwebs. Trails of light arced before his eyes. Nothing he could do now. They were at the mercy of gravity, which kept applying itself until they slammed squarely into something hard.

All movement stopped.

And a deep blackness engulfed him.

CHAPTER 69

STEFANO WALKED WITH ASCOLANI OUT OF THE MONASTERY'S MAIN gate. The car that had just left was one moment speeding down the road, its headlights leading the way, and the next skidding out of control, then disappearing into the trees.

He heard bangs.

Headlights extinguished and darkness resumed control.

"We need to get down there," he said.

"First, I want to know what happened here."

"People could be hurt."

"Father Giumenta, I have the situation under control."

Which meant there were others here. He caught an edge in the voice. He'd pushed too far. "My apologies, Eminence."

"Quite all right. Now let's find the prior."

They headed back through the gate and into the office.

"Wait out in the cloister for me," Ascolani said.

Stefano exited, but managed a quick look back through one of the windows. Ascolani was tapping on his phone. He finished, pocketed the unit, and headed his way.

The klaxon had stopped and there were now more brothers up and about, moving in and out of the doors, the cloister alive with light. Ascolani led the way and they were told the prior was inside the church. There they found him with five other men, including a lay brother in a white cowl, along with a woman whom Stefano assumed to be Camilla Baines.

"It seems that one of our documents has been stolen," the prior said.

"From the sixteenth century?" Ascolani asked. "Signed by Pope Julius II?"

The prior nodded. "Its significance?"

Ascolani shrugged. "We will have to ask the thieves that."

"Apparently one of them was Cardinal Jason Richter," the prior said. "What would he be doing here, stealing?"

"As I mentioned earlier," Ascolani said, "this is Entity business."

"That is not good enough, Eminence." And no respect laced the use of the title. "This facility is under my control and I want answers. As I just made clear to my lay brother, this breach is extremely serious."

"I have told you all I know."

"Then I will report this to our prior-general in France, and he can speak with Rome."

"As you wish. But please know that all of those inquiries will end up with me."

"Then give me some answers. One of my brothers has been shot. He's bleeding."

Ascolani shrugged. "I am sorry for that. The document that was stolen. Was it protected?"

The prior nodded. "Inside a stiff plastic sleeve."

"How did all these people gain access?" Stefano asked.

"Apparently, one of the lay brothers is close friends with Signora Baines here."

"Excuse me."

And Ascolani stepped away, toward the far side of the church, focused again on his phone.

Thomas stood from the roadway.

He'd taken out the car and sent it over the side. Its headlights had reached him, so the occupants could be aware of his shots. His phone vibrated and he read the text message that just arrived.

Retrieve a document that was inside that car. Protected by a plastic sleeve. Advise if it was destroyed or you have it.

He hustled to where the car had been last seen. A total cloaking darkness dominated. He heard hissing from below. He propped the rifle against a tree and used the light from his phone to make his way down the embankment. The car had flipped over. Battered from the fall, it was now lying at an angle against the trunk of a thick cypress.

Vapor seeped upward.

No movement from inside the vehicle and no sign of the occupants outside the car. He made his way closer and caught the thick waft of gasoline. He found Malone and Cardinal Richter inside the car, both not moving. Dead? Didn't really matter. He raked the light from his phone across the destroyed interior. Both men were still strapped into their seats. Richter's right arm was bent at a sharp angle, a deep gash in the forehead, blood caked to his hair. He aimed the light across the interior and caught a reflection.

A plastic sleeve.

Lying at Richter's feet.

That had to be it.

He rounded the car's smashed front end and climbed up where he could reach down, past the cardinal, and retrieve the sleeve.

The gasoline odor seemed to be escalating.

He doubted, though, it would catch fire.

Without some help.

Stefano's patience was reaching its limit but he realized he was not in charge. Far from it. He was apparently only along for the ride.

"Signora Baines," the prior said. "You are a trespasser."

"I was invited here."

"The lay brother will be severely disciplined for extending that invitation. It is contrary to our rule. You both conspired to steal a document from our protection. I could have you arrested, but I will be satisfied with you leaving here and never returning."

"I will also take my donations and generosity with me."

The prior shrugged. "Do that. We will survive. As we have for centuries. Without you."

The woman clearly did not appreciate the rebuke. "Might I remind you that I own all of the lands surrounding this monastery. Lands you currently farm."

"We will learn to live without them. And by the way, you are not the only person who is generous to this order."

Baines turned and motioned.

She and the other men left.

The prior seemed agitated. How could he not be? The entire essence of the order had been violated. And especially so here, where precious records were kept and maintained. The treachery of the lay brother was particularly disturbing. That man might well be expelled.

"I assume, Eminence," the prior said, "that you are not going to tell me the significance of the stolen document."

"I do wish that I could but—"

"I know. I know. It is Entity business."

"I will say that every effort will be made to locate it."

"That is appreciated."

"Now we must take our leave."

Ascolani motioned.

And they both headed for the church doors.

Thomas informed Ascolani by text that the document had been retrieved and was intact. He'd then asked what to do next and the instruction was clear.

Make sure they are not found alive.

The easiest way to do that seemed to be to take advantage of the situation itself. A car had gone over the bank, rolled, then crashed into a tree. The gas tank had ruptured and the inevitable had occurred.

A fire.

Only this one needed a little help.

He retrieved the rifle and aimed for the car's rear end, which he centered in the nightscope. He fired one round.

Then a second.

And the car ignited in flames.

CHAPTER 70

COTTON'S ATTEMPT TO FIGHT BACK TO CONSCIOUSNESS WAS LIKE peeling a scab from a sore. Every heartbeat sent new waves of pulsating pain through his skull. *Breathe. Keep the lungs in rhythm. Check the extremities.* Both arms and legs moved and had feeling. As did his fingers and toes. Nothing seemed broken. But bouts of pain came from bruised flesh. Relief, disbelief, and a touch of anger all tumbled through his mind. He recalled the drop over the side of the road and the tumbling. Then the crash. And stillness. He'd partially come to once before with a light piercing his face. Bouncing on and off. He'd managed a peek through a tight squint and caught sight of someone inside the car. Searching. And the face. Seen only for an instant. But enough. The same man from the train and in Siena. Here? He hadn't been able to stay awake long and had lapsed back into the darkness.

Now he forced himself to come awake.

"Cardinal," he said. "Can you hear me?"

"I... hear you."

"You okay?"

"I think so. But my arm hurts. I smell gasoline."

He did too. The odor hung heavy in the air, clammy and close. Not good.

"Do you have the pledge?" he asked Richter.

"It has to be in here somewhere."

But he knew that was not going to be the case. The man from the train had come and retrieved it. Why else would he have searched? He released his seat belt and slipped out of the harness. Which hurt. He was below Richter, the driver's side of the car resting on the ground. "You need to climb out first."

Richter released his seat belt.

He wondered why the man from the train had not finished them off.

He heard a swish in the distance, then something pinged off metal.

What the hell?

Another pop.

And the rear half of the car erupted in flames.

THOMAS WAS SATISFIED.

It would take only a few moments for the fire to heat up and the car to be engulfed. The gasoline would feed it and obliterate everything. Job done. He headed for his car and laid the rifle across the back seat.

His phone vibrated with a text.

Return to Siena. Bring it to the fountain in the campo and wait for me there.

He climbed inside.

And drove away.

COTTON WAS HAVING TROUBLE BREATHING. HEAVY SMOKE BROUGHT an ache in his chest with each inhalation.

"We need to get out of here," he said to Richter.

"I am trying."

He helped Richter free himself of the shoulder harness. The cardinal then used his good arm and climbed from the car, coughing from the smoke. Cotton started hacking too as he followed Richter out.

They moved away to fresher air.

The fire was spreading, flames licking the night. Although on television or in the movies wrecked cars always explode at just the right dramatic moment, that rarely happens in real life. More a slow and steady burn that's hard to stop. Hot too. Fed by gasoline. Intense enough to melt metal. And the smoke. That was what could really get you.

"Stay here," he said to Richter.

And he risked going back to the car. He had to know if the pledge was there. So he held his breath and plunged inside the destroyed interior cabin for a quick look. Nothing there. Gone. He returned and led Richter farther away and into the trees, putting more distance between them and the car. Moonlight gauzed the ground and partially lit the way. Thankfully the underbrush was thin, the trees scattered. He swallowed hard, an empty feeling shooting up from his gut.

"What happened?" Richter asked when they stopped.

"Someone was lying in the road. I think we had two blowouts from rifle shots. Then we had a visitor."

He told Richter about the man on the train who'd come to the car.

"You never mentioned that guy to Stamm," Richter said.

"It wasn't important at the time. You've got a nasty cut on your forehead." Which wasn't actively bleeding, but still needed some attention. "How's the arm?"

"Jammed up, but I don't think it's broken."

His head felt light, his mouth dry. The events of the past few days seemed far away, easy to believe it all a dream.

But it wasn't.

Now what?

CHAPTER 71

STEFANO DROVE THE CAR AS HE AND ASCOLANI LEFT SANTA MARIA di Castello. His distrust of Ascolani had magnified tenfold, and he found himself remembering more of his Entity training. *Good actors make good spies.* Absolutely. Role-playing was essential. Sometimes critical. But he'd been taught that eventually any impersonation could be penetrated. No one could keep the fiction up forever. *Like identical twins. They cannot be the other for long.* Ascolani was indeed a good actor. He played his part as a senior prelate to perfection, revealing next to nothing about his innermost thoughts. But Stefano had caught that faintest curl of a smile on the old man's lips as he'd read whatever had last appeared on his phone.

Definitely good news.

And now they were headed away from the Carthusians. Down the road, back toward the valley. He'd seen splatters of flickering light off beyond the asphalt, down the embankment.

Fire?

"I have people dealing with this," Ascolani said as they drove past. "We need to return to Siena. Immediately. All will be fine here."

So they had not stopped.

Nor had he believed a word Ascolani had said.

THOMAS ENTERED THE CAMPO.

He'd returned to Siena, driving through a light rain that had enveloped the countryside. He was tired. Some sleep would be welcomed. He'd parked beyond the city walls in a public lot that was only about half full. People were still out and he could hear the far-off celebrations of music and shouting. But the rain had probably placed a damper on some of the festivities. He'd taken a moment and examined what was inside the plastic sleeve. Some sort of document. Aged. Brittle. Signed. Still legible, though in what appeared to be Latin. He wondered about its importance, but knew he would never be told.

Which was okay. No concern of his.

He left the car and walked into town. The rain had stopped but the cobbles were slick with moisture. Inside the campo the racetrack was illuminated only by the ambient light from the surrounding buildings. It had served its purpose and was now just an eyesore. A fountain occupied the highest point of the ancient sloping plaza. He looked around and did not see Ascolani. He had no idea where the cardinal was, but he'd certainly been close to that monastery as the orders he'd received were quite specific. He had an urge to pray, so he sat on the fountain's edge and closed his eyes, offering up a Hail Mary and an Our Father.

Which calmed him.

He hoped this assignment was over and he could shrink back into the shadows, where he preferred to dwell.

Maybe by tomorrow at this time he would be back in England.

STEFANO KNEW THE CAUSE OF THE NAMELESS FEAR THAT HELD HIM IN A firm grasp. Disappointment. He'd been lied to and used, expected to go along, obey, be swept up by the strength of the Entity's zeal, surrendering himself to Ascolani's unexplained actions without question. Yet he could not. Even worse, he could not just walk away. If it meant the end of his career with the Entity, then that's what it would be. But he was going to honor his oath of service and learn the truth.

It had started to rain a few kilometers out of town, but had stopped by the time he dropped Ascolani off just outside Siena's walls, watching as the older man walked away.

"Head back to Rome," Ascolani ordered. "Your mission here is complete."

"What did we accomplish?"

"Exactly what was necessary."

More aggravating obtuseness.

So he'd quickly parked the car and headed off in foot pursuit. His mind seethed with an assortment of conflicting emotions. A burgeoning excitement, a chilly dread, an irrational anger. He could not fall victim to fear and paranoia, as those two could dog every operation and usually caused failure. He also had to resist the urge to better demonstrate his own brilliance with unnecessary foolishness. He was a priest. Ascolani a cardinal. The second most powerful man in the Catholic Church. He was taking enough chances already. What he was doing now was clearly wrong. A termination offense. He'd be banished to some parish far off the beaten path. Forgotten. He'd thought about heading back to Rome and talking to the right people, then waiting for everything to clear itself up naturally. But would it? No. This had to be pursued. Here. Now.

By him.

Alone.

He followed Ascolani at a distance, mindful that the damp streets were clearing of people, though the city remained awake and alive, seemingly not surrendering to sleep. He imagined that, as with the Calico Storico, it would take a few days for the adrenaline to work its way out of Siena's veins. The tourists and visitors, though, would be gone by tomorrow, if not already.

He broke his pace with halts here and there and short dashes accompanied by checks back over his shoulder just in case he was more prey than predator. He always smiled at books and television that depicted the complex ways of trailing people with unmarked cars, relays of footmen, and frequent switches. Overkill. None of that was needed if you were just careful. And besides, the last thing a self-important prelate like Ascolani would think was that a subordinate was watching him. He noticed, though, that Ascolani took a circuitous route through the wet streets, turning corners and doubling back before finally ending at the campo.

A hundred or so people were there, getting their last look at the racetrack, which would almost certainly be gone tomorrow. Ascolani headed for the open center, which had earlier been filled with tens of thousands of spectators. He stopped at the fountain and talked with another man.

One Stefano recognized.

From the pictures he'd taken.

From the Palazzo Tempi.

THOMAS BOWED HIS HEAD IN RESPECT AS ASCOLANI APPROACHED. "Eminence."

He then handed over the document.

Ascolani took a moment and admired it. "What happened with the car?"

"It was burning when I left. Malone and the cardinal were inside, unconscious."

"There is one more thing we must do," Ascolani said. "Before your mission is complete." The cardinal drew close. "There is a man. Eric Casaburi. He is the secretary for Italy's National Freedom Party, a member of our parliament. His photograph will be easy to find. I want him eliminated."

He nodded.

"Of course, additional payment will be promptly deposited to your account," Ascolani went on, "for this added service."

"How do I find him?"

"That will be the easy part. Head to Florence. I will get him there. Bring your toy. I will be in touch."

And the cardinal walked off.

STEFANO WAS FILLED WITH CONFUSION.

Ascolani's conversation was short and ended with the other man handing over what had to be the Pledge of Christ taken from Santa Maria di Castello. It was similar in size and shape to what he'd seen outside the church being held by either Malone or Richter. Ascolani accepted the document and headed off, exiting the campo by way of one of the many streets. The other man lingered a moment then walked off too, not coming anywhere near where Stefano was concealed. He should follow. But caution urged him against that.

He could not risk detection.

He was still waiting on Daniele's contacts within the Siena police to report on any identification from the pictures he'd taken. He checked his phone one more time. No message on that subject yet. He had to do something. But what? Since he could not turn to anyone within the Curia, he decided that it was time to find someone outside that arena. Someone he could trust without question. Someone who was no friend of Ascolani's. Only one name came to mind. The man who'd originally recruited him.

Charles Cardinal Stamm.

Ascolani's grip within the Curia was massive, reaching into every department and all the way to the pope. No way for anyone to know friends from enemies. All of them, like good spies, would be acting, trying their best to play their parts to perfection, no one wanting to make Ascolani an enemy.

But Stamm?

He had a multitude of friends and enemies too. Number one enemy on the list? Ascolani. So he decided to follow the order given to him earlier and return to Rome.

And find Stamm.

CHAPTER 72

STEFANO HAD RETURNED TO ROME.

But not to his rooms inside the rectory for the Archbasilica of the Most Holy Savior at the Lateran. Instead, he'd driven straight to Cardinal Stamm's apartment, but found no one there. He had to be careful and not attract attention. Eyes and ears were everywhere, and he could not afford to alert Ascolani. He needed to get in contact with Stamm, but the number he'd once called was no longer functioning, and had not been since Stamm's termination. Surely Entity headquarters had contact information, but he could not ask. Too risky. So he retreated to street level and called Entity headquarters to inform them that he was back in Rome and available.

Standard procedure.

He thought about the next step and decided to call a member of his rapid response team. The priest was not only a subordinate but also a friend who thought highly of Cardinal Stamm. Perhaps he might have contact information?

"Is there trouble?" he was asked.

"Not at all. I just need some institutional knowledge the cardinal should have. We were always encouraged to use that source, if need be."

That explanation worked and he was given a cell phone number that was, to his subordinate's knowledge, still current. He stared at the number on the screen. He was about to defy a direct order from his director. But there was no turning back now. Yet he was chilled by something Cardinal Stamm himself once told him, and few other recruits, the day they were all sworn into service.

"There once was a convent that existed in northern Italy. Up in the Dolomites. A beautiful place. But that region has always been dangerous, vulnerable, all of the villages intentionally built on easily defended hilltops. Sadly for the nuns, their convent sat on low ground. So they placed their safety in the hands of God, but they were not foolish. If raiders came they would ring an alarm bell that summoned armed men from the nearby village to come to their aid. One night the nuns decided to find out how much they could depend on the locals to protect them. So they rang the bell. The men up on the hill, safe inside the village walls, leaped from their beds, snatched up weapons, and scrambled down the slopes to battle nonexistent raiders. The nuns were pleased with the test. Their would-be rescuers not so much, having lost much-needed sleep. Three nights later raiders came for real. The nuns woke and rang the bell. The men of the village heard the clang but went back to sleep, tired of being tested. The raiders slaughtered the older nuns, then dragged away the others to sell as slaves. The lesson? Don't ring the bell unless it's for real."

He typed a text.

Eminence, this is Father Stefano Giumenta. I am ringing the bell and sounding the alarm, like the nuns in the Dolomites. Below is a picture of a man. Do you know him?

He decided to keep the first contact simple, reminding Stamm of the story, sending the picture, and hoping for the best. Three minutes later a reply came.

Why is it important?

He replied. This man is a problem.

Five minutes later a response.

Come to me. Now.

His answer was never in doubt.

Where?

COTTON ALLOWED THE COBWEBS INSIDE HIS HEAD TO CLEAR. HE DID not think he'd suffered a concussion, but you never knew about a head injury. Richter seemed okay, besides the twisted arm and gash to his forehead. The bleeding had stopped and the cardinal seemed fine.

"None of this was ever mentioned at seminary," Richter said.

He smiled. "I would hope not."

"You saw a man in the road, holding a rifle?"

"I did. It was the same man from the train. The same man who was inside the car, searching for the pledge."

"Who now has it."

That was true. But who did the man work for?

He fished his phone from his pocket and saw that it had survived the crash. Tough units. Specially made for the Magellan Billet, and given to him by Stephanie Nelle. He unlocked the screen and saw that there was service. Thank goodness. He entered a code that the phone recognized and dialed Stephanie Nelle's direct line for a phone she carried with her twenty-four hours a day. She answered immediately and he reported what happened.

"We need to get to Cardinal Stamm," he said. "He's nearby at a Tuscan resort."

"I'll get a car to you from your phone's GPS."

"We'll be waiting."

"You armed?"

The gun was still nestled at his spine. He'd made sure to bring it with him. "I am."

"Good."

He ended the call.

They were near the highway on which they'd driven to Santa Maria di Castello. A few minutes ago three cars had left the monastery. Two first together. Then a single vehicle. All three sped down the highway and away into the night, not stopping to investigate what was apparently burning down below the roadway. Which spoke volumes. No way to see who had occupied the cars. But one or more surely held Camilla Baines and her Golden Oak minions.

The night was calm and warm.

Peaceful, despite the chaos.

A lot was happening.

Thank goodness he'd worn his patient pants.

Cotton's watch read 10:20 P.M. when the car that had retrieved him and Richter turned off the main highway and headed into the woods on a dirt lane until finally reaching a cypress-lined avenue that ran alongside a golf course. He'd caught a glimpse of several greens and tee boxes in the headlights. The car climbed a short incline and stopped before a lit villa on the grounds of Castiglion del Bosco. Richter explained that the resort had assimilated an actual medieval village, and that Stamm apparently liked it there.

Which had made him smile.

The building before them occupied a rise and surely commanded a high-priced view of the countryside. It looked like a two-story stone farmhouse that had been transformed into a multi-bedroom hideaway, the very picture of a Tuscan villa, including stone walls veined with greenery, a ceramic-tiled roof, and a lovely flower garden. There was also a shaded terrace and pool, both lit to the night. A Land Rover Defender was parked out front. Inside were comfortable Tuscan-style furnishings combined with the latest in technology, including a huge flat-screen television. Stamm was ensconced before it watching a European football match.

"Sit," the older man said as they entered. "There are liquids on the cart. Wine. Whiskey. Soft drinks. Help yourself."

"We need a doctor for Cardinal Richter," he told Stamm.

"Signora Nelle informed me. One is on the way." Stamm eyed Richter. "It does not look that bad."

"It's not," Richter said.

"I was not entirely frank with you back in Rome," Cotton said.

Stamm muted the sound on the ball game. "Do tell."

And Cotton described everything that had just happened along with the complete story of what had occurred on the train, including the killer.

"We need to find out who he is," Richter said.

"That will be easy. I hired him. Years ago."

Cotton stepped over and lifted the remote control for the muted television, hitting the OFF button.

"That was rude," Stamm said.

He sat in one of the chairs. "Eminence, we've had a rough night. I'm tired. Hungry. And a bit frustrated. Cardinal Richter needs a doctor and I should be back in Copenhagen selling books. So tell me about the man you hired. Who is clearly a professional killer."

"His name is Thomas Dewberry. A person with no morals, deep religious convictions, and, as you say, unique skills."

"You hired someone like that?" Richter asked.

"I hired a person who could provide retribution for those who most definitely deserved it. The world is a dangerous place. Violence exists. There are times when prayer and 'turning the other cheek' simply do not work. We had to be prepared to deal with that contingency. If not, we would simply be a toothless tiger. So I recruited Thomas. But he was only dispatched to political hot spots, locales where the law was nonexistent and those drastic measures were needed—where violence had already occurred against us. They were all retaliatory strikes. Not offensive ones. Never."

"Clearly Ascolani has expanded his use," Richter said, taking a seat too. "Your man is right in the middle of framing me."

"And I am sorry for that. Ascolani is making a play for the papacy. The pope is going to retire. He's made up his mind. Ascolani surely knows that. I am told he has already applied pressure to at least eight other cardinals who were either papabile themselves or capable of influencing others. Simple blackmail, mainly. The hardest pressure was saved for you, Jason."

"Lucky me."

"I assume the fact that you are yourself papabile, popular, and also a close friend of the pope made you special. So Ascolani wanted you disgraced. Tainted. Made radioactive. Perhaps even excluded from the coming conclave. I have also learned that one of the defendants in the bribery trial was offered a deal. Implicate you, and things would be much easier for him. He accepted that deal, lied, and the money was planted to reinforce the lie. That defendant worked in the Secretariat of State. Ascolani surely had great power over him."

"Aren't you a wealth of information tonight," Cotton said. "How long have you had this intel?"

"Not long. There are many within the Curia and the Entity still loyal to me. I was also able to access a special financial account. A personal slush fund I long ago created and used for decades. Ascolani inherited control of that account when he assumed the Entity's leadership. I have learned the money used to frame you came from there."

"It seems you have all we need to clear my name," Richter said.

"Unfortunately, Ascolani closed the account and the money is now in the possession of the Swiss Guard, removed from your country residence in Dillenburg."

Cotton's brain raced with possibilities. "Ascolani had Dewberry take us out and get the pledge."

"That would be a good assumption."

"So what now?" Richter asked.

"This is not over," Stamm said. "Not yet, at least."

Cotton heard a car outside and rose to look out the window. "You expecting someone?"

"I am. And he may be the answer to our problem."

CHAPTER 73

STEFANO STEPPED FROM THE CAR.

He'd driven straight from Rome. He should be tired but he was far from it. Adrenaline coursed through his veins, clearing his thinking and readying him for action. He supposed it was the boldness of youth, but he told himself to stay vigilant. His phone had provided navigation to a high-end hotel and resort known as Castiglion del Bosco. He'd heard of the place and knew it existed, but had never before visited. Stamm had directed him to come to a building away from the main hotel labeled Villa Biondi.

Which he'd found.

Three men emerged from the villa's front door. Stamm, Cardinal Richter, and the American, Malone. Seemed he'd stumbled his way to a party. They introduced themselves and shook hands.

"Stefano was one of my recruits," Stamm said. "An excellent operative who now heads the Entity's rapid response team. He is currently disobeying a direct order from his superior, Cardinal Ascolani. Come, let us sit on the terrace. The night is lovely. We need to talk. And we need to hear what Father Giumenta has to say."

They all rounded to the one side of the villa and a covered terrace that accommodated more than enough comfortable chairs. A lit pool stretched out before them in a pale-green tint. Overhead stars shimmered like splintering candles, small brittle fires, fragile yet eternal.

"The man whose picture you sent is Thomas Dewberry," Stamm said. "He is a contractor the Entity employs from time to time. Sadly, though, Ascolani has expanded Thomas's use."

Stefano said, "There's a dead jockey in Siena. Thanks to him."

"Add him to the list," Malone said. "There's a dead Swiss Guardsman in Cologne, along with a woman on a train. Then Dewberry tried to kill me and Cardinal Richter."

"Dewberry was inside the Palazzo Tempi during the Palio, with a high-powered rifle. He shot that jockey," Stefano said.

"While trying to kill me the first time," Malone added.

"I suspect Thomas is not happy with all the risk taking," Stamm said. "He is a careful one by nature."

"I assume Dewberry is a ghost in any and all official records," Malone said. "He exists nowhere."

"He is quite adept at not being seen." Stamm faced Stefano. "You are not the nuns ringing the bell, just as a test. This is real."

He knew that.

And was glad to know Stamm thought the same.

"Ascolani has to be stopped," Richter said. "He cannot be allowed to become pope."

Stamm nodded. "I agree. But we also have an additional problem."

He did not like the sound of that.

"As we all know, Eric Casaburi wants to apply pressure on the church through a sixteenth-century *Pignus Christi*. To do that he has been compelled to take several steps. First, he violated the tomb of Anna Maria Luisa de' Medici inside the Medici Chapel. Then he appeared at a church in Panzitta, where Pazzis are buried, and wanted to open the tomb of Raffaello de' Pazzi. The local bishop passed that request on to Rome."

"He says he is a Medici," Richter said.

"He just might be," Stamm said. "Casaburi had a recognized

DNA expert with him inside the Medici Chapel. He most likely wanted another sample from the Pazzi tomb. I suspect he is trying to establish not only a connection, but that he is a *legitimate* royal Medici heir."

"That would mean Anna Maria and that Pazzi were legally married," Malone noted.

Stamm nodded. "Precisely. Which does strike at history. Medici and Pazzi were not families that mixed together. Far from it, in fact."

"Does Casaburi have a copy of the pledge?" Richter asked. "The one we saw expressly said there was another that the Medici retained."

Stamm pointed a finger. "That is what we have to find out. The copy Ascolani has is surely ashes by now. A shame we do not know its terms."

Malone smiled. "We do."

And they listened as Malone recited the pledge, word for word.

"So you really do have an eidetic memory?" Stamm asked. "Quite a gift."

"It can be."

"Casaburi, though, needs the actual document to make his case," Richter said. "Which is good for us."

Stefano sat back in his chair and stared up, beyond the terrace covering, at the velvet sky, which extended in every direction for what seemed like forever. So peaceful. Beautiful. Comforting.

"Ascolani is headed to Florence," Stamm said.

"You have eyes on him?" Malone asked.

"Not the most reliable. But some. Casaburi is at his family's home in a small village east of Florence. Where he goes in the morning will be instructive."

"It would be nice to know where Dewberry is," Malone said.

"I believe I can help there," Stamm said. "Thomas is managed by an intermediary. A duplicitous individual known as Bartolomé. I know how to contact him. I can exert pressure there."

Stefano had no doubt. Stamm was an assertive leader who

placed a great deal of faith in his subordinates. He remembered something Stamm had once said. An African proverb. His way of teaching. *Every morning a gazelle wakes up. It knows it must run faster than the fastest lion or it will be killed. Every morning a lion wakes up. It knows it must outrun the slowest gazelle or it will starve to death. It does not matter whether you are a lion or a gazelle, when the sun comes up you had better be running.*

He'd be ready to run in the morning.

It was good to be back on the right team. Stamm was a man of heart with a cultivated mind, a clear conscience, and a perfect command of himself. He also could see that Malone was thinking. He knew little about the man besides the fact that he was an American intelligence operative. But Stamm seemed to have great respect for him, which spoke volumes.

"Okay," Malone said. "Find out where Dewberry is, then we'll go from there."

CHAPTER 74

Florence, Italy
Thursday, July 3
10:50 a.m.

Eric hustled inside the Basilica di Santa Croce and moved through the main church, heading for a door at the far end of the nave. He'd driven from his home village to Florence, making a series of phone calls along the way, learning how and where to gain access to the Santa Croce's records. He'd been told that the archives were kept on site in a secure location, the materials dating back to the sixteenth through the eighteenth centuries all digitized. Good to know. Might make things easier.

He found the archives and spoke with a young clerk who directed him to a desktop computer and located what records they had for the middle part of the eighteenth century.

"There are some for that time period," the clerk said. "But nothing complete. So many record purges have occurred. Bad management lost even more. But you can scan these to see if what you are looking for is there."

He sat before the computer and studied the images. Written in the Florentine style. Dates were important. Anna Maria's father, Cosimo III, died in 1723. Anna left Florence in 1724 to get away from her brother, retiring to the countryside to supposedly live alone. Raffaello de' Pazzi died in 1725. Best guess? Any marriage had to have occurred between 1723 and 1725.

So he started scanning the images, looking for those dates.

Thankfully, the entries were noted in relative chronological order. A few scattered ones appeared here and there with differing dates. He focused on the ones for marriage. And there were many. The clerk had explained that the Catholic Church had been the official record keeper for most of Europe, up to the time of the Protestant Reformation. After that it kept only records that concerned the church itself, such as those who were born, baptized, married, or died within the faith. From everything he'd ever read about Anna Maria she was a devout and faithful believer, an open supporter of the church. It made sense that she would properly marry.

He clicked through the images.

Leaf after leaf.

He'd heard back today from party leaders who were inquiring about the Vatican's support. Other parties were also lobbying for the Holy See's tacit endorsement. The elections in nearly every district were going to be tight races. Every vote was going to count. The margins for error would be in the low single digits. He'd assured everyone that he could deliver the Holy See. If he failed? Most likely his party would lose, with no chance at the prime minister's seat. And he would be out as secretary, relegated to doing nothing more than what he was told. His own election was not set for this round, so he would keep his seat in parliament. For whatever good that would mean. He would essentially be nothing. Right back where he started.

His mind had drifted and he forced himself to focus on the screen. He could not afford to miss anything important. He'd tried to call Camilla Baines. Twice. And received only a recording to leave a message. Perhaps he should travel south to Siena and find her? Worth the trip? Definitely. He had to have that pledge. But at least he knew that it existed and was now back out in the world.

He kept scanning.

And saw an entry.

A M Luisa - Raffaello de' Pazzi
Matrimonio 18 June 1724

Incredible. That was it. Some degree of anonymity was achieved by using Anna Maria's initials, along with no surname. But there was no mistaking that a marriage had been recorded for June 18, 1724. A lawful union. Proof. Verification of what Anna Maria herself had written. He decided to draw no attention to his find, but snapped a quick picture with his phone, then closed the file. The record was not going anywhere. He now had all the pieces.

Save one.

Maybe he should drive to Siena.

He left the archives and retreated into the warm morning. Piazza di Santa Croce was nearly back to normal after the Calcio Storico, the last of the sand for the ball field being hauled away.

His phone vibrated.

He did not recognize the number but answered anyway. It might be Camilla Baines again.

"Signor Casaburi."

A male voice. His senses went to full alert.

"I understand you gave Cardinal Richter until tomorrow to provide you an answer. I have one now."

"Who is this?"

"The person who can deliver what you want."

"How did you find me?"

"Is that important?"

"Actually, it is."

"Your office in Rome provided the number."

Now he was even more suspicious. But he wanted to know, "What is your answer?"

"That all depends on you."

COTTON WAS WORKING A PLAN THAT HE WAS MAKING UP AS THEY went. Stephanie had managed to locate Eric Casaburi through a cell phone track that led them to the Basilica di Santa Croce. He stood within the Pazzi Chapel adjacent to the basilica. Impressive place. Above the altar he studied the famed astrological fresco, or at least what was left of it. He knew the story that there was an identical one in the Medici Chapel—the same star configuration on the same night, July 4, 1442.

Richter had told him all about Casaburi, who sounded like an opportunist politician trying to find the fastest way to power for himself and his party. Richter also explained that people tried all the time to get the church to help with elections. Nothing new there. But few tried to actually blackmail the Vatican. This man had played with fire.

His phone dinged.

Stephanie.

"Casaburi's phone is near you," she said. "He's headed away."

"And Ascolani?"

"He is near the Duomo and he just called Casaburi."

"Casaburi's moving toward Ascolani?"

"It seems that way."

"Looks like they're doing our work for us." Then he asked the main question. "Where is Dewberry?"

Stamm had been good to his word and made contact with Thomas Dewberry's intermediary, Bartolomé.

"I explained that Thomas was about to meet his fate and he had a choice to make. He could join him or not. Of course, he pointed out that I was the one to hire him in the first place. I assured him that was not the issue. Instead, the issue was how loyal he was going to be."

And like most co-conspirators, Bartolomé sold out his benefactor, providing a cell phone number where Dewberry could be reached. But they also learned that Ascolani had provided Dewberry with a burner phone for direct communication between the two. There was no way to learn that number, but they could track Dewberry's personal phone.

"He's there," Stephanie said. "Near the Duomo too. You think he will try to kill Casaburi?"

"I certainly hope so."

And he ended the call.

CHAPTER 75

STEFANO REALIZED THAT IF THIS DID NOT PLAY OUT AS PLANNED, HE would surely be arrested and tried for an offense against an officer of the Holy See. The repercussions would be swift and certain. Ascolani would see to that. No mercy would be shown. He'd hoped to one day be a bishop. Cardinal Stamm himself had begun as a priest-clerk, moving to a field officer then all the way up to head of the Entity. It felt good to be working with Stamm again. When the pope had forced Stamm's retirement, there'd been a genuine sense of loss within the Entity. Everyone respected the old Irishman. Then, when Ascolani assumed command, a sense of disbelief had permeated the air. Never had the secretary of state held that position. The conflicts of interest were inherent, but apparently no voices of concern had been raised.

Or not enough at least.

Ascolani was right in the middle of something far beyond the bounds of his official duties. And using a hired killer? That was unconscionable. He supposed, though, that was what ambition did to good judgment. He flushed all those disturbing thoughts from his mind and concentrated on the clangor and rush of the Piazza del Duomo around him. The ancient piazza was less open space and more a grand stage for the architectural gems that filled it. Florence's famed Duomo, with its signature vermillion dome, stood to his left isolated, free from attached or adjoining buildings. The same was true for the much smaller Baptistery before him, with rows of tourists lined up outside its main doors waiting for entry. The great bell atop Giotto's Campanile tolled for noon, as it had done for all of Florence for over five centuries.

A gust of wind swept across the open space. The day was warm, the pavement soaked in sunlight. Malone had asked him to reconnoiter the piazza focusing on the surrounding buildings that housed shops, restaurants, and boutique hotels.

Which led them here.

ERIC ENTERED THE PIAZZA DEL DUOMO.

The voice on the phone told him to be here, at its center, by noon.

"I will be wearing a white hat," the voice had said.

"Why should I come?"

"Because Cardinal Richter cannot give you what you want. I can. We can make a deal."

That last part intrigued him.

So he'd had no choice.

But to come.

THOMAS WAS MOVING FAST.

Ascolani had called an hour ago and instructed him to assume a concealed position with privacy, and without witnesses, that overlooked the cathedral square. He carried the shoulder bag with the rifle tucked inside and was making his way toward a small hotel that occupied a spot where the Via de' Martelli drained into the piazza. Four stories. With plenty of windows from rooms that overlooked the piazza. Ascolani's instructions had been crystal-clear. *Use your toy and deal with Casaburi. Do not miss this time.*

The jab at his failure in Siena cut deep. He was not accustomed to disappointing his benefactor. But that task during the Palio had been fraught with difficulties. This one would be much easier.

He kept walking.

Plenty of people filled the streets. Surely most of them tourists, here to enjoy the sights. Everything throbbed with activity. He checked his watch. 11:45 A.M.

He had fifteen minutes to be in position.

COTTON STUDIED HIS PHONE AND THE PULSATING BLUE DOT, WHICH indicated that Thomas Dewberry was nearby. How close? Hard to tell from the dot. He was utilizing a special Magellan Billet program that could track a cell phone, once the relevant information for that phone was input. Which Stamm had obtained from the intermediary. He also had information on Ascolani's Vatican phone, which indicated it was in the Piazza del Duomo, which opened at the end of the street about a hundred feet away.

He turned and backtracked down the street. At an intersection he hooked left and kept walking. The blue dot was ahead of him. Somewhere. A red dot indicated Stefano's phone's location.

Which he headed toward.

ERIC WAS UNSURE ABOUT THE UNEXPECTED TURN OF EVENTS. HE'D acquired some new, unknown Vatican ally.

Or was it a trap?

He spotted an older man, dressed casually. Pants. Shirt. Sneakers. Looked to be in his mid- to late sixties, a close-curled head of steel-gray hair crowning an imperious, finely chiseled face. He stood straight with his hands behind his back, balanced on the balls of his feet, the posture finely taut. The face cast a gloomy, almost tyrannical expression. Atop his head he wore a white hat with a wide brim that shaded the sun.

He approached.

"Signore Casaburi, I am Cardinal Ascolani."

He knew the name, just not the face associated with the name. The Vatican secretary of state. Just one rung removed from the pope.

Yes, this man could deliver.

"You have been collecting DNA," Ascolani said. "Are you directly related to Anna Maria Luisa de' Medici? And to Raffaello de' Pazzi?"

"I am. I know with certainty about Anna Maria. For Raffaello? I still need a sample, but I am confident it will show a connection too. I just discovered that they were married at Santa Croce."

"Seems all you need now is the pledge. Sadly, the church's copy is gone."

Which explained why Camilla Baines had gone radio-silent. She had nothing to bargain with. Still, "Thankfully, there was a duplicate."

"But you obviously do not have it, or we would not be standing here talking."

He caught the arrogance in the observation.

"I am wondering," Ascolani said. "Did you actually think you could extort our support for your party?"

THOMAS ENTERED THE HOTEL DUOMO.

A rather dull, faintly antiquated place too small for any convention or gala, but fashionable and surely overpriced. He'd checked the local geography earlier, after Ascolani's orders, and determined this would be the best place to do what had to be done. No doorman, only an elderly bellboy and a reception desk staffed by a young, dark-haired man focused on a computer screen.

To his right rose a flight of wooden stairs. To his left lay the entrance to a restaurant. The place was quiet. He headed for the restaurant and watched as the clerk abandoned the front desk and disappeared through a door into a back room. No one else was in the small lobby. He approached and studied the wall behind the desk with its pigeonholed slots for keys and mail. From the room numbers he noted there were four stories, ten rooms to a floor, the keys there for many of them signaling unoccupied. All of them overlooked the piazza, so it did not matter.

But height did.

He stepped around the counter and snatched a key for one of the fourth-floor rooms, then headed for the stairs just as the clerk reappeared through the door.

He came off the stairs on the fourth floor.

Silence reigned down the narrow corridor to the door for Room 408. Along the way he passed a set of emergency stairs that led back down to the ground. Good to know they were there. They would provide an excellent escape route. The hotel was definitely an older establishment, the floors creaking hardwood beneath a thin carpet runner, the walls flaking plaster, the room doors wooden with actual keys to lock and unlock. He tapped on the door for Room 408.

No answer.

He inserted the key and released the lock.

Inside was a pleasant space with two windows and a double bed with nightstands and lamps on either side. A wardrobe and dressing table rounded out the comfortable, but dated, furnishings. A small upholstered sofa sat before the windows and would make a perfect firing platform.

He locked the door, then slid the canvas case from his shoulder and removed the rifle, quickly assembling it with the bipod extended. The settee was too close to the window so he slid it back about two meters. He rested the weapon atop the back and sighted through the scope, parting the curtains enough so he could see below. He scanned the piazza through the scope until he found Ascolani, in a wide hat, standing near its center. Exactly where the cardinal said he would be. He'd already familiarized himself with Eric Casaburi from photos on the internet.

Both men were there.

Ascolani's instructions were clear.

"I will touch the right side of my head in some way to signal for you to be ready. Take the shots when I touch my left side."

He decided to leave the window closed until the signal came.

So he settled in and waited.

STEFANO KEPT MOVING THROUGH THE MIDDAY CROWD, WHICH EBBED and flowed. Knots of tourists followed their flag-waving guides in tight schools across the piazza. The more people, the more difficult it would be to find Thomas Dewberry. People seemed to be either enjoying the sun or searching for shade. Off to his right, toward the center of the piazza, he had already spotted Ascolani, who was now talking with Eric Casaburi. Both he and Malone had seen photos of the politician. Hundreds of people stood between himself and them, no danger of being spotted. Malone was behind him, searching the side streets. He checked his watch. 12:05 P.M.

The sun was high in the sky, reducing the shadows across the cobbles. The center was as bright as a stage under spotlights.

Malone appeared about fifty feet away and he hustled over.

"The tracker is stationary, and has been for the past few minutes," Malone said. "He has to be inside there."

Malone motioned to a four-story corner building.

The Hotel Duomo.

"Given what happened in Siena," Malone said. "I don't like this."

CHAPTER 76

ERIC WAS DETERMINED TO HOLD HIS GROUND.

Machiavelli was right.

The lion cannot protect himself from traps, and the fox cannot defend himself from wolves. One must therefore be a fox to recognize traps, and a lion to frighten wolves.

"I am a legitimate heir of Anna Maria Luisa de' Medici, herself the heir of Cosimo de' Medici III. I am of their royal blood."

"Congratulations," Ascolani said. "It will make for an interesting historical footnote. But hardly relevant anymore."

"I know where the Medici copy is located."

"Then produce it."

"I shall."

"Of course, if the church becomes an advocate for the National Freedom Party, then that debt is forgiven? Correct?"

"Seems like a win/win for all involved."

Pigeons fluttered to and from the flagstones, oblivious to the crowds.

"Your political party is a hollow group with no substance," Ascolani said. "You merely say what the people want to hear. You have neither the ability nor the desire to change anything. Why would you? There would be nothing then for you to complain about."

He resented the insult and told himself to keep his temper. But what he'd just heard was not wrong.

Men are so stupid and concerned with their present needs, they will always let themselves be deceived.

"Your political party lacks the skills to ever build anything meaningful," Ascolani said.

"We might surprise you."

Ascolani shrugged. "I truly doubt that."

JASON FELT THAT EVERY MUSCLE IN HIS BODY WAS TAUT TO THE breaking point, his mind a maelstrom of unspoken emotions. Malone had told him to stay back, out of the line of fire, and let them handle things. Which sounded okay. At the time.

But not anymore.

Ascolani had actively tried to destroy him.

Then he'd also sent Dewberry to kill him.

He could not let that go.

So he entered the Piazza del Duomo.

And headed for its center.

THOMAS KEPT THE RIFLE'S SCOPE FOCUSED ON ASCOLANI, WHO WAS deep in conversation with Eric Casaburi. A round was loaded in the chamber, the weapon resting on its bipod atop the sofa back. He'd have to fire shots quickly and accurately. Within a few seconds of one another. The sound suppressor would mask the retort and, with so many people out there moving in every direction, it would take a few moments for the bystanders to fully comprehend what had happened. Hopefully a panic would ensue that would allow him the moments needed to break the weapon down, slip it back into the case, and make his escape. He would have to close the window, but slowly so as not to draw any attention. Replace the sofa too, then leave using that second set of stairs he'd noticed a few minutes ago. Also, take the room key with him. Leave nothing that could be traced to him. He'd been careful to touch little and wore a thin pair of latex gloves to further mask his presence.

Ascolani reached up and rubbed his right temple.

The signal to get ready.

He left the rifle and approached the window. Slowly he raised the lower sash enough for him to fire through the opening. He left the sheers hanging, parting them only enough to give him a clear view below.

He returned to the rifle and refocused through the scope.

Waiting for the order to fire.

COTTON STARED UP AT THE HOTEL DUOMO.

The tracking dot showed that Dewberry was here.

Stefano had described a black Stealth Recon Scout rifle he'd seen inside the Palazzo Tempi back in Siena, which had been removed from there by a priest and delivered to Ascolani. That was a high-tech powerful weapon, also equipped, as Stefano reported, with a high-pressure sound suppressor. Dewberry had apparently used that weapon during the Palio, killing a jockey in the process. In another really public place.

A window on the fourth floor opened.

About halfway.

"You see that," Stefano asked.

"I do. That hotel is air-conditioned and nobody else has a window open."

They both continued to stare upward.

The blue dot still pulsated right over the hotel.

"This is getting too risky," he said. "Go get Casaburi out of the piazza."

"And you?"

"I'm going inside."

CHAPTER 77

Eric was tired of being patronized. So he said, "The church needs to seriously consider my proposal."

"Why would we do such a thing?" Ascolani said. "Even if you achieve a majority in parliament your party will never last. Eventually, all populists grow tiresome on the people, especially once they realize that nothing ever is done."

"Our party will be this nation's salvation. Every poll shows that the people favor our message. The president will have no choice but to offer us the prime minister's seat."

"Only after you win thirty-eight additional seats in parliament."

He resented this man's condescending attitude. "When I retrieve my family's copy of the Pledge of Christ, the situation will be different."

"Do you truly think that a five-hundred-year-old document will carry any legal weight?"

"It is not just a document. It is a solemn pledge of Pope Julius II, sworn before Christ, in perpetuity. If that carries no legal or moral weight, then what does?"

And he believed that.

"Anna Maria Luisa left writings," he continued. "Many. She detailed how she felt about her life and her child. Contrary to what history says, she did birth a son. A legitimate royal Medici heir. She wrote of the pledge and wanted her child to have, as she said, that *sacred promise*. It is only a matter of time before I have the Medici copy."

"I assure you, we will have no problem ignoring it."

Eric had made a career out of reading people. And he was good at it. How they carried themselves. Gestures. The way they stood or sat.

And above all, the eyes.

The promise given was a necessity of the past. The word broken is a necessity of the present.

More Machiavelli.

And on target.

Cardinal Ascolani's ball-bearing-like eyes took on a metallic sheen and beamed with the confidence of a cold heart.

Which momentarily frightened him.

COTTON ENTERED THE HOTEL DUOMO AND APPROACHED THE reception desk, staffed by a younger man.

Stefano had headed off into the piazza. He liked the young priest. He seemed like a decent man who'd taken a huge chance coming to Stamm. He'd listened last night as Stefano explained all that he'd seen and suspected. The priest had a good pair of eyes and ears. Which every good intelligence officer needed. Clearly, Cardinal Ascolani was heavily involved in something that was most certainly illegal. Stamm had made clear that Thomas Dewberry had never been used to carry out extortion or the killing of a prelate. That would have been unthinkable. Having a man like Thomas Dewberry nearby? That was nothing short of dangerous.

This whole thing was drifting out of control.

"How many rooms on the fourth floor?" he asked the hotel clerk in Italian.

"Ten."

Outside he'd counted twenty windows in a row. "Two windows to a room?"

The clerk nodded.

He again visualized the hotel's exterior in his mind and did the math, determining that the window had opened in the eighth room. He then glanced behind the clerk and saw the cubbies for each room. "Who is in Room 408?"

The look on the clerk's face seemed to signal that there was going to be no response. He fished a one-hundred-euro note from his pocket and handed it over. The younger man accepted the offering and said, "No one. It is empty."

Now he knew why the guy had so easily taken his money.

"Why is there no key?" he asked, pointing to the cubby.

The clerk had no reply and just shrugged.

Room 408 was not empty.

Somebody had opened the window.

But was it a threat?

THOMAS KEPT HIS RIGHT EYE PRESSED TO THE RIFLE'S SCOPE, FINGER ON the trigger. He could tick off two shots in a matter of a few seconds. The high-powered rounds would then do the rest of the work. Just make it a solid smack in the chest. Which was no problem. The target was brightly lit and easy to center. The next signal would be to fire.

But the two men were still talking.

No matter.

He was ready.

COTTON CLIMBED THE STAIRS TWO AT A TIME AND FOUND THE FOURTH floor. He'd passed no other guests and there were no cleaning carts in the corridor before him. He'd thought perhaps Room 408 was being serviced, but that did not appear to be the case. He was not sure of anything, except that he had a bad feeling. He reached back and found the Beretta, keeping it down at his side, shielding it with his leg, finger on the trigger. The hardwood flooring beneath the runner creaked with each step as he navigated the narrow hall. His senses were on full alert, listening for anything unusual.

He stopped to the side of the door.

For Room 408.

JASON'S GAZE RAKED THE PIAZZA, SEARCHING FOR ASCOLANI. Malone and Father Giumenta were here. He knew they'd told him to stay back.

No way.

He spotted Ascolani, standing with Casaburi. Fifty meters away. Enough. He was a cardinal in the Roman Catholic Church. Held in high esteem. Respected. Time to start acting like one.

He marched toward them.

ERIC WAS DONE WITH THIS ENCOUNTER.

A waste of time. Nothing was being accomplished. So he said to Ascolani, "We will wait until I present the pledge to the church for payment, then we can debate the legalities. Here is not the time or place."

The cardinal shrugged. "We have many ecclesiastical lawyers who can advise us on the proper course."

"I'm leaving," he said.

THOMAS WATCHED THROUGH THE SCOPE AS ERIC CASABURI WALKED away and headed toward the Baptistery. Ascolani casually reached up and touched his left ear.

The signal. *Take the shot.*

He shifted the rifle to his left and centered Casaburi in the crosshairs. People, though, were in the way, coming in and out of the field.

He waited.

A moment longer.

Now.

He squeezed the trigger.

The round left the barrel with a swoosh, the gases that caused the customary crack of an exploding shell muffled by the sound suppressor.

The bullet zipped through the air and found its mark.

He fired again.

CHAPTER 78

ERIC HAD NEVER FELT ANYTHING LIKE THAT BEFORE. FIRST A SHARP pain at his spine, and his body jerked forward as though from the force of an explosion. Then another pain and his chest exploded. Blood and guts spewed out onto the pavement.

Trails of light arced before him.

His legs caved under him and he knew it had not been an explosion, but a blow to his spine.

His head spun.

The world around him winked in and out.

He fought to stay conscious. He heard a scream.

Then something else cut through him. At his shoulder. He lost all sense of equilibrium and collapsed to the pavement, smacking his chest and face hard.

The last thing he saw, before a deep blackness engulfed him, was the clear blue sky overhead.

JASON HEARD A SCREAM AND TURNED.

Casaburi was staggering. Red stained the man's chest and the people around him were reacting by giving him a wide berth, many starting to flee. Casaburi jerked again, then spun backward and hit the ground with a dull thud, not moving.

Ascolani was walking in the opposite direction.

Which left him in the middle of the piazza.

Alone.

Exposed.

THOMAS WAS PLEASED.

Two shots. Two hits. Casaburi was down. Surely dead.

He looked up from the rifle and focused out the window. People were fleeing in all directions. Ascolani headed away from where Casaburi lay. Then he spotted someone else. Really? He focused through the scope. He was right. Cardinal Richter. Here. Alive.

Another failure with the burning car?

His finger went to the trigger.

STEFANO SPOTTED CARDINAL RICHTER. IN THE PIAZZA. EXPOSED. HE began to run, his legs stretching effortlessly as they had on the calcio ball field.

Casaburi was down.

Shot. Twice.

Ascolani was fleeing the piazza about thirty meters to his right. He called out to Richter but there was too much commotion, too many people darting in every direction. If Dewberry was inside the Hotel Duomo he'd have to wait until the field was clear to fire.

Unless he didn't care who he shot.

COTTON HEARD SOUNDS FROM INSIDE ROOM 408 AND KNEW WHAT they were. High-pressure exhaust.

He banged on the door. Hard.

No answer.

He tried the knob. Locked.

No sense being subtle.

He raised his right leg and kicked the door.

THOMAS WAS STARTLED BY BANGING ON THE DOOR.

Then the knob rattled.

He needed to finish. Now.

People began to clear. He centered Richter in the scope.

And fired.

STEFANO RACED ACROSS THE CHAOS ON THE PIAZZA, SHOVING PEOple aside. Richter was beginning to leave, but he was still an easy target.

So he kept running.

Then leaped from his feet and tackled Richter hard.

Taking them both to the ground.

THOMAS GRIPPED THE RIFLE AND LIFTED IT FROM THE SOFA, SWINGing around just as the room door burst open. He leveled the weapon and fired two rounds through the open doorway. There was no leaving this room by the windows, no balcony, no ledge. His only means of escape was to deal with whoever was forcing their way inside.

Yet nobody was there.

Cotton had anticipated that Dewberry would not be happy with the intrusion. What would he do? Simple. Use the rifle. So he stayed to the side of the doorway, conscious of the fact that Dewberry's high-powered weapon could inflict a lot of damage at close range. Even worse, the hotels olden walls would offer little to no protection.

Which Dewberry seemed to instantly realize, readjusting his aim and sending rounds through the walls, which thudded into the other side of the corridor. Cotton kept retreating down the hall until he was beyond the corner of the room. He'd only have a moment. So he had to make it work. He fell to the floor with his legs limp, allowing them to stiffen slightly as he landed, forcing his body into a forward roll that ended him on his belly. He reached up and banged the wall with the Beretta. Dewberry reacted as expected and fired at the noise. Cotton used the moment to wiggle forward to the door's edge.

He gritted his teeth and lay on his back.

One. Two. Three.

He rolled away from the door into the corridor and came to his knees. In one fluid motion he pivoted into the doorway and aimed the gun. Dewberry stood across the room—thick shoulders, strong neck, flat stomach, tapered waist—with the rifle at chest level. It would take a moment for him to realize the situation and readjust his aim.

Cotton fired once.

The sharp crack of the Beretta splintered the stillness.

He fired again.

Both shots neat holes to the chest.

Dewberry was thrown back, groaning in pain, still holding the heavy weapon. Cotton stood and sent the third round into the head.

Dewberry's lifeless body crumbled to the carpet.

Cotton entered the room and kicked the rifle clear of Dewberry's loosened grasp. He kept the gun aimed. Ready. But no more shots were needed. Dewberry was dead. He stepped to the open window and stared out at the piazza. Most of the people had fled. Casaburi's violated body lay lifeless, face down. Richter and Stefano were about fifty feet away, slowly coming to their feet.

Stefano tossed him a thumbs-up.

All good.

Apparently, any shots at the cardinal had missed.

Ascolani? Nowhere to be seen.

No matter.

They knew where to find him.

CHAPTER 79

VATICAN CITY
FRIDAY, JULY 4
11:14 A.M.

JASON ENTERED THE APOSTOLIC PALACE AND WALKED STRAIGHT TO the second floor and the offices of the Secretariat of State. He'd not called ahead or made an appointment. No need. He'd come on authority of the pope himself as his personal representative.

He'd traveled yesterday from Florence back to Rome and was there when the Swiss Guard briefed the pope. Father Giumenta had accompanied him, and together they explained all that had happened. He owed his life to the young priest. No question. Using information that Cardinal Stamm had unearthed, inquiries were made to other cardinals, some of whom confirmed that Ascolani had made improper overtures to them attempting to influence their votes in any upcoming conclave. That was strictly forbidden by canon law. With the combined testimony it had been easy for the pope to order Ascolani's immediate removal.

"I am truly sorry," the pope said to him. *"For all that happened to you. I was given false information, which I trusted and relied upon. That was my mistake. Can you forgive me?"*

He could understand how it happened. The Vatican secretary of state was more like a prime minister than a foreign representative. The job came with myriad responsibilities that included supervising the Curia, drafting papal documents, writing speeches, organizing ceremonial rites, regulating access to the pope, choosing people to be promoted to official posts, managing church money, and making countless other operating decisions without consulting anyone. The job was a gatekeeper by which everyone had to pass before seeing the pope. The opportunities for abuse were endless, and Ascolani had taken full advantage.

"Consider it forgotten," he told the pope, *"if you will grant me one small thing."*

And his old friend had gladly complied.

He informed one of the assistants in the outer office that he had come to see Cardinal Ascolani. That had brought an immediate rebuke, the clerk saying that the secretary of state was busy, with no time to speak to anyone.

"I am here on order of the pope," he made clear. "And you may check with the papal secretary to verify."

And with that he brushed past and opened the door to the private office. The space, like Ascolani's apartment, was a monument to extravagance. The walls were Italian marble dotted with priceless Botticelli paintings depicting the life of Moses. Ascolani sat behind an impressive ornamental desk, his face impassive in a high-backed gilded chair, dressed in a plain black cassock.

Jason stopped before the desk.

The clerk had followed him inside. "I am sorry, Eminence. But he just barged in."

"It is okay," Ascolani said. "You may go."

The clerk left, closing the door.

"We have two problems," Jason said, mimicking what Ascolani had told him a few days ago in the Vatican Gardens. He pointed a finger. "More accurately, *you* have two problems."

"Really? Please explain. I so want to hear."

"First. Thomas Dewberry is dead."

No reaction at the use of the name came from Ascolani. The face remained the color of bone, sallow, bloodless, the lips forming a smile of contempt. "Is that supposed to be important to me?"

"It should. He worked for you. Or more accurately, he killed for you. He shot Casaburi yesterday, then he himself was shot dead."

"Your allegations against me are baseless and false."

"We retrieved a mobile phone from him. There were multiple calls, along with text messages, which we retrieved. They paint a clear picture of what was happening in Siena and Florence. All messages from you to Dewberry. Also, the priest you sent to retrieve the rifle from the Palazzo Tempi in Siena has provided a sworn statement, as has the second priest who removed it from Siena and delivered it to Dewberry outside Santa Maria di Castello. Dewberry then used it to try to kill myself and Cotton Malone, and then did use it to kill Casaburi. That makes you an accessory to murder."

"Again, that seems like wishful supposition."

"And it would be except for one additional fact. We have the sworn affidavit of the man you used as an intermediary with Dewberry. He says, under oath, that you ordered that I be killed."

"Seems he may have incriminated himself with such a statement."

He shrugged. "True. But he was granted full immunity from prosecution. Which he was more than willing to accept, considering that Thomas Dewberry is dead. He had no desire to take all the blame himself."

Ascolani said nothing.

The walls were surely closing in. No other way could the situation be viewed. He and Cardinal Stamm had thought this through in precise detail, trying to anticipate any and every move a manipulator like Ascolani would make.

"Ascolani fears you," the pope said. *"You are most papabile, and your fellow cardinals know that. Two Germans have made it to the papacy. You could be the third."*

Those words had shocked him. Of course he'd brushed aside the praise, urging the pope to not resign and continue to serve. But the argument had fallen on deaf ears.

"What has happened here makes it even more imperative that

I stand aside. I was deceived, and things could have turned disastrous. The church needs a new direction with younger, more vital leadership."

"The pope has ordered your immediate removal from the Secretariat of State and the Entity," he said to Ascolani. "You have also been suspended from any and all ecclesiastical duties."

Ascolani stood. "I think I have heard enough. You may leave."

He smiled. "When the pope suspended you, he also apologized to me. I, of course, accepted that apology with one condition." He paused. "That I be allowed to bring you the news."

"And you have. Now get out."

"As you wish." He turned, walked back to the door, and opened it. Two Swiss Guardsmen entered, along with Cardinal Stamm. Jason faced Ascolani. "I told you there were two problems. The first is that you have been removed from office and suspended. The second is that you are now under arrest."

Ascolani pointed at Stamm. "These are your actions."

"No, Sergio. They are entirely yours."

"You hired Thomas Dewberry. He was here when I assumed control of the Entity."

"That I did. But I used him in only the most dire situations and always in a defensive posture with the full knowledge and consent of the pope. Unlike you, I have nothing to hide. Men like you are a threat to all of the faithful in every parish of this world. The church has no need of you."

"The great new sin of modern times is the unwillingness to become involved. At least I am not guilty of that."

"No, Sergio. You are as Jesus said to the Pharisees. *If a man knows to do right and doeth it not, to him it is a sin.* Take him."

The Swiss Guard motioned for Ascolani to come with them. But the older man stood still. Jason enjoyed watching Ascolani's formidable will reach its limits. "Please. Make this difficult. I so want them to physically carry you from this building. They would like that too. After all, you also ordered the killing of one of their own."

A moment of silence passed between them.

Finally, Ascolani relented and stepped from behind the desk, leading the two guardsmen from the office. He and Stamm watched as they left through the outer door.

"Sadly," Stamm said, "the church seems cursed by weak men with huge ambitions who rise to power. None of them recall what St. Augustine said. *The sufficiency of my merit is to know that my merit is not sufficient.*"

"I am glad that's over," Jason said.

"It may be here, but not in Florence."

CHAPTER 80

Florence, Italy
Saturday, July 5
7:00 a.m.

Cotton opened his eyes to the early-morning light that flooded the hotel room. He'd found a room at the Westin and decided to stay over a day or two. There was some unfinished business. Loose ends that required tying up. He lay on the bed and stared at the ceiling, his thoughts bounding about. The danger was over and some deep, unbroken sleep had sharpened his wits.

It was a new day.

He rose, showered, and shaved.

The hotel had provided all the amenities needed. Yesterday afternoon he'd made a couple of stops at some men's clothing stores and bought new underwear, pants, and a shirt, which would get him by today and tomorrow. He should be back in Copenhagen by Monday.

Ordinarily after pulling the trigger, he was a bit introspective. Unlike in movies, television, and novels, killing came with consequences to the psyche, though this time those had been tempered by the fact that there'd been no choice. None at all. Thomas Dewberry would have never laid down his rifle and surrendered. One thing and one thing only would have stopped him.

Which Cotton had done.

The local *carabinieri* had arrived in the Piazza del Duomo and found Eric Casaburi's bloodied body. The hotel had called them to the scene of what happened in Room 408 and Cotton had no choice but to stay and answer their questions. He'd been taken into custody but released when Stephanie Nelle appeared at the police station with a representative of the Agenzia Informazioni e Sicurezza Interna, Italy's version of the FBI.

Always good to have friends in high places.

It had taken a few hours but they finally located the vehicle that Eric Casaburi had been driving when he arrived at Santa Croce. Inside they had found an old wooden box filled with nine handwritten volumes. Experts from the local university confirmed they were written by Anna Maria de' Medici. Some sort of diary that she'd maintained. That information had interested both the Swiss Guard and Cardinal Stamm, who also arrived and assumed operational command *on the authority of the pope.* Apparently he was back in the good graces of the pontiff. As was Richter. Who'd traveled back to Rome to brief the pope. Cotton had spent last evening reading Anna Maria's writings. He was especially intrigued by her last entry, which might well lead to the Medici's copy of the Pledge of Christ.

He stepped over to the window.

The fresh touch of an early sun seemed to invite a walk. So he left the hotel and navigated the streets, heading for the Pitti Palace. Father Giumenta had been waiting for him downstairs in the hotel lobby. They needed to finish this. Today. Together.

In 1550 the first Medici grand duke, Cosimo I, bought an unfinished palace that covered the northern slope of the Boboli Hill, on the southern bank of the River Arno. It had been started more than eighty years before by a man named Luca Pitti but never finished. Cosimo not only completed it, but also added on and created what became the royal palace, from where the Medici ruled Florence for the next two hundred years. Its distinctive style, solemn and grand, spread throughout Europe and became the standard for a Renaissance royal dwelling. Today it was called the Pitti Palace and was no longer a residence. Instead it was a museum, art gallery, and cultural center visited by millions of people every year.

"You think it is here," Stefano asked him.

"It seems like the right place."

The pledge was secured with two writings, one for Rome, the other for our family. I leave that pledge to you alone. It does not belong to the people of Florence. Instead, it rests safely under a watchful eye and this verse will lead the way.

Then Anna Maria had offered—

Know the darkened world has long missed the night and day, which while the shade still hung before his eyes, shone like a guide unto steps afar. Ne'er will the sweet and heavenly tones resound, silent be the harmonies of his sweet lyre, only in Raffaello's bright world can it be found. Auguror eveniat.

Clearly a riddle.

Compounded by something else they'd learned.

Cardinal Stamm, who'd been given temporary command of the Entity, had dispatched two field officers to the village of Panzitta, where a Pazzi family burial crypt existed. Eric Casaburi had visited there recently and was shown something of interest. A copper plate from inside the grave of Raffaello de' Pazzi with Latin writing on its back side. An odd verse that had yet to be understood, the thinking being it was something personal to that particular Pazzi.

Ne'er will the sweet and heavenly tones resound, Silent be the one nature feared, and when he was dying, feared herself to die. Forever silent be his harmonies, only in his third son's bright world be justice found. Auguror eveniat.

He'd immediately noticed the similar diction and syntax with *Ne'er will the sweet and heavenly tones resound.* Along with the Latin phrase at the end. *Auguror eveniat.* I wish it will come. That could not be a coincidence. The words were identical in the two separate writings. The only logical explanation? The same person wrote both. Since they knew Anna Maria wrote one, she surely wrote the other too. A search of the records at Santa Croce had revealed what Eric Casaburi had also found. Raffaello de' Pazzi was the husband of Anna Maria. Father of a male Medici descendant, surely with a direct DNA link down to Casaburi.

The dots were beginning to connect.

Time to form the complete picture.

He stopped outside the Pitti Palace. They were here before the site opened for the day and thousands of tourists arrived. It was one of the most popular spots to visit in all of Florence. A grandiose, oblong building, three stories high, longer than several football fields, with windows spanning its length and two great wings on either side that formed the great central block, framing out the famous Boboli Gardens. A security guard waited at the main entrance along with Stephanie Nelle.

Cotton walked over. "I see you are still here. Out in the field. That's a rarity."

She smiled. "You need adult supervision."

He grinned and introduced Stefano.

"I heard what you did saving Richter," she said to the young priest.

"Just doing my job."

"Running into the line of fire from a sniper is a bit more than doing your job." She pointed at Cotton. "Did you tell him to use that line? *Doing my job.* That's what you always say too."

"But it's true," both he and Stefano said together.

She shook her head. "You two seem perfect for each other. A couple of loose-cannons-on-the-deck, with a propensity to go rogue."

Cotton shrugged. "And the problem?"

"Exactly," she said. "Do you have any idea how many strings I had to pull to get this kind of access?"

"I think it might be worth it. Shall we," Cotton said, motioning.

And the three of them entered the palace.

CHAPTER 81

STEFANO, ALONG WITH HIS TWO NEW AMERICAN FRIENDS, ENTERED the Ammannati Courtyard, which cast a clear feel of imperial Rome with its array of Ionic and Corinthian columns. Many a spectacle had occurred right here through the centuries, the palace long identified with the ruling families of Florence, whether they be Italian, French, or Austrian.

He was impressed with Stephanie Nelle. He'd never before known or been associated with an intelligence agency head outside of the Entity. She was confident and self-assured but not cocky or arrogant. She listened far more than she spoke, which was always the sign of a good leader. Malone seemed to greatly respect her too. She'd arrived yesterday and worked all day with Cardinal Stamm. Cardinal Richter had previously left for Rome to deal with Ascolani. He'd been told that the secretary of state had been relieved of his office, suspended from duties, and arrested. The pope had ordered all of that, along with reappointing Stamm as head of the Entity. Stamm had ordered Stefano to stay in Florence and assist the Americans with whatever they might need. Malone had worked most of yesterday on deciphering the writings of Anna Maria de' Medici. It was impressive the amount of knowledge the American carried around in his brain.

"I collect information," Malone had said. *"I like facts of all kinds. I accumulate them like some folks keep coins or stamps."*

That and the internet had allowed them to steadily solve a three-hundred-year-old puzzle.

Eric Casaburi died instantly from his wounds, so nothing more would be learned from him. But blood and tissue samples had been preserved from his body. Cardinal Stamm had ordered the bishop who oversaw the village of Panzitta to allow the tomb of Raffaello de' Pazzi to be opened and a DNA sample taken. They utilized the same expert Casaburi had used with Anna Maria. Late last night the results were delivered. Casaburi was definitely DNA-connected to Raffaello on the paternal side, confirming his parentage back to 1743. That and what they'd found among the archives at Santa Croce seemed to prove that Casaburi was a legitimate heir of a royal Medici.

The only thing missing was a properly executed Pledge of Christ.

The church's copy was gone. Ascolani had said he destroyed it. Maybe so. Maybe not. No matter. He was never going to acknowledge that it still existed. So they focused on finding the second copy belonging to the Medici.

And Malone thought he knew exactly where it was located.

COTTON LOVED PUZZLES.

They challenged his mind.

And this one had been a great swirling maelstrom of possibilities.

Yesterday he and Stefano had reviewed everything and formed some conclusions. He'd informed Stephanie and told her what was needed. She'd never wavered a moment and assured him it would happen. Now he followed her as she led them into the palace where a middle-aged woman waited. She was introduced as the museum curator, in charge of all the palace collections.

And they were vast.

Room after room of paintings and sculptures, along with fine china, silver- and goldsmithery, furniture, and other royal fittings. Most came from the Medici, part of Anna Maria's Family Pact, but much more had been added in the centuries since the family's demise. She led them through the palace to a space identified as the Room of the Jewels. An object sat atop one of the glass cases. About two inches long and that much wide. A small cradle, gold enameled with pearls and diamonds.

"I thought you might like to see this," the curator said. "It is one of the many jeweled trinkets that Anna Maria Luisa de' Medici bequeathed to Florence. It was given to her by her husband, Johann Wilhelm, Elector Palatine, as an augury for the announced, and much desired, birth of an heir. Sadly, that never came true as she miscarried. I was told yesterday about what you have discovered. If you look close, between the two rockers are the words AUGUROR EVENIAT. I wish it will come."

"The same thing she wrote in her diary," Cotton said. "And what was also inside the Pazzi tomb."

The curator nodded. "Precisely. It seems you may be on the right track."

He'd done some old-fashioned detective work and, together with Stefano, pieced together a theory.

In 1512 Pope Julius II did in fact borrow ten million gold florins from the Medici family, which its then-head Giuliano de' Medici negotiated. That transaction was evidenced by a Pledge of Christ, which Julius provided with his seal and signature. A promise in perpetuity. Payable on demand. Not your ordinary promissory note. But nonetheless enforceable provided that the demand came after July 1532, twenty years after the original promise, and was made by Giuliano de' Medici or his heirs, successors, and assigns. Two copies of the pledge existed. The church's had been accounted for and was assumed destroyed. The Medici copy?

That was the rub.

Presumably Giuliano de' Medici took possession of that document. But Giuliano died in 1516, sixteen years before the pledge could even be demanded. He was succeeded as family head by his nephew Lorenzo. The mantle of power as the lord of Florence kept being passed down from Medici to Medici until Cosimo I became the first Grand Duke of Tuscany in 1569. That royal title was made possible by both the Holy Roman emperor and Pope Pius V.

Pius himself crowned Cosimo.

And a deal was made. There had to have been.

History noted that Pius V was instrumental in having the Tuscan grand duchy created. The Medicis also wanted full assurances that it would never be taken away. They had already survived two banishments from Florence. Now they wanted their power solidified.

So it was agreed.

The pledge would not be enforced so long as the duchy remained inviolate.

If this deal had not occurred then why would the Medicis, who were bankers in the business of making loans, forgo collecting what had to be the largest single debt ever created? There had to have been an agreement, especially considering that from 1475 to 1605 four separate Medicis were pope—Leo X, Clement VII, Pius IV, and Leo XI—none of whom ever moved for the Vatican to pay the debt. To keep that threat in place the Medicis had to have safeguarded their copy of the pledge, since it was their fail-safe against anyone trying to take their duchy. If that happened they could immediately invoke the help of the Roman Catholic Church, which would either have to protect the royal title or pay the debt, which was accruing at a rate of 10 percent for every year after 1532 it remained unpaid.

So where had they hidden the document?

Anna Maria wrote that—

The pledge was secured with two writings, one for Rome, the other for our family. I leave that pledge to you alone. It does not belong to the people of Florence.

So she seemed to have had the document in 1743. The next sentence in her diary was clear. *It rests safely under a watchful eye and this verse will lead the way.*

Which made the next verse critical.

Know the darkened world has long missed the night and day, which while the shade still hung before his eyes, shone like a guide unto steps afar. Ne'er will the sweet and heavenly tones resound, silent be the harmonies of his sweet lyre, only in Raffaello's bright world can it be found. Auguror eveniat.

Along with the words from Raffaello de' Pazzi's grave.

Ne'er will the sweet and heavenly tones resound, Silent be the one nature feared, and when he was dying, feared herself to die. Forever silent be his harmonies, only in his third son's bright world be justice found. Auguror eveniat.

Lots of clues there.

And thank goodness for the internet.

At first he'd been baffled by *now only in Raffaello's bright world can it be found.* Was that a reference to Raffaello de' Pazzi's grave? Yes and no. Anna Maria had been clever, recognizing the double entendre, which had taken him and Stefano a little time to see.

The answer came from the Pazzi's grave.

Silent be the one nature feared, and when he was dying, feared herself to die.

It had taken only a few seconds of an internet search to know where Anna Maria had found those words.

From the inscription on Raffaello Sanzio da Urbino's marble sarcophagus, placed there when he died in 1520. His name in English was much shorter. And far more well known. Raphael. One of the greatest painters and architects of the High Renaissance. The actual inscription was an elegiac distich written by another cardinal, Pietro Bembo. HERE LIES THAT FAMOUS RAPHAEL BY WHOM NATURE FEARED TO BE CONQUERED WHILE HE LIVED, AND WHEN HE WAS DYING, FEARED HERSELF TO DIE.

Anna Maria had recognized that her second husband and the great painter had the same first name. Clever her use of that coincidence.

Once he'd zeroed in on Raphael, the next link from Anna Maria's warning that *Only in his third son's bright world be justice found* was easy to decipher. Giuliano de' Medici, who made the loan to Julius II, was a third son. And only in Raphael's bright world can *it* be found. A simple Google search had provided the final piece of the puzzle.

In 1515 Raphael was commissioned to paint a portrait of Giuliano di Lorenzo de' Medici. It was to be sent to Philiberta of Savoy, the aunt of Francis I of France, to whom Giuliano had become engaged. The couple had not yet met, so the portrait was created to provide her an idea of his physical appearance. The match had been a political one. Pope Leo X, Giuliano's brother, himself also Medici, was hoping to cement an alliance between the French and the papacy through marriage. At that time portraits were often part of the diplomatic arrangements for such dynastic marriages. So Giuliano sat for the painting.

They left the Room of the Jewels and walked through the various galleries. They passed through the Rooms of the Planets—Venus, Apollo, Mars, Saturn, and the last one, Jupiter.

Where they stopped.

The curator explained that, for the Medici, the space had been used as a throne room where the grand dukes held public audiences. Which made sense as the walls were richly decorated, full of frescoes, white and gilt stucco works, and plumes decorated with shells.

On one of the walls he spotted Raphael's portrait.

"It has hung here, inside the Pitti Palace, off and on since 1743," the curator said to them. "Its provenance is fairly known."

They listened as she explained that the portrait was sent to France to serve its purpose, but was returned to Florence after Giuliano di Lorenzo de' Medici married Philiberta in 1515 and became the Duke of Nemours. The French were grooming Giuliano for the throne of Naples, but he died prematurely in 1516. A further connection to Giuliano could be found in what Anna Maria had written.

Know the darkened world has long missed the night and day, which while the shade still hung before his eyes, shone like a guide unto steps afar.

Giuliano was buried in the New Sacristy of the Church of San Lorenzo. Michelangelo himself crafted the tomb with a sculpture of Giuliano holding the baton of an army commander. At his feet reclined the figures of Night and Day. Night, a giantess, twisting in uneasy slumber. Day, a herculean figure, glancing wrathfully over his shoulder.

Night and Day.

Cotton stared at the portrait hanging on the wall.

Giuliano cast a deflected, sidelong glance, fashionably dressed in the French style with a black doublet over a scarlet vest and a cloak of grayish-green brocade bordered with fur. He wore a wide-brimmed hat tilted to reveal a gold hairnet beneath. His right arm rested on a parapet, the hands holding a folded missive, a pictorial device used at the time to show attentiveness to office. He had just been appointed captain-general of the church by his brother Pope Leo X, the fact alluded to with the Castel Sant' Angelo in the background beyond a drawn curtain. He also sported a beard, which was customary for the French. After his death the painting stayed with the Medici and was part of the initial bequest from Anna Maria to Florence in the Family Pact.

Cotton motioned. "All roads point to this painting. Only in Raphael's bright world can it be found."

"You think there's something hidden there," the curator asked.

"I think it's worth a look. Anna Maria seemed to enjoy symbolism. She chose this painting for two reasons. First, it is of the man who made the pledge. Then second, notice Castel Sant' Angelo in the background. That was where the popes kept their treasury. She's sending a message."

"I find it fascinating that this particular painting could prove so important," the curator said. "It is inscribed in the lower left corner."

Cotton stepped close and saw the letters R.S.M.V. "Is that Raphael's notation?"

"It is. But though it is recognized as a Raphael, most art historians say it was painted by students in his workshop, not by the artist himself. Hence why Raphael's more common signature, Raphaello, is not there. All of which diminishes the painting's importance and value. There's even a copy that belongs to the Metropolitan Museum of Art in New York. For decades there has been a debate as to which is the original. We have used ours here as a placeholder. The painting that is normally hanging in that spot is being restored. This one just temporarily fills the empty space."

"Cotton is convinced there might be something there," Stephanie said. "That's good enough for me. We need to take a look."

The curator motioned. "The alarms are off, and I have been instructed to accommodate your wishes."

Cotton and Stefano approached the painting and lifted it off its wall hooks. It measured about three feet by two feet, enclosed in a heavy wood frame with carved ornamentation, painted a burnished gold.

"The frame is not original to Raphael's time," the curator said. "But everything else is."

They laid the frame on the floor atop a drop cloth that had been waiting for them, with the painting facing downward. This way they could examine its back side. The painting itself, a tempera and oil, had been created on canvas, which was stretched on a wooden frame.

But Cotton immediately noticed something and pointed. "Why is the back covered?"

"It is not unusual," the curator said. "The piece of wood there is clearly old. We have seen that before."

"We need to remove it," Cotton said.

The curator seemed hesitant, so he said, "I thought you were asked to accommodate our wishes."

"But not to destroy something."

"It's a filler painting. Like you said, with little historical or monetary value. And there'll be no damage to the other side."

Cotton watched as one of the museum attendants carefully examined the back of the painting. He'd been summoned by the curator and told to bring tools. The young man used a small chisel and began to work it between the solid backing board and the frame itself. Some splintering occurred as it was forced apart. Not unexpected. But minor.

Then he noticed something.

The chisel could only penetrate about half an inch.

He bent down and examined the gap the attendant had generated. "There's some sort of tab in there. Inserted into a slot in the frame. You're going to have to work all the way around so the backboard comes free in one piece."

Which was precisely what the attendant did, twisting the chisel and freeing the tab that extended out on all four sides. The wood creaked from the pressure of the tab's release. It took a few minutes for the backing to be readied for removal.

The attendant was excused, and the curator dropped to her knees.

With both hands she worked the backing away from the frame and exposed a thin cavity beneath.

A holding spot.

Lying inside against the back side of the canvas was a piece of vellum, identical in shape and size to the one they'd seen at Santa Maria di Castello. Cotton bent down close and saw that it was written in Latin, signed with a *G* by Julius II, like the other, with the odd Medici mark drawn in the lower left corner.

The second copy of the Pledge of Christ.

Right where Anna Maria pointed.

"Incredible," the curator muttered.

Cotton carefully lifted out the document, this one not in a protective plastic sleeve. He placed his open palm beneath the sheet to provide support, mindful that he did not wear gloves. The vellum seemed intact, and the writing was still clearly legible.

"What are you doing?" the curator asked.

"He is doing what I asked," a new voice said.

Cardinal Stamm entered the room, dressed officially in scarlet, a gold pectoral cross against his thin chest, looking every bit like a prince of the church. The old man drew close and examined the document.

"Anna Maria seems to have either known it was there," Stamm said, "or placed it there for her son to find. Hidden with Giuliano de' Medici, behind the Castel Sant' Angelo. How ironic. The Medici who made the loan protected the collateral."

Stamm motioned and a priest entered with a slim, hard-sided leather briefcase, which was opened. Cotton gently laid the document inside, and it was snapped shut.

"That is a historical document belonging to this museum," the curator said. "I was not instructed to allow any removal."

"This document will be placed in the Vatican archives," Stamm said. "There it will stay, safe and protected, until a lawful Medici royal heir appears to claim it."

Cotton smiled. "Of course, no one knows it exists, except us."

"Actually, there is a woman in a village about an hour from here who also knows. But she is not long for this world and few, if any, will pay her any mind."

"So no Medici heir will ever appear," Cotton said.

Stamm shrugged. "That is not my problem. I have done all that the church should do. The document will be properly preserved. What else may or may not occur is of no matter to me."

And with that the cardinal and the priest with the pledge left. Before they did so, though, Stamm said, "Father Giumenta, I'd like you to come too."

"Of course." The young priest turned and shook Cotton's hand. "It was an honor to work with you."

"The honor was all mine," Cotton said. "You take care."

The three prelates left.

The curator seemed flustered. "I will have to report this."

"Good luck with that one," Stephanie said. "That cardinal is not someone who makes irrational moves. I assure you, he's cleared it all with the right people."

"We will see about that."

And the woman left the gallery.

"I appreciate what you did," Stephanie said to him. "You went above and beyond. Running in the Palio? And you won it? That's one for the record books."

"The horse won. Not me."

"You did good. I appreciate it all, Cotton."

She stepped across the room and admired some of the paintings. He'd known her a long time. They'd been through so much together. He owed her more than he could ever repay. He also knew that she hadn't come all the way to Italy because of the Pledge of Christ. Something else was wrong.

So he waited.

"What are you going to do about your supposed daughter?" she asked him.

"I'm still not sure. Maybe that ghost should be left undisturbed."

"Is that what you want?"

"I'm not sure what I want. I'm still processing."

"You know what I would do."

He did. "And I'm leaning in that direction."

"I have a problem, Cotton. A big one."

Finally. To the point.

"I hate to ask. But I need your immediate help."

His answer was never in doubt.

"You've got it."

WRITER'S NOTE

For this novel Elizabeth and I visited Tuscany, including Florence, Siena, San Gimignano, and Castiglion del Bosco, as well as witnessing the famed Palio. It's a wondrous part of the world, definitely worth a visit. Previously, on several occasions, we toured the Vatican at length.

Time now to separate fact from fiction.

Aspects of the prologue are taken straight from history. Pope Julius II was indeed ill in 1512, facing the last few months of his life. The Vatican was also in dire financial straits thanks to a combination of Pope Alexander VI (Julius' predecessor), who spent lavishly, and Julius' many wars, along with his massive building projects and enthusiastic support of the arts. At the time the Medici were likewise banished from Florence thanks to the poor decisions made by Piero the Unfortunate. They wanted to return. The Vatican needed money. But to my knowledge, there was no loan nor any Pledge of Christ given. Those were my inventions.

As to the locations throughout the novel: Dillenburg (chapter 1) exists, and there was indeed once a castle that overlooked the town. It's now gone other than its stone watchtower. The diocese's residence there is my invention. Cologne Cathedral is a marvel of the world (chapter 13) and one of my favorite places. Siena is a wonderful medieval city that oozes an Old World feel. Its Porta Camollia is real (chapter 29) and harks back to the days when the

Medici ruled Siena. The cathedral is an architectural gem, alive with the black-and-white striping of its pillars and walls, along with some incredible marble floors (chapter 30). The octagonal pulpit described in the prologue not only exists today, but was also there in the time of Julius II.

The bad blood between Florentines and Sienese that started in the fifteenth century remains, and I was given a firsthand look. While in Siena for research I was talking to a local bookstore owner familiar with my books. I told her I was writing a Cotton Malone novel featuring Siena, and she was thrilled. But when I informed her of the title, her attitude totally changed.

She was not pleased.

Not at all.

San Gimignano (chapter 61), though a bit touristy, is still fun to visit. Castiglion del Bosco is one of the world's great hotels (chapter 43). The Basilica of San Domenico in Siena (chapter 56) houses the head of St. Catherine, who is a local icon. The Basilica of the Holy Cross at Santa Croce, in Florence, houses the Pazzi Chapel (chapter 31). The starry ceiling fresco that only partially exists inside the Pazzi Chapel is indeed identical to the one inside the Medici Chapel of San Lorenzo. No one knows why the two identical frescoes were created and retained by two families that despised each other. My explanation is wholly fictional.

Italy's political system has always been complicated and fragile (chapter 3), a real challenge to develop any semblance of a working coalition. Becoming prime minister is likewise difficult (chapter 66). This, more than anything else, accounts for the large number of failed governments (chapter 66). Sixty-eight different ones since 1947. My addition of the National Freedom Party is totally fictional.

Calcio Storico is perhaps the most violent game in the world. It is an ancient spectacle that Florence has long enjoyed. Every year at the end of June the games are played in the piazza before the Basilica di Santa Croce. The match in chapter 2 is accurately depicted, including the miracle goal made by Stefano Giumenta, which was modeled after one made in a real match.

The drink called the Beverly in chapter 8 is real. Once mass-produced, it now exists only as a novelty at select stores in the United States. One of those is Club Cool at Epcot in Walt Disney World, where you can sample it for free. I assure you the taste is quite memorable, but it grows on you. The restaurant La Giostra is one of Florence's best (chapter 11). Its co-owner is a colorful individual reflected in the character of Daniele Calabritto (chapter 34), the owner of my fictional La Soldano in Siena.

The Vatican Bank has a long and checkered past riddled with secrecy and corruption (chapter 9). To this day Vatican finances remain a mystery, and no one outside of a select few within the Curia actually know the church's true financial status. This was all explored in much more detail in *The Malta Exchange*. The Vatican archives, on the other hand, have been subjected to repeated theft and purging (chapter 20).

So much has been lost.

Pius V was a memorable pope who started the first Vatican intelligence agency, which eventually became the Entity. Never is its existence either acknowledged or confirmed, but it does exist. Before Pius was pope, when he headed the Inquisition, he led a group of "black monks" who wreaked havoc on Rome (chapter 16). He was banished by Pius IV and took with him into exile a host of documents. What those were, and what became of them, no one knows. He lived in exile for six years, but not at a Carthusian charterhouse. That was my invention. Pius V did, though, have deep connections to the Medici and was instrumental in having them granted the duchy of Tuscany (chapter 37). Was that connected to any deal not to enforce the collection of a loan secured by some Pledge of Christ? No one knows.

But it made for a great plot element to the story.

The Order of Carthusians has existed since 1084. They have always enjoyed a certain independence and a light hand from the church. To this day they retain a unique form of liturgy known as the Carthusian Rite. They are one of the best-run and most successful monastic orders. Their monasteries are known as charterhouses. Twenty-three exist around the world on three continents. Eighteen for monks, five for nuns. Their headquarters is located near Grenoble, France, and is known as La Grande Chartreuse. Two charterhouses sit in Italy, but Santa Maria de Castello (chapter 60) is my invention.

Carthusians have, since 1737, produced one of the world's most unique liqueurs. The recipe was given to them around 1605, and remains a secret. There are two versions of Chartreuse. Yellow and Green. Its La Tarragone du Siecle cost around $75,000 per bottle, or around $1,200 a glass. Revenues from the production and sale of its liqueur finance the Carthusians. A friend of mine recently enjoyed some of the pricey Yellow Chartreuse. He told me, *I would compare it to grappa. Sharp and powerful, burning your nose hairs, at first, then an intense warmth as it hits the back of your mouth. Oddly soothing, before you are reminded of the sharpness in an aftertaste, along with a pungent residual smell.*

Here's another fun fact. When Pius V (here he is again) in the sixteenth century decreed the Roman missal mandatory for all Catholics of the Latin church, he specifically exempted the Carthusians, an exemption they continue to enjoy in modern times.

Interesting, the distinction shown them.

The Pazzi Conspiracy is a historic fact (chapter 24). The information noted in the story about it, including its bloody aftermath, is accurate. The harsh repercussions for the Pazzis, including their banishment and bankruptcy (chapter 40), happened. Ironically, all their murderous actions accomplished was to forever taint the Pazzis and strengthen Medici control over Florence.

The observation in chapter 51 that Medici rule was anything but benign is both true and sobering. They definitely had their share of enemies. The Pazzis did enjoy a certain degree of resurrection after the Medici were banished from Florence in 1494. But they were never again what they were prior to the attack. Pazzi and

Medici remained apart. My connection of Anna Maria de' Medici and Raffaello de' Pazzi, in a secret marriage, is wholly fictional.

Front and center in this story is the famed Palio. It is indeed one of the grandest, and oddest, horse races in the world. Everything Camilla Baines tells Cotton Malone about the race is true. The luck of the draw as to a horse, the randomness of the starting positions, and the duplicity of the jockeys happens. There are seventeen *contradas*, each of the neighborhoods acting as its own political and social entity. I invented an eighteenth called the Golden Oak. Allies and enemies exist among the *contradas* that change from year to year. The celebratory dinners noted in chapter 42 happen the night before the race (I attended one). The track itself is created inside the Piazza del Campo. Dirt from the surrounding countryside is hauled in and packed tight to create a treacherous race course. Both horses and jockeys are routinely injured. One hundred and five rules govern the race. Most are there simply to ensure an even playing field among the ten participants. But short of physically interfering with another jockey's grip on the reins, you can pretty much do anything to stop another from winning. It is an amazing spectacle and well worth a visit to Siena during the two times each year the race is run.

This novel focuses on the Medici. First, I had to learn the correct way to pronounce the name. Americans tend go with *Med-EE-chee*. Italians, though, pronounce it *MED-i-chee*. They were an amazing family that managed to rise from nothing and dominate both Florence and Tuscany from the fourteenth to the eighteenth centuries. Along the way they became Italy's leading bankers, pioneers in a burgeoning financial industry. Eventually they integrated themselves with many of the dominant ruling families across Europe. Florence was always their epicenter, and what became known as the Pitti Palace was both their home and their royal seat (chapter 80).

The symbol shown in chapter 63 was used by the Medici to authenticate their documents. What it means, or represents, no one knows.

The painting shown in chapter 81 of Giuliano de' Medici is real. Whether it was created by Raphael or students at his workshop is a matter of debate, as is whether the version at the Pitti Palace or the one at the Metropolitan Museum of Art in New York is the original. The Pitti Palace, though, does use its copy as a placeholder, as described in chapter 81.

A host of notable Medici were buried within the Church of San Lorenzo and its sacristies (chapters 18 and 21). Giuliano de' Medici lies there in a magnificent tomb, with representations of night and day carved by Michelangelo himself. Anna Maria Luisa de' Medici is also buried within San Lorenzo. She was an extraordinary woman. Truly, as history notes, the last royal Medici. All of her family history described within the story is true. Only her second marriage to a Pazzi, and the birthing of a child, were my additions. Her diaries (chapters 44 and 47) are likewise fictitious. The Family Pact (chapter 27) was her creation and endowed the city of Florence with all of the books, art, and artifacts the Medici owned, expressly providing that they never leave the city. Everyone who visits today to see those treasures owes her a debt of thanks. The tiny jeweled cradle described in chapter 81, with the inscription *AUGUROR EVENIAT*, I wish it will come, is on display in the Pitti Palace museum. It was a gift to Anna Maria from her first husband. Sadly, she miscarried that child.

The Medici, though, have not rested in peace. Their graves have been periodically violated. First covertly for centuries by thieves, then overtly by science. The first formal intrusion occurred in 1857 when many of the tombs were opened, inspected, and inventoried. Similar investigations occurred periodically over the ensuing centuries. The 1966 flood of Florence caused much damage. Another detailed investigation happened in 2013, this one utilizing all of the modern techniques. Anna Maria's tomb was one of those opened. A copper plate, similar to the ones described in chapter 53, was found in not only her grave but others too.

The Medici were, as a family, justly called great. Great in their extraordinary abilities. Great in their imagination. Great in their unparalleled love for learning and art. Great in their abounding energy and vitality. Great, above all, in allaying fierce political passions that few others could pacify. They were, at their core, Florentines, and loved Florence with a deep passion. History notes that, when they eventually became grand dukes, they did not rule from a distance, receiving the surplus revenue of the state, spending their wealth elsewhere, interesting themselves little in affairs of state.

Quite the opposite.

To obliterate their memory from Florence would be impossible. Wherever you turn there are reminiscences of them. Everywhere in the crowded museums and galleries and in the churches, you see pictures, statues, bronzes, gems, vases, inlaid tables, costly cabinets, and other objects of art innumerable, many of which were acquired by some member of the Medici family, all bequeathed to Florence, for the enjoyment of all, by Anna Maria de' Medici. Then, as you stand in the magnificent mausoleums, where their lives ended, surrounded by great porphyry monuments, each one finished with the workmanship given to a costly gem, it's easy to see that the Medici were not ordinary people. Not in the least. But, unlike in the novel, there are no more royal Medici.

Sadly, the family went extinct in 1743.

They were not perfect by any means, as they ruled as despots and murder was not foreign to them. They waged war with abandon and took no pity on their enemies. They rose from obscurity to first become merchants, then bankers, lords of Florence, and finally grand dukes. They flourished for three centuries, then vanished. And old Italian idiom was in many ways their motto.

In bocca al lupo. Crepi il lupo.

Into the wolf's mouth. May the wolf die.

A way of saying "Good luck."

Which in my tale Anna Maria wished for her son.

But it also was the way the Medici lived life.

ABOUT THE AUTHOR

Steve Berry is the *New York Times* and #1 internationally bestselling author of nineteen Cotton Malone novels, five stand-alone thrillers, two Luke Daniels adventures, and several works of short fiction. He has more than twenty-six million books in print, translated into forty-one languages. With his wife, Elizabeth, he is the founder of History Matters, an organization dedicated to historical preservation. He serves as an emeritus member of the Smithsonian Libraries Advisory Board and was a founding member of International Thriller Writers, formerly serving as its copresident.

For more information you can visit:

SteveBerry.org

Facebook.com/SteveBerryWriter